30.95   12/7   31476248

P9-BXY-285

THE GAME OF OPPOSITES

This Large Print Book carries the
Seal of Approval of N.A.V.H.

The Game of Opposites

Norman Lebrecht

THORNDIKE PRESS
A part of Gale, Cengage Learning

SNYDER COUNTY LIBRARIES, INC.
ONE NORTH HIGH STREET
SELINSGROVE, PA 17870

GALE
CENGAGE Learning

Detroit • New York • San Francisco • New Haven, Conn • Waterville, Maine • London

GALE
CENGAGE Learning

Copyright © 2009 by Norman Lebrecht.

Grateful acknowledgment is made to Evžen Hilar for permission to reprint "May 1945" by Dagmar Hilarová, translated here by Norman Lebrecht. Reprinted by permission by Evžen Hilar.

Thorndike Press, a part of Gale, Cengage Learning.

ALL RIGHTS RESERVED

This is a work of fiction. Names, characters, places, and incidents either are the product of the author's imagination or are used fictitiously. Any resemblance to actual persons, living or dead, events, or locales, is entirely coincidental.

Thorndike Press® Large Print Reviewers' Choice.

The text of this Large Print edition is unabridged. Other aspects of the book may vary from the original edition.

Set in 16 pt. Plantin.

Printed on permanent paper.

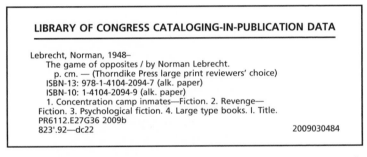

LIBRARY OF CONGRESS CATALOGING-IN-PUBLICATION DATA

Lebrecht, Norman, 1948–
    The game of opposites / by Norman Lebrecht.
      p. cm. — (Thorndike Press large print reviewers' choice)
    ISBN-13: 978-1-4104-2094-7 (alk. paper)
    ISBN-10: 1-4104-2094-9 (alk. paper)
    1. Concentration camp inmates—Fiction. 2. Revenge—
Fiction. 3. Psychological fiction. 4. Large type books. I. Title.
PR6112.E27G36 2009b
   823'.92—dc22   2009030484

Published in 2009 by arrangement with Pantheon Books, an imprint of Knopf Doubleday Publishing Group, a division of Random House, Inc.

Printed in the United States of America
1 2 3 4 5 6 7 13 12 11 10 09

In memoriam
Myriam (1932–2006)

It was May
And all the blossoms burst forth;
Blue lilac spindles spread their
fragrance.

May imposed itself on the land
And everyone touched freedom,
As a blind man, the face of a loved one.
— Dagmar Hilarová, "Mai 1945"

■ ■ ■ ■

Part One:
Flight

■ ■ ■ ■

CHAPTER ONE

At four in the morning, an hour before the cement mixer is due, Paul creeps downstairs in woollen socks and pulls on his trousers in the wood-panelled tavern bar, the air heavy with the past night's conviviality. Fumbling past the silent coffee machine, a stair light winking off its curved steel wall, he brews himself a small black pot on the old crusted hob and sips the scalding bitterness through a rock-hard almond biscuit, the last of the batch that Alice baked for Easter. Crossing the room once more, he caresses the coffeemaker with trailing fingertips.

The coffeemaker was Paul's dearest possession, his defining object. He had picked it up "on the black" and trundled it for miles on the back of a jeep before unwrapping it in front of a twitter of village wives, his masculine perversity gratified by their shrieks of dismay. He had hoped the contraption would cause alarm, and it satisfied his wishes to the full. To the huddle of black bonnets around the bar, Paul's machine was a pulsing threat, a disruption to the natural order. There was no telling the harm it might do. A man in need of strong coffee after a hard night's lambing in the fields would be lured away from hearth and hob by this sibilant hussy. One sip, and a husband was lost. The ladies had read of such things in picture magazines and were not about to permit them in the village. "Take it away, landlord," shrilled the butcher's wife, "before I ask Father Hitzinger to denounce it this very Sunday."

It cost Paul three rounds of free tastings to convince the bonnets that his novelty was innocuous, its dainty servings so different from their kitchen dispensations as to pose no challenge to their domain. A real man, he explained, would always require a large dose of the handmade. His tiny shots of steam-pressed coffee were meant for visitors, for city people jaded by luxury and condemned to a vapid quest for extreme sensation, effete couples who came to the inn for cynically themed "country week-ends." This machine was strictly for what Paul called "passing trade."

The ladies, receptive to slick assurances,

flattered by his attention, and emboldened by the fierce extract that surged through their child-worn frames, turned bold and mildly flirtatious, as people do when free drinks are being served. "It is a fine beverage, landlord," declared the market carrot seller with the comically jutting bosom. "It is hot and aromatic and rasping to the tongue, but it is not what we *around here* call coffee, oh no. Coffee is what we *grind* by hand, with the grime of our fingernails and a fleck of sweat from the brow. When you want *real* coffee, landlord, boiled through and through and served in a *man-sized* mug, just knock at my door and I will show you proper *coffee.*"

"And if her gimpy old man is out in the fields," cackled a wrinkled head scarf at the fringe of the throng, "our Regina will show you plenty else besides."

"Shut your cesspit, Elsa," snapped the carrot woman. "The landlord is a Christian gentleman. He does not need to hear such filth. I apologise for the feeble *old lady,* landlord. This posh coffee of yours has gone straight to her head."

" *'Old'?"* squeaked her antagonist. "She and I were in the same class at school. She's got a prolapsed womb and can't stand up straight for arthritis. I'll give her old. . . ."

13

"Ladies, ladies," soothed Paul, shepherding them to the door and bolting it when the last was gone, his plan fulfilled. Soon no man within miles would be unaware of his acquisition or incurious to see it in action, eager to sacrifice another slice of rural lore for the benefits of modern convenience.

As if in response to the women's sensitivities, Paul hung a sign on the machine the next morning, saying that it was out of order, awaiting a vital part. For a whole month, it stood bare and idle on the bar top, like a villain in stocks on assizes day, an object of casual derision. Two days before its reinauguration, Paul posted a notice outside and took on extra hands behind the bar to cope with the anticipated rush. At the second unveiling of the miraculous steam machine, the Laughing Hind was packed so full with unfamiliar faces that its wooden beams seemed to bend outwards to accommodate them all. Rye farmers in mud-caked boots jostled lumberjacks from deep in the forest. Poachers were drawn from their traps and goatherds from vertiginous mountain huts. All converged to inspect a mechanical intruder which, rumour had it, was about to change a staple of their existence.

They rallied much as their great-grandparents had gathered a hundred years before to watch curls of smoke from the first locomotive, aware that the steady tread of their lives was under attack, that a man might no longer earn his keep from the shearing of sheep, as his womenfolk spun wool and his sons repaired the looms and shod the village horses. The puffing iron carriageway would render their rustic crafts redundant and all would be forced to work in dark factories while the land returned to wilderness and foxes copulated on their parents' graves, as the priest of that day thundered from his pulpit. His gruesome fears proved, by God's mercy, to be greatly exaggerated, thanks to a hostile gradient which even mountain folk found intractable and an absence of commercially extractable mineral resources. A century later, at the coming of the coffee machine, the nearest railway station was still hours away by winding road and the village existed much as it had done since legendary times. The surrounding slopes were coated in virgin oak, uncut by fire lanes. Crested eagles, the last of their species, nested balefully on craggy heights. Hyenas howled at night. Pagan rituals were whispered in forest glades. Ramblers, ornithologists, and election-year politicians who reached the village on a bone-rattling detour from their cardinal occupations marvelled at its remoteness. It was a place where no radio signal was received and a person could sit all afternoon in a beer garden without hearing so much as a cough of internal combustion. "Paradise it is," sighed the Christian party cheerleader over his frothing beer jug. "The crucible of our civilisation," agreed the contented Socialist candidate.

The villagers smiled thinly at these pitiful compliments, the perfumed words of city folk who could not milk a goat to save a dying child. What did their paper-white fingers know of the skin-cracking struggle to hack sustenance from hard rock, their fat bottoms of hoar frost at dawn in a December earth closet? Waiters who replenished their tankards and chambermaids who turned the corners of their eiderdowns knew the cost in quotidian brutality of a picture-postcard charm. They did not ooh and aah at the loveliness of a living thing before it was killed, stripped, and eaten, its bones crushed for manure, its offal fed to the chickens. Paul, stomping through blood pools big as duck ponds in his backyard, warned his staff to mask their contempt for the visitors. Personally, he told them in a low voice, he would cheerfully suffocate townies who drooled at dinner over a dish they had photographed a couple of hours earlier frolicking in the field. Someday, he would frog-march their fat asses into a tour of the slaughterhouse before he admitted their hungry faces to the dining hall. "Good for you, landlord," chimed an ancient jug washer. "Come the millennium, we'll choke the parasites with their duck pillows and bury them in a compost heap."

Paul's righteous anger endeared him to the village as a man whose instincts were in the right place — who, although he came from "over there," was at heart one of them, a straightforward man who valued the simple life. They loved the landlord's colourful phrases, so much more quotable than the priest's dull, repetitive homilies. *Drooled over a dish they had snapped an hour earlier in the field.* Now that's telling 'em: so apt, so true.

So when the first election came around after the war, the village voted overwhelmingly to elect Paul as mayor, in preference to official party candidates, confident that he held its interests at heart and could squeeze the ministries for permits and subsidies to support their rural heritage. Paul, from the day he arrived, had proved that he could work the mechanisms of government the way a potter worked his wheel. He had time for every villager and limitless patience for those who, for one reason or other, lagged behind the growing prosperity. He was, both in smile and in deed, a caring and capable leader.

What the village did not see was the rage that welled within the landlord, now mayor, as he went about his duties. Every aperitif he poured for city guests, every souvenir walking stick he sold them brought up on a parallel screen in his mind's eye the same people being dragged out dead and broken from the rubble of an apartment block laid waste by aerial warfare. Try as he might, Paul could not block out visions of urban destruction. An inner voice assured him that it was only right and proper that buildings which had watched stone-faced as certain residents were selected for eviction and death should themselves be pulverised by high explosives falling from a starry sky. The nocturnal destruction of cities upon their inhabitants seemed to Paul a just and necessary punishment for their daylight indifference to murder. He hated the city, hated it as one who had witnessed its nameless cruelties. The village was his refuge from the city of his past.

But the village, haven that it was, was no

less complicit in recent crimes. Where the city had turned a blind eye, the village had sat and watched a daily march of death from the top of the hill, through its main street, past the Laughing Hind, and down to the bedrock quarry. Paul had been one of the head-bowed marchers not that long ago. Forty minutes down in the morning, fifty-five up at night. In a village where no leaf falls unnoticed, every evil done is an evil known. Ignorance is impossible, innocence an untenable defence. The village had not been blind to murder as the city was; it had seen all and said nothing. The village must be made to pay for its impassivity. It merited retribution. Paul, now mayor, was in a position to inflict it.

He began to alter the landscape, to transform it beyond hope of recognition, so that grandsons and daughters in decades ahead should never reconcile the view that met their eyes with sepia photographs in family albums. Every defining feature was to be changed. Pasture would be turned into housing estates, primal lakes into parking lots. The washhouse would become an electric Laundromat, the smithy a gas station; the neighing of horses would give way to a growling of jeeps. Paul ripped wooden frames out of gabled windows. He bricked over wells, kicked over earth walls, and enforced city laws on child labour that put family farms out of business. He imposed safety regulations on peasant handicrafts, condemning them to extinction. The village, unaware of his motives, danced beneath his fluorescent filaments in the light of an equinox moon.

Dismayed at the lack of resistance, needing some sign that his measures were causing pain, Paul pushed through a cross-valley merger of two villages which loathed each other with such historic fervour that girls from one could not marry men from the other without being branded harlots and driven from their homes. The plan aroused a ripple of opposition, all too easily overcome with bland promises. In a matter of months, two enmities were welded into a new town so anodyne that Paul named it New Town and filled its pre-fabricated houses with itinerants who smudged what remained of the indigenous character of the two villages and their connecting valley.

And still his rage burned white, perhaps because there was no-one to share it. Like a mad Roman emperor, Paul built a needless town on a high mountainside without anybody demanding to know why. His was a triumph made hollow by stealth. Paul had

rewritten the map and torn up his work-
ings. By suppressing his punitive intent,
Paul succeeded in effacing not just the village but his driving role in its effacement.
By the time he was done, people could
barely describe the old washhouse and
smithy, let alone remember who it was that
had ordered their demolition. The history
of Paul Miller, which a historian will one
day struggle to uncover, is made the more
poignant by his complete disappearance
from the scene.

In future times, if drinkers at the Laughing Hind were asked for a symbol of Paul's
rule as mayor, they would omit to mention
the new roads he laid out, the centrally
heated public housing, the cottage hospital,
the school he furnished with an Olympic-
length swimming pool, football pitches, a
language laboratory, and all pedagogic aids.
These amenities are all forgotten as, across
the rims of trademarked beer glasses (no
jugs or tankards anymore), old fellows
point, with wavering fingers, at the emblem
of Paul's glory, there on the half-marbled
bar top: the huffing, hissing, spitting coffee
machine, the ultimate non-necessity. The
machine, one of them points out, was the
landlord's pride and joy, the last thing he
touched on his short sojourn on this

troubled earth, rest his dear soul.

What kind of man was he? the historian asks. Popular, they say. Just that? Yes, popular, a good man, well liked. Was he tall, short, fat, thin? On the thin side, not too tall. Hair? A bit thin, maybe. Nothing out of the ordinary.

"What became of him?"

"Shame, it was, terrible shame."

"What happened? Did any of you see anything?"

Heads shake, lids fall like blinds on watery eyes, and the drinkers lapse into a dialect so thick, it could be sewn as curtains. Paul's legacy has evanesced into nothingness, faded to white. *Popular* and *coffee* are all the historian gets for his beers, useless and inconsequential as an advertising slogan. Paul has made himself a nullity, the man who never was.

The small black pot stops its bobbling on the rickety hob. In the breathless silence, Paul takes his cup to the sink, rinses it under the cold tap, and upends it on the draining board. Returning, he stops at the coffee machine, bends at the knees, and plants a farewell kiss on its motherly mound. In pitch-darkness, he feels for his jacket on the wooden coatrack, his boots in the porch, and, opening the front door with both hands to mute the squeaky hinge, pulls it shut behind him.

This is the hour that Paul knows best. Too late for owls, too soon for cockerels, it is the time when free men sleep and only slaves jump to attention.

Paul was up most nights at this hour, unable to shake off the habits of servitude. His eyes would snap open, his legs would swing over, and his feet would reach for the floor in a response — "Pavlovian," he told Dr. Kovacs — that had been drilled into him before, in the life he talked of to no-one, not even to Alice, who slept through his disturbances, her measured breathing beckoning him back to bed, her warm body to a merciful forgetfulness that he longed for but could not embrace.

Paul resisted the comforts of love. He would stand night after night at the window, staring at the pane and beyond into a raven blackness that stretched from the crest of the hill where the camp had been, down the village street, past church and inn, and down to the quarry, where men like him once slaved and died. Camp-inn-quarry. Quarry-inn-camp. The route had been drummed into his feet, tramped dawn and dusk, down and up, eyes to the unyielding ground, any upward glance an invitation to assisted suicide by means of a bullet in the back of the neck. He knew the Laughing Hind at first acquaintance by the number of paces, thirty-eight, that it took to cross its perimeter length, from stable to grinning shield, pickaxe on his shoulder, calluses swelling on his broken feet, killer dogs at his heels. He knew the inn by the clink of summer drinkers in its garden, their backs turned away from the march of the damned. He knew the Laughing Hind as a place he dared not look. He knew it as a relief denied.

And now he stood nightly on its topmost floor, ruler of all that lay beneath — the inn, the village, the whole goddamn valley. "Come to bed," Alice would murmur from the depths of sleep. But Paul stood frozen at the window, his eyes tramping the old trajectory, camp-inn-quarry, quarry-inn-camp, up and down, down and up, dawn and dusk. He stood and stared until he started to shake, trembling with cold and shame, rattling with worthlessness from head to toe. To settle his treacherous limbs, he crept down a flight of stairs to Johann's room, the boy's catarrhal sighs a slow assurance that some good had come of the shaming things his father had done, the hateful thing he had become. Johann was his refuge from the past, his hope of salvation, his *apologia pro vita sua.* Johann, his son.

They named him for a saint who baptised a saviour, or so Alice declared, genuflecting at the font. Paul had said nothing. He often said nothing so that he could listen to a soundless noise in his head. What he had heard at the font was his mother's name, Johanna, a saint unknown to Alice or anyone else in his present life. Johann to Paul was short for Johanna. To Alice it was a name without burdens, for she knew nothing of his mother's martyrdom.

Alice shortened the name as soon as the baby began to smile. "Jo-jo-jo," she crooned, then "Hans-hans-hans." The soft consonants sat better with her tune. Paul heard her sing "Hans, hans" over Sunday lunch. He clutched his throat as if he had swallowed a wasp and rushed, choking, from the room. "Hans," Alice was still singing when he returned, "Hans, hans, hans." Paul, in a firm tone, asked if she would not mind calling the baby by his full name. Alice declined. Such a sweet little thing — she would call him whatever she liked. She was his mother, wasn't she? Johann is his name, said Paul. We agreed on it. So what? snapped Alice.

The argument sputtered between them like an oil lamp, flaring intermittently. Alice

25

could not understand why Paul reared in fury at what was, for heaven's sake, a sound as common as Kurt, Karl, Klaus, Heinz, Franz, or Paul itself. Paul, flustered, said it was a question of taste; her stub of a name was inadequate for their beautiful boy. Johann was a dignified name, one he could wear with pride. Alice replied that Johann was fine for a man but pompous for a boy; he would get teased for it at school. Hans would do for the time being. Paul fled the table once more, hand to mouth. *Hans,* an exhalation that ended in a serpentine hiss, the sound a rabbit made when you snapped its neck, was an evil noise. It made his flesh crawl, his feet twitch in terror.

The next time he complained, Alice blew up. "What's the matter with you? What in hell's name is wrong with Hans?" she yelled, and Paul, doubled up in an agony of confusion, fled outdoors into the chirruping night, hurtling down the hill to the valley of the dead. It had to stop, her Hans calling; he had to make it stop. There would be more bodies in the quarry if she didn't stop. What was he to do?

He considered taking Alice into his confidence, including her in his abhorrence of the name by telling her all about Hans and the things he had done. But even as he

26

contemplated letting openness into their marriage, he knew that the past lay beyond its beyond a love that began at the zero hour and must never look back. He could not change their rules of engagement by exposing Alice to an unforgiven past. He cared too much for her to make Alice choose between then and now, between her village and her man. And if she were forced to make the choice, he was not altogether sure which way she would turn. He was trapped in the silence of their pact, unable to reach out, or to retreat.

It fell to Alice to make a conciliatory move, taking his right hand between her lips in bed and biting the fleshy mound beneath the thumb, a prelude to love. Alice was wise, as country girls are, in treating male distress with the elixir of sex. She would not allow a domestic quarrel to fester overnight. Paul was just as keen to make up, but he needed to resolve his feelings in words before plunging into love. Alice, yawning, rolled over and fell asleep before his statement was finished, leaving Paul stranded and alone. At his next session with Dr. Kovacs, he avoided any mention of the name row until he got stuck in one of those interminable silences that are supposed, according to the theory, to bring out buried truths.

"You had a convulsive reaction when she used the name Hans?" asked the therapist.

"Correct."

"Coughing, retching, shortness of breath?"

"Correct."

"It sounds like a conditioned response."

"Meaning?"

"The name provokes a reaction; it's cause and effect."

"I have explained the cause."

"Indeed you have. But you react only when the name Hans is attached to your son. You do not convulse, I think, when Alice mentions Hans the plumber, Hans the goatherd. Hans the village half-wit. Why do you think that is?"

"The others mean nothing to me. I cannot let my son bear an evil name."

"What if it is not evil?"

"What do you mean?"

"One person never sees the whole picture. You experienced a series of incidents over a certain period. You blame your suffering on a man you called Hans. But what if this Hans is no worse in relative conduct than, say, Hans the plumber?"

"That's ridiculous. Hans the plumber repairs taps and toilets. The Hans I knew killed men for pleasure."

"What if he were not responsible?"

"He was mad, you mean?"

"Or acting under orders."

"That's no excuse."

"It might be to Hans."

"Are you asking me to understand him? Is that what I come here for?" cried Paul, rising from his seat.

"Let's agree that Hans is evil incarnate," said Kovacs, unmoved.

"Fine," said Paul, sitting down.

"Nobody is worse than Hans."

"Correct."

"How about someone who helped him?"

"Bad, but not worse."

"Someone who encouraged him?"

"Likewise."

"Someone who might have stopped him? Who could have stopped him to save lives?"

A fit of coughing propelled Paul out of his chair and left him in a gasping huddle on the floor in a far corner of the room. "I think that's enough to be getting on with," said the doctor, scribbling a note and blotting the ink with exaggerated care on his pad.

Most nights when Paul came home from the analyst, he liked to make love to his wife, who was generally willing. The release numbed him into a sleep that ran through until morning, leaving him to think that the therapy was doing him some good. On this occasion, though, he slept no longer than an hour before his feet hit the floor and he was back at the black window, running the shrink's question over and over in his head. What if Hans was not the worst? Who could be more culpable than Hans? A man who might have stopped him and didn't. Who should have chased him, caught him, brought him to justice. Someone who shielded him behind a false name. Now who might that be? Who let Hans get away? Who stayed on in this valley of the shadow of death as if nothing had happened? Who let Hans live? What kind of monster? Why, there he is, staring at you out of the window-pane, the most evil man alive.

Paul glared at his image until it blurred. Then he began to shake as he never shook before. The tremors did not stop until he swore, on Johanna's sainted memory, to put an end to Hans. He would deal with Hans without delay and regardless of risk, even if it cost him Alice, his son, along with the sham of his second life, as mayor of the idyllic village.

CHAPTER TWO

Hans was the commandant's name; everybody knew that. They knew it by rumour, by inference, from overheard snatches of guard conversation. The prisoners relied on such scraps, since names were prohibited items, punishable by death. Guards were addressed by rank and never looked in the eye. Prisoners, heads bowed, caps off, hands behind back, said Yes-Corporal, No-Corporal, Right away–Corporal. To identify themselves, they shouted out a number, the one tattooed on their left arm, below the elbow. They had this in common, guards and prisoners: the absence of names.

Anonymity was the guards' insurance against a day of reckoning, when those who survived would come in search of vengeance. The guards knew the war was going badly, that the end was near. The prisoners, sensing their fear, called it hope and collected curriculum vitae. They eavesdropped on guards and filched letters from waste-paper bins. A market was created in personal data. Maretzek, the comrades' boss, paid for a guard's birthplace in bread and tobacco. Finkel, the romantic nationalist, offered his morning soup for a date of birth. Milman, the dissident pastor, promised eternal life for an addressed envelope. In the long, low huts where the prisoners slept and no guard dared to brave the stench, men from every land of occupation jigsawed together profiles of oppressors, reclaiming invisible identities.

A bowl of soup, equivalent to a day's strength, was weighed against the risk entailed in obtaining a name, and the risk was mortal. Paul had seen a man flayed to pulp across a stone bench for shouting "Hans is coming!" and another shot on the spot for having a guard's name written on his palm. Among the offences that could cost a man his life, the possession of a name ranked with attempted escape. The rules were enforced by the shadow they knew as Hans. Shorter than most of his inmates, bristle-headed in a knee-length leather coat that made him seem shorter still, Hans walked with a limp that rumour ascribed to a war wound. He walked alone, unescorted, inviolable, unforeseen. On summer nights, he would sharp-shoot men from his upper window and call the dogs to finish them off; in winter, he patrolled the camp on silent snowshoes, heaving any curfew breaker into a water barrel and leaving the poor wretch to freeze overnight. Hans was the law in camp, a law unto himself.

"He, too, will hang," growled Maretzek in Paul's ear as, eyes to the front, they stood on the parade ground, watching Finkel swing on the gallows for some hapless misdemeanour. "You can help us, Paul. Get us addresses, his family, friends. The people's security bureau will do the rest, when the day comes."

Paul was what was known as a privileged prisoner. He did not hack rocks. A lucky choice of vocation allowed him to spend much of the quarry day in a cabin, designing an underground storage system for the wonder weapon that was going to help Hans win the war. The tunnel he was drawing and revising would house the weapon in specified conditions of temperature and humidity, to avoid spontaneous combustion. So long as Hans needed Paul's skills to perfect the silo, Paul could expect to live. He would have liked to drag out the project with minor errors and slow-motion working, but errors when discovered were punishable with death, and Hans, across the cabin, kept a corner of his eye on Paul, barking out a threat if he suspected a slackening of effort. Much of the time, Paul just drew and drew, aiming to turn himself into backdrop, a beat-up sofa in the far corner of the cabin. Much of the time, he succeeded.

He, alone among the prisoners, got close to Hans — close enough to kill him. The opportunity arose every day when, after lunch, the commandant took a snooze at his desk. Paul, had he been so minded, could have taken the knife from Hans's tray and plunged it into his throat. It would have got him beaten to death by a rush of guards, but fellow prisoners were urging him to do it. Killing Hans, preached Pastor Milman, would delay the wonder weapon and save many lives. At the next hanging, Maretzek attacked Paul. "It's your fault," he hissed; "you could have stopped that." Paul, though, was no hero. His emaciated stick of an arm was, he told himself, too weak to carry out an assassination, and his sacrifice would, in any case, not hold back the war effort. Another Hans would see it through; there would never be another Paul.

Each cabin day as he faded into furniture, hope grew in Paul's heart that he might outlive the camp. Hans was his ticket to a future life; he was not going to jeopardise that chance with a reckless gesture. He would rather be alive than an honour plaque on the wall of his university dining hall. He kept his head down and his arm busy on paper, raising neither until Hans was gone from the cabin and he was alone.

One such rainy afternoon, while Hans was taking a party of army brass around the site, Paul exploited his solitude to stare out of the streaked window at a chain gang, soaked to the skin, lugging sledloads of slate into the mouth of the unfinished tunnel. A river flowed at the foot of the gorge. The opposite slope was decked in primal foliage, old as the universe. On the near side, the incline was slashed white by a quarry, disfigured for all time to come. Paul tried to find a moral in that stark contrast, but his brain had lost all power for philosophy.

Sliding off his chair, he sidled across to the commandant's desk, keen to see how Hans organised his work. The desk was organised along conventional lines, two piles on either side for incoming and outgoing mail and a folio-size blotting pad dead centre to absorb surplus ink on the authorising signature. On top of the outgoing pile was a cardboard personnel file, of the stationery-shop kind to be found in any firm that

employed more than a dozen staff. Paul
tried to read the name on the cover but
could not decipher it because a wristwatch
had been left across the dossier, a semi-
precious Swiss job — a Tissot, by the look
of it.

Paul used to own a Tissot, a thirteenth-
birthday gift from his mother. He had lost
it at the strip-down parade on entering the
camp. Paul had cherished his watch, winding it up last thing at night, checking as he
awoke that it was on the bedpost, where he
had left it. His Tissot had no numerals, the
hours faintly indented at its perimeter, a
delicate suggestion of the slippage of time.

Hans's watch was meatier, more manly,
with a heavily scratched glass cover that left
only the hands visible and a steak-thick
leather strap, criss-crossed in a runic pattern. It was worth more than a man's life to
touch that timepiece, but temptation drew
him closer and closer. Cocking an ear for
approaching footsteps, Paul took the watch
in his palm and tested its heft as a prospective customer might in a jeweller's shop. It
made him feel powerful, holding Hans's
watch, and at the same time contaminated.
He put the watch down with a shudder, and
as he did so, the name on the file leapt to
his eyes in the twenty watts of an overhang-

ing lightbulb.

"Hannes Joachim Kerner," it said. Not Hans, but Hannes — more Nordic and esoteric than Hans, possibly snobbed up to give an illusion of aristocracy. And there was a surname as well, a priceless find. Paul's heart hammered a tattoo of terror on his ribs. He had unlocked the secret of secrets, the name which, after the war, would be the hanging of Hans. His chest swelled. Chilled as he was by fear of getting caught, he knew that his life, short or lasting as it might be, would never be the same again. The knowledge beneath his fingertips had ended his slavery, his state of impassivity. Paul was a free man once more, free to make decisions and determine a course of action.

Aware that he could be suddenly disturbed, he skim-read the dossier, taking in cogent phrases, discarding detail. Unfit for active service, said an army discharge certificate for H. J. Kerner. Reason: left leg and lung weakened by infantile poliomyelitis (so, not a war wound after all). Hero of the Great Struggle, proclaimed a Party commendation, rubber-stamped with famous signatures that ran all the way up to the top. A glossy photograph showed Hans saluting the leader, man-to-man, at a mass investiture beneath sky-high light columns.

The ensuing pages squirmed with intimacies, an orgy of information. A set of divorce papers (domestic violence cited), reports from a state children's home on a mentally retarded child, a police record (assault on two boys, case quashed by a Party tribunal), the map of a bifurcated farm and — what's this? — a ministerial order to subsidise the owner in feed and seed. All was laid out before Paul's incredulous eyes.

The land deeds were meat and drink to a man of Paul's profession. They showed that Hans owned one tract around the quarry (a paternal legacy) and another (on his mother's side) on the crest of the hill, in a forest clearing. Both were wretchedly infertile, yielding by way of income little more than their cost in tax. It did not take much for Paul to work out that Hans had persuaded his Party pals to lease his useless legacy — the quarry site for tunnel, the hilltop for a labour camp. This was, by any measure, a brilliant deal. In exchange for uncultivable land, Kerner acquired wealth and power. He was not only commandant of the labour camp but owner of all within, free to do as he pleased — so long as he delivered in the tunnel on time and on budget.

A welter of correspondence described the

recruitment of guards at convalescent homes for wounded soldiers. Prisoners came from the state agency for conscripted labour, purchased by the truckload for a few coins a head. Replacement orders for "breakages" and "waste disposal" revealed the death rates, 96 one month, 142 the next. The euphemisms reminded Paul of collusions back home, where his uncle, a master of palm greasing, was the middleman in grubby deals between lazy landowners and underpaid municipal officials. It pleased Paul to find graft and corruption flourishing at the summits of a regime that trumpeted a ruthless purity. It signified structural weakness, a portent of downfall.

Listening for footsteps, hearing nothing but the patter of rain on the cabin roof, Paul flipped back through the file, searching for something he might have missed. He worried that the material was too clear-cut, too one-dimensional. Could it be a hoax? Was Paul being set up? Was someone, a mutinous guard perhaps, trying to plant false rumours about Hans? Had hunger unhinged Paul's critical mind? He reread the dossier, cover to cover. The leader salute was no fake. The deeds confirmed that Hans had friends on high. It did not matter how the file had come to be left on the desk. What mattered was that Paul had the facts of Hans's life in his trembling hands and the opportunity to use them to incalculable personal advantage.

Shutting the dossier, replacing the Tissot across it, Paul scuttled back to his desk to reroute a service lane in short, brisk strokes, consigning to memory by whispered repetition every salient fact from the file, eager to get out of the cabin before the commandant remembered what he had left on his desk. The sketch done, he delivered it in teeming rain to Hans, who, taking the paper scroll in one hand, cuffed Paul with the other across the skull, the blow rendered painless by practised anticipation. In the dance of slave and master, the slave was choreographer.

That night, scratching a louse bite in his bunk, Paul silently recapitulated his findings. First names first: not Hans but Hannes, a limp suffix, a dragged leg, a sigh, and a lisp. The supererogatory syllable softened the man's dread. This was not so much a mad beast as a harassed contractor running a delayed operation with a disloyal team. In different circumstances, Paul might have felt a tweak of sympathy for the project manager.

It was a tough job, construction, with no second chance. He was almost inclined to

40

offer the commandant expert advice, when emptiness gnawed at his organs and he remembered who was who in this situation, he and murderous Hans.

The file, he knew, could feed him for months. Bread from Maretzek and soup from Finkel's people. Loaves of fresh bread, great tureens of soup. He could taste them on the tip of his tongue, feel them slip down his throat in gulps and into his concave stomach. Cravings howled at him, as an infant screams for the breast. He would do anything to placate those needs, anything except put his life at risk. That stopped him short. With the acuity of an actuary, he calculated his chances and rated them low. If Hans's real name got into circulation, it would be swiftly traced to the source. There were traitors in the camp, known as *shtinkers*, who would sell their own brothers for a slice of liver sausage. Hans would remember leaving the dossier on his desk and have Paul dragged to his dungeon. It was more than Paul's life was worth to share the information, much as he desired the nourishment, the prestige, and the solidarity that would be his in exchange. He would have to keep the Hannes name to himself.

Feeling guilty at letting the others down, Paul convinced himself that it was not in their interest to know the truth. Hans was the name they had pinned on an enemy. Any other name would confuse starved minds, sap resistance, and deplete the will to live. Paul, empowered by knowledge, felt that he was responsible for upholding camp morale, for reinforcing the bonds between men, founded though they were on myth and misapprehension. The things the other men shared — the Hans name, the common dread — these things were worth more to the human spirit than actual fact. Regret it though he might, he would not divulge the contents of the dossier.

That decision set Paul apart from his fellow sufferers. He owned fact; they indulged a fantasy. He had light; they fumbled in murk. "Hans will hang" was Maretzek's daily mantra. "Vengeance is mine, saith the Lord," chanted the Professor at dawn ablutions. "A life for a life," preached Milman. "Hans's for ours."

"Kill him it today!" hissed Maretzek as Hans, not long before the end, stamped on the pastor's fingers that clung to the cliff edge of the quarry. That night, Paul had a dream. As a boy, his mother had taken him every Friday to a fleapit to see none-too-recent American films on an old projector that kept breaking down, either stopping in mid-frame or screwing the image to one side so that faces were lengthened and half the screen was left blank. Paul, more delighted by the breakdowns than by the silly plots, imagined that an unseen story was being told on the empty half of the screen. He could see the story inside his head and hear the salient voices. It was his private movie world and it came to his rescue many times when he got into trouble at school or work and he would stop the reality reel and run his personal version instead. The trick came in handy on the parade ground when men were hanged and he could see them bright and laughing in a different state of being, on the other half of the screen.

On the night of Milman's murder, Paul harked back to a Harold Lloyd movie he had seen with his mother, where the hero was clinging to the arms of a giant clock at the top of a skyscraper. On the other screen, he saw Hans and himself hanging from opposite arms of an outsized Tissot. Paul was dangling from the hour arm at nine o'clock, ticking upwards second by second towards the apex of noon, from where he could scramble onto the safety of a roof. Hans was on the long arm, heading for a perpendicular abyss at the stroke of the half-hour. Paul knew that he must hold himself at the opposite extreme from Hans. He must be as far from Hans as it was possible to be if he wanted to escape. He must not be like Hans in any way, or he was doomed. If Hans scowled, Paul must smile. If Hans ate, Paul must starve. If Hans killed, Paul must renounce killing now and for evermore. He must be the opposite of Hans.

Paul awoke next morning with more clarity of mind than he had known in months. He understood that if he killed, he would become Hans; therefore, *he must not kill.* Let Maretzek rage and the Professor sulk. If he wanted to be Paul, *he must not kill.* Dawn after dawn, he repeated that rule to himself amid the vengeance chants, smiling not so much with moral superiority as with an iron sense of purpose. He knew what he must not do.

And when the day of freedom broke, when prisoners awoke and found the watchtowers unmanned and the double gates creaking in the wind, Paul stayed alone in his bunk as Maretzek and the Professor led a pack of avengers on the guards' accommodation block. Striped skeletons chased ghosts with self-made knives and shards of stone, ransacked beds that had been warm an hour before. All they found was Hans's idiot valet, asleep in his iron cot, a teddy bear on his pillow. They bludgeoned him to death anyway and surged on to the food stores, which gaped empty, every last can removed in the guards' retreat. Exhausted, prisoners pounded bleeding fists on cupboard doors and howled at the sky. Fights broke out over a sack of turd-like potatoes found in a scullery. Maretzek, firing the valet's pistol, claimed the turds for "the people's pantry." Chaos mingled with misery at the dawn of liberation.

"What now?" said Paul when the Professor crawled back into the bunk they shared, panting with exertion.

"Now nothing," said the thwarted avenger.

"Are we liberated?"

"No, but close," cried Maretzek. "I heard artillery fire."

"Shall we go out to meet them?"

"Who cares?" said the Professor, his pale cranium shining in spring light.

They called him "Professor," though he was no more than a lab assistant from a Balkan capital. Mircea Vitse, his name was, or so it had said on the clipboard when the men in black arrived with a conscription list for voluntary labour.

"But I didn't volunteer," Vitse had protested. "There must be some mistake."

"No mistake," said the chief thug. "The

penalty for not volunteering is five years in a labour camp. You're sentenced. Get moving."

Paul was seized that same day in a different country, frog-marched out of his uncle's office, and pummelled onto an open-topped truck. He did not protest, accepting his fate as if it were self-inflicted. They met, Paul and the Professor, on a forced march uphill from the quarry, brandishing ironic banter as whips snapped at their legs.

"You're designing an escape chute," quipped the Professor.

"No, I'm helping them dig to invade Australia," laughed Paul. "What's your job?"

"I'm supposed to curate the weapon that will bring victory. But their scientists haven't managed to mix the right potion without fritzing their balls, so for the time being I am compiling temperature charts for elements of the periodic table."

"The weapon, will it combust?" asked Paul, thinking of wall thickness and foundation depths.

"It is more likely to bring us out in boils," smiled the Professor. "The devil's spawn are experimenting with a bubonic plague virus, among other mediaeval reversions."

While the two friends made deskbound calculations, others carved slate for the silo.

The rock-face work was murderous. Men dropped from heat, cold, and hunger. There were frequent avalanches. The guards veered from bullying to a playfulness that was even more dangerous. A man accused of slow working was made to carry a full load of slate to the cliff top, where, harried by dogs, he jumped or fell. Hans turned this torture into sport. Two men would jump together while the guards laid bets on which would land first, and whether on his feet or head. "Skydiving," it was called. The other prisoners, summoned to watch, welcomed the respite from hacking and stacking. Three rounds of skydiving could take an hour out of the unending day and tire out the savage dogs.

The dead were carried at close of day in sombre quickstep, quarry-inn-camp, up the road, past the Laughing Hind, the church, the shops, to the lime pit outside the camp, where each corpse was lifted up to have its arm number ticked off a list, then tipped into the mass grave. The living were counted through the gates one by one and made to stand on parade for an hour or two while they were counted once again for Hans's meticulous bookkeeping. Roll-call gave Paul the time to map his surroundings. The camp was built as a set of squares. Four blocks of service units — kitchen, sickbay, store-rooms, torture cells — enclosed the parade ground. Row upon row of prisoner barracks made up the next square, itself surrounded by the guards' block and its herbaceous borders, which presented a respectable façade to passers-by, unlikely as anyone was to pass so far off the forest path in violation of the KEEP OUT notices.

In the last months of war, when the roads were bomb-cratered and dead workers could not be replaced, the skydiving stopped. So did Paul's cabin privileges as every last prisoner was hurled into a frantic effort to finish the tunnel. "I'm glad I volunteered," coughed the Professor through a lungful of slate dust. "I should hate to have to perform such unpleasant work under duress."

"It will provide research for your doctor-ate." Paul grimaced.

"I have no wish to be doctored."

"They will make you rector of the acad-emy when you get home."

"My dear Pavlov," said the Professor, "has anyone told you that you are full of shit?"

"Pavlov" was the Professor's name for Paul.

"Why Pavlov?" Paul demanded.

"After the Soviet scientist who made his

dogs salivate as he withheld their food."

"Am I withholding something?"

"You know what you know."

"What does that mean?"

"You play your own game. You stand apart and observe us like laboratory rats."

Paul had met the Professor's type before, clever, bitter men who by reason of poverty or personality faults had failed to attain a good degree and earned a pittance in white coats as scientific auxiliaries, despising men of lesser minds who were addressed as "Doctor." The Professor was a mass of resentments, a man of preposterous self-esteem who always used long words where short would do. At university, he would have been an impossible colleague; in camp, he was life itself. Many times that perishing last winter, he saved Paul from collapse at the quarry face. He taught him to save energy by bedding his sled with bracken to make the guards think it was full. "Minimum effort, minimum, minimum," he mumbled. "Three centimetres," he chimed on the evening march. "Don't lift your feet higher; save strength."

Paul repaid his friend with grateful deference. He may have outranked the Professor in academic qualifications, but the bald technician had vital life skills, garnished with a rare gift of irony. Each night in their upper tier, the two men broke bread on a spread handkerchief, pretending they were dining at a gourmet restaurant.

"May I replenish your water glass, Professor?"

"Thank you, Pavlov. Another morsel of this delicious baguette?"

"I'm quite full, thank you."

Other inmates crowded round for a front-row view of the comedy. They were a pair, Paul and the Professor, and their antics provided an illusion of normality. After the tablecloth was folded away, each crumb lifted off with a damp finger and placed on lips to avoid waste, the Professor would sit in his corner, honing a knife, while Paul held open surgery at the edge of the bunk. Word had got around that Paul held two anomalous doctorates, in psychology and architecture, and prisoners looked to him for help and advice. Tamas, the brawny Hungarian, commissioned him for a fistful of vegetable peelings to design an extension to his father's brewery. Angelo wanted to learn how to reproduce a drawing of two naked nymphs he had seen in the Uffizi Gallery back home. Twenty-year-old Janko confided that he felt sexually attracted to men. Vremi, from the Ukraine, feared his foot rot was turning gangrenous. The Professor himself, blade in hand, asked Paul, once the last of his clients had gone, what he ought to do about a little domestic problem, a flat-chested, pasty-faced year-two biochemistry student with whom he had shared a stairway closet during a militia raid, an encounter which resulted in an unintended pregnancy, the consequence (he complained) of his partner's previous inexperience and lack of precautions.

Benignly and with serene patience, Paul addressed each request on merit. For Tamas, he knocked up a lean-to with storage for hundred-litre barrels. For Angelo and anyone else who cared to attend, he gave a Sunday-morning class in life drawing. Janko he told not to worry, saying he would lust once more for big breasts the day he left the camp. Vremi's wound, he lanced with the Professor's tool, drawing out the pus and bandaging it with the dinner-table handkerchief. The Professor, he congratulated on becoming a father, even with so unappealing a mate as the virgin biochemist.

"What am I to do about the child?" fretted the Professor.

"First, get out of here alive," said Paul. "The rest will fall into place. You may find when you get home that motherhood has

51

turned the girl into a Mona Lisa and you won't believe your luck in landing such a beauty."

"I've never had any luck worth believing," grumbled the Professor.

"You have a child."

"I never wanted one."

Paul changed the subject, wary of giving offence. His alliance with the Professor was founded on mutual need and respectful distance. "Like frock-coated diplomats in a cannibal kingdom," in the Professor's creative allegory, they maintained a pretence of civilised conduct in the narrow bunk. Feet to face they slept, an intolerable proximity. Each morning they congratulated each other on being one day closer to the glory of a single bed.

"What now?" said Paul as the Professor rose from his shroud of liberation gloom.

"We wait," said the Professor.

"How long?" cried Tamas. "There's nothing to eat. If we are not out of here in a day or two, we're dead."

"What do you suggest, dear Pavlov?"

"Why don't we get out and forage, go down to the village and knock on doors for food," Paul suggested.

"Are you crazy?" said Janko from the bunk below. "Do you think farmwives will give us eggs and milk and a bed to sleep in? They'll shoot the first of us that opens a gate and set the dogs on the rest."

"And who's to say that Hans isn't out there, sitting in the forest with a bottle of schnapps and a rat-a-tat machine gun?" rumbled Vremi. "We're best off staying here. The liberators can't be far. That rumbling is cannon fire, not thunder."

A hush fell upon the bunkhouse as men wrestled with unaccustomed freedoms of decision. The Hungarians were all for getting out without delay, but Paul urged them to listen to Janko, who, in his market town before the war, saw urchins stone a stray Gypsy child to death. If there was one thing that united peasants of the world in ways that Karl Marx had not foreseen or Maretzek could admit, it was xenophobia. Men in camp stripes could expect no favours from country folk who had buried their heads until now in beer mugs as the death march passed through their village.

"Janko's right," said Paul. "Let's wait. If no help arrives by daybreak, we'll go out and beg." That night, the men talked in the future positive, a forgotten tense. Janko wept at the thought of embracing his widowed mother. Angelo described his plans for reunion with Renata, up in the hills with partisans. He wished he could show them a photograph of his lovely fiancée; instead, he circulated a naked drawing he had made under Paul's tutelage, expatiating on her pale olive complexion, her oval black eyes, her classical contours, and her vociferous enthusiasm for the act of love beneath the naked sky, a description that Paul interpreted as a generous effort to distract his friends from racking hunger, impotence, and the fear of morning.

Andras and Tamas keened a ballad of Balkan treachery in the centre of the hut. Marek, the Pole, ruminated aloud on car repairs. Dragan, the Serb, filed his spoon handle to a lethal point. Nils, the Norwegian, sat still at the door as a fisherman beside an ice hole. The hut was a united continent of the dispossessed.

"What about you, my Leonardo?" piped Angelo, addressing his art teacher. "What will you do?"

Paul had no home, no plans, no-one to see.

"Where will you go?" pressed Janko.

"Canada, maybe. There is a cousin in Vancouver, on my mother's side. . . ."

"It's a land of plenty," said a disembodied voice.

"Plenty cold," said the Professor, and a

shiver gripped cadaverous men beneath their sketchy blankets.

"Who will go out first tomorrow?" asked Angelo.

"Let's draw lots," proposed the Professor. "No point all of us getting shot together."

"One man," said Maretzek, "the most presentable, should scout the area and bring back what he can. When the rest have eaten, we'll make a second sortie."

"Any volunteers?"

"Might as well be me," said Paul. "I speak the language and I have the least to lose."

"Let's sleep on it." The Professor yawned. Consensus settled on the blockhouse night, the last that Paul would endure.

A full hour ahead of dawn, he was up by force of habit, rushing out for roll-call before he remembered that the counting was over, the counters gone. He lingered at the wash tap, alone beneath the diamond stars, buttoning his jacket to the throat against the cold. Returning to the hut, he felt Janko's eyes upon him from the bunk below.

"I'll go with you," whispered the young man.

"Better not, safer on my own."

"Don't take risks."

"Don't worry, I'll be careful."

"Be quick."

"I'll do my best."

"Bread and cheese and eggs and jam . . ."

"As much as I can carry."

Bending low, Paul kissed Janko on the crown of his head, realising at that moment that Janko's stammered confession of homoerotic urges had been a shy declaration of love for the man who bunked above. Janko grabbed Paul's hand, kissing it hard at the knuckles before shoving him off, out into the hard, empty world.

Paul walked through the gates of the inner camp, past mounds of earth and tripwire trenches and through the electrified outer fence, one of its sections having been wrenched off at a crazy angle by a fleeing vehicle. Looking neither right nor left, he entered the forest at a steady tread, the soles of his feet knowing each step, every bend in the road, every rut in the surface, the spot where Grunwald was shot, where Goran dropped, where Varady was ripped apart by exultant sheepdogs. On either side of him, oaks and conifers rolled down endless slopes. He smelt mushrooms in the undergrowth but could not see a thing or trust himself to tell edible from deadly. Another odour tweaked his nostrils, the reek of animal dung. There were wolves in the woods — he had heard their howling — but his fear of the wild was annulled by a headier sensation, a thrilling solitude. Alone and unwatched, Paul became a naughty child, eager to break rules. He relieved his bladder in a thin stream against a fat tree and, buttoning up, flung his slave's cap into a thicket. His head rang with exhilaration. He had been to Dante's hell and come forth physically whole and without blood on his hands.

He was free to do as he pleased, go where he chose. He need never descend or climb this hill again. He could get food for his friends, or forsake them. No-one could touch him; no-one need ever know. He was free, free, free. Quickening his pace in descent, he counted steps as if this were another forced march. He passed the church at eight hundred sixty, and the doctor's house, where a light glimmered above the staff and serpent emblem. He thought of pulling the doorbell but decided against it, thinking that the doctor, if he were true to his oath, might be more approachable in daylight. The doctor, of all the villagers, would surely be his best bet for sustenance.

He headed on, faster. One thousand and forty-one steps, forty-two, forty-three, he saw the luminous grin of the Laughing

Hind and remembered the smell of giant waste bins beside its kitchen door. A good place for scrapings, for fruit and vegetable peels to chew, which might stop his legs trembling until he could go to the doctor and the priest and beg for a token of human decency, if such a thing existed in a place that turned its head away from the dead and dying.

His strength fading, Paul lifted the iron lid of a waste bin and looked inside. The bin was empty, clean as a cat's bowl. They must have fed the tavern leftovers to pigs the night before or spread them on a compost heap. The second bin was the same, and the one beyond. Paul's sunken eyes filled with tears. There was not even a mouldy cabbage leaf for a man to gnaw. The sky was going grey at the edges. He looked for a window that might let him into the kitchen for a gulp of water, a rummage around in search of crumbs. He saw a loose latch on an upper vent and used the last wrench of a muscle to haul his frame onto the window ledge. As he wriggled one gaunt arm into the gap, his leg slipped on the ledge and he crashed to the ground, dislodging a bin lid as he fell. "Who's that?" quavered a voice, the last voice he would hear for days.

CHAPTER THREE

They had an unspoken agreement, Paul and Alice, never to refer to their first meeting by word, gesture, or anniversary gift. It was their particular secret, a marital intimacy so private that they refrained from sharing it again, even with each other. Neither could remember who had requested the silence, whether it had been invoked by Alice out of modesty or Paul out of shame. Either way, neither of them ever alluded to the moment they had met. Paul assumed that Alice did not want to be reminded of the state he was in when she found him, half-dead and more animal than man. It must be hard for her, he thought, to look at her husband, the landlord and popular mayor, and remember him as the mephitic thing she hauled up from the ground and fed from her hand like a fallen bird. Paul, for his part, declined to revisit his act of betrayal, the forsaking of his desperate friends for the solace that he found in Alice.

Staunch and self-contained, Alice never once, in a domestic row or sentimental mood, reminded him of his debt to her. She saw him as he was now, not then, and Paul sealed her unseeing with a complicit kiss. He knew that if she were ever to glance on him as she had done that day — a rag doll, soiled and starving among the waste bins — he would be unmanned. Their life was built on the rock of her respect. If she were to appraise him with the pitying gaze of first acquaintance, the rock would turn to chalk and crumble beneath them. She held the keys to his confidence and never jangled her ownership. Paul loved Alice as much for her tact as for any other facet of her resolute nature; and if he could not swear before God that he loved her as he had never loved another (not that she ever asked), he could at least reciprocate her love for him with an appreciation of her estimable qualities — unless, as so often happened, she beat him to the compliment.

"Dearest," she said one summer's evening as he sketched at his pad while she, sitting at the linen basket, slipped wooden ball into sock after sock, darning any toe hole that came to light. "Dearest," she said, "I am so proud of you."

"Proud? What of?" asked Paul, half-fearing reminiscence.

The grandfather clock ticked off sonorous seconds in the hallway and a horse clip-clopped metronomically up the hill. A warm breeze fluttered the curtains, wafting in the dusty smell of drying hay from the fields that meandered down to the clear river. Alice bit off a cotton thread with creamy front teeth and patted the darn into place. A strand of straw-yellow hair slipped over her eye. She pinned it methodically back, her actions neat and sparing. "I was just counting," she said, "all the changes you have made to the village, the innovations you brought to our tavern. . . ."

"But you run the inn, not me," he protested mildly, inviting contradiction.

"It couldn't flourish without you." She smiled. "All the ideas are yours — the hotel wing, the weekend tourist package, the coffee machine. Who in this province ever tasted espresso before? Now they come from miles around just to look at our coffee machine, as if it were a Michelangelo. You have made the Laughing Hind somewhere people want to drop into, even if they don't need a drink. It is a place to have breakfast, read the papers, meet friends, have a party, or sit alone, and that's all down to you, my love. Even Papa can see that."

Later that night in bed, coiled around her contented back, Paul would wonder how Alice might respond if he were to share with her the thing that had returned to haunt him, tugging him awake at the dead of night, the dread of Hans. She would, if he started to talk, listen without interruption and, when he had finished, assure him of her unconditional love, her limitless support, in that wonderful way that came so naturally to her. Together since that first grey dawn, they formed a front against the world. Paul knew that he could do whatever he needed to and Alice would be right behind him. Alice, without pretending to understand more than a fraction of Paul's complex thoughts, knew with full certainty that he was right, that he was hers, that he would never leave her.

A cloud scuttered across her brow.

"What is it, dearest?" Paul murmured, folding away his sketch for the new school roof.

"I'm worried about you waking up every night," said Alice. "Is it something to do with, you know, the waterworks? Maybe you should see Dr. Walters?" Paul shook his head twice, irrevocably.

"Papa had that trouble," she continued.

"The doctor sent him to the university hospital. They took a, what do you call it, a roentgen and found a little lump on the — you know what. They kept him in a week after the operation, and when he came home, he was right as rain — well, as right as he'll ever be."

"My insomnia is nothing to do with a urinary malfunction or any cyst or growth," said Paul, using medical terms to conceal his irritation. "It's nothing to be concerned about. A passing phase, probably due to overwork, too much on my mind. It will go away on its own, my love. Anyhow, you know I couldn't bear to be cooped up in a hospital. I don't respond well to barred windows and strict regimes."

Alice, hearing his shutters descend, handed him a tangle of green wool to hold while she rewound it into balls. It was a wiry mess unfurled from an old sweater and was required — waste not, want not — for reknitting. Arms outstretched, Paul looked down on her bobbing head and busy shoulders and saw a woman doing as her mother and grandmother had done before her, doing the best for her man and her house. Alice belonged to a time before. Her horizons were the valley walls, her ambitions close to hand. He could not tell her of the makers of great cities and deep ideas, because she had never ventured beyond the valley nor, so far as he was aware, held any book but the Bible in her hand for longer than it would take to read the title. Had he met her in his former life, he would not have known what to say to her, and any physical spark between them would have been quenched by the gulf of cultures. It was a measure of how far he had detached himself from that past that he now found Alice desirable and interesting, her unworldliness a positive virtue. He had no need to converse with her about architects and philosophers. He had cancelled his subscription to the restless intellect and its learned journals. All he wanted for the rest of his life was to watch the river swell in spring and ebb in summer, the meadows shaven by harvest renew their bounty next season, his son rise from knee height to head. Above all, he longed to relax in the gift of a love that came from Alice as easily as wool from a sheep or, as it now did, from a frayed sweater. Alice was Paul's safe place, her alto voice his lullaby. Hearing her count rotations of wool, or sing to Johann, or boss the kitchen girls, or chatter to Lisl behind the bar, Paul was lulled by her ample, earthy tone, her physical robustness. Hers was a bell that first tolled in the ears of a dying Paul, prostrate at her feet, and, dimly heard, gave him hope of revival.

"What is it?" was the second thing he heard her say, after the timorous "Who's that?" She was standing above him, her scullery boots, beside his chin, smelling of acrid ammonia.

"Are you hungry?" she demanded. "You must be hungry. Wait. I will fetch you something."

The sound reached him blurred and delayed. He tried to unclick his tongue from a parched palate and twitch a leg to show he had heard, but the message did not travel from brain to limb. He managed to blink and she nodded acknowledgement, raising one open palm in mute gesture: Wait there. When she was gone, he separated her words into syllables and joined them back together, desperate to work out if the girl was about to help him, or turn him in for liquidation. Her voice had been warm, her diction clear, her meaning direct. Still, something jarred. A false pronoun, that was it. "Are *you* hungry?" she had said, using the formal *Sie* in place of the childish *Du*. She had addressed him as an adult, a free man, a person of consequence. He had not been spoken to that way since the day of his arrest. Overwhelmed, he tried to raise an arm in salutation as she returned.

"Don't move," the girl commanded. Squatting beside him and lifting his head into the crook of a strong arm, she spooned cold water from one bowl, warm vegetable soup from another, alternately angling them into the cavern of his mouth, careful not to feed him too fast or scorch his tongue. The ninth or tenth gulp caused him to retch, a hacking up of phlegm mixed with morsels of carrot. She did not flinch, wiping the bile off her apron and waiting for him to resume. She seemed accustomed to invalidity. When he could swallow no more, she lowered his head into her lap and let him rest.

"Did you escape from the camp?" she asked, fingering his striped jacket in the light of the kitchen window. "Are they searching for you?"

He shook his head, signalling with open hands that the fences had been breached, that he was out on his own and no danger to anyone. Pinkness creased the horizon.

"Come," she said, holding him beneath the arms, "let's get you up."

Her grip was sinewy, but there was nothing in his legs, and he flopped fish-like to the ground. She propped him against the wall and assessed him with an objective eye, making up her mind what to do next. Paul stared at the ground out of prisoner habit, fearing to influence her decision in case it was the wrong one. The girl was young — seventeen, eighteen — crop-haired, smooth-skinned, and evidently well nourished beneath a capacious, shapeless kitchen overall. Her voice was steady, her actions calm.

"Let's get you inside," she said. He sneaked another look at her. Eighteen, maybe nineteen. Hair not cropped but tightly bunned against her skull to effect a sexless, androgynous look, sensible in such wild times. Remarkably, she showed no fear of the male intruder: He must seem puny and pathetic, he realised.

A cart trundled somewhere along the road, its hinges creaking. Paul scrambled to his haunches, as if to flee. "Stop," said the girl. "It's not safe for you to be out in prisoner clothes. I'll get you something else to wear and keep you indoors until night-fall." She pulled him up and dragged him inside, down a corridor, and, finger to her lips, up a wooden staircase. At the second flight, she switched her grip and lifted him bodily, one arm around his neck and the other beneath his knees, carrying him to a room at the top, beneath the eaves. "This used to be the cook's," she panted, "but she got called up last year to feed the troops, so there is just me and Papa left at the inn, us and a few old hands who help out in the evening."

The attic contained a single bed with a striped mattress flush against the sloping wall, a small desk by the window, pitcher and bowl, mirrored cupboard, chamber pot. No electric light or running water. The girl opened the curtains and whipped a brocaded cover off the bed. "I'll bring you water to wash in, and some clothes," she promised. "More to eat, as well." He sat down on the bed, which hardly flinched at the slightness of his weight. "I'm going to lock you in," she explained. "No-one much comes up here now, but you never know. If you need" — she indicated the chamber pot — "use that."

He flopped back onto the mattress and, to the sound of the key turning, sank into nullity. When he woke, the day was dying at the window and the road was deathly still. Some slices of crisp bread and cheese sat upon a wooden tray, beside a cup of coffee substitute, stone-cold. He gnawed a sandwich and sipped the black liquid until his gut rebelled and he rushed for the pot. As he evacuated the last spurt, the lock turned and the girl entered with a steaming basin of water that she put on the wooden floor, with a chunk of soap and a towel. Unembarrassed by his skinny shanks and the putrid stench from the commode, she asked if he was feeling better. Paul, stripped of privacy and pants, reverted to slave status. He muttered an apology, eyes down.

"No need," she said. "Time to get washed and changed."

"And then?"

"We'll see how things look."

Fixing a candleholder to the desk, she lit the wick while he stripped off the rest of his striped garments and washed his upper body over the bowl on the floor before lowering himself into the water to let it lick around his lower parts. He looked down and saw his ribs jut through parchment skin, his concave belly, his straggly manhood. The girl showed no embarrassment, holding a towel as he rose and wrapping it around him. He started to shake. She held him tight to her heavy sweater, sharing warmth. "It's all right," she said. "You're safe here."

"Shall I go?"

"No, stay the night. You're in no fit state to leave."

Dropping a woollen nightshirt over his

head and arms, she draped the bed with an extra eiderdown that she brought from the cupboard. The legs of the bed rattled with his trembling. "You'll be all right," she said. "Get some more sleep; there's nothing to worry about. It will all be over in a few days and we can start to look ahead."

He was coughing in spasms when she returned with a bowl of clear broth. "You'll live," she assured him.

"How do you know?" he enquired.

"I nursed my dying mother," said the girl expressionlessly. "You're not that sick."

For three days and nights, his fever raged, and when it was over, so was the war. The girl brought him news of the surrender with a bowl of leek soup and a yellow tulip in a tall glass. Paul, once she had washed him head to toe with a damp flannel, staggered to the window on his own two legs and saw tanks grumbling down the road, their crews waving bare-headed from the turrets. A white flag covered the shield of the Laughing Hind. The rest of the village was, so far as he could see, deserted. After the last tank had gone by, the girl inched open a window to let out stagnant air, but no fresh gust blew in. All was still outside, time and nature suspended.

A jolt of conscience hit him like an electric

shock from the camp's perimeter fence. What had become of the men he left behind, the ones he had promised to bring food and drink? He had betrayed them, left them to die. He tottered on his feet, and the girl — Alice, her name was — led him by the arm back to the bed. He asked if she knew what was being done for liberated prisoners from the labour camp at the top of the hill. She gave him a slow, frugal look, assessing how much he could take. Paul repeated his question. Some of the men, she said, had come out scavenging. One of them, a Czech, had been shot by a farmer's wife he tried to rape. Dear God, prayed Paul, let it not be Janko.

The village, said the girl, was terrified of the inmates. It was not the fault of the local folk that the fellows had been mistreated. People felt sorry for them, but what could they do? It was a serious offence to help a prisoner. One woman, a war widow, had been sent to jail for sneaking food to one of the striped wretches who had been sent to bring in her harvest. Another was shot for hiding an escapee in her barn; there were posters about it all over the village. She spoke as if Paul were not a recent prisoner but a guest at her inn, filling him in with the gossip. People, she continued, were hoping that these poor men would be sent home right away, wherever it was they had come from.

"And what if they have no homes to go to?" Paul demanded. "What if their homes and towns were burned with their families inside?"

"We know nothing about such things," said Alice, pressing strips of ham and lettuce between two slices of bread that she held to his lips. Paul opened his mouth and said nothing more.

Alice spent the first days and nights of liberation in his attic, despatched there by her father to keep her out of sight of sex-starved soldiers. "He doesn't know *you're* here, of course." She giggled, implying by her levity that he did not count as a rampant man. She wore a thick-knit sweater and dungarees, her hair trapped beneath a workman's cap. With her broad shoulders and big boots, there was no femininity to her, nothing to arouse desire. She joked with Paul about her attire, asking if she could play Joseph, the carpenter, in this year's Nativity play. She seemed more child-like than before, heedless of the world and its turmoil. She brought him news and tittle-tattle — about the mayor, who had vamoosed with silverware from the church;

about the mule that went missing from the Bauer farm and was found half-eaten; about the farm's owner, who, violated by a black soldier, shot herself soon after. Rumours swirled. Some said this was the same woman who had shot the marauding Czech prisoner the day before.

"Serves her right," grumbled Paul.

"Franziska Bauer, her name is. My mother's cousin," said Alice.

At night, she bedded down on Paul's floor in a khaki sleeping bag, asking if he minded and promising with a giggle not to snore. He noticed in morning light that she slept with a thumb in her mouth and a doll at her side. Awake, she chatted to him most of the time, requiring no more than a vague smile by way of response. She asked once or twice if she was boring him, apologising and saying that she did not get much chance to chew the fat with anyone these days. Ever since her mother died, she and Papa had clanked around each other like the ghosts that lived in those ornamental knights in armour on the staircase. The boys were long gone — Karlheinrich shot by resistants in the Balkans, Franz-Josef missing on the Russian front. The boys never even knew that Mamma was ill. They were spared her merciless ordeal, an agony unrelieved by drugs because Dr. Walters was out of analgesics and no relief was obtainable, even on the big-city black market. Papa had pawned his father's watch in exchange for a fistful of pills that turned out to be chalk. He wept at Mamma's bedside, saying that he had failed her in all their years together, and she, poor thing, had not the strength to contradict him. Alice was the one who attended day and night, holding her mother's hand as life drained away. She had never talked about it to anyone before, come to think of it.

They were taking a walk along the top-floor corridor, Alice holding Paul by the arm to help him get his strength back, she said, Paul getting the measure of the building, as he liked to do wherever he stayed. It gave him confidence to feel the proportions of height to breadth and hear the foundations sing out their depth from beneath the ground. He understood the language of buildings and took in their dimensions intuitively as he walked up and down along an upper floor.

Alice was chattering away happily about her family sorrows. Papa, never a man with much to say, had gone mute on Mamma's death, restricting his communications to barks and oaths. "He's like — what d'you call them, the monks of silence? Trappists, that's it, the ones who only speak one day a year." She laughed.

"Why won't he talk to you?" asked Paul.

"Maybe I remind him too much of Mamma."

Most nights, she said, Papa matched the demon drinkers downstairs schnapps for schnapps until his head hit the tabletop. Alice kept to the kitchen, washing up with the old codgers. Her friend Lisl was away, sent for safety to her married sister in Pringsheim, across the gorge. There was no-one for her to talk to. She was bored, bored and out of her element — "like a nun in a brothel." She giggled. Some of her remarks were designed to amuse. Others were lost on Paul, couched in teenage dialect, a generation beneath him.

They were back in the attic before he asked what she thought would happen next. "There's a curfew," she reported. "The Americans are here, issuing orders. They requisitioned the Black Horse in Pringsheim as military headquarters. We could be next; that's Papa's big fear. He's petrified we're going to be shut down."

If they closed the Laughing Hind, she warned, "it will be the end for us." The inn had a cellar full of flour and potatoes. They had eggs from the hens at the back, and a few hogs left to slaughter. Mamma, foreseeing hardship, had seeded a garden bed with carrots and spinach. They could get along pretty well so long as they lived above the tavern and kept it open. If the inn was taken over, there would be no home or income, no food, nothing to do, no reason to get up in the morning. Papa would die and she would go out of her mind, or out of the village at any rate.

"The military authorities have notified us of a visit," she announced. "Papa is so scared, he has taken down the knights in armour — military symbols, you see — and he's in the bar this minute painting over the black-and-red decor in shades of lavender, like a ladies' toilet in a grand hotel." Alice could not stay serious for too long.

She was shaking out his bed, plumping the pillows, straightening the eiderdown. Paul stood at the window, staring at the empty road. "Shall I get us an extra chair?" she suggested. "You must have somewhere to sit other than the bed. Isn't it time you told me your name, by the way? I didn't like to ask before."

Paul stretched his arms and walked around the attic cell. A decision was looming, and he needed to get the blood circulating round his sluggish brain. Things were about to change. Strangers would come crawling over the inn, asking questions when they found him. He shrank from confrontations with bureaucracy, sympathetic or inept. He needed to devise a role that would allow him to stay safe in this place until he had enough strength to decide what to do with the resumption of his life.

"I can help you," he told Alice.

"How?"

"I can talk to the Americans when they inspect. I speak a little English, from school. I will tell them that you hid me when I escaped from the camp."

"Are you crazy? If you tell them that, half the village will treat us as traitors and the other half as madmen. They won't believe you anyway."

"Why not?"

"Because hardly anyone helped prisoners; it was too risky. Those who did were sent away, or strung up as a warning to the rest of us."

"You did. . . ."

"Only at the last gasp."

"Enough to save my life," said Paul, slumping onto the bed.

The girl stared at him from the opposite side of the room.

"I'd have to tell Papa about you. . . ."

"You weren't planning to tell him?"

"I hadn't decided. I rather like having you here as my little secret. I'm not sure he'd understand."

"Well, you'd better do something, because he's sure to find out when they search the place."

"What should I say?"

"That you hid a man who will put in a good word for you with the occupiers. Tell him also that I won't be staying long."

"You're not strong enough yet to leave," protested Alice.

"That's for me to decide," said Paul.

His curt reply underlined the age gap between them, fifteen years, at Paul's guess, and shifted the balance of authority, revising their relationship from helper and helpless to airy young girl and experienced older man. Alice grasped the reversal and was not in the least bit pleased. She banged about the room, tidying up before going off to fetch a chair. Paul, unprompted, asked for a block of paper, a ruler, a compass, and pencils. She brought back her old school satchel and then flounced off to help Papa with his emergency painting and decorating.

All day long, Paul sat beneath the window

and drew as he had not drawn in years, for pleasure and for profit. He sketched a shelter for the giant kitchen bins, hiding them from scavengers, human and animal. He rearranged the front yard of the Laughing Hind, inserting delivery bays, customer parking, flower beds, and a water fountain. After a short nap, he reconfigured the attic, utilising its roof space to create an adjoining washroom, with running water from an overhead tank. He cut a skylight into the ceiling and drew in a power line to the nearest electricity pylon. Finally, to illustrate the full potential for luxury accommodation, he sketched in recessed cupboards, Sun King furnishings, and a four-poster double bed of the kind he had seen on weekend visits to ducal palaces in the town where he grew up. The walk along the corridor had given him all the structural information he needed.

"That's amazing!" exclaimed Alice, arriving with their supper tray.

"It's what I do." Paul smiled.

"Are you an artist?"

"An architect, of sorts."

"May I show these to Papa?"

"That's what I intended. Have you told him yet?"

"No."

"Take the drawings. Tell him they are suggestions for modest improvements to the property, a little thank-you from a fugitive you looked after. Then introduce me."

"As soon as we've finished eating."

"Good girl. Get me some clothes, as well. I can't meet your father in a nightshirt four sizes too large."

Alice put a hand to her mouth, stifling a giggle. She came back with a shirt and trousers that were only twice Paul's size, the sleeves flapping around his flute-thin wrists and ankles. "I can take them in for you," she offered.

"Don't bother," said Paul. "Let's get the introductions over and done with."

The two men came together on neutral turf — not in Paul's attic nor in Papa's bar, but in Alice's domain, the capacious kitchen.

"Hofmann," said the landlord, extending a hand, into which Paul's vanished as if amputated. Papa was a barrel of a man, bulging at the midriff, a fearsome blunt object beneath a closely razored skull.

"Malinowski," murmured Paul.

"My daughter brought me your drawings."

"Did you like them?"

"Are you a draughtsman?"

"An architect, actually. An analyst of buildings. I was wondering if there is anything I can do here, by way of repaying your daughter's kind hospitality."

"The inn is very old," said Hofmann, "four centuries, five. Always in our family. Bits of it are falling off."

"I can look at that," said Paul. "I'll test the wood for worm and conduct a structural survey. If it requires major repairs, I'll supervise the builders. I am familiar with mid-Renaissance buildings and I'd guess that any degeneration can be made good."

His professional patter skimmed off Papa's skull like hailstones.

"My daughter," said Hofmann, "thinks you can save us from confiscation."

"I can try."

"How?"

"I'll tell the occupiers that you hid me here, saved my life."

"I didn't."

"Your daughter did."

"She is a reckless child."

"She is a Good Samaritan," said Paul.

"They are coming tomorrow," grunted Hofmann. "At noon, the district commander with his quartermaster sergeant. They are going to seize the inn."

"I'll be here to meet them," said Paul.

Exhausted by the confrontation, his legs crumpling, Paul let Alice lead him back to the attic and feed him a cup of broth. "Sleep now," she said, reasserting control.

He awoke, to find a white shirt and brown suit hanging from his chair. "My younger brother's," said Alice. "Try it."

The suit was three sizes too large. He tightened the belt to the last notch, but the moment he let go, the pants flopped to the floor. "Never mind." Alice smiled. "I'll take them in."

Ten minutes before noon, six vehicles screeched into the forecourt, a small invasion. "Papers, on the tables in front of you!" yelled the quartermaster sergeant, slamming his Remington bolt-action rifle onto the tavern bar. Paul, cowering beneath a decorative stag's head, opened his palms in mute transparency.

"Papers!" demanded the sergeant, puffing out a cigarette cloud from a neck twice as thick as Papa's. Paul rolled up his left shirtsleeve to expose a row of blue numerals.

"Camp?" rasped the sergeant. Paul nodded.

"Where?"

Paul inclined his head towards the hilltop.

"Shit, we liberated that place," muttered

the sergeant. "What the hell you doing here? I thought we counted off all survivors."

"I escaped," said Paul.

A lieutenant strolled over, one bar and a flak jacket beneath a dented combat helmet. "Where are you from, sir?" asked the officer, taking in the tattoo.

"Up, over there," said Paul, his English fragmenting in fear.

"Political prisoner?"

"Not political. Social degenerate they called me."

"Intellectual?"

"Inter alia."

"How long?"

"One and half, two years."

"Sheet," said the officer, his upper cheeks smooth as a baby's thighs. Can't be more than twenty-two years old, thought Paul.

"We'd better get you out of here right away," said the officer. "Get you a medical check, some decent rations, and send you home on the first available convoy."

"Not get out, please," stammered Paul, lost for English words. "No home."

"What do you mean, no home?"

"Home is boom-boom, gone. Nothing, all dead. Here is home. I escape from camp, I hide here. . . ."

"You're kidding me," exhaled the sergeant.

"These guys kept you under wraps?"

"No," said Paul. "Not under wraps, under roof. . . ."

"Well, I'll be damned. They could have gotten hung for that."

"Correct," said Paul. "Very brave people."

"Let me get this straight," said the baby-cheeked lieutenant. "You escaped the camp and these guys hid you here, while the guards were drinking downstairs?"

"Correct."

"When was this?"

"Days, weeks, I . . . don't remember."

"What's your name, sir?" asked the lieutenant.

"Malinowski, sir, Paul Malinowski."

"And where are you from?"

Paul named a town, so close to his country's western frontier that it had fallen within half a day of the invasion.

"Fancy that," said the lieutenant.

"You know it?" he asked.

A grin like a quarter watermelon split the lower half of the officer's face. "Sir," he exclaimed, "I am Lieutenant Edward Wierzbicki, Allied commander in these parts!" He pronounced the name *Weirds Biccy,* offending Paul's didactic ear.

"Wierz-beetsky?" he ventured.

"That's absolutely right, sir. My *Dziadzia*

used to pronounce it like that. He came from a farm outside Miss Lowicky, not all that far from your hometown."

"Myslowice, ten kilometres to the south-east," said Paul.

"Damn right. Mr. Malinowski, we could have been goddamn picket-fence neighbours a century back, just fancy that. I can't wait to tell my folks I met what they'd call a 'landsman.' You are one helluva brave man, sir, and I'm proud to meet you."

"I am not brave," said Paul. "Hungry, frightened, desperate . . ."

"I understand, sir, and I salute your courage. It must have taken guts to survive in that camp, and even bigger guts to get out. I can't imagine how you did it through three fences and trenches, but you can tell me sometime. If my *Dziadzia* hadn't gotten the hell out of Miss Lowicky when the harvest went bad in '92, that could have been me in the camp, and I don't know if I'd have been as brave as you. Right, Sergeant?"

"Yes, sir."

"You got my respect, Mr. Malinowski. You need anything else, anything at all, you ask right out for the commander. Got that, Sarge?"

"Yes, sir!"

The grandfather clock in the corridor

tolled a slow noon.

"What am I gonna do about you?" said the lieutenant.

"I stay here," said Paul.

"You can't stay here, sir. My orders are to shut all bars with immediate effect and take the landlord in for questioning."

"I am landlord," said Paul.

"Is true," interjected Alice. She was standing halfway down the bar and exhibiting an unsuspected grasp of English. "He is new landlord."

"Can I see some paperwork?" said the quartermaster.

"I show." Alice nodded. "He — is landlord. All signed."

"I can't leave this place open." The commander sighed. "We're closing all the bars to stop my troops from fraternising with the locals."

"Maybe leave open — just for troops?" proposed Paul.

"Now there's a thought," said the sergeant. "The boys need a place to drink after a hard day's soldiering, sir. We could leave this guy in charge, under our authority."

"I pour beer, for soldiers," said Paul.

"Mr. Malinowski . . ." The lieutenant sighed.

"Yes, sir?"

"You'd better come with me, sir."

"I stay here."

"Sure, but I need to get you kitted out with some ID, PDQ."

"What is IDPDQ?" quavered Paul, thinking of Roman legions and Julius Caesar and *Quo Vadis* and crucifixions.

"You'll find out PDQ." The lieutenant laughed. "Hop in the jeep and I'll give you a lift to HQ."

"HQ?"

"Headquarters, my friend."

"And PDQ?"

"Pretty damn quick."

"My friend," the lieutenant had called him. The ploy had worked. Paul had an ally in power, a protector, if he played his cards right. And the inn could stay open.

The former wedding suite of the Black Horse at Pringsheim, all pink walls and flounces, had a contour map on one mirrored wall and a pile of manila files crawling up the left-hand side of the lieutenant's desk like poison ivy. The Black Horse had been transformed in great haste from welcoming to forbidding. Military police in pillboxes guarded four corners of the forecourt, checking papers. The ground floor had been partitioned into offices; the upper floors served as officer quarters. Lieutenant Wierzbicki complained that his room was damp and the plumbing rudimentary, nothing like the dorm block at West Point. He was about to grumble some more, when he remembered the conditions that Paul had endured and apologised for being such a "pampered prick." Paul missed the colloquial meaning of that term but understood that in the hierarchy of suffering he ranked above the lieutenant and could use his superiority to advantage. It did not escape his notice that the commander, whether because they were "landsmen" or for some other imagined affinity, was prepared to treat him as a special case. Paul had graduated from the privileges of Hans to preferential status with Wierzbicki. Perhaps, thought Paul, he had an aura that was trusted by those in power.

A mug of coffee, its aroma so heady that Paul nearly fainted, steamed on the right-hand side of the bridal dressing table that served the lieutenant as a desk.

"Sure you won't have one?" asked Wierzbicki.

Paul shook his head, fearing his entrails might rebel. He sucked a sugar cube instead and sniffed his breath behind a cupped hand to make sure it had stayed fresh.

"Take a form," said the lieutenant. "Pick a name."

Paul stared back, uncomprehending.

"Take any name you like, sir, and I'll put my stamp on it. Any name within reason, unless it's Dwight D. Eisenhower or Winston Churchill. It's your second baptism, sir."

Paul's bewilderment deepened. He caught most of the words, but the meaning refused to jell. The textbooks that had taught him English conversation were decades out of date.

"Don't quote me" — Wierzbicki smiled — "but I'm giving you a once-in-a-lifetime chance to start over. A fresh identity. No past, no debts, every man's dream."

"I see," said Paul, half-seeing.

"It's not just a name; it's a way of life. Me, I got a Polack name that gives me no headaches in Iowa, where practically everybody's from someplace else, but you, you gotta decide where you want to be and get a name to match. Folks around here might not take too kindly to an -owski, if you catch my drift. Got it?"

"I think so."

"Wipe the slate clean. Erase the traces. Be who you like. Lots of bad guys are on the run under false names, so why shouldn't

89

you start over, as well? Pick a name, friend. Take my advice: Keep it simple. Go for something that blends in."

"Miller," said Paul.

"Excellent," roared the lieutenant. "Works in English, German, Swedish, even French — could be Catholic, Jewish, or E-piscopalian. First name?"

"Paul."

"An apostle. Title?"

"Doctor."

"Is that for real?" Paul nodded, watching the man's eyes narrow with respect for a degree he had earned more by dogged application than from any brilliance of mind.

"Actually, two doctorates," he bragged. "Seven years' psychology, followed by five more in architecture. I could not make up my mind."

The lieutenant, uninterested, stamped a form, picked up the phone, and summoned the unit photographer. "Coffee?" he repeated.

This time, Paul could not resist, submitting to a rush of vegetal energy that almost knocked him sideways. "Cream?" said the lieutenant. Paul had forgotten about cream. "L-lieutenant?" he stammered.

"Yes, Doctor?"

"Can you tell me what happened, when

90

you entered the camp?"

Edward Wierzbicki rose from his round-armed chair, plucked his valeted trouser creases, blew his nose into a checked handkerchief, and lit himself another cigarette, though one still curled in his ashtray. "Not much to tell, my friend," he muttered, running a nicotine-stained finger inside a soft khaki collar. He looked, Paul thought, like a door-to-door brush salesman at the end of a no-sale day.

"I should never have obeyed orders," said the lieutenant. "We were halfway up the valley when a signal came from brigade. 'Stop right there; await asbestos suits.' 'What for?' I queried. 'Haz chem,' said brigade. 'What's that?' 'Hazardous chemicals, stored in an underground weapons dump.' Three days we hung around, waiting to enter the concentration camp. Finally, I said, 'Fuck it. We're going in, suits or no suits.' "

"And what did you find?" said Paul.

"Gates wide open, prisoners lined up beside the road as if they had been waiting for us in a welcome delegation. Mostly dead. Some were twitching. Close-up, I saw it was just maggots. Then the smell kicked in. Chief medical officer threw up over my boots. Staff sergeant, veteran of the Bulge, passed out like a fallen tree. Someone shouted that there were men alive in the huts, eyes blinking. We carried them out on pallets, one by one. I set up a field hospital on the square.

"There were no rules for this kind of thing, no guides for liberating officers. I told the meds to put those with a chance of life on the right, the dead and dying to the left. Some would not let go of a dead brother or best friend. They bit the hands that came to save them. My big brave men, from the bottom of their hearts, broke open cans of condensed milk from their battle rations and poured the stuff down gaping throats. Too thick, too sweet. There were spasms. Men died. Prisoners were seeping with dysentery, riddled with typhus, tuberculosis. We did our damnedest, but they kept on dying. Two hundred and seventeen in three days. They were dying faster in our care than in captivity. On the fourth day, I gave an order to pile the dead on pyres, poured ten cans of gasoline, and stood well back. I torched the huts as well, burned them off the face of the earth. Got a reprimand from brigade for destroying evidence."

"And the ones who survived?" asked Paul, pressing him.

"Those that could be moved, I had driven them to a sanatorium we'd found in a forest a few miles to the north, a rest-cure palace for political bosses and military brass of the old regime. State-of-art medical equipment, swimming pool, silk sheets, champagne on ice, record players."

"A shock to the prisoners." Paul smiled.

"A bigger shock for the staff, I can tell you. I made every scar-faced doctor and every white-capped bitch of a nurse personally responsible for six patients. 'If one man dies or complains,' I told them in very slow English, 'you . . . go . . . to . . . concentration camp.' They got the message; they knew all about concentration camps, those sisters of mercy. I check in on them every day. Our survivors are getting better treatment than millionaires in Baden-bloody-Baden — excuse my French. They're gonna live, damn it."

"And the haz chem?" said Paul.

"Nothing there, just an unfinished tunnel in the valley."

Smoke from two cigarettes intercurled above the makeshift desk like Oriental dancers on the cover of a honeymoon brochure that Paul had glimpsed in a long-ago shop window. Paul, not much of a smoker, had accepted a Camel out of curiosity, teased by a mirage of dry, hot, empty lands evoked by its pack. The inhalation singed his throat and he choked back a cry of pain. A tear trembled at the corner of his eye and his nose itched, but the smoking brought the men close, the lieutenant's warm hands touching Paul's chin as he cupped the steel lighter to his cigarette. Their bond was sealed in the searing of a flame.

The lieutenant was describing how soldiers blubbered like schoolgirls over skeletons that they found in the camp's torture cellar. He was using Paul as his father confessor. Paul was in a position to grant absolution.

"You did what you could," he told the young warrior. "You saved lives."

"Nah," said the lieutenant, moisture welling in jaded blue eyes, "we failed."

"How?"

"We never caught the perpetrators."

"Not your fault," said Paul.

"We never caught a fucking one of them," confirmed the sergeant, entering the room with Paul's laminated identity card at the end of an elongated arm. "Two full generals and a junior minister we yanked outta soft bitches in that sanatorium. We put them for a few hours under a sunlamp with some easy questions to answer. Amazing grace. Not one of them had heard a word about concentration camps, not even the one six

94

miles down the road. Shocked, they were, horrified, a-fucking-ghast. I had myself a good kick at one of them, always wanted to break a general's balls. Not that it did any good. I told the Loot here we shoulda shot every second one of them on the spot."

"That'll do, Sergeant," snapped the lieutenant. "We do it by the book."

"Before I lit the fires," said Wierzbicki once the Remington bearer had withdrawn, "I rounded up some folk from the village and brought them to the camp to see for themselves what was done on their doorstep. The old priest, the grave digger, the blacksmith, a few farmers' wives. I asked them in my best West Point manner what they knew about this facility, so close to their cosy homes. They shook their heads like wooden toys and said it was all military, top secret, six months in the pokey if you strayed off the forest path or looked the wrong way. A shot in the head if a herdsman entered the quarry. That's all anybody knew. It was nothing to do with them, oh no.

"So I showed one woman a receipt she had signed for slave labour. 'Oh, we only did this to help the poor fellows, give them some work on our farm at harvest time, fatten them up a bit, give them some pocket money.' I showed the blacksmith an order from his foundry for clamps and wall chains that we'd found in the torture cellar. He said, 'Business is business.' You know what? I couldn't even hold the guy in a cell for a night without a smart-ass brigade lawyer screaming down my phone to let him go. Justice was his bloody job, not mine, got it, Lieutenant? I found myself in the same position as the village folk: nothing I could do against the mighty machine without getting into trouble."

He paused for the space of two puffs, tapping the table with browned fingertips. He looked, Paul thought, touchingly vulnerable for a man whose work was fighting and conquest. There was something appealing about him in both senses of the word — he was an agreeable young man and one who was crying out in search of reasons for the things he had seen and done. He could use some guidance, spiritual and practical, from a person of greater experience. But that was none of Paul's business. He had tangles of his own to resolve. Slavery had distorted his analytical faculties. Freedom consisted of a flurry of questions to which he had no ready answers from the moralities of an obliterated past.

"Let me give you some advice, Doctor," said the lieutenant, lowering his voice as he rose from the ridiculously ornate chair. "If you come across a perpetrator, don't call the U.S. cavalry. You understand?"

Paul gave a faint nod of the head. "If you see one of the brutes who ran that camp, do what you have to do, and let me know when it's done. I cannot deliver justice under the laws of occupation, but I won't stand in your way, and I can help to make things disappear, if you see what I mean. There is such a thing as natural justice."

He signed Paul's papers in a flowing hand and shouted through the open window for the sergeant to drive him home. "Can't let you walk the streets until I have made them safe, my friend. Anything you need, just ask — you hear me? Stay in touch."

"Thank you, Lieutenant," said the re-named Paul Miller, clutching his impeccable papers, wearing his new identity like body armour.

CHAPTER FOUR

The inn was packed with other ranks, raucous with masculine relief. Beer spilled from tabletops in the low-beamed room and a mouth organ played blue notes through a fug of Lucky Strikes. "We've opened for the military," yelled Alice, rushing up the bar to welcome Paul. "Papa is so happy. He says it's thanks to you."

"No, Alice, to you," shouted Paul, bringing a flush to her cheeks. Her hair was bare and she was wearing an embroidered blouse, through which a hint of cleavage winked at khaki customers. Papa growled a wary greeting from the far end of the bar. Paul nodded, unwilling to be drawn into further complicities.

The sergeant had been telling him on the bumpy ride what a useful fellow he could be. "It's like the crossing of the Rhine," he shouted, "and you're the only bridge left standing. Think about it, Mr. Miller, just think about what I am asking."

He was, it appeared, in a unique position. The occupying force was forbidden to speak to the indigenous residents except by way of orders and restrictions. The locals had no means of communication with their new masters. Paul was a heaven-sent go-between. "Think about it, sir," yelled the sergeant. "Guy wants to buy piece a jewellery, guy wants to meet a girl, you make the link, you collect a reward. Lady has too many eggs in her hen coop; she tells you, you tell me, and everybody's sunny-side up at breakfast. Got it?"

Paul, clinging to the side of the jeep and trying not to throw up, was in no state to argue with the massive quartermaster. "The thing you learn in the army," said the sergeant, "is how to make it work all around. Orders are just orders. You get nowhere obeying them — look what happened to us when we hung about at the gates of the camp. You got to work a way around the orders. That way, we all stay alive and get happy. Are you with me, sir?"

Exhausted by the social effort and the clattering drive, Paul, after one sip for common courtesy, set down the brimming beer jug the sergeant had thrust in his fist and slunk into the kitchen, where a toothless crone called Tante Anna ladled him a bowl of stew and watched each forkful as it entered his mouth, her eyes grudging the comestibles as they slipped down his oesophagus, her eyes fastened to his meagre wrist as it rose and fell in a slow parabola, bowl to mouth, mouth to bowl. Irritated by her fixed scrutiny, Paul left the food half-eaten and stepped out into the early-evening chill. He needed to be alone, and being alone still felt forbidden. He would have to accustom himself in small helpings to the luxuries of liberty. Bit by bit, he was becoming whole. Soon, he would be ready to leave. There were too many evil memories to keep him here. A few steps up or down would show him that here died one friend and there another. If he walked to the top of the hill, he was back at the camp; down, and he was in the quarry. The mountain view from his loft window was glorious, the mental map unspeakable. He needed to decide his future, somewhere far away, and soon. In the meantime, he had the commander's protection, the sergeant's collusion, and the gratitude of the innkeeper's daughter, temporary as such things were.

Drawing a deep breath of twilight air, he felt the skin crawl at the back of his neck and swivelled round to catch two ragged children — supperless, by the look of them — staring at him. He mimed the act of eating, hand to mouth. They nodded with eager squeals and he went inside to fetch the remnants of his stew, but when he came out with two round bowls, they were gone, vanished in the descending gloom. He wondered why they had run off. Was he, in their powerless eyes, an object of fear? Had he crossed some barrier from victim to victor? Was he still the same man, or had events turned him into a chameleon that changed colouring to suit its circumstances? If he was free, why was he being watched? If he could walk away from hell, why didn't he run from here? He was not free; that was the truth of the matter. Eyes were upon him at all times. Even out here in the dark, the spinster aunt would come looking for him, followed by Alice, her father, the lieutenant, the sergeant, the village waifs, and every idle pair of eyes in the valley. He was still a prisoner, a slave to others' expectations.

That settled it. He had to get away, and without delay. Climbing up to the attic, he lay down on the bed to map his plans. He would get up in the dead of night, steal into the bar, clear out the tills in the tavern room, and flee before dawn. With clean papers and civilian clothes, he could take himself onwards by foot and by ship to a remote corner of the earth, where the reconditioned "Paul Miller" might start a life without a past.

He napped for a couple of hours and, as the last jeeps roared out of the forecourt, slunk downstairs to see where the cash was kept. Alice was alone in the bar, wrapping bunches of green-backed notes in elastic bands and jotting the total on top of each bunch. She greeted him with a tired smile and, clinking jugs into the sink, asked if he would help her with the drying up. The crone had gone home and Papa had found happiness upstairs in a bottle of Jack Daniel's that he had got off a soldier in exchange for a crooked cross, a leftover from the fallen regime. Hearing her laugh about the emblem removed Paul's last qualm about his intended theft, a crime that ranked low in the list of crimes committed by the last regime. It was almost a moral duty, an imperative, to steal from a people that had ransacked the whole continent. He was looking forward to making off with the bundles that Alice was shoving into the drawer behind the bar where she kept the corkscrews.

Hanging up the last of the tankards, the girl sat Paul in an alcove to polish wine glasses while she prattled of the night's excitements, the thrilling days ahead. Lisl, her best friend, was back from Pringsheim, full of hair-raising experiences — "She was *that close* to being raped!" — and eager for adventure. Practically every soldier in the bar asked Alice to go with him for a walk in the woods, and she played along until they had paid for a few drinks, at which point she flashed her mother's wedding ring on her middle finger and pretended to be "engaged." One of the fellows spoke her language comprehensibly and seemed more intent on civilised conversation than a grope among the trees. "But he's forbidden, officially, to talk to me," Alice said, "and Papa would have a fit if he saw me out walking with an enemy soldier! He thinks I'm such an innocent."

Alice had lost all interest in Paul, that was for sure. She had not bothered to ask about his interviews at military HQ, or about his arrangements with the commander and his sergeant. He had become part of the furniture, once more, and it suited him to stay that way. Alice's hair swung free and golden. She must have washed it for the soldiers and dressed up in her Sunday best, besides. Not that Paul was jealous. He had paid his debt in full by getting the inn reopened.

"Is there anything I need to know about my duties as landlord?" he asked as the flow of chit-chat dried up.

"Throw out the late revellers, don't get into fights, and remember to lock the cash drawer," she recited, tossing him a bunch of keys from her belt. It was all too easy.

"I'm done for." The girl yawned. "Sunday tomorrow, long lie-in, thank God." She hung the last of the glasses on an overhead rack and turned out the lights, switch by heavy switch, on a square fuse box beside the front door. "I'm off to bed." Paul replied that he had taken a nap and was not quite ready. "Take your time," she said. He called "Good night" to her swinging mane.

Sitting in the alcove in watery moonlight settled his nerves, each creak of the ancient inn affirming his insignificance in the greater scheme of things. He was just another wayfarer in the turbulence of centuries, one of thousands who had taken refreshment between these walls. The ticktock of the grandfather clock echoed his intimations of ephemerality, removing any obligation to justify his existence by way of action or achievement. He was, because he was. He mattered no more than the cockroach that was crawling up the side of the bar in search of crumbs. A week before, he might have tried to catch the insect and pop it in his mouth, storing its crisp protein as a defence against starvation. Now he greeted it as kin, his scuttling cousin in the game of life.

With the moon at its zenith, Paul stretched and rose, feeling his way in darkness to the staircase. He climbed three flights in stocking feet, his right hand gliding up the polished banister. He opened the attic door and, finding Alice's sleeping bag gone from the floor, dumped his clothes as he shed them — jacket in a corner, trousers and shirt on the chair, the rest in a higgledy trail. He washed face and teeth with water from the pitcher, leaning over the blue-veined bowl, and drew the curtains wide so that he would wake at first light. Then he crawled under the eiderdown, wriggling to find his body's dent in the mattress and touching, as he sunk to the middle, the paralysing contact of bare skin.

"Hello," she whispered. Paul froze to the undersheet, numbed by the pounding of blood in his head. He could not remember when he had last touched living flesh (the dead he remembered all too well), or how it felt. His instincts were unwired, his limbs askew. A part of him looked in from outside and saw a dry skeleton lying with a voluptuous young woman, naked from head to foot, an absurd conjunction. Velvet lips kissed his shoulder blade, moving up to the cleft of his chin and murmuring encouragement as they reached his ear. Her hand took his left palm and placed it on her breast, where it sat cold and lumpen as a sculptor's mould. Her lips were on his mouth, unflinching from the foul odour of malnutrition. "Come," she said, shifting her hips so that she lay beneath him, moist-breathed. But he, like a bird caught in barbed wire, hovered motionless above her, not daring to move for fear of being torn apart. Calmly, as if leading a lamb to the shearing, she reached up and stroked his back in vertical lines, his nape, his shoulders, his ribs, whispering that he must not be afraid, that this was meant to be. Her fingers were at the cleft of his buttocks, moving round to the cave of his belly and down to the wild stubble below. His nerves splayed out like electric wires bursting from a live socket, loose and full of danger. He tried to gather them in, to control the power, to exert his will to say yes or no, but her hand strayed one fathom lower and he was helpless and spent, shamed in his debility and indecision. "Never mind," the girl murmured. "We can do it again."

He fell into a dreamless sleep at her side

and half-awoke hours later with the drifting moon in his eyes, aware of amends to be made. Duty-bound, with few preliminaries, he held himself above her and, bursting through barbed wire, entered her forcibly, drawing a cry of pain. He retracted, apologising, but she held him fast, raising her hips to find his rhythm and wrapping her arms around his waist until a breath caught at the back of her throat and her lower body heaved in release, her arms splayed at either side. Paul would, with time, anticipate and adore that catch in her breath, a sound known to no other man. The sound was Alice to the core, her gift of love, the most that this discreet person allowed herself to express by way of sensual deliverance. He had known, in another life, lovers noisier and more exuberant than Alice, hedonists like his architectural intern, who shrieked at climax, horse riders like his uncle's mistress, who mounted him in boots. Never, though, had he known a partner so guileless as Alice, so direct. Even in that first lovemaking, unable to guess at her motive, he pulled back and marvelled at her self-assurance, her absence of doubt, her absolute composure in the writhings of love. "Better?" she said, planting a kiss on his brow. Better, he concurred, much better.

They made love again in broad daylight, his objective mind amazed at his own stamina, his beauty-starved eyes feasting on her ample contours. This time, her hands locked hard onto his hips to prevent any thoughts of escape, until a dry cry of submission croaked from his throat and Alice stroked his cheeks with soft assurances of safety, a litany of lovingness.

Many months later, long into their marriage, as she lay in his arms one Sunday morning after love, Paul asked Alice what had prompted her, that virgin night, to give herself to a virtual stranger. "I knew what I was doing," she retorted.

"Did you know I was about to leave?"

"I guessed you were thinking of it. Anyway, I wouldn't have let you."

"How could you have stopped me?"

"I was going to hide your clothes. Burn your papers. Break your legs. You were mine; that much I knew."

"Your prisoner?"

"My prize. My reward."

He laughed aloud at her possessive indignation. "But why me?" he persisted. "You could have struck it lucky with an American officer. I was no catch for a young girl like you. Too scrawny to stand up straight, bad breath, too old, a foreigner, full of rage . . ."

"You were beautiful," she said, a finger to his lips. "You were a revelation. I saw in you the beauty that comes from great suffering, the beauty that you see in pictures of our Lord."

"That's blasphemy," said Paul, half-shocked.

"Not to me. You were a saviour that came in my hour of need, the answer to my prayer."

"A romantic wish . . ."

"No, a hardheaded peasant mentality. I knew what lay ahead. There were no men worth having in the valley. The good boys had died, and the ones who crawled back from the war were damaged in body and mind. I could have caught a foreign soldier, but that would have been whoredom. My plan was to reopen the inn, rebuild the family, renew hope. God heard my cry and delivered you to my doorstep."

"Why me? I was not much to look at. . . ."

"I saw dignity behind your misery, and strength in your gaze. I saw a man dying for want of love yet terrified of affection. I saw a man of pride who refused to take a free meal. I saw someone like me, someone who does not look back in futile nostalgia or waste his time on earth. Someone who works around the clock so long as there is work to be done. Someone who is not led astray by vanities. I looked at you and saw great qualities. Was I wrong, dearest?"

"That's a lot to live up to," said Paul, impressed.

"I saw a man — a real man, not the boys I knew in the village or the soldiers who wanted a fumble. I saw a man of character, a man I could love without making the apologies that my mother had to make for Papa. My man, that's what I saw. My man."

She asked for nothing in return, then or ever after, no equivalent pledge of love, no song of songs in praise of her effulgent beauty and manifold virtues. She had no need for assurance and no ear for flattery. Paul had never met a person as self-possessed as Alice, as certain of her actions and her place. His love for her paled beside hers for him. It was a paltry thing, hardly worth having, a second-hand love, a halting, sputtering stream of brackishness, inexpressible without hesitancy. Yet she demanded no more, proud and content with precious little, proud of her man and content with her choice. He was, he insisted, not much of a lover, physically or emotionally, but she swore to make him whole, and, over time, he relaxed his defences and conformed to the role that she wrote for him, in life as in bed.

Their lovemaking was a rising curve of discovery. As his frame fleshed out, Paul would find himself aroused by a stray thought of Alice and seek her out in the busy kitchen. She, smiling, would leave instructions to the cooks and lead him outside for what she announced as "an inventory assessment," to the pantry or the barn, where they climbed into each other with a minimal mussing of clothing and hair, so that both were back at work within minutes, their pact renewed. He searched for words to express his gratitude for her ease in love, her assimilation of intimacy into a working day, but she stilled his lips with a shushing finger, shy at being cherished for actions that came to her as easily as a smile. He had no eye for other women. Alice suited all his needs, fortified his self-esteem, and afforded him a place of safety.

And when, in the grave hour before dawn, he shot out of bed and the guilt crawled up his leg at the window like a whining mongrel, she would love him back to sleep no matter how long it took, steeling him to face the world from her impregnable tower. She was fearless in his defence, starting from their first Sunday morning, when she informed her father of their intimacy over

111

breakfast and then went out and displayed their togetherness at Mass to everyone in the village, people who had known her since the cradle and crossed themselves at the mention of her mother's name even as they speculated through stale breath what the saintly Maria would have thought of her Alice sharing her bed with a man twice her age, shameless as a vixen in heat and not even married.

"And what about you, Hedwige Bauer?" Alice snapped at a garrulous farmwife who made a face as she walked by arm-in-arm with Paul and Papa on the next market day. "What are your moral standards? Your boy, the little Richard, now he doesn't look much like Fritz Bauer, does he? Remind me — where was Fritz the year Richard was born? On the front line, that's right, while Hedi went waltzing with a fat tax collector." "Enough, Alice," said Papa Hofmann, tugging her away and apologising for her sharp tongue. The Bauers were big customers and little Richard had a confirmation party coming up. But Papa was not backward when his daughter's proprieties were cast into question. Tante Anna, wondering why Alice was sharing a bed with the foreigner, was sacked on the spot, and when one of the backroom drinkers told an obscene joke about a stick-insect and a nymphomaniac, Papa hauled out a nail-studded club from behind the bar and threatened to stave in the skull of any useless old gelding who insulted his family. Paul spotted what looked like rust stains down one side of the weapon and knew it had been used before in anger, probably more than once.

Papa Hofmann kept out of Paul's way on the whole. In the back room, with buddies from an earlier war, he drank himself to oblivion. In the bar, the soldiers grew rowdy and libidinous, ignoring posters on the walls warning of venereal disease. Alice let her necklines fall and her smile stretch as vacantly as the hind's on the shield outside. It made the men buy more drinks, she told Paul, who trusted her. Paul busied himself in the backyard, cleaning out a hen coop and cutting a hole in its side for natural light so that he could use it as a temporary office. On a drawing board that Alice purloined, he sketched an outline of the inn and its environs, marking the parts that might need attention. Lacking the proper tools, he took a skewer from the kitchen and a ladder from the yard, making a slow circuit of the building and plunging the blade at methodical intervals into exposed seams of woodwork. Marking the results on a pad, he found the structure to be sound, in need of nothing other than minor repairs with a gouge and mallet, followed by a coating of tar that he and Alice applied, on parallel ladders, in brazen view of the drinking soldiery. "Come on!" cried Alice, jaunty in a skirt that barely covered her knees. "Who's man enough to join me up here for the best view in the valley?"

The first soldier to run up her ladder fell flat on his back, upended by a smear of machine oil that Alice had surreptitiously drizzled onto the lower rungs. Another contender followed, then more, amidst mounting merriment. With a wink at Paul and a shout of free beers to anyone who helped him finish the job, Alice made a swishing descent to raucous applause. She was good at getting men to do her bidding, confident in her feminine amplitude. Paul, watching her flirt, admired her the more for knowing that, to keep the soldiery entertained, she had to suppress an innate modesty that inhibited her from removing her underclothes in front of him or naming bodily parts during foreplay. Avoiding public displays of affection, she put on an exuberant front to camouflage their love, allowing Paul to linger unheeded in her shadow until he was ready to face the world.

■ ■ ■ ■

Once the repairs were finished, Paul scaled
the wobbly ladder to oil a hinge on the inn's
shield, a decrepit bracket on the sign of the
Laughing Hind that squeaked on windy
nights and disturbed his fragile sleep. Two
rungs from the top, he found himself shaking with vertigo and surveyed the undulat-
ing surroundings, the village top and bottom and the river down below, as a means
of calming his fear. Once he was down, he
swore, he would make an effort to walk into
the village, a resolution which, simple as it
sounded, allowed him to descend rung by
rung in safety to the deserted ground. He
had a self-defense plan. Instead of replacing
the skewer in the cutlery drawer as Alice
had instructed, he slipped it into the right-
hand inside cuff of Franz-Josef's old jacket,
just above the wrist, so that it would come
easily to hand when he stepped out-of-
doors. It seemed a sensible precaution. The
woods were reputed to be full of wild men
— convicts bombed out of city jails, old-
regime diehards, and rampaging camp
survivors, as well as wolves and feral dogs.
The streets were not safe, either, even in
daylight, with drunken troops on the loose

115

and the military police nowhere to be seen until a brawl was safely over. Alice had told Paul not to be in a hurry to enter the village, but he had ghosts to settle and time on his hands.

The morning he stepped off the inn's land for the first time, he picked a posy of wildflowers and laid one on every spot uphill where he had seen a man die. Walking with eyes half-shut, he counted his steps by rote, looking neither right nor left, identifying the bakery, the butcher's, the grocer's, and the tannery by their smell. He got as far as the blacksmith's before the roaring furnace melted his resolve and drove him back, quivering, to the chicken crate. He sat there sweating until the attack abated. Then he sketched a chart of his cardinal fears, grading them from blue to red in ascending order. Least dangerous were the village tradesmen, cowed by occupation and keen to avoid disruption to business. No shop owner would draw attention to himself; shops were blue. Next up were xenophobes and returning soldiers who, nursing grievances, might greet an ex-victim like himself with a sour look but nothing more; colour them light blue. Former camp inmates were unpredictable: An unforgiving fellow like Maretzek might assault him in broad daylight, but Paul reckoned he could handle other stickmen, tinted pink. His greatest fear was of running into a former guard, worst of all Hans himself. Guards were red, Hans vermilion.

It was for such dreads that he carried the skewer up his sleeve, for such eventualities that he needed a plan. If he saw a guard, he was going to walk straight past him and call Wierzbicki from the telephone at the nearest shop, clutching the skewer in front of him until the forces of order arrived. As for Hans, he would simply run away and hide in the chicken crate. Hans was a law of his own making; there was no telling what he might do if he saw Paul and recognised him as a witness to his crimes. The skewer would be of no more use against Hans than a mediaeval lance from the stairwell, and Paul himself would be paralysed in terror. The deepest, darkest shade of red did not begin to convey the degree of danger that was represented by Hans.

Yet, once his hands stopped shaking, he was able to rationalise the risk. Hans would not enter the village. There was a reward on his head and a wanted poster on the wall of the police station. He would not get more than five items in his shopping basket before the arrest warrant was executed by a military patrol. Hans could not come back and walk free. Paul had nothing to fear.

That same afternoon, he stepped out into the village once more, this time with his eyes wide open. He visited the ironmonger's for nails and brackets and, on the doorstep, was stopped by the roly-poly baker with a slice of fresh poppy-seed cake. At the next store, the greengrocer thrust a giant cabbage into his arms. Beneath the sign of the staff and serpent, the wrinkled doctor with the walrus moustache asked Paul if he might drop by sometime to inspect his leaking roof. Word had got round that he was good with buildings.

Faces smiled wherever he turned. Paul had to remind himself that these were the same faces that had turned away as he was whipped twice daily up and down their main street, but that thought faded as, one after another, men and women came out to make his acquaintance, proclaiming themselves charmed by his quaint accent, his quick mind. He must stop for a coffee, some homemade apple cake, a little schnapps, they said. Tempted by a sense of transgression, he accepted here and there, letting himself be ushered into "our humble abode," "our little hovel," "my grandmother's parlour." Across oak tables, he exchanged remarks about the rain, the crops, and the cake, aware that these country dwellers were not listening to a word he said but were watching through hooded eyes the tilt of his head, the splay of fingers around his cup, the crumb upon his lower lip. Satisfied, their faces opened to him slowly like sunflowers at noon. Paul was not sure what he had done to win their friendliness, but it struck him that he might have cultivated in the camp a magnet of popularity, the aptitude to be liked without having to do very much to earn it.

Swaggering with self-worth, he was checked by Alice's caution that men and women who dragged a living from mountain soil gave away nothing without expectation of reward. When the baker shoved cake in his mouth and the ironmonger refused to charge for a fistful of nails, this did not mean they had fallen (as she had) for Paul's shy smile and sharp intellect. It meant they thought that he could facilitate some matter on their behalf with the occupying authorities, having heard that he was on friendly terms with the lieutenant. Requests soon trickled in. The baker needed extra coal rations for his oven, the laundress a travel permit to visit a sick aunt. The seamstress was out of thread. The doctor required an affidavit testifying to his alleged victimisation by the former regime, a certificate without which he was not allowed to bind a broken limb or attend another village birth, though nature, vegetal and animal, had not ceased to bring its abundance of both to his shining black door. A slip of paper would legalise his practice once again and allow the doctor access to a supply of medicaments. "How urgently do you need this?" asked Paul.

"If you were in labour," said Dr. Walters, "you wouldn't ask."

Each week, Paul called on Lieutenant Wierzbicki with a sheaf of petitions, hard-luck stories, and barefaced lies. "What would you do with these?" asked the lieutenant.

"Tear most of them up," said Paul, scrambling to his knees to gather a pile of files that had been brushed off the bridal dressing table by the commander's weary gesture.

"Can't do that," said the lieutenant, bumping heads with Paul beneath the desk.

"Then stop dealing with individual petitions. Delegate bits and pieces to a junior."

"I can't," said Wierzbicki. "I'm where the buck stops."

"The buck?"

"Responsibility."

"Perhaps I can put the petitions in order for you? Three piles — 'Desperate,' like the doctor; 'Maybe,' like the seamstress; and 'Forget It,' like the fat baker."

"That sounds like a good idea."

"I am trained in structural thinking."

"In that case," said the officer, summoning another brace of canteen coffees, "let me ask you to apply your structured mind to my most burning issue."

The valley was afire with spring fruits, carpeted with strawberries and wild apricots. Blackberries burst forth from brambles and the orchards were dropping half-ripe apples. A vagrant could live for weeks on the windfall, and many had moved in — individuals and families uprooted from the east, kicked out of their homes with an hour's notice and nowhere to go, three generations crammed onto a laden cart and nag. The valley bed was thick with travellers, riding broken axles and what remained of their luck. In turn, grey-skinned, and blank-eyed despair, they came and went in waves, unhindered or noticed unless they got arrested or dropped dead. Displaced persons, said the lieutenant, were a transient hazard. Soon the flow would slow down. The harvest, on the other hand, was a flaming crisis.

In a few weeks, the grain would be high, and there were no hands to bring it in. Any men of farming age were infirm, limbless, captive, or drunk. The women lacked muscle and know-how. The lieutenant had asked for volunteers at a nearby prisoner-of-war camp, but though a dozen POWs were keen to get their shirts off in the open fields and within sight of women, brigade said it would violate some international convention. Wierzbicki ran his hands through a full head of wavy fair hair.

"So what would you do?" he asked Paul. "Myself, I've been trained to lead men in war and bring most of them home safe and sound. Nothing in my book tells me how to be an occupying power when the crop is ready and every hick kid in Iowa knows what needs doing. If we don't get the harvest in PDQ, the valley starves. Simple as that. There will be dead babies in the river come winter. I can't see brigade flying in extra rations when hunger turns to fucking famine — excuse my French. So what am I to do, Doc? You're a college man. What's your best shot?"

Paul had seen Papa Hofmann hammer locks onto the doors of his cellar, where the reserve stocks were kept. "Whatever happens to the harvest," swore Hofmann, "no-one in my house will go hungry." The valley, he continued through a mouthful of nails, had seen such times before. It was a historic thoroughfare. At the end of every war, it got clogged with human driftwood, angry, frightened, hopeless people who did not know where they were headed and stole all they could carry until winter drove them off or wiped them out. "A man first looks after his own," muttered Papa. The lieutenant, on the other hand, had broader responsibilities and was looking to Paul for something more than sympathy. He had used the word *apostle* on hearing Paul's name, and Paul, trained in psychoanalytic method, heard a hidden meaning. The lieutenant was a lost soul of simple origins, searching for someone he could look up to for moral leadership. Paul examined the officer's open face over the lip of his coffee cup and warmed to his inchoate personality. He, Paul, fresh out of a concentration camp, was in a position to shape this young man's character. As a survivor and a teacher, he could not resist.

"You have two problems," Paul told the lieutenant, "harvest and refugees."

"I know."

"One is problem, the other solution."

"How does that work?"

"Get refugees to bring in harvest. Give them roof over heads and three meals a day. Good houses for best workers."

"Neat." The lieutenant smiled. "But where do I find houses, and who cooks the meals?"

Finishing his coffee with exaggerated concentration, Paul paused before answering, walking around the room and staring out of the window, increasing the other man's expectation. He had not been nicknamed Pavlov for nothing.

"I could," he said over his shoulder, as if testing a hypothesis, "I could, if you agree, Lieutenant, make a dormitory at the back of the inn — tin roof and communal washrooms, very simple — for thirty harvest workers and families."

"How would you feed them?"

"We have big kitchen at Laughing Hind, caters three hundred at weddings. Harvest wives do cooking and cleaning."

It was the lieutenant's turn to impose a time-out, testing the proposition against his rules and regulations, anticipating an onslaught of brigade objections.

"What's it gonna cost?"

"Nothing."

"How do you figure that out?"

"You supply building materials from army surplus. I fix accommodation."

"And the food?"

"You provide potatoes, flour, meat. I work out and tell you how much. We take vegetables from garden, fruit from orchard, fish from river. No more needed."

"So where's the catch?"

"I don't understand."

"What's the kickback? Who gets fat on my hog? Whose barrel gets my pork?"

"Sorry, I don't understand, Lieutenant."

A sunbeam burst across the lieutenant's face, spontaneous as a salmon's leap. "Of course you don't, my friend." He chuckled. "You're nothing like the hustlers I have to deal with every day. You're an ivory-tower college thinker with no idea how to grease a wheel, let alone the skin of my palm. You've no idea what people offer me the moment that door is shut — gold, girls, boys, any price I care to name."

"I am still not understanding," repeated Paul.

"I know, my friend, and that's why I call you 'my friend.' You're one straight man in a crooked valley, and I am grateful. I'll have a think about your scheme and get back to you ASAP."

"ASAP?"

"It's like PDQ, pal, only slower."

A locker-room confraternity settled on the

defaced bridal chamber, a prickle-shaved amity between pink walls. Paul looked at the lieutenant and marvelled at his innocence. Wierzbicki squinted at Paul with an attitude of frank respect.

"Those workers are gonna need somewhere to hang out after hours," he noted.

"That is correct."

"I guess I could let them use the Laughing Hind, easing the restrictions?"

"That would be convenient."

"In recognition of your help."

"A quid pro quo."

"Quid pro quo: something for something," cried the lieutenant unexpectedly. "I know my Latin. I was raised a Catholic. Are you saying this is payback for you after all?"

"No," said Paul, shaking his head. "I mean it is good for the inn, the people that saved my life."

"I can understand that," said the lieutenant. "So, what are your plans?"

"Stay here, for a while."

"And then?"

"No idea. I am a leaf on water, waiting to be moved on by the next wave."

Paul was never short of a good metaphor, and the lieutenant took his time savouring its imagery. " 'The next wave,' huh?" he repeated.

"That's correct."

"And we are all bobbing on that surface."

"I think so."

"That's one very true word." The lieutenant sighed. "We are leaves on the water, waiting to be moved on. You and me both, brother, you and me both."

Chapter Five

By the middle of harvest month, the air heavy with chaff and thunder rolling round the hills, Alice was in full bloom and there was no concealing her condition. She wore a full-sail summer dress and tossed a cheeky wink at the spinsters and the war widows who twitched their disapproval as she swept past them, last as ever for Sunday Mass. Her pregnancy was a swell of pride, a sign that she, for one, was not going to mope away her youth or wait for permits and certificates before the cycle of life could be resumed. Arm in arm with her friend Lisl, she stuck out her belly and pranced past the frowners in the low pews, contemptuous of their sorrows, her well-being unconfined.

The village had expanded. There were thirty harvest families in the tin hut behind the Laughing Hind and more in shacks beside the road. The inn hummed day and night, and Paul had to be reminded by the lieutenant to keep the noise down after dark and the numbers within safety levels. To keep a closer eye on things, Paul moved his desk from the chicken crate to a clothes closet in the entrance hall, a cramped space where Alice joined him at snatched moments when her hands were empty and her skirts could be hoisted for love. Distracting Paul was fun for the girl, proof that he loved her more than his work. Most of all, she liked to sit around after a quick bout of love and watch him struggle with a structural drawing, resolving issues with swift thrusts of his right arm, like a fencing champion at full tilt. His absorption was intense, fiercer than in love. She guessed it was an escape from the pits of memory, and the relief it afforded him was visible. For the first time since he had crashed into her bins, Paul slept most nights past daybreak and woke, blinking, in their attic bed. High summer drove the pallor from his cheeks and slowed his step in torrid heat; he was adapting to the rhythms of the land.

As the last sheaves were gathered, the fields cut bare, the lieutenant informed Paul that he was on the move. His unit was being merged into general headquarters and he was taking charge of a wider stretch of territory. It meant that his visits to the village would be infrequent. "Thank you, Lieutenant, for everything," said Paul.

"It will be Captain by next week."

His departure, rather than diminishing Paul's authority, seemed to increase his value to the village and, with it, his responsibility. He whisked off a memorandum to Wierzbicki, warning of the stress placed on local services by the increased population. There were seventy extra children in the coming year's school intake; Dr. Walters had tripled his patient load; bacteria levels were rising in the water supply; the roads had been rucked up; four policemen were needed to stem pilfering and petty brawls; and Paul himself could use a clerical assistant to process requests to the commander, as well as a public registrar for births, marriages, and deaths.

Captain Wierzbicki replied by return mail. He allocated a locum and nurse to the doctor's surgery, three more teachers, two gendarmes, and a secretary for Paul. "But don't ask me for more," he wrote, "because there ain't nothing left in the budget but two paper clips and a wad of gum."

Paul wrote back, attaching an ambitious plan to use the harvest crew on winter road repairs and house building. "You'll never get that through," said Alice, reading over his shoulder as she adjusted her lower garments. To his own surprise, he did, and before the month was out.

The speed with which Paul's wishes were granted, in contrast to the congestion of most requests, drew grumbles from late-night drinkers about the alien who had put a bastard in the inn girl's belly and filled the village with thieving foreigners. A glance from Papa Hofmann in the direction of the studded club melted the grouching into unfocussed obscenities, which dissolved, in turn, into sycophantic smiles the moment that Paul entered the bar, another twelve-hour day of selfless service behind him. Alice asked him to stop work earlier, but the longer he wrestled with paperwork, the easier it was to defer a decision about his own future once he left this village limbo, as leave it he surely must.

He could not stay forever in this place of degradation, where every inch of road was steeped in blood. He had repaid his debt to Alice, and if he were to slip away, she and her child would be provided for by the inn's swollen income until another suitor came along, someone more suitable as her life's partner than a freed slave with a sack of grievances. It would be a kindness to Alice if he left the field clear to a better man, one of her own type, one who aroused neither pity nor guilt, who let her sleep nights unbroken, without standing in admonition at the black window. He was, as he had told Wierzbicki, getting ready to move on.

"I want us to get married once the harvest is in," said Alice without preamble as they strolled in a heat haze after supper beside the summer-slow stream.

"W-what did you say?" stuttered Paul, feigning inattention to cover his confusion.

"We must get married," she repeated slowly, as if to a child.

"Are you s-sure?"

"Without a doubt." She smiled. "You are my missing half, dearest, my heart's desire."

"B-but . . ."

She put a finger to his lips and, one by one, eliminated obstacles and objections. True, there was no need for them to marry. The old morality was dead. There were village wives who had conceived while their husbands were at war and girls who had fallen pregnant to passing uniforms, some by consent, some by force, some not knowing which of eleven men the father might be and praying as they went into labour that the child would inherit one of the better characters. No stigma attached to these accidents of war, nor did Alice hold herself above those less fortunate or prudent than she. On the contrary, she said, seeing her getting married would give light and hope to the girls who were left to bring up their babies alone. It would show that love could arise at the lowest moment and with the unlikeliest of partners. She wanted to set an example. She wanted the village to witness her transition from girl to woman, to accept her in her mother's place, to announce by her marriage to this outsider that there was no room in the world for foaming prejudices and past hatreds. And she wanted the Church to consecrate her act of welcome to a stranger, as it sanctified Rebecca at the well and Rahab on the walls of Jericho.

"What about your father?" Paul demurred.

"Papa will be pleased."

"He doesn't like me, you know. . . ."

"Why should he? You have taken his child and filled her with your love. He is jealous and angry. But he'll get over it. Or not — it's up to him. My mother would have loved you, and that's what matters to me — as it should to him, if he remembers. Ask him for my hand the moment we return. He won't dare to refuse."

Paul raised her fingers to his lips, buying time. A decision was being thrust on him.

133

What was he to do? He did not want to deceive Alice with false pledges of eternal love; neither could he bring himself to let her down. He was drawn, torn, stretched in every direction. Running out of excuses, he drew Alice down to the riverbank and stared into her clear green eyes with troubled insincerity.

"This is all wrong," he declared.

"What is wrong, dearest?"

"It's wrong that you should ask me to marry you. I am the one who should be on my knees, begging you to be my bride, you, the beautiful and compassionate, you, Alice, my golden-haired saviour."

"Don't be melodramatic," she said, pushing him aside. "I'm not marrying a poet or a politician. It's you I love, Paul the wise, Paul the man of few words."

"Alice, will you please marry me?" he whispered, holding her hand to his cheek.

"Immediately and without delay." She chuckled, kissing him in wet pecks all over his head, his brow, his chin, and, languorously, his lips.

He gave himself to her enthusiasm, sweeping guilt and doubt from the corners of his mind. He could make this work, he assured himself. It was no great passion, unlike the passion he had known once before, but he could settle for Alice and her love, given freely like water from a well, life-restoring at his hour of need. Alice had earned his devotion, if that is what she really wanted.

"Let's make an announcement," she cried, leaping to her feet.

Papa Hofmann received them in the back room with bluff guffaws and hooded eyes. He thumped Paul across the back with a ham-size fist, broke the neck of a schnapps bottle on the rim of the table, and made his prospective son-in-law throw back a giant slug of the firewater, roaring with glee as he choked. Alice, scolding her father, mopped snot from Paul's nostrils as he blinked through tears, awaiting formal consent. But the barrel-shaped man was giving nothing away, any more than a bear, motionless in a forest clearing, announces its intention to attack or repine. A decade apart in age and a civilisation in outlook, Paul and Papa glared at each other in mute and mutual incomprehension until Alice told them to get on with it, or she'd announce it herself.

Hofmann countered with a run of questions. How old was Paul? So old, huh? Been wed before? Harrumph. Parents alive? Religion? The final answer seemed to hit the spot, for Papa pronounced himself delighted that Paul, for all that he was a foreign fellow, was a son of the one and only true Church, baptised and confirmed, not an adherent of reformist heresies nor — heaven forbid — a soul in damnation, one of those godless deniers. Storming into the saloon and banging his fist on the bar, he gave a rafter-rattling bellow and announced Alice's engagement to the crowded room, drinks all around.

Banns were posted and a date was set for the first Saturday in September. Old Father Hitzinger, who had sprinkled baptismal water over the infant Alice and her mother before her, summoned them for instruction. A swish of threshing machines pervaded the nave, the rhythms of God's fixed seasons. "A time to sow seed, and a time to gather in harvests," said the dishevelled priest, egg stains on his cassock and a sole flapping loose on one boot, a bloodshot eye settling on the bride's bulging midriff. "A time to keep silence, and a time to speak," warned Alice.

"Such a clever girl," said the priest, sighing through beery breath. "She knows Scripture better than I do."

"And believes every word," said Paul with spousal pride.

"You will need a best man," Alice reminded him as they walked home.

"I thought of asking Dr. Walters," said Paul, who had found a friend, of sorts, in the village. Visiting the doctor to view a hole in the surgery roof, he had tripped over a box of books in the attic and, winded, sat down on a bare joist and fingered the spines of long rows of hardbacks, almost all of them banned by the last regime. There were four such boxes, some two hundred books. The doctor was, on this evidence, a heavy reader and, by inference, a dissenter.

Opening a book, Paul was handcuffed by cold print. There was once a time when he could not walk to the park without a book in his pocket or sit at table without an open page before him. Novels were his refuge, his secret garden. He had never lived before in a house without books until he entered the inn, where the only volume to be found was a family Bible that Alice read aloud on Sundays, selecting lurid episodes and relishing their gory outcomes. Paul had been broken of his reading habits in the camp and had lived many months in freedom without recovering the escapist urge. If any change in his behaviour proved that he was no longer the same Paul, this did. He had lost the need to lose himself in stories and ideas.

He must have been sitting on the beam

for half an hour with a biography of Freud open on his right knee and a volume of Heine on his left before the doctor brought him down to earth with an offering of herbal tea and currant cake. As they sipped and nibbled in the hush of an incipient storm, Paul wondered how a man of such independent mind and amiable disposition could have watched the march of death pass his front door without hurling himself in its path. He was the only cultured soul Paul had met in the village. Did art and science count for nothing when terror raged?

Before he could frame a leading question, the doctor began to explain himself through a curled moustache that seemed, the longer Paul looked at it, quite ludicrously walrus-like. Walters, it appeared, was an exile, evicted from his city practice after allegations were made against him by a sluttish sixteen-year-old, whose illegitimate foetus he had refused to abort. "She did me a favour, that Lore," said the doctor, his eyes crinkling with humour. "She spared my family the bombing and the hunger and put us within reach of nutrients that flower in the woods and swim in the brook. We grew healthy in the village while my city friends paled. My children are all quite plump, except for Lisl — you've met her — who

138

feeds, like I used to, on good books."

"I was the same at her age," said Paul.

Indicating a broken rafter in the roof, he offered to send over a repairman from his workforce. At a clap of thunder, the two men descended to the ground floor, reciting Heine's version of "The Erl King" in antiphonal verses and speculating on the possible effects of the poet's syphilitic invalidity on the tone of his later works. "He might have done better with a homeopath than with the leeches and sawbones of conventional medicine," said the doctor. "Myself, I completely altered my therapeutic practice after I came here. For want of a city pharmacy with a stock of chemical preparations, I would spend my lunchtimes picking plants and berries in the woods. With mortar and pestle, like Goethe's Faust, I made potions for every common condition. I treated like with like, in the manner of Samuel Hahnemann, and did less harm than good, as I was pledged to do by Hippocrates. There were no side effects and the only complaint was that my potions tasted bitter — I could never lay hands on enough honey or sugar rations."

Paul sipped the last of the acrid tea and pronounced it excellent.

"Nettles." The doctor beamed. "I plucked

and dried them myself. *Urtica urens,* very beneficial for gout and arthritis, not that such things should trouble a man your age. Anaemia, though: You look a bit pale. Another cup?"

"If you think it will do me good."

"That depends what you mean by 'good.' "

The doctor, Paul discovered, delighted in paradoxes. He had read all the philosophers — Spinoza, Marx, Nietzsche, Freud, Jung, Wittgenstein — and suffered from a lack of café disputation. In the city, he'd had a regular table at the Imperial and a convivial circle of intellectuals, two of them literary critics on the morning newspaper. Here, he had no-one to argue with and he was losing sharpness of mind. His wife read nothing but romances, and his children, Lisl excepted, read nothing at all — taking to the country life "as if to peasants born." The only other literate soul in the village was the wretched priest, and he was no more than a ragbag of superstitions, jumbled and half-forgotten with decrepitude. Paul was a treasure, a rare find in the wild. Stroking his iron grey moustache with ecstatic emphasis, the doctor led him back to the attic and begged him to borrow any book he liked. "Books," he declared, "we can share without either of us suffering loss — that, my dear fellow, is the beauty of it."

Paul ran his fingers down the serried works of Thomas Mann, an author banished for his principled humanity. Next to *Death in Venice,* four times as thick, lay *The Magic Mountain.* "My favourite," cooed Walters. "It works both as narrative and as a parable of the sickness in society. It even suggests, to a degree, why we got ourselves sent to the mountains, you and I — for the protection of society and our personal security. . . ."

"Were we?" snapped Paul. "I don't remember anyone being concerned for my safety and protection. Quite the contrary, in fact."

"In the city, they would have shot you on the spot," said the doctor.

"You know that, do you?" sneered Paul.

Rage flared inside him like a gas jet. How dare this man make presumptions about his fate? What did he know about city massacres, and what had he done about them? More to the point, what had he known, or wanted to know, about the whippings and killings outside his village front door? How could he reconcile his duty of care to humanity with the back he turned on dying men? What right had he to compare the mild inconvenience of his relocation to the mortal agonies of the quarry?

As swiftly as it erupted, the jet died. Paul was in no position to criticise. The doctor had put survival first, just as he had done in the camp. A free mind among morons, he had declined to risk his children's lives by making a pointless show of solidarity with the downtrodden, any more than Paul had risen in protest when Hans staged a hanging or a skydiving. The difference between him and the doctor was one of degree: Walters had kept his family and slept in his own home; Paul had lost his loved ones and been crammed in a concentration camp. Each had found a way of rationalising his inaction. One walked in the woods and read books in his attic, blotting out external horrors; the other lazed in a warm construction cabin as his friends were worked to death. The doctor was not to blame for Paul's suffering. Paul was not even sure that Walters was aware that he had been one of the death marchers who passed his door. He must see so many drifters in his surgery these days, so many dull eyes and shame-filled pasts. All he could do was take each patient at face value and make no assumptions until he had heard a story, often as not untrue.

Ashamed of his outburst, Paul murmured an apology and, in the same breath, asked the doctor to do him the honour of serving as best man at his wedding to Alice, the innkeeper's daughter. Walters, with a cry of delight, declared that nothing would make him happier. His youngest daughter, the well-read Lisl, was to be bridesmaid; to officiate at God's altar with his own sweet child would be rare glory indeed. Taking Paul's cold hand in a plump paw, he led him to the parlour for a celebratory libation of elderflower wine and an introduction to his slight, grey-fringed wife, whose reticence wafted like sour milk. "I have been asked to ride shotgun at Alice's wedding," boomed Walters. "That's nice for you, dear," said his wife, mopping up a spillage of wine. "So much to do," cried the doctor, "and so little time."

It was years, he declared, since he had last acted in this capacity; he needed a list of duties. Attend here, stand there, and afterwards at the feast deliver a ribald address to the guests, right? He had better get his opera suit steam-cleaned and decide which buttonholes to pick for himself and the bridegroom. Blood-red poppies, he thought, to annoy the priest. His speech, a Socratic discourse, would fly so high over the heads of the peasantry that some would request a copy of the text and try to memorise his pseudo-classical apothegms for further repetition. Oh, such fun, such fun. He was so grateful to Paul for asking him, restoring morning sun to an old man's heart.

"Not so old," reproved Mrs. Walters, "and watch out whom you offend in that speech. We can't afford to lose any more patients to that young louse in Pringsheim."

"On second thought," said the doctor, "forget *The Magic Mountain* — it's too morbid for the occasion. My engagement gift to you will be another work by Mann, *Joseph and His Brothers,* in a scarce first edition. I see you in a certain light as Joseph, the son who was sold into slavery and saved his new land from seven years of famine."

Paul read *Joseph* one chapter a night and was unmoved. Bumping into the doctor at the bakery, he refused to simulate enthusiasm. "The writer doesn't make me care for his characters," he said.

"That's just the point," said Walters. "Mann is not concerned with anyone's likes and dislikes, least of all his own. Like me, he has a job to do. I am not interested in most patients and may not care for their habits and attitudes. But I don't allow indifference to occlude my attention to their condition or affect the care I give them. Every now and then, I am rewarded by some fortuitous insight into human nature."

"Some simple goodness revealed in suffering?" said Paul.

Shoppers jostled them on the kerb of the shopping parade. "Goodness," replied the doctor, ignoring Paul's scepticism, "does not cross my surgery threshold. It gets left in the waiting room with the mothers and the nannies. If I stopped to see good or bad in my patients, I could not address their complaints with clinical detachment. I treat all who come to me with complete neutrality."

"The thief and the priest are the same in your eyes?"

"Don't talk to me about that priest," snapped Walters. "He's a hopeless drunk. Should have been pensioned off years ago. If I've told the bishop once, I've told him a dozen times. Ah, good morning, Father. Come to collect your breakfast roll, I see. Good to get some solids early in the day with your usual liquid diet. Have you met our Mr. Miller?"

"I am marrying him the week after next," said Hitzinger, wrinkling his nose with a grimace of resentment and distrust.

"Just checking." The doctor grinned. "Making sure you hadn't forgotten."

The pace of preparations picked up and

145

Tante Anna was restored to favour to fit the expanding Alice into her mother's wedding dress. The spinster sniffled as she worked about her "poor dead Maria," until Alice stormed out in a bursting lace bustier and Paul was called to promote reconciliation while being shrieked at by both women to look away from the dress, which would bring them all bad luck if he caught so much as a glimpse before it sailed down the aisle. Peace restored, he let Tante Anna truss him up in Franz-Josef's best suit, taken in by two sizes, and then into a wing collar that looked as if it had once belonged to a Hohenzollern princeling. It had been in the family for five generations; six said Alice, no five said Anna, and the row resumed. Two sows, Selma and Greta, were slaughtered for the wedding feast, their screams reaching Paul at his drawing board and making him swear never to taste ham again. Lisl squeaked around Alice's skirts, trim as her mother, unaffectedly curious about her friend's impressive catch. "Father insists you read this before the big day," she said, pressing into Paul's hand a well-thumbed edition of Arthur Schnitzler's mildly salacious memoir, *My Youth in Vienna.* Lisl always seemed to have a book to hand.

A week before the wedding, Alice moved

downstairs to her old room, leaving Paul to sleep on a cot in the corridor as he supervised the renovations. His workmen equipped the loft with en-suite bathroom, built-in cupboards, and a king-size four-poster bed, all made to Paul's specifications. On the eve of his nuptials, he reoccupied the finished quarters, exercising a strut of bachelor liberties — the right to fart without apology and to scratch an unwashed crotch. There was no men's party on his pre-nuptial night. Paul had no-one to carouse with, no-one to tease him over lost freedoms. As much as he was marrying Alice, he was pledging himself to this place, to people who had turned a blind eye to murder. Why did he not see that, was he as blind as they were? Torments raged behind his sleepless eyes. How could he live here in peace and love? What kind of creature was he to choose comfort ahead of retribution? He was a traitor to everything he held dear, to his homeland, his language, his mother, his true love. He was a renegade, a collaborator, a scavenger, a sewer rat, the lowest of the low.

All night long, Paul tossed to and fro on the presumptuous four-poster. And when sleep brought blessed relief, he found himself thrust onto a parallel screen into another time and place. It was the same time of year, the breathless heat before war. Alice would have been a kid back then, one of those pigtailed girls he saw in newsreels, shrieking *heil*s in a faceless mob. And he, featureless, too, was an academic in a factory town, a teacher of platitudes, balding, pasty-faced, and on a road to nowhere. He'd had this dream before, and he knew he could not evade its dreadful end.

CHAPTER SIX

Back then, before he knew the meaning of pain, Paul was cycling through the town centre on a Monday morning, the beginning of a week no different from the one before, his thesis successfully defended but stubbornly unpublished. Interest was waning in Alvar Aalto, his subject. Aalto, a Finn, designed white-light transparent structures, as different as any building could be from his hometown's pseudo-Baroque showpieces or its few proto-modern blocks, marred as they were by architectural incompetence and the collusion of commercial developers with corrupt officials. Paul hated the look of his town. A bracing dose of Aalto would offset those curlicued lintels and inutile window ledges, adding a suggestion of contemporary thought. Paul knew, though, that he had left it too late. There were tanks massed on the western border, a potshot away, and nobody wanted to talk about bold, bright campuses with lots of glass.

The university had told him to incorporate military architecture in the course he taught — trenches, tank traps, and so forth. When he declined, feigning ignorance when he meant indifference, the rector cut his hours and ordered him to justify his retention by teaching his other discipline, the qualification in psychiatry that he had taken to please his parents before they consented to his choice of vocation. The rector's offer was singularly insulting. He was supposed to be teaching year-one psychology to a pack of ignorant teenagers — a subject he found antipathetic, for it offered no remedy to his personal situation. He was a man at the hair-loss end of his twenties, living with elderly parents and without hope of love in a town that belched grime and held modernity in grim contempt. He needed to get out. Exiled to the wrong department, he fired off applications to other universities, but, as he had never fawned over influential colleagues at sinecure seminars, his missives went unanswered. All exits were blocked. He was going to have to teach convent-raised virgins the erotic theories of Sigmund Freud without offending the brittle faith that kept them notionally intact for holy matrimony. He looked ahead to the new academic year with an apathy verging on despair.

To keep his eye in and augment a pathetic pay packet, Paul undertook small commissions for his uncle, a smoke-wreathed building contractor whose thriving practice was erected on a scaffold of social contacts. Uncle Antoni was a man without scruple, or sons; if Paul played his cards right, he would become his heir. That rich prospect depressed him even more than his academic and social isolation. Love was beyond Paul's reach. Girls bypassed him at parties, deterred by his lack of small talk. He knew three jokes, and they were so trite that his parents banned him from repeating them at home. He always forgot to light a girl's cigarette or let her pass first through a door. He did not know how to make the first move. He was, his mother lamented, a hopeless case — a diagnosis that Paul took as a perverse compliment, singling him out as an interesting specimen of human malfunction.

It was with these glum thoughts in mind that he was on his way to see a client of his uncle who wanted an illegal extension to his sock-weaving sweatshop, when an army truck, travelling at twice the permitted speed, clipped his rear wheel and sent him head over handlebars into the opposite lane of Warsaw Street. By the grace of six milli-metres, an oncoming four-seater slammed on its brakes with a squeal, the fender groaning metallically in the air above Paul's numbed head. A corpulent couple leapt out, brandishing fists at the military vehicle, which accelerated and turned a corner, out of sight. The pair, dressed for café society in wide, garish tie and giraffe-high heels, turned their attention to Paul, absorbing him into their marital warfare.

"Ring a doorbell, and get them to call an ambulance," barked the man.

"Don't tell me what to do," cried the woman. "I've done my first-aid course. I shall give him the kiss of life."

"Don't be an idiot. He has been knocked off his bike, not bloody drowned."

"Who are you calling an idiot? Do you know how to perform a tracheotomy when a casualty stops breathing?"

"He will certainly stop breathing, Adina, if you start kissing him in that vile perfume."

"It came from Paris and cost a fortune."

"I know, I know, don't I just know."

"Stop being a complete pig, Mitek, and loosen his collar."

"Help me lift him into the car and let me

drive him to hospital."

"Are you crazy? You could damage his spine. He will end up paralysed and sue you in court for every penny you have got. Have you considered that, Mitek?"

"He will end up dead if we don't get him to a doctor. Now please, Adina, for once in your contrary life, do as your husband says."

"Don't say I didn't warn you."

Paul must have passed out again, because he came round in a white room to the sound of the couple arguing whether they had done the right thing, brought him to the right place, whether they knew him from somewhere. He looked awfully familiar. Wasn't he that clumsy boy of Johanna's?

"Thank you, Mr. and Mrs. Gastwirth," said a brisk young woman in a crisp white coat, "I'll take over now."

"Dear Ewa, we have every confidence. You will let us know how he is?"

"I will drop by and tell you tonight, at the end of my shift."

"We want the best for him, poor fellow. Money's no object."

"Was it your car that knocked him down?"

"Heaven forbid. How can you think such a thing? We saved his life, Mitek and I. He would have been crushed to death. Now please look after him. We need every young man to be fit and ready, should the worst come to the worst."

Through a veil of pain, Paul heard the doctor asking his name, address, job, what day of the week it was, where it hurt. Her fingers pressed lightly around his skull, then more firmly on his shoulders and arms. When she touched above the elbow, he gave a yelp. "Sorry," she said. "You may have broken it. We'll get a roentgen."

He was wheeled up one corridor and down another. In the hours it took to x-ray his arm and process the films, he was fed sips of water by a nurse in a giant white cap that looked like a sea-going yacht. Nothing to eat, she said haughtily; they might have to operate. It was late afternoon when the doctor whom the café couple addressed as Ewa returned with his X rays, regretting the delay, explaining that she had been detained in theatre by a multiple skull fracture of great complexity.

"Another traffic accident?" surmised Paul.

"Everyone is driving like lunatics," said the doctor. "The tension drives them insane." She had good news for him. A clean break, six weeks in plaster, no need for surgery. Her only concern was his aching head and initial confusion. Concussion could not be ruled out. She had decided to keep him in overnight.

Paul shook his head to assure her he was fine, making his temples throb and his left arm screech in agony. He explained, as if to a dim new student, that he suffered from a mild form of claustrophobia, which made it inadvisable to confine him in a hospital. He would drive the nurses mad; he was not designed for communal living. "Let me go home," he pleaded. "My parents will be worrying. They are not young. Patch me up for the night. I will come back tomorrow to show that I am still alive."

The doctor seemed impressed by his excuses. "All right," she conceded. "I shall send you home with a painkiller, which you must take before bed. But I want you back here at ten o'clock. Is that clear? Five minutes late and I will send the Gastwirths to fetch you. They have already phoned three times to find out how you are."

She wound the hot plaster sheets on his arm, explaining that the orthopaedic sister had gone for the day and she was due herself to go off shift. Her hair was rich and dark, her movements brisk and sure. He wanted to look into her brown eyes again, to resume the duel of wills, but she was impersonality personified. He was of minor interest to her, a simple fracture, a routine repair. "Where do you live?" she demanded, slipping his left arm into a cotton shoulder sling.

"Moniuszko, fourteen. Are you testing me again for concussion?"

"No." She smiled. "I thought I'd see if it's on my way home. Give me ten minutes to get changed and I can drop you off. It will save you getting bumped about on a bus."

"Don't forget you have to report to my rescuers."

She laughed, a ripple running upwards through her gaunt frame. "The Gastwirths? They are a comic pair, aren't they? Kind-hearted and never satisfied. They nearly became my parents-in-law last winter. A lucky escape."

"For you?"

"For all of us."

The heat hung heavy on the hospital parking lot as she rolled down the windows of a large black car, its roof painted white and emblazoned with a huge red cross. Paul, recognising French elegance, identified the machine as a Traction Avant, probably of the 11 series, five or six years old. Never having learned to drive, he admired automobiles objectively, as a eunuch might appraise feminine nudity. "I have the Citroën on loan during the state of emergency," she explained. "It seats eight, but the backseat flattens out to carry a large number of casualties if there is an aerial bombardment. Nobody knows what's going to happen or when, just that it seems inevitable. One of the matrons said to me, 'Whatever you want, do it today — tomorrow may never come.' "

She was not, Paul decided, his type. Her features were too close-set, her complexion jaundiced, her eyebrows untamed. There was a hint of down on her chin. Not that he was likely to be mistaken for Rudolf Valentino. Years of uninterrupted study had left a pinch to his lips and a pallor to his cheeks. His shoulders slumped and he exuded little physical energy. Looking at himself in the wing mirror of the TA-11 as it sallied through the hospital gates, he saw an unkempt specimen of manhood, a confirmed bachelor. No wonder girls at parties gave him such a wide berth.

The doctor drove as she had worked on his arm, in concentrated silence. At traffic lights, she neither tapped the wheel nor fiddled in the glove box, but sat with perfect composure, at ease with herself. She wore no lipstick and smelt of surgical hand soap. Her fingernails were neatly trimmed, the cuticles shining like half-moons on a starry night. As she turned the corner into Warsaw Street, Paul found himself falling in love. Why at this junction, two streets away from home, he would never know, but as the big vehicle swung into the main lane, the localised ache in his arm gave way to a severe existential pain and he made a forthright bid for her attention.

"Excuse me, Dr. Ewa," he said, "may I ask you something?"

"Go ahead."

"Are you married?"

"Lots of men ask that" — she smiled, staring straight ahead — "some before I even examine them, some with a wedding band on their hand."

"I apologise for the impertinence, but I require the information."

"For what purpose?"

"For important personal reasons."

"What are they?"

"I am single, and extremely eligible. Desperate, actually."

The car rocked with her giggles and he saw, in the mirror, a flicker of interest. "I will give you an answer at ten o'clock tomorrow," she said, helping him out of the car and towards the entrance arch of his apartment block. He longed to take her in the crook of his right arm and raise her oval face to his. He had been in love before, but never so instantaneously. She offered him her hand, and he remembered, for once, to bring it to his lips, touching it to his cheek before he let go. She smiled, waved, drove off.

After that, things happened very fast. At ten the next morning, Dr. Ewa checked his head and found no concussion. "A small kiss would stop the throbbing," he suggested. "Not here," she shushed, which he took as a promise.

She agreed to meet him at noon at a stand-up kiosk in the park. He bought them each a stuffed pastry and they strolled down to a bench beside the lake, feeding the crumbs they had saved to the ducks. Paul talked with passion about city planning. Ewa showed him how to set a broken bone. When she put a hand on his arm, he covered it with his palm, and she did not seem to mind. Before long, they were in confessional mode. Ewa admitted she was far too thin, the aftermath of a pneumonia brought on by long working hours and bad relationships at work, where the director put her on general duties even though she was an orthopaedic surgeon specialising in paediatric care. Her social life was vacant. She was twenty-eight years old, a long way from

home, an old maid, almost. The Gastwirths'
son, a salesman in the family antique shop,
had kindly offered to marry her, but he was
spoilt, uncultured, and reedy-voiced. She
liked slim men, well read, resonant. She
could never marry an ill-stocked mind.

Paul undressed his own predicaments. He
had no friends and few interests outside
architecture, design, and the theoretical
aspect of human psychology, being some-
what terrified of the practical. He was a
lecturer at the university and had a second
job with his uncle, but life was passing him
by. If he liked a girl, she walked away; either
that or, if he mentioned psychology, she
would recite her complexes and expect
instant Jungian analysis while propping up
a wall at a faculty party. He had no dream
girl in mind, just a vague feeling that
someone existed for him out there. That
vagueness had just turned to certainty. Ewa
was his destiny. He was not bothered by
looks, dowry, or pedigree — though he
hastened to add that she was beautiful and
brilliant, bringing a blush to her sallow
cheeks. He had no prejudices or expectations. His mother came from a home so
poor that girls sat at spinning wheels at
seven years of age, and from a religious
minority that was always under threat. Ewa

replied that in her home they would thin the supper soup with water until there was enough to go round; in case he hadn't noticed, she belonged to the same troubled ethnic group as his mother.

He demanded that she meet his mother — meet her right away, for there was no time to lose. Who knew what might be a week from now? Ewa said they must not get rushed into decisions by the general mood of despondency and panic, to which Paul replied that he paid no attention to what others thought. He knew in his heart that they were made for each other. Ewa squeezed his arm. They passed the fleapit with the ever-splitting screen and were strolling down a parade of shops, glancing at window displays. A pyramid crested on a travel agency poster. "Nice place for a honeymoon," said Paul. Ewa rose on tiptoe and kissed him on the cheek. She had entered into his fantasy. "Are you sure?" said Paul with a searching look. "At this moment, yes," said Ewa. "I may have doubts later on, but it feels ordained that you and I should meet here and now, on the edge of a precipice. My life has been stalled by my own hesitancy and the malign intentions of others. I am ready to trust my instinct. You are the nicest man I have met in a long time, and you make me laugh. That's a good start."

Entering his parents' shabby apartment on the fourth floor of a well-worn block, he introduced Ewa without preamble as his fiancée. "Arthur," said his mother, "get some glasses." His father rummaged beneath the kitchen sink and came up, red-faced, with a dirty-rimmed bottle of plum brandy and four cut-glass goblets. Ewa placed a hand over Paul's glass. With his sore head, she would not allow him anything stronger than lime cordial. His father, clinking toasts, told Ewa that once, before his early retirement with a heart condition, he had been the town's registrar for births, marriages, and deaths. He knew everyone by name.

"Except singletons like me." Ewa smiled.

"Not for long," said Arthur, crooning a love song to his second brandy. Ewa joined Paul's mother in the kitchen, comparing recipes as they set out the evening meal. She ate heartily at table, assuaging his mother's undisguised anxiety at her pinched waistline.

"Give the girl more potatoes, Johanna," said his father.

"I have already eaten a field and a half," protested Ewa.

"More gravy?" said his mother, spooning

liberally.

The betrothed couple held hands on the sofa as the radio crackled with cross-border incidents and intimations of war. Ewa agreed, as they walked out to the car, to marry Paul without delay. She would take him that weekend to her father, who was the spiritual leader of a small congregation in the capital, two hours away by train.

"Will he accept me?"

"He has long since written me off as a bride. He will hug you to his chest and make you dance a *kazatzka* with him inside a ring of clapping disciples."

"But I am of another faith. I was baptised. . . ."

"It won't matter. Your mother, Johanna, is of our people, born in a village whose name he will know. My father will join us in marriage on Saturday night in the light of candles, beneath a holy canopy, and before a hundred male witnesses, so there can be no going back on our vows. Are you prepared for that?"

"I can't wait," said Paul. "And when we return, my father will perform the civil ceremony at his old desk in the town hall, the one he has rehearsed at our table ever since I was a little boy: By the power of the authority vested in me by the state, I pronounce you, my son, man and wife, with — insert name — the bride of your heart."

He kissed Ewa beneath the crepuscular entrance to the apartment block, out of sight of the snooping concierge. She nestled into his chest, a sparrow in a storm, utterly trusting. Only when he fumbled with her shirtwaist buttons did she pull away.

"Don't be afraid," he implored.

"I'm not," she purred.

"Don't you want me?"

"More than you know."

"What, then?"

"Let's wait a few days more," she said. "We have the whole of our lives."

He took her hand, touched by her chastity, so different from the brazenness he met each day in the university and at his uncle's office. Ewa was waiting for him. As he kissed her good night, he heard a murmur in her larynx.

He went to the station in the morning and bought a pair of first-class tickets for the Friday dawn train. As he packed — dark suit and tie, two shirts, razor, brushes, and underwear — his mother brought him a photograph of a large family sitting outside a thatched hut. "That's my father, with the long beard, my mother in the head scarf," she said. "Show it to Ewa's family." Paul went to bed early and slept as if anaesthetised.

Explosive flashes broke the night. Aircraft shuddered overhead and glass crunched in the avenue below. Paul rushed to the window and saw enemy tanks, shredding matchstick objects in their path. Behind them came armoured cars with megaphones, ordering citizens to stay indoors. Paul's parents joined him at the window, huddled together in fear. He put the kettle on and brewed a pot of coffee. Ewa would be finishing her night shift about now. He telephoned the hospital, but the line was dead. His parents sat hand in hand on the sofa, conjoined by dread. There was nothing useful to be said. As the day wore on, the wireless played martial music, interspersed with prohibitions. Anyone who did this or failed to do that would be shot. Order would be maintained at all costs.

The rattle of tank treads abated with dusk and the streets fell silent, the lamps unlit. Paul flung a jacket over his arm sling and went out in search of Ewa. Slinking past the concierge's portal, hugging the shadow of street walls, he loped along in the direction of the hospital. Muffled howls reached his ears a hundred metres out and he quickened his step. Seeing the forecourt barred by armed sentries, he slipped around the rear, where as a boy, bored and solitary, he used to hang around watching ambulances come and go and orderlies wheel out tall bins of soiled linen from a sunken cellar entrance. He found the cellar door at the foot of stone steps and gave a grimace of satisfaction as it yielded to his shoulder. Through the morgue he strode, onwards to a flight of stairs, which led up to the marbled main lobby.

Unconfined howls directed him to the emergency room, a depot of broken bodies and blurred activity. Ewa's face, grey with fatigue, lit up. Throwing him an orderly's brown coat, she instructed him in ten curt words to conduct triage, to sift urgent cases from those that could wait. Soldiers and civilians, old and young, screamed for attention. Paul surveyed the room and devised solutions. He called all relatives to step to one side and divided them into groups, one to remove the dead to the morgue, the next to fetch mops and clean the floor, the third to take notes as he interviewed each casualty and pinned a priority letter to coat lapels — A for immediate, B for secondary, C for can wait. Within half an hour, he had the gangways clear, the floors clean, and three queues lined up for Ewa, her student, Jacek, and five haggard nurses. "Have you eaten?

Drunk?" he demanded. They shook heads. Paul sent the mother of a plump boy with a superficial face wound to load a trolley with coffee and sandwiches in the canteen and operate a mobile food station for the medical staff.

The night passed in unremitting effort, punctuated by intermittent loss. Ether and morphine ran low, and Ewa saved what was left for children. Adults, speckled with shrapnel, were strapped to the table, swabbed, and cut in a single motion. Single-handed after Jacek collapsed, Ewa stitched up the last emergency as sunlight broke through the makeshift blackout.

"How many?" asked Paul, but she had lost count of all the incisions and amputations. The only patient she talked about was the young coal miner she had lost, struck by a cerebral haemorrhage just as she finished saving his terribly tattered leg.

"You deserve a medal," said Paul.

"It's what I've been trained to do." She shrugged, shoving an angry strand of black hair beneath her green cap.

Relief was arriving by enemy convoy, two surgical teams and fresh supplies, followed by a daytime torrent of human suffering. Ewa briefed the incoming shift before taking Paul down to a basement locker room, where they fell onto separate cots. "I love you," he whispered, his eyelids closing.

Awake once more and eager to serve, they climbed the stairs, grabbed a sandwich, and, still munching, walked into the scuttling path of the head of surgery. "Out," he hissed at Ewa. "You must go. New racial laws. They made me identify minority staff. If they find one, they say, they will arrest me and shut the hospital. You must leave. It is dangerous for us all." Paul opened his mouth to protest, but Ewa squeezed his hand and told the director in a low voice that she was available when required. A passing nurse burst into tears. Ewa, kissing her farewell, took Paul by his good arm and led him back into the bowels of the building, where, waiting for nightfall, they held hands and said very little, because little needed to be said. Love connected them invisibly, like an electric current.

Under cover of night, they left through the morgue and, dodging roadblocks, reached Paul's home by a two-hour detour. "We must get away," said his mother once they had washed and sat down. "They have come knocking on doors, demanding papers. Anyone of foreign or minority birth is given two hours to pack. The Goldvichts, upstairs, and the Kaplans have been taken."

"And you?" said Ewa.

"My husband opened the door, showed them his certificate as town registrar, and swore that he was a widower, living alone."

Over broth, they plotted flight. Paul's father said they must reach his younger brother, Andrzej, who owned a sports shop in a mountain resort and knew the goat trails across the southern border like the lines on the palms of his hands. "Let's sleep on it," said Paul, giving up his room to Ewa and curling up on the lumpy sofa.

He was awakened by a pounding on doors all over the building. Peering from behind net curtains, he saw neighbours in smart hats and coats being beaten into line with rifle butts and kicked with riding boots, then marched off to the yapping of dogs. There was no time to lose. The concierge, who kept a list of residents, would soon betray them. "We must get Johanna and Ewa to the mountains," said his father.

"But how?" Paul demanded. "There are no trains, and there's a strict curfew."

"I have the ambulance," said Ewa quietly, "and a full tank of gasoline."

"Where is it?"

"Parked round the corner."

Car owners had been ordered to surrender their keys, but Ewa's Citroën had a red cross on its roof and doors, and the troops thought it belonged to an international relief organisation. "It got me through several barriers when I brought it here." She smiled. A plan cohered around the family table. Ewa had enough gas to reach Andrzej's resort. She would drive the ambulance. If they got stopped, Arthur would pretend to be having a heart attack. Ewa would blare her siren and, head to the wheel, drive through the sentry post at speed. Risky, said Arthur. It's our best chance, declared Johanna.

"What about me?" asked Paul.

"You stay here," said his father, "in case we run into trouble. Talk to my brother Antoni. Ask him to fix you a set of false papers. Stay here and wait to hear from us."

"Where will you be?"

"In Andrzej's chalet, God willing, where we went on holiday when you were a boy, remember? It is a simple hut," he informed Ewa, "earth closet and no electricity — but isolated. No-one will know we are there except my brother, who lives alone."

"You can't leave me here on my own," cried Paul with mounting petulance.

"It's for the best," said Johanna. "A young man in the car would arouse more suspicion than a hospital doctor and a pair of old patients."

"You have a broken arm," Arthur added. "You'd be useless at changing a tyre."

Paul protested. He argued, rationalised, pleaded, blustered, contradicted, and finally appealed to Ewa to take him along. His voice had taken on a whining tone and he saw himself, of a sudden, as a boy of four or five, having lost his way while picking berries in a forest and feeling utterly abandoned.

"It won't be for long," said his mother, mussing his hair. "We know you can't manage without us."

"I will never let you leave me again," he swore, clinging to Ewa that night, fully clothed on his bed. "I know," she whispered. "You are part of me, now and forever." He woke, to hear her dressing in the dark. "We have the whole of our lives. . . ." she whispered, touching his lips with a cold forefinger. Minutes later, he heard the French engine purr below and the car crunch quietly on its way.

Alone, he slept late and turned idle. His mother had left food in the pantry for a month of siege. Paul pottered about the apartment, omitting to shave or wash dishes. He left a genealogy book open on the table to make it appear as if his father were around, in case of more searches, but the curfew was being lifted, and by the end of the week people were returning to work. Paul called on Uncle Antoni at his office. Over the wireless they heard that the university had been shut down. Antoni offered him a partnership on the spot and took him to lunch at a plush restaurant where leading businessmen were meeting officials of the new administration.

Paul plunged himself into work, the first to arrive and last to leave. It kept his mind free of constant worry and established him as his uncle's successor. Two months passed before Antoni slid him a set of false papers under the desk, apologising for taking so long. By way of amends, he produced a travel permit that would allow Paul to go south on compassionate grounds to visit a dying grandmother. He could join his loved ones as soon as he heard from them. "God bless you, Antoni," said Paul. "Father said you would not let us down. I'll go to the station and check the connections."

"Hang on a minute," said his uncle. "This has just arrived."

It was a letter from his uncle Andrzej, the rugged mountain guide, a man of few words. Andrzej trusted his dear brother and beloved nephew were in the best of health and sent them his warmest greetings.

Should they be thinking of paying him a visit, he advised strongly against it, as the weather was inclement and accommodation would be hard to arrange.

"What does he mean?" said Paul, alarmed.

"It sounds like trouble," said Antoni, "Give me a few days, I'll find out."

Some days later, Antoni called Paul back to his inner office and shut the door.

"Terrible news," he said. "There was an incident as they arrived at the resort."

"My parents? My fiancée?"

"God rest their souls."

"All three of them?"

"I'm sorry, my boy."

"Do you know what happened?"

Anton shook his head, side to side, as if there was nothing more to say.

Paul shook hands with his odious uncle, the sweat of collusion leaking into his palms. He tidied the top of his desk, locked the drawers, and took a walk through the park, imagining that Ewa's footsteps were imprinted beside his in the gravel path. He went home and tried to mourn, but no tears came, nothing but a hacking snuffle. He stayed away from work for three days, and when he returned, his conduct went into reverse, as if a switch had been thrown in his control box from positive to negative.

Assiduousness gave way to laxity, punctuality to lateness, seriousness to glassy levity. He cracked off-colour jokes, repeating them in a louder voice when no-one laughed. His drawings were imprecise, his designs unsafe. Danger dangled from him like a charm.

Women, previously allergic to Paul, were drawn to his new persona like vultures to carrion. He brushed them aside, wanting nothing from the rest of the human species. Spurned, they lingered against his wall of impassivity, fired by some mothering urge that they could no more restrain than he could ultimately resist their temptation. He succumbed in due course, first to the middle-aged receptionist at his uncle's office, then to the interior designer in the adjoining room, to two skittish stenographers, to the wife of the head of the psychology department, to a reed-thin oboist from the workless symphony orchestra, to his office intern, a stranger in the stairwell of his parents' apartment block, the waitress from the kiosk where he had lunched with Ewa, the nurse who had kissed her farewell in the hospital lobby. There was a principled dignity to his acquiescence. He never once took a woman before she was fully willing, waiting for her to raise a hand in proposition, and then for her physical desire to overflow before he despatched her with austere detachment.

Of all his would-be comforters, only Jadwiga, his uncle's pencil-heeled mistress, yielded more than superficial satisfaction, and his conquest of her was filled with such rage that he almost strangled her during coitus. Drawn to powerful men, Jadwiga was more impressed than deterred and urged him to ever greater indulgence. "My lion," she called him, stroking his bare haunches in the modern house that Antoni had built for her. Paul barely heard her endearments or felt her touch. His mind was on the nurse of the night before, his closest memento of Ewa.

Legends of Paul's lotharioism spread around the town, earning him a notoriety that was indistinguishable, in a state of abject defeat, from actual heroism. Under military occupation, Paul did as he pleased and showed a stony disregard for consequences. Women would stop him in the street and ask him to light their cigarettes. Young men spoke of him as a role model. Cowled monks who would recoil in normal times from carnal sin blessed his sullen defiance as a sign of national resistance. Even enemy officers accorded him respect, recognising in his sexual rampage a resonance of their own decadence. While others supped on meatless gruel, Paul received gilt invitations to champagne parties in former palaces where licensed killers in black uniforms danced with blondes in blank looks. He stood by the wall, tall glass in hand, courting nothing and nothingness. The more women loved him, the less he felt liked. Each fresh coition aroused a surge of self-repugnance.

Relations with his uncle turned brittle as Jadwiga click-clicked between them, until she hightailed it out of their lives, replacing them with a death's-head colonel in a white silk scarf. "Easy come, easy go." Antoni smiled, his arm around Paul's shoulder. "Keep your nose clean, son," said his uncle, "and we'll get through these difficult times, together. People always need builders, remember that. And women always respond to a show of disinterest. It never fails." Paul's mother used to call Antoni "the slime," when his father was out of earshot.

Paul responded to Antoni's camaraderie with a rising curve of outrageous conduct. He gave away his three-piece suit to a street beggar and went to work in a bizarre combination of peasant shirts and patent-leather shoes. He sang patriotic dirges in a loud, flat voice and held the eye of passers-by in a scornful vise. He flaunted his contempt, and Antoni could do nothing to defuse him. Paul knew too much about his uncle's business and could potentially, with a calculated indiscretion at Sunday lunch, apprise his aunt Grazyna of the slime's multiple treacheries.

Nor was he done yet with competitive infidelity. No sooner had Antoni's eye settled on Helena, a brunette intern, than Paul reeled her into his embrace — her, and the concierge's daughter, Mrs. Kaplan's unmarried niece, three ex-students in a week, a tall girl on a tram, and others too numerous and indistinguishable to recall. As time passed, he wondered if some of his lovers had not been figments of a damaged fantasy, fevered rumours that a town mill had ground into credible fact. Jadwiga, Helena, and the compassionate nurse, he remembered with warmth and clarity; the rest blurred into a cavalcade of passing flesh, aware though he was of the change they had wrought in him. The sexual pariah had become an erotic magnet, the outcast a saviour, the leper a hero, just like the miraculous tales his mother used to read from the Old Testament. He began to understand the flimsiness of fame and appreciated that, sooner or later, he would face nemesis, no doubt at the hands of malevolent Antoni, who was smarting from humiliation. Paul knew that Antoni must retaliate and was not much bothered how, when, or why. He had lost all reason to care. Except for a nagging ache in his left arm, he felt nothing.

So when, one afternoon while Antoni was out for lunch, gendarmes dragged Paul out of the office and threw him onto an open truck, he guessed that, after four years of studied forbearance, his seamy uncle had finally run out of patience. It was not unusual in those unnatural times for people to say of family delinquents that what they needed was a short, sharp spell in a concentration camp. Paul felt no resentment towards Antoni for turning him over, not even a twitch of satisfaction that he had pushed his slippery uncle to the limits of self-interest. Antoni might have convinced himself that he was sending Paul away for his own good, in order to get him back in a better state of mind. More likely, he had sacrificed him to eliminate a risk to his own skin and perhaps to collect a reward of some kind. Either way, Paul maintained a façade of imperviousness as he landed bodily on the back of the truck. He felt sure that, whatever lay ahead, there could be no pain on earth greater than his guilty self-reproach for the fate of his loved ones.

He soon learned that there could. Whipped along rutted paths in wood-soled shoes, starved to the point where he saw soup mirages, festering with infected sores, Paul experienced a degree of physical suffering that matched the existential. He responded with unforeseen resistance, a refusal to succumb. Where this strength came from, he did not know. Nothing in his upbringing had prepared him for endurance, nothing in his expensive education for savagery on such a scale. Unlike the God-fearers in camp, he did not resign his soul to an almighty will; unlike the politicals, he had no dream of power; unlike fellow intellectuals, he found no solace in analysis. He awoke each day to the knowledge that he was being punished for good reason. In the worst agonies, flogged across a stone bench on Hans's command for miscalculating the height of a lintel, he accepted in staggered breaths that he deserved every one of the forty strokes for letting Ewa and his parents go out alone and unprotected. He could not give up his life until he had shared the fullness of their suffering, for which he was solely and irredeemably responsible.

It was all his fault. Had he not brought

Ewa home, she might have fended for herself and escaped. His parents could have got by on Antoni's false papers while Paul kept his head down at Antoni's desk. If, on that sunny Monday morning, he had not been sunk in self-pity on his bike, he would never have been knocked off, never have been taken to hospital, never have met Ewa, never have conjoined the three lives he held dearest to an inevitable death. A rational voice piped up from time to time that the escape had been Ewa's plan, endorsed by his mother and accepted by unanimous consent. He could not be held accountable for a collective decision, taken with proper calculation of risk and eyes wide open. Ewa and his parents would not wish Paul to torture himself. It was insane that he, the survivor, should suffer. He knew that was what his mother would have said. But no amount of knowledge and reason could palliate his need to assume the full burden of guilt once a trustworthy account of their fate had been brought to his door.

It had taken his straight-talking uncle Andrzej the better part of a year to obtain a travel permit from the obtuse bureaucracy of military occupation, and it was two days before the anniversary of the disaster that he arrived to present his testimony. Paul collected the wizened mountaineer from the station and walked him in silence to the apartment, his woollen breeches and old-fashioned peaked cap attracting sidelong looks from properly suited pedestrians who jostled past on the crowded pavements. Reaching home, he sat his uncle on the settee with a glass of water, which was all his visitor would accept by way of refreshment after his tiresome and terrifying journey, punctuated by spot checks and violent threats. Andrzej, his face furrowed by sun and laughter, placed one hand on each knee, dark veins protruding, and waited for a request to proceed. Paul sat on a straight-backed chair, arms to his sides, and gave an imperceptible nod. As Andrzej began, Paul leaned forward to catch the words as a murderer inclines his head to hear his sentence, cocked for the inevitable, the emptiness ahead.

Andrzej had seen the drama from behind the heavy door of his little store. He began by begging Paul's forgiveness for not having tried to save them, for standing frozen in the shadows, nailed to the floor. Paul reached for his uncle's hand and asked him to tell all he had seen, but no sooner were the words out of his mouth than he regretted them, remembering that Andrzej described each shrub and bird he passed on a walk in the woods with the pedantry of a naturalist and was unlikely to spare him the parts he least wished to hear. True to his fears, the kindly uncle recounted every detail.

It appeared that Ewa's plan had worked perfectly, or so Andrzej was told by Arthur in the four days he lay dying. The three fugitives had left the city beneath the flaring red cross and passed unchallenged, saluted even, through several barriers as they puttered into open country. Unmolested along empty lanes, they pulled into a clump of trees beside a stream to fill their water bottles, eat lunch, and stretch their limbs. Barely had they left the road than a military convoy roared past, a close call. They decided to spend the night in the copse and complete their journey the next day. Ewa made Johanna and Arthur comfortable on the fold-down backseat, and then napped as best she could in front. In benign morning, the ambulance set out once more, passing one sentry post after another, climbing with the last of its fuel to the entrance of Andrzej's resort town, a popular enclave of family hotels and rainy-day diversions — a casino, a heated swimming pool, and rows upon rows of souvenir and sports shops.

The town was under martial law, its tourists dispersed by the invasion. Eight or ten soldiers milled at the gates, as if awaiting orders. Just as Ewa prepared to drive through, one of them raised a gloved hand and stepped into their path. Arthur, lulled into false confidence, let out an involuntary yelp and clutched his arm. "He's having another heart attack," cried Johanna. Ewa rolled down her side window and, screaming "Medical emergency!" swerved around the soldier, burst through two barricades, and shuddered to a halt in a market square where the Angelus bell was tolling noon and a mediaeval scene was being played out in deadly earnest.

An officer in grey-green field fatigues stood in front of the town hall, tapping his thigh with a restless riding crop. "I am waiting," he said, each syllable bouncing off the surrounding hills with a mocking triple echo.

"I wish to know, know, know," said the lieutenant in schoolmasterly fashion, "the names, names, names of those men who broke into my armoury last night and stole three rifles and a quantity of ammunition, nition, nition. Once I have the names, I give you my word as an officer that no action will be taken against innocent persons. But time is short. Unless I have the names in two minutes precisely, icely, reprisals will follow, hollow, hollow."

Andrzej, cramped behind his shop door, where he had been reaching for a sunhat, turned his eyes to the church clock. Its large hand clicked once from four minutes past vertical noon to five, and again to a deadly six. A pile of potatoes tumbled off a stall, rolling comically to the centre of the square. No-one moved. The lieutenant, tapping his thigh, ambled around the stalls, from tomatoes to lettuce to onions, placing a black-gloved hand beneath one chin after another, staring into blank eyes. Andrzej's knees rattled, and he gripped an upright pair of skis for support. The air curdled as it entered his lungs. Just as it seemed as if God himself would have to break the silence, a vehicle with red crosses on its roof and sides came hurtling into the square and Andrzej saw erect in the backseat the ashen face of his dear sister-in-law Johanna. He wanted to rush out and greet her, but his feet were set in cement. It was the thigh-tapping lieutenant who reached the car first, throwing open the driver's door.

"A timely arrival," he declared, yanking a young woman in a white coat out of her seat, grabbing her by the back of the neck like a miscreant cat. "I am a doctor," croaked his captive. "I need to get this man to hospital. He is having a heart attack. It's an emergency, a matter of life and death."

"Mine is also an emergency," said the officer, bantering.

"Red Cross," choked the woman in a white coat.

"One hundred and first Cavalry," said the lieutenant, as if he were being introduced over cocktails. "Step this way. Let me show you how my regiment deals with a life-and-death emergency. Corporal!"

An artilleryman clicked to attention.

"Select ten women and line them up against the wall."

Stall keepers were dragged, despairing, from their pitch and shoppers from the sides of the square. "Not just the old ones and fat ones," ordered the lieutenant. "I want some who are young and pretty, sweet girls with their whole lives ahead." A white-faced parade was arrayed before the town hall. "Let me add two of mine to make an even dozen," said the lieutenant like a man selecting mushrooms at market. He shoved Ewa and Johanna to the end of the line.

"Firing positions!" Six soldiers placed gun barrels on a mound of cheeses.

"So what have we here?" said the lieutenant. "Wives, mothers, maidens, even a schoolgirl. My compliments, ladies. In other circumstances, I might kiss your hands and ask for a dance. I wish you to know that we are not barbarians. We do not kill the innocent. But unless our weapons are recovered, there will be innocent deaths on our side, and I have a duty to prevent that. So, ladies, last chance, please, which of you is going to whisper to me the names of your munition thieves?"

He walked down the line, theatrically placing his ear to one pair of tight lips after another. When he reached Ewa, the last in line, he stared into her eyes and paused. "So, what have we here? A sister of mercy, yes?"

"I am a doctor," said Ewa, her voice traversing the square.

"Where is your holy cross of Christ's mercy?" demanded the officer. Reaching into her white coat, he rummaged around her neck for the obligatory ornament and came out empty-handed.

"Empty your pockets," he commanded.

The town clock tolled the quarter hour as the young woman extracted handkerchief, keys, coins, and identity card from either side of her coat. A final item glittered in her palm, its chain dangling.

"What have we here?" cried the officer, holding up a six-pointed gold star.

"A gift," protested Ewa, "a keepsake from some friends who recently emigrated."

"Really?" smirked the lieutenant. "You expect me to believe so feeble a lie? What have we here?" he repeated, raising his voice across the square. "An impostor. Not a doctor at all, but a racial parasite. One of those who provoked war between our two countries. A shameless traitor, carrying the secret symbol of her dirty tribe. Shooting is too merciful for such a creature. I shall resort to a more exemplary remedy."

At this point, on the settee, Uncle Andrzej changed his tone. He stopped quoting every spoken line and proceeded to paraphrase the rest of the encounter in dry, short sentences, drained of emotion. The officer, he resumed, hurled the David star to the ground and crunched it beneath his heel. Taking the lapels of Ewa's coat and dress in either hand, he ripped smartly downwards, so that she stood naked but for a pair of undergarments. With a gesture, he ordered her to remove them. When she stared up in bemusement at his impassive face, he slapped her twice around the cheeks and tore at her flimsy covering until she stood bare and defenceless in the square. He motioned at her to stand against the church door. A stool was brought from within. She was made to mount it. A hammer was fetched from the hardware store, and nails. It was a mild day in early autumn. A breeze ruffled the market awnings. Somewhere, a dog barked, a chaffinch trilled. Two soldiers held Ewa's bare arms and a third drove a pair of long, cold nails into her elbows and another into her knees. The stool was kicked away and she slumped forward, coal black hair jutting out of her chalk flesh in accusing clumps. Townspeople turned away in shame and disgust. An order barked out like a shot. "Face front, all of you. Anyone not facing front will end up beside the louse."

Starting at the end, the lieutenant walked down the line of women in front of the town hall. Pistol in hand, he asked each woman a curt question before shooting her squarely between the eyes. Paul's mother, the newcomer, was shot unasked. As he reloaded beside the seventh hostage, a prayer-gabbling grandmother in a canvas apron, a brace of black horses cantered up to the far end of the square and two officers leapt to the ground with a clatter of spurs. "We've caught the thieves," one shouted.

"Excellent," said the lieutenant. "Just in

time for lunch. You can all go home now," he told the rest of the women. "Off with you now, shoo, shoo."

One of the riders, a captain, jerked his head towards the naked woman nailed to the church door. "What's going on, Hans?" he demanded. Without waiting for a reply, he strode over, released a shot into Ewa's skull, and told a sergeant to clear up the mess. The clock tolled the half-hour.

"That's all I can tell you," said Andrzej, hauling himself up from the settee and stumbling over to put a wiry arm around his nephew, who sat upright on his chair. "I saw it all from my doorway and I did nothing. For that, I cannot forgive myself. . . ."

"Thank you, Uncle," said Paul.

"For what?"

"For having the courage to come and tell me. For bearing witness. For making me feel as if I was there. I should have been there, you know. I should never have let them leave the city without me."

"What could you have done if you had been there?"

"I could have died with them."

"Come, my boy, what good would that have done?"

"We would have been together."

"The girl —"

189

"My fiancée, Ewa . . ."

"— she did not make a sound. Not a whimper. She bore her trial with dignity."

"Thank you, Uncle."

"Everyone in our town said she acted like a saint. . . . They pray secretly to her memory."

Paul could bear to hear no more. His Ewa, so bashful that she had asked him, her beloved, to turn his back as she changed clothes in a dark room, had died exposed to the eyes of male strangers. Thinking of her nailed to a church door drained Paul of the last of his faith in the human race and its right to exist upon God's good earth. It sucked him dry, too, of emotion. He felt no urge to shout and keen and tear his hair, knowing it would do no-one any good. Nothing would.

"What happened to my father?" he enquired, completing the inventory.

"I carried dear Arthur from the car into my shop and called the doctor," said Andrzej. "I made him comfortable on the bed upstairs. After putting a stethoscope to his chest, the doctor shook his head. Arthur lay beside the open window, listening to the birds he so loved. He hung on, drifting in and out, determined to tell me all that he knew so that I could convey it, one day, to you. 'Tell Paul,' he said. 'Paul must know.' His heart gave out on the fourth night and I had the sad honour of burying my big brother, the hero who protected me from schoolyard bullies and was always there in my hour of need.

"Johanna and your girl had been flung, with the other women, into a trench at the far end of the churchyard, close to where they fell. The night Arthur died, three friends and I entered the cemetery and, by the light of a crescent moon, disinterred our martyrs, your mother and fiancée, taking them with Arthur to the freedom of the mountains, to my chalet garden, where we spent those happy summers together, the best of our lives. I laid Arthur and Johanna in a joint plot, the girl in a space beside them. The gentians will grow around them in spring, and tiger moths will flutter in summer. You will come and visit."

"I will, Uncle, thank you," said Paul, knowing he never would.

"When my time comes," sighed Andrzej, "I have asked my friend to lay me beside them."

There was no more to be said. Andrzej refused to spend a night in the polluted city. Paul asked if he wanted to drop in on Antoni on their way back to the station, only to see his uncle's lip curl with contempt. There was no love between the brothers, one close to the land, the other poisoned by city wiles.

At the station, Andrzej stood with tireless patience while his papers were checked over and again and soldiers abused him as a swinish nuisance. As they hugged farewell, Paul whispered a final question.

"What was his name? Do you know his name?"

"I made enquiries," said Andrzej. "I heard from one of our local gendarmes, a friend of mine, that the lieutenant had been put on a charge for damaging church property and shipped out that night to Silesia. Witold didn't know his name. But I heard the horse rider, the one who shot your fiancée, call the torturer by a Christian name. Hans, he called him. That I heard clearly. 'What's going on, Hans?' he said."

Paul had never met a Hans. The name meant nothing to him. It rang no bells in his memory, except as the forename of a Danish storyteller, a German mastersinger, and the chap who invented the Geiger counter. Hans had been a neutral name for Paul until this railway platform moment, when it was seared on his brain like a mark of Cain. Hans from now on would signify

192

the ultimate in awfulness, a viral evil that lurked below a thin veneer of civilisation. Hans was the antithesis of conscience, the devil in uniform, a bottomless fear, an infinity of iniquity. And later, when, by the grace of providence or coincidence, Paul wound up himself under the authority of another Hans, he would decide that the name had to be generic, a label for the most odious, the worst of the worst.

Defining Hans gave Paul no relief from fear and misery, but it did afford some respite from self-loathing. Paul could not be the most hateful and contemptible creature alive, so long as Hans was alive — unless, that is, Paul was keeping Hans alive in order to spare himself the unsought title. So long as there was a Hans, Paul could maintain his pretence of human decency and, maybe, pursue a normal life. Hans existed to save his sanity, to preserve him from self-annihilation.

These bleak and truthful thoughts, on the night before his wedding, taunted Paul in his handmade bed, reminding him of every theft he had committed against another camp wretch to stay alive, every other life he had sacrificed in lieu of his own, every time he had silently prayed that the next man to be picked for skydiving would be someone other than him. And every time, he, who did not deserve to live, had been saved, while the innocent died.

Hans preyed on his mind that pre-nuptial night until Paul, in a frenzy of despair, leapt out of the giant four-poster and banged his head upon the unforgiving wall mirror seven times, as if by mystic ritual, cracking it ceiling to floor. He stared into the split halves of his face, searching for cathartic resolution and finding none. It took some minutes for the blood to trickle down his brow, and when it came, in halting rivulets, Paul welcomed it as a libation, a primordial benediction on the multiple betrayals he was about to commit.

CHAPTER SEVEN

The wedding morning broke beneath a
scowling cloud and spits of rain. Paul's suit
and shirt were laid out like a shroud, and
he had to stuff the jacket shoulders with
last-minute newspaper balls to stop it from
looking outsized. Dressing robotically, he
repeated under his breath the responses he
was expected to make in church, and those
he must at all costs suppress. When Dr.
Walters came to fetch him, he looked so
pale that the best man made him sniff smelling salts and drink a short brandy before
hoisting him onto the beribboned wedding
cart. The sun burst through in benediction
as he dismounted at the church gate. The
doctor took him by the arm and thrummed
a calming cadence into his twitching bicep.

The ceremony passed in white murmurings. The Latin declamations were familiar
from boyhood, but beneath them burred a
susurration of chatter in a language that he

associated with danger and death, the oppressor's tongue. He wondered what people were whispering about him, and he looked upwards for reassurance, but all that met his eye was a naked white body on the cross, representing Ewa. At the moment that he was joined in the sight of God to his bride, Paul shivered and sweated like a malaria victim in the grip of delirium, unable to tear his eyes from the crucifix. Alice clung to his hand with warm, strong fingers, transfusing him with volts and ohms of her confidence. He neither felt her hand nor heard the priest at his practised ministrations. He was not in a church but in a court of law, on a charge of complicity to murder. He would not leave this place alive.

At the sealing of the bond, when crackly Father Hitzinger invited him to kiss the bride, Paul sank to his knees at the altar, begging God's forgiveness and the mercy of a painless death. Alice, thinking him overcome by piety, knelt beside him, reciting the rosary. Paul rocked back and forth. Hans, hans, hans, went the rhythm in his head. Hans the first, Hans the second, and himself Hans the third and worst. The first two had done what a Hans had to do. He, Hans the third, was making a Hans of himself by mingling his blood, the blood of martyrs, with the lineage of murderers.

"Come, my love," said Alice, raising him with one hand and stroking his cheek with the other. "Let's face the world." A sun shaft lit the aisle for their procession. Alice clung to his right arm and Dr. Walters murmured encouragement at his rear. Cool air stung his eyes. Men grabbed his hand; women bussed his cheeks. The doctor punched his shoulder and pronounced him a lucky chap. Papa Hofmann slapped him sickeningly between the shoulder blades.

"Come," whispered Alice, skipping around the rear of St. Ignatius and down the sloping churchyard towards a trim plot on which he saw from afar the name "Maria Hofmann," engraved in gilt on a death-white headstone. Alice tended her mother's grave with trowel and flowers twice each week. She had never brought Paul before. This was her way of including him in her sorrow. He leaned over and kissed the crest of her veil, touched by her wish for him to meet her mamma's approval.

As they cuddled beside the tombstone, he sensed a spectral presence. Scorning superstition, he stepped in front of Alice and cried out, "Who's there?" A skeletal vagabond stepped out from behind a pine tree, dressed in what had once been an army uniform, its fabric worn colourless and threadbare. The collar was gone, the jacket torn. One sleeve hung empty. A boot cracked open; the mouldy toes stank at twenty paces. "Franz!" shrieked Alice, hurling herself at the intruder and pummelling his chest with her fists, enraged beyond coherence.

"Alice?" quavered the stranger under a shower of blows. "Is it you?"

"Of course it's me," screamed Alice, "and this is Mamma's grave, God curse you. She gasped her last breath thinking you were dead, you worthless piece of pig shit. We never heard a word from you. The telegram said you were missing in action. Where have you been? Why didn't you write, you filthy swine? Why did you let Mamma go to her grave thinking both her boys were dead, you stinking dog?"

Paul had never seen such fury in Alice, her lips spittled and her face bright red, yet her body amply in command of her emotions. She flung herself once more at the soldier, who, tripping on a kerbstone, would have fallen to the ground had she not caught him with both hands and held him upright like a rag doll. From hitting him, she began shaking the poor waif and rattling his scarecrow bones until, her rage assuaged, she opened her arms and clasped him to her wedding dress, her prodigal brother returned from the presumed dead.

The guests, hearing the disturbance, came running into the cemetery, young and old. "A miracle!" squeaked Tante Anna, slipping on rain-greased gravel and ending up in her preferred position of supplication, arms raised to the skies. "Franz-Josef!" squeaked Lisl. "God be thanked!" cried Papa Hofmann, reaching for his risen son with ham-fists that shook for want of strong drink. "The Lord giveth, and the Lord taketh away," intoned Father Hitzinger, finding himself amongst graves and picking what he thought was an appropriately funereal verse. "Blessed be the name of the Lord," responded the doctor, who had twice warned the diocese about the old man's wandering concentration and received no reply. "He quickeneth the dead" — beamed the priest, white surplice tails waving in the rising wind — "and bringeth the resurrection."

"This is my boy Franz-Josef," boomed Papa Hofmann, seizing Paul by the shoulders and bringing him face-to-face with the newcomer. "And this," said the barrelman to his son, "is our Alice's Paul."

The bridegroom shook his brother-in-law's left hand, staring into grey cavities for a clue to his nature, to whether he had spent the war as cannon fodder or as an oppressor of men. The fellow dropped his eyes, a pair of empty wells, sunken in defeat.

"Mamma . . ." mumbled Franz-Josef.

"She said she would greet you among the angels," sobbed his father. "She kept the telegram beside her deathbed, along with your photograph and Karlheinrich's, her boys who waited for her in heaven."

"It won't be the first time you let her down, Franzi," snapped Alice. "She won't have been surprised to find you absent from heaven, just as you were always late for meals and school. But look at you — we can't have you standing here like a starving dog. We had better get you home, and something inside you."

"That's what Mamma used to say. . . ."

Alice flung a sheer white arm round his neck and led her limping brother in a cavalcade of guests to the wedding carriage, forgetting Paul in the excitement. He perched on a headstone and let the breeze dishevel wild hairs at the back of his neck. Rather than feeling excluded, he felt morally uplifted. It was plain that he would never belong to these folk, which meant that he had not betrayed his own. So long as he had one foot on the threshold, ready for flight, he knew that he belonged someplace else and could return there some day. He was a sojourner, just passing through. Before long, he was joined by another stranger, Captain Wierzbicki, full of regrets for missing the ceremony due to a four-star general's snap inspection.

"It was not all you missed." Paul smiled. "The bride's one-armed brother came back from the dead and got carried off as guest of honour in my place."

"That's terrible," cried the captain.

"Not really," said Paul. "He's one of them."

"Where does that leave you?"

"A bystander, amused but not upset."

"Would you like me to have the guy checked out with War Crimes?" asked Wierzbicki.

"Not necessary." Paul shrugged. "He doesn't look the type."

"There isn't a type."

"I know, but he looks harmless."

"I'll run a check anyway. Anyone else you'd like me to look into while I'm at it?"

"If it's not too much trouble, a lieutenant in the Hundred and first Cavalry, first name Hans." Paul named a date, a time, a town, a half-hour of terror.

"That's not much to go on." Wierzbicki

frowned.

"It's all I have."

"I'll do my best — no promises. Haven't found that other Hans of yours yet."

The feasting was in full frenzy when the groom reached the inn with his military escort. Franz-Josef was seated in the bride-groom's gilded seat, villagers queuing up to touch some limb of his to confirm that he was no apparition. Beer spilled from giant jugs and a blood-and-soil song was choked off as they entered. Papa Hofmann was plastered across a table and Alice had taken charge, telling the barmen to keep the ale flowing once the last slices of pork ran out. A peck on Paul's cheek, and she vanished into the kitchen. Dr. Walters launched into his speech, unheard amidst the hubbub. A three-tiered cake was brought out with fan-fare.

"Congratulations," said Wierzbicki.

"I'll be fine." Paul smiled.

The band moved outside and struck up a waltz. Bride danced first with groom, then bridesmaid with best man, interchanging and proceeding socially down the guest list. The captain took Alice for a twirl, mutter-ing stiff formalities into her ear. "I will make him happy, you know?" she replied.

"I hope so," said Wierzbicki. "He deserves

a double dose of happiness."

Lisl swept Paul off on a wave of chatter, taking him to task for hanging back at the cemetery and coming late to the feast.

"You are always just out of things, Paul," she scolded.

"Am I?"

"You seem to be judging us."

"I don't judge. I observe people, just as your father does, but less clinically."

"He tries to heal them. You look down on us."

"That's unfair. Not on Alice, surely?"

"I should hope not," said the girl.

Wierzbicki cut in and took the bridesmaid for a tentative whirl.

"Are we all criminals to you?" demanded Lisl.

"Of course not," he replied.

"Then loosen up, put your hand around my waist, and imagine, just for a moment, that I am the girl of your dreams."

"That's so sweet." The soldier beamed, his cheek to hers.

"Just for a moment, I said," admonished Lisl. "Just to bring a flash of fantasy and romance into this overcast day. There, that's enough now."

"You're pretty smart," said Wierzbicki. "Not like other girls around here."

"You're pretty quick to draw conclusions," replied Lisl.

"You speak good English."

"I like to read. One of your men gave me a book of stories. By O. Henry. Funny name. I liked them. Can you recommend something similar?"

"I'm not much of a reader."

It was getting late and the captain had a long drive back to base. "What can I get you as a wedding gift?" he asked Paul as they stood beside his jeep.

"Get me Hans," said the bridegroom. "Any Hans."

That night in bed, Paul rolled over to the wall and pleaded tiredness. Alice touched him playfully between the legs and found him inert. "Never mind," she chuckled. "We've got the whole of our lives."

He recoiled as if shot. "What did you say?"

"We have the whole of our lives. . . ."

"Don't say those words," cried Paul. "They don't belong to you. Don't say them."

"What's the matter, dearest? What's wrong?"

"Nothing. I'm tired. I'm sorry. A bad memory."

"Sleep now. You will feel better in the

morning."

Those words, *the whole of our lives,* were Ewa's, her pledge to him. Alice had no right to usurp them, no right to take her place. But Alice knew nothing about Ewa. He must be going mad, confusing two women, conflating two worlds. He was no longer sure that he had heard Alice use those words. He may have imagined it. He was hearing voices; he had to get away. He did not belong. Every breath he took here was a betrayal. He must get out, no time to waste, out while he still had some grip on reality and the means of escape. He would leave at dawn, he decided, doomed to wander for the rest of his days. A hundred years hence, children in the village would be sung to sleep with the ballad of the bridegroom who vanished on his wedding night, a mythical relative of the Flying Dutchman.

At five in the morning, he woke, to find the bed empty and Alice gone. How tactful, he thought, so much easier for him to escape. As he scrambled into trousers, Paul heard a noise behind the new bathroom door, a keening sound. He knocked and, getting no response, burst in, to find Alice crouched over the sink, blood spattered on the floor and walls, on the tasteful grey-and-white tiles she had so carefully chosen. "The baby?" he whispered. Alice clutched her midriff and reached for his hand. "I'll fetch the doctor," he said.

In undershirt and bare feet, he ran uphill to the surgery, hopping from one grazed sole to the other while yesterday's best man packed his portmanteau with needles and pills and panted with him down the slope towards the grinning hind.

"Bed rest for a week," said Dr. Walters an hour and a half later, wiping his hands on a towel that turned several shades of red before sitting down to a breakfast of pink ham and scrambled eggs that Papa Hofmann put in front of him.

"The baby?"

"Gone, I'm sorry. . . . Twenty weeks, twenty-one . . . I cleaned out the tubes and gave her a shot. . . . Alice is sleeping. She's a healthy girl. In time, she will have more babies, God willing."

Paul heard him out white-faced, Papa Hofmann with surly resignation. A howl rose from a corner of the room, an animal cry. Franz-Josef, unseen in an alcove, was venting raw lament, mourning all his losses — his mother, his arm, his youth, his wink and his grin, and now this unborn kin, a soul consigned like his own to limbo. His cry was feral enough to distract the doctor from his breakfast, one eyebrow cocked. Papa Hofmann uncorked a bottle of schnapps, his fail-safe remedy.

Lisl walked in just then, sent by her mother to direct the doctor to another call. Taking in the frozen tableau, she walked over to Franz-Josef and held him in her arms. The howling muffled, she glanced up at Paul and beckoned him over. With a hand on his shoulder, Paul promised Franz-Josef that Alice was going to be all right, that she would not die like his mother, that one day she would bear a girl with their mother's name. Blowing his nose, Franz-Josef clutched Paul's right hand in his left, his head on Lisl's breast, the three of them united in sorrow. Paul felt nothing but pity for this maimed young man, who was unable to tie his shoelaces, unfit for most inn duties, dependent for the rest of his days on the kindness of strangers. He was, like Paul, dispossessed and emotionally disabled. He was a Franz, not a Hans, nothing to be afraid of. Paul brewed them a pot of acorn coffee and drank with his brother-in-law to an ersatz alliance of desolation.

A week later, when Alice descended, her husband and brother had carved out roles. Franz-Josef would run the bar, Alice would look after catering, Paul would write a business plan, and Papa would pursue other interests. The Black Horse at Pringsheim was struggling to reopen. The owner was a forty-year-old widow, Mathilde Zumsteig, willing to enter a partnership of some sort with the Laughing Hind. "Why not?" said Alice. "It takes a competitor out of the market."

"Better still," said Paul, "it creates economies of scale."

"What's that?" demanded Hofmann.

Paul explained the mechanics of bulk buying and how a larger enterprise could flourish on slimmer margins than a small one.

"You mean lower prices?" said Franz-Josef.

"Exactly. And the more inns we own, the sooner we can cut prices and the more customers we will attract. This is a good time to start buying inns, forming a chain of inns across the valley to be ready for the tourist rush."

"It'll be years before the spenders return," growled Papa.

"That's why this is such a good time to start," enthused Alice, "when property is cheap and business slow. Go over and see if Zumsteig will sell us a half-share in her inn."

"Are we agreed on that?" asked Paul.

Alice and Franz-Josef raised their hands in assent.

"It's none of our business," said Paul weeks later when Papa packed his cut-throat razors and, after a final skull shave in the overhead bar mirror, removed his personal effects across the gorge to the Black Horse.

"The dirty dog," said Alice, "crawling into a widow's bed at his age."

"He deserves a second chance," said Paul emolliently. "He's drinking himself to death over here. Maybe the widow can dry him out. Anyway, we have a partner over there and a stake in the profits."

"I don't like that Zumsteig," grumbled Alice. "She smells of onions."

"Must be a good cook," teased Paul.

"Not as good as me," flared Alice. "Garlic is much better than onions."

"Maybe she's . . ." Paul grinned, mimicking a pair of swaying hips.

"Come upstairs and I'll show you who's good at what," said Alice, grabbing him by the hand, a gesture he did not resist.

Wierzbicki came by to say goodbye. His discharge papers had come through and he was heading home, he said, to a small town in Iowa. The disburdenment of authority had lifted the fixed frown from his brow and left him in a chatty mood. "What's the first thing you'll do when you get home?" asked Paul.

"I am going to crack open a bottle of beer and swig it on the porch." His friend smiled. Paul, remembering a pre-war film, visualised a prairie home with a timeless veranda and Mark Twain in a panama hat snoozing in a rocking chair at noon.

"And then?"

"Dunno. My pa wants to give up running the gas station. He'd like me to take over."

"And you?"

"Dunno. I guess I want something more. I've seen a lot of life and a lot of death and I'm kinda scared I might get bored in a nowhere town of five hundred and eighty-three people where nothing much has happened since Teddy Roosevelt whistled through in oh-twelve or so."

"What are the possibilities?"

"There's the GI bill. . . ."

"What's that?"

"Uncle Sam is offering to pay to put me through college."

"I used to have a rich uncle," mused Paul.

Wierzbicki erupted in full-throated laughter, delighted at the misapprehension. "I'm so sorry." He hiccupped, clapping Paul rhythmically on the back as if he were a baby to be burped. "I got so used to your fine mind that I talk to you like a buddy and I forget you don't get half the things I'm saying."

"I understand five hundred and eighty-three and Theodore Roosevelt," said Paul, faintly wounded.

"I know you do, pal. Lemme spell it out. The U.S. government, Uncle Sam, has kindly offered to send a million guys like me back to school."

"To study what?"

"Well, that's what I am thinking. What would you suggest?"

"I am the wrong person to ask," said Paul. "First, I tried medicine. After two years, frustrated with how little we can cure, I turned to psychotherapy. I read Freud, Jung, Adler, Reich, Ferenczi — and each declared that the others were not only completely wrong but scoundrels besides. During my exams, I made drawings to relieve the tension. Everything I drew came out like a building. I took the sketches to my analyst, who was also my academic supervisor. He said, 'Why don't you try architecture?' Ten, eleven years I studied for two doctorates. Now I serve drinks in a bar. What good am I for career advice?"

It was a mild autumnal evening and they were sitting in the beer garden with a brace of wine glasses, a half-full yellow flask, and a plate of salted nibbles before them.

"What's the best part of architecture?" asked Wierzbicki, munching a salted bread stick.

"The dimension of beauty," said Paul without hesitation. "Aalto, the great Finnish modernist, said that form in buildings must follow the dictates of the surrounding nature, and beauty will flow from that."

"I like that!" exclaimed the young officer. "Most buildings where I come from are thrown up as cheap as can be. I'd kinda like to factor in a — what did you call it? — a dimension of beauty. Maybe I'll study architecture. I saw a course listed in Chicago."

"You can make a difference, you know," said Paul, his enthusiasm mounting. "You have leadership experience, my friend, and a healthy idealism. You have good instincts, a grasp of structure, and a desire to put things right. You can make the world a better place, if you like."

"I guess. . . ."

"But don't do it because of me," warned Paul. "I am no example to anyone."

"You may be wrong there, pal," murmured the returning hero.

"How will your father take it?" asked Paul.

"He won't be happy. He's been on his own since Ma died and is none too well. But I got a sister nearby, and her bum of a husband can hang around the gas station selling Cokes and hot dogs while I get me an education at Uncle Sam's expense."

"I congratulate you," said Paul with grave formality

"I'll keep you posted," said his protégé.

The young wine fizzed in the embers of sunset. Their time was running out and both men knew they would never see each other again.

"That Hans you asked about," said Wierzbicki, resuming his official tone and lowering his voice. "I've got his name: Hans Kruger. There is a file on him, thick as your arm. He is wanted for the massacre you mentioned, and for another in Sanislawow. A captain of the same name is wanted for slaughtering half the adult males in a French village. We dunno if these two or three are the same guy, or if they are alive or dead. It's a common name, and those guys had damn good getaway routes. All I can tell you is that the files are marked 'Priority' and the police of three nations are involved."

"And the other Hans?" asked Paul. "The one that was here, Hannes Joachim

Kerner?"

Wierzbicki shook his head. "I checked him out against the files that we took from the camp site. Two of his deputies went home to the Baltic, where the Soviets strung them up outside an opera house. Another guard got shot dead by our patrols. Six are in custody. The rest are anywhere you care to guess. Kerner has vanished without a trace. Not one sighting since the night he skedaddled from here. With blood on his hands and the booty he stole, he could have bought a passport to oblivion. By this time, he is probably living the life of Juan Diego del Riley in some Latino banana republic where the president likes his liver sausage rare."

"I'm sorry?"

"Me, too. He's gotten away; that's the long and short of it. War Crimes has a file on him, but I gotta tell you its arrest rate is about as high as Chicago's when Al Capone was king. Don't hold your breath to see him hang is what I'm saying."

"Thank you," said Paul.

"For nothing."

"No, for everything. You have been a good friend to me."

"And you to me. I would never have gotten a promotion without the advice you gave me on the harvest and the refugees, and it was the extra pay that set me thinking about getting a better job when I'm back in civvies."

The moment of parting had come. "Be happy, my friend," said Wierzbicki, kissing him old country–fashion on both cheeks.

"For me," said Paul, withdrawing from his embrace, "happiness is not an option."

A year passed and, at the same lowering season, as the leaves reddened and Lisl, heavy with child, married Franz-Josef at the church of St. Ignatius, Alice absented herself in mid-service to give birth, with assistance from Dr. Walters, to a sturdy eight-pound boy. They baptised him Johann after the saint in the Bible (said Alice) and Karl-heinrich for her brother who had fallen in France. It seemed a heavy burden of expectation for one newborn to bear, but as Father Hitzinger vacantly sprinkled consecration wine on the baby's head instead of baptismal water and Dr. Walters made a mental note to report him yet again to the indolent bishop, Paul looked down on his son's pale cranium and gave thanks to the heavens that something so pure and beautiful could atone for his catalogue of compromises, errors, and shortcomings. The boy's brown eyes belonged to Paul's mother, Johanna, giant irises that opened wide at the sound of Paul's voice. The name, too, was his mother's, though he never told that to Alice. It was unnecessary, he decided. By calling the boy Johann, he had struck a root in this secondary life and expelled all thoughts of flight.

He was an active father, excessively involved. At the baby's first mutter, he would leap out of bed and take him to Alice for suckling. Paul loved to touch the child, to change his clothes, to talk and sing to him, to promise him a life happier than any his father had known. Alice tolerated his interceptions with a moue of pique, resenting the inference that he knew best when the baby was cold and hungry. But such was Paul's delight in Johann that she could not be cross with him for long, cherishing his adoration for the red-cheeked apple of their improbable love.

As seasons flipped like pages on a wall calendar, one cycle, then another, Lisl gave birth to twins, a boy and a girl, and the inn bawled with infant life. Lisl erected bookshelves along the upper corridor and Paul found diversion in the novels that she borrowed from her father and forgot to return. Walters came by nightly to play with his grandchildren and would stay for a beer or a meal.

"It may not be easy for Alice to have another baby," he warned Paul. "She had a hard time with Johann, you know. Don't be impatient."

Perhaps, thought Paul, that was why Alice had lost her appetite for love and wriggled away from his approaches. He protested at first but, acceding to her wishes, modified his habits to less frequent, less fervent intercourse.

One night, awake at the window, he saw a shaft of light cross the forecourt and, fearing a break-in, crept downstairs with knife in hand. He pushed the panelled door of the tavern room slyly open and saw, at a corner table, his sister-in-law, Lisl, sitting in a nightgown with a handheld torch, reading a thick volume. "It's Franzi's night to get up with the babies." She smiled. "I needed time away, to be with myself."

"I'm s-sorry to interrupt you," stuttered Paul.

"Not at all. Have you read this?" She held out a Vicki Baum potboiler, all high society and hotel bedrooms.

"Not my sort of thing."

He flipped a main switch, bathing her alcove in light, and, while boiling a kettle on the bob, surveyed his sister-in-law from a safe distance. Lisl's eyes were fireflies. They danced and darted, whereas other pairs that Paul met, dulled by sun and snow, took in the world with ponderous reticence. Her hair shone black and short in a sullen field of yellow cornflowers, framing her olive-skinned face in crescent moons. She stood out in the village by pigment and attitude, and showed no wish to conform. Paul poured two camomile teas, a gift from the doctor's herbarium, and carried them on a tray to her table.

"Did your father manage to get hold of the new Thomas Mann?" he enquired.

"He is still waiting. The book was published in America and Sweden, but it's not out here yet in his native land. You know what it's about?"

"Good and evil, shades of black and white. Doctor Faustus, the hero, sells his soul to the devil, but not for the usual reasons — youth, virility, attractiveness, wealth. He swaps it for a talent to compose music in a very modern, unmelodic way."

"Why would he want to do that?"

"To eclipse every composer that came before, as Bach did, and establish himself as the father of all that follows in the future."

Lisl wrinkled her nose and worked her

eyebrows close in concentration.

"It's an allegory, isn't it?" she ventured.

"What do you think it is depicting?"

"My guess is that it's about our country, about its need to destroy the past and start again, always looking for the elixir that will allow us to override good and evil — to act like the sons of gods, released from ordinary values."

"That's very perceptive," said Paul, impressed. "You haven't even read the book."

"I read a lengthy essay and discussed it with my father. It seems to me that no book that appears today can be read in isolation. Even a children's book carries buried traces of where the author has been these past fifteen years. Literature is a mirror of our inner selves, someone once said. What do you think, Paul?"

Paul was thinking about the milk-heavy breasts that unbalanced Lisl's symmetrical slightness. Weeks of celibacy brought sexual fantasies unbidden to mind. He was easily aroused and Lisl was close and desirable.

"I think I hear Johann crying," he said, rising to his feet. He needed to unplug the illicit contact. He could not indulge his lively sister-in-law in an intimacy he could never share with his devoted wife. Paul wished Lisl good night and went up to bed, head jangling. It had been years since he had last engaged in abstract thought, and it was a bracing sensation, like the first icy river swim of springtime. His intellectual apparatus, idling in a garage for years, had just sparked to the touch. It longed for the open road of free thought, the hair-ruffling thrill of a fast run with the windows down, but Paul could not let it out, for fear that the intrusion of high ideas would foster discontent with his village life as well as an indecent proximity to Lisl, whose disenchantment with the abject Franz-Josef was becoming all too audible. There had been slamming of doors and pouting of lips. All was not well with his in-laws, but Paul knew better than to get involved. He decided, instead, to keep his distance from the heaving Lisl and his mind out of heavy books, reminding himself with a pinch to the thigh that the inn was a public feeding station, not a philosophy circle or the national library. He was an innkeeper and a town builder. He must not let his placid present be invaded by the turbulent past. Any temptation of the cerebral kind would distance him from Alice and diminish his bathetic delight in the constant novelty of Johann, who was babbling away — "Bah, bah" — and crawling at unsupervised high speed into every inconvenient cranny.

So, with husbandly common sense, Paul gave a wide berth to Lisl's bookshelves and stocked the vacant spaces of his mind with technicalities of urban planning and the nitty-gritty of local politics. His new houses had straggled down the valley and up the opposite slope, all the way to the historic Pringsheim border, reviving ancestral enmities and breeding a swell of resistance. There were murmurings in both inns. Papa Hofmann warned that the Pringsheimers were up in arms and preparing to march on the state capital to block Paul's unification. He needed to move fast and sure. With the unerring skill of unearned popularity, he cycled around Pringsheim for three whole days, smiling and joking with total strangers, persuading leaders of the revolt to meet him in the back room at the Laughing Hind, where, amidst overflowing tankards and a flurry of promises, they endorsed his vision for the valley. A week later, he summoned elders of both communities to a festive dinner at the Black Horse. After a sumptuous meal cooked by Mathilde Zumsteig, who was younger and friendlier than Alice implied, both communities agreed to join forces under Paul's leadership to seek the enhanced status and state funding of a new town, to be known provisionally as Neustadt. The extra subsidy, one greybeard mumbled with a sly grin, would buy a horse and cart for every farmer. A rash of self-interest speckled the white tablecloth.

A toast was proposed to Paul Miller, who, rising to reply, sensed a decisive shift in his standing. He was no longer well liked in a "Take him or leave him" sort of way. Over the course of the two meetings, it was his presence, rather than his arguments, that prevailed, melting hearts and minds. He had the aura of authority and, besides, a mysterious musk that made men and women like him on sight. He was no longer good or bad, dull Paul or bright, but a new Paul risen from the ruins, a Paul whose presence could warm up a room. How else could he account for the friendship of Wierzbicki and Franz-Josef, the doctor and Lisl, Hoenig the baker, and that grinning carrot seller who never let him pass her stall without some cheery ribaldry? People liked him for being himself, and he kept trying to call them in evidence when the prosecutor stabbed an icy finger at him in the hour before dawn, proclaiming his worthlessness. But I am well liked, protested Paul. Save your breath, replied the accuser. If you are

well liked, tell the court this: Why is the accused so consumed with self-hatred that he
cannot sleep a night without rushing to the
window? To that charge, Paul had no
answer.

A second shaft of insight came towards the
end of the feast as Mathilde Zumsteig
decorated his apple strudel with a dollop of
double cream, applauding his success at
merging the two communities. As the cream
plopped onto the centre of the slice, Paul
knew that he was way out of his depth. He
could cope, on the strength of education
and experience, with repairs to the sewage
system and the electricity pylons, but he
had no idea how to unite one grid with its
neighbour or whether such a move was
feasible and desirable. His design portfolio
was limited to factory extensions and fantasy houses for the disgustingly rich. His
ignorance of town planning was extensive.
How many streetlights to a side road, and
at what intervals? What was the optimum
occupancy for a housing estate? How was
public transport scheduled and funded?
With no answer to any of these riddles, no
solid knowledge of urban infrastructure,
social integration, population flow, industrial
development, and environment protection,

he was applying to build a brand-new town and was bound, in time, to be exposed as a fraud. The rules he knew were years out of date and belonged to another jurisdiction. He needed to acquire a crash course in current practice and a network of contacts in the government mechanism to guide him through a minefield of paperwork.

"I know people who can help," said Dr. Walters over a late-night schnapps. "Why don't we take a trip together to the big city?"

"At this point," said Paul, "I need to know what to ask before I meet anyone. I have to get my head into the university library for a few days and then into the city-planning department."

"I could set up appointments while you are in the library," said Walters.

His enthusiasm was unexpected. Paul had heard the doctor swear that he would not set foot in the city until he received a public apology for his eviction and an offer of compensation for the loss of his practice. For a man who rarely spoke above a ruminative murmur, the doctor would shout and bang on the table when the city was mentioned. Yet now he was offering to join Paul on what sounded like a pleasure trip down memory lane. It made no sense to Paul, who changed the subject.

Walters, however, kept pressing him. "There is a good symphony orchestra," he said. "There are bars. We can pretend to be men about town. . . ."

Paul listened with half an ear to his blandishments until the time came to book his ticket, and then the dismay on the doctor's face at finding Paul was travelling alone was so heart-rending that Paul reproached himself for failing to grasp the depth of his friend's need. He made a mental note to bring him back a compensatory gift.

Alice was less resistant. He told his wife that he aimed to spend one week on research and a second meeting city engineers and planners to arrange statutory instruments that would, once agreed, give her village a geographic importance greater than it had known since the Hundred Years' War. Alice took down a trunk and packed clothes for a fortnight, tucking sausages and cheeses between the folds so that he would not starve to death on hard, paved streets. She wrote to a Hofmann cousin, ordering him to meet Paul's train, and, the night before his departure, she made love with wholesome vigour, as if to drain him of any energy and curiosity he might have felt towards the loose girls of the capital, who, rumour had it, had grown even more depraved under occupation than under the notorious decadence of the former regime.

Though she wept to see her husband walk out of the door, Alice was by no means unhappy to be rid of Paul for a while, to have their lovely son to herself, to call him, unrebuked, whatever Hansy name she liked. She looked forward to having the four-poster to herself and sitting up as late as she liked with Lisl, talking of girlish things and probing to see what was wrong in her marriage. She had held the upper hand with Lisl since their first day at the village school and was confident now of placating her friend's dissatisfaction with Franz-Josef. She would have a word with her brother as well, tell him to pull himself together and make more of an effort towards his pretty wife before she dumped him for someone better. These domestic deficiencies would be ironed out while Paul was away, so that he could return to a smiling household, a thriving enterprise, and a loving wife, whose ferocious pride and encouragement were the foundation of his achievements and public esteem.

One foot on the taxi fender, Paul bent over his little boy's sweet head and promised to be home before Johann cut another tooth.

It was the first time he had left the valley since his arrival as a slave, and his hands trembled in his lap as the old Daimler taxi trundled down the hill and through leafy ways on the bumpy drive to the railway junction. It was an hour to the station and three hours more, with two connections, to the capital. Paul, who, as a student, had never thought twice of catching a train from his industrial town to the elegant, ominous, and frivolous centre of government, now felt like a country lad on a mediaeval crusade, facing risks to life and tests to his faith. He was about to reenter a dangerous world, a world where a ghost glimpsed in shadows could shatter confidence and jeopardise survival. Alert and not a little afraid, he mumbled a prayer he had learned on his grandfather's knee, a prayer about hazardous journeys and safe returns: *And Jacob went upon his way and there he was met by angels of God.* The prayer stilled his nerves, but, leaving the last bend in the valley, he found himself wishing that he had taken the doctor as his companion, to protect him from the unknown. The doctor, he suspected, had an ulterior motive for wanting to come along, but Paul had powerful reasons for taking this trip on his own. Boarding the train was a breach with the

camp. It was his first act as a free man, unwatched and without concrete obligation.

■ ■ ■ ■

Part Two:
Fight

■ ■ ■ ■

SNYDER COUNTY LIBRARIES, INC.
ONE NORTH HIGH STREET
SELINSGROVE, PA 17870

Chapter Eight

The railway terminus was a girdered shell, bombed to the edge of utility, its platforms a bridgework of planks on which in-coming passengers picked their way precariously towards a roofless forecourt. The hubbub was overwhelming. On top of the huffing and whistling of steam engines, the squealing of brakes, and the clangour of cargo, there was a wailing of mendicants, the screams of abandoned children, the shouts of hawkers. Nothing, in close-up, was quite as it seemed. A legless beggar turned out, in proximity, to be sitting on a healthy limb, folded behind a fake stump; a crying infant was being taught by its mother or sister to simulate abandonment; and goods that were being shouted out for sale were nowhere to be seen. The merchandise was always just around the corner: "Follow me, sir. This way, please." Paul, warned by wall signs to avoid rogue traders, trod a wobbly line in the rubble towards the great architrave of an exit, a dictatorial landmark left bizarrely intact by a tonnage of wartime bombs.

Suitcase in hand, scanning the crowds in vain for the Hofmann cousin whom Alice had ordered to meet him, he picked up a smell so acute that it pierced all the sweet and foul odours of milling humanity and cast him back to childhood. He could not put a name at first to the aroma, but it put him in mind of Marcel Proust and his madeleines, the evocation of a boy in heaven. He sat down on a bench at the wall of the forecourt and gave himself up to savouring the smell as he tried to place it.

Some kind of hot beverage, a kind of coffee, sharp as a bread knife and blessed as sweet wine, but where in his infancy, and when? Closing his eyes he conjured up an image of an old woman in a tight head scarf, no stray hair to be seen. She is roasting green beans in a rotating drum above a fireplace. Once the beans are done, she scoops them out of the drum and pounds them in a pestle, singing under her breath a cracked and dolorous melody. As Paul observes from chair height, the head of the house, grey of beard and twinkle-eyed, enters the room in a wide-brimmed hat and hangs his greatcoat on a peg by the door.

The woman, without a word of greeting, measures a pinch of the powder into a chipped white bowl and pours hot water over it. The old gentleman murmurs some words beneath his breath and brings the bowl to his lips with a beatific sigh. Paul clings to his grandmother's apron, sharing the old man's joy in his breakfast. Paul's mother, young and submissive, sits at the table, chopping vegetables, locked in frugal dialogue with her parents. Leah, they call her, not Johanna. Leah's siblings, young and old, filter through the fragrant kitchen. Paul's face is stroked, his hair ruffled, his cheek pinched. Yesterday he wept alone in the woods, abandoned; today he is invulnerable, universally loved. He asks his grandfather for a story and climbs in expectation onto a bone-hard knee.

A knock at the door. A man stands outside in a brown hat, suitcase in hand, eyes fixed on paper-pale Leah. The suitcase rests beside the doorpost. Terse words rise above the twittering of ‘crickets. His father stretches a hand far into the room. Grandmother turns her back. His mother rises, hesitates, takes the hand. They step outside. The suitcase sits accusingly on the doormat. The coffee reeks of cold anxiety. His grandfather's knee trembles; he teaches the little boy to say a prayer for long journeys. Grandmother's mottled hand, purple veins outstanding, clears the breakfast dishes. She says a few words to her husband in a foreign tongue; he replies in long sighs, sigh-igh-ighs. A beardless youth, an uncle or cousin, offers to take Paul for a walk. They reach the door just as his mother and father, faces flushed, return hand in hand. All is well. They will leave straightaway. They are going home.

Riveted by the memory, Paul wondered how he could have forgotten so important an event, an existential crisis in his parents' marriage: his mother's flight, his father's deferential pursuit, his grandparents' despair. Four, five years old he must have been, and what was it about the smell of coffee that brought the scene back? Why was the memory buried so deep? What was he scared of? Substituting Proust for Freud, he asked whether his tender psyche had been damaged by his parents' rift, whether he had been torn by the clash of cultures, and simultaneously formed. His father had belonged to the walled-in world of men in suits and offices; his mother had been rooted in a village of beards and head scarves, amongst people who had not changed their ways in centuries, encased in unshakeable faith. He had seen them pulled apart and rejoined, the foundation of his existence unstitched and reunited before his welling black eyes. How had that conditioned the person who grew up to be Paul?

Tracking back in family legend, he reminded himself how they had met, Arthur and Leah, creatures from different constellations. There was some story of an operation. His mother, rushed to a cottage hospital with stomach cramps; his father, a junior admissions clerk, abandoning his post and running helter-skelter to the home of the head of surgery, hauling him out of a Sunday snooze to perform an emergency appendectomy. There was a photograph somewhere of his mother, age sixteen, her black hair beautifully braided, sitting up in bed in a morbid convalescence ward, sipping water from a transparent glass. Parted for a month from her immutable family, she was visited hourly by the clerk, who fell in love with her otherness, as she did more slowly with his ordinariness, his air of belonging to a larger, more inclusive humanity than her own self-enclosed clan. They eloped to the city on the day her father was due to collect her, telling each other that love and goodwill would triumph over cultural difference. As it did, to the end.

Theirs was a tale of two tame creatures in a unique act of rebellion, and Paul had heard it told many times on birthdays and anniversaries with minor variations and many plum-brandy toasts. Now, in the hubbub of a railway station where nothing stood still for a second, he saw with dazzling lucidity the source of his outsiderness, his stubborn unbelonging — the reason that two Pauls warred within him, one craving acceptance, the other knowing it could never be granted. His identity hinged on that framed instant, the moment his father stood at the door, splitting his sapling son down the middle, one green half in either world. What chance had Paul of wholeness? They, his mother and father, had cracked him in their palms like a walnut and held him together with a solvent they called love, sabotaging his chances of finding himself. He let out a roar of rage at Arthur for coming after them and another at Leah for yielding to his pleas, forsaking her own kind and never seeking further reunion, denying her son one vital half of his rightful self. Paul craved his grandfather's blessing, the trembling of his knee. Anger coursed through his veins like raw alcohol, rapidly pursued by a corollary sensation — a mighty relief that he had found the right to hate his parents, something he had never done while they lived, or had dared to contemplate since their terrible death. He rose from the station bench, consumed by catharsis, healed by a whitening balm of Proust's madeleine and Freud's analysis.

Encouraged by two of the great behaviourists, he followed the trail of a third — Ivan Petrovich Pavlov, who had proved that dogs salivate at any sound, sight, or smell that they associate with food. Paul followed the Pavlovian smell of suppressed memory to the left-hand exit of the broken station and, lugging Alice's sharp-cornered suitcase, to a kiosk window in the outside wall where a bulge of uniforms strutted like a flock of penguins on an Antarctic ice cap. OFFICERS ONLY said the sign. Inside stood a silvery monster, eructing white puffs of pungent steam.

"Excuse me, sir," Paul said to a light-blue airman with pips on his shoulder. "What is that machine?"

"It's a fucking lifesaver, that's what."

"What does it do?" Paul persisted.

"It pumps hot water at high pressure through coffee grounds. *Capisch?*"

"Is that its name?"

"G-a-g-g-i-a. Italian guy. I think he owns the patent."

"Achille Gaggia," said a sonorous voice from behind the window. "A genius in Milano, a maker of miracles." The mellow tone, the hyperbolic phrase, both were unmistakable.

"Angelo?" choked Paul.

"Leonardo?"

Bursting through a crowd of sky-blue, the former block mates fell into an embrace that was almost a dance, swaying with thanksgiving at finding each other alive.

"You made it!" cried the coffee dispenser, touching Paul's face in disbelief.

"Just about." Paul smiled. "And you — look at you, a doctor in a white coat."

"That's right, a healer of thirst."

"Can we get some service down here?" twanged a voice at the far end.

"A moment, sir," cried Angelo. "I have the honour of a visit from a great artist, my teacher in art. *Mio caro* Leonardo, you will drink some coffee?"

"It says 'Officers Only.' "

"The 'Only' is at Angelo's discretion; I make the rules. Tell me, Leonardo, what are you doing here in this wicked place? You must tell me everything. No, first you must drink. A small cup. Smell, then drink very slowly. Good, no?"

Paul sipped, and fell speechless. A dependent coffee drinker who made do with acorn stew when nothing else was to hand, he had smelled nothing stronger since boyhood nor tasted any liquid so restorative, the caffeine shooting through his nostrils to the top of his head and down to the far corners of his travel-weary frame. He was intoxicated in the literal sense of the word, his mind and body disordered by the toxins he had imbibed, to the point where he was ready to pick a fight if that's what it took to get a refill.

"Another?" said Angelo, observing his changing facial expressions, a slide show of sensory satisfactions.

The second cup set him jigging on the spot with high energy and a burned tongue, jabbering inconsequentialities until Angelo advised him to slow down, eat a biscuit, drink a glass of water, wait a few moments until they could sit together and catch up. "I close right away," declared Angelo, hanging up an OUT OF ORDER sign and chivvying his customers to drain their dregs and go. "No more Paradiso today," he cried; "the angel is back tomorrow."

Waiting for the iron shutters to descend, Paul felt a knot of dread clog the last of the coffee in his gullet. He was not ready for social niceties with camp comrades, let alone prepared to handle pertinent questions. Watching Angelo finger the knobs on his machine like a church organist at introit, Paul saw him in a parallel frame, crawling along the ground between two kicking guards, dipping a crust in guttered rainwater, doubled up at the latrine trench with bloody dysentery. He saw Angelo as he was on the day of arrival, cocky in the head bandage of a fighting partisan defeated by superior forces, and again at the end, cadaverous but vivacious, preserved by his fighting toughness and his irrepressible capacity for badinage. He remembered, word for word, their last blockhouse colloquy.

"You never went home?" asked Paul.

"I went home, and it was no longer home."

Manhandled by liberating soldiers into a red-crossed field ambulance, Angelo had used the last of his strength to escape and hide in the maze of the camp, cowering in a cell block until he sniffed an opportunity. A bread van pulled into the camp, dispensing fresh bakes to the starving multitude. Angelo, quick on his feet, vanished into the top rear tray, lapping up the crumbs. When the door was slammed and the van pulled out, he gave a silent cheer. He was no longer amongst the counted. The van drove to a depot of sorts, where the doors were flung open. Pushing himself to the back, Angelo avoided detection until the last tray was removed and the vehicle was ready for restocking. As the soldiers went for fresh supplies, he slipped away with a loaf of black bread beneath his shirt and hid in an army washroom, which seemed handsome and luxurious. Locking himself in a cubicle, he finished his bread in small bites and slept a few hours against the wall, undisturbed by comings and goings.

When the washroom was quiet, he stepped out. The depot consisted of a bakery and a vegetable store, which delivered supplies to an occupation army. Angelo, rake-thin and with no identity except the camp numeral on his arm, hid in a packing case at the back of a vegetable truck and was bumped towards the careless chaos of a postal sorting centre, where he stole a few bars of chocolate and hid in a mail sack with the destination "Bergamo." Across the mountains he rode, stopping at town after town, listening in tears to the lilt of his mother tongue and calculating the right moment to jump off, when the driver stopped for a beer.

He wandered into fields, where insects

hummed and butterflies sipped and peasants crossed themselves at the sight of him,
a walking scarecrow. Taken in by a bachelor
farmer to share his evening meal, he
savoured each mouthful of pasta, the red-
ness of tomatoes, the purple skin of aub-
ergines, the minced flesh of field animals,
the icy clarity of springwater in a dirty glass,
the sparseness of basic needs. In the morning, a benign sun on his beaten back, he
stumbled the last paved miles home.

His welcome was as exuberant as he could
have wished for — his father wailing thanks
to the Saviour, the neighbours rustling up a
feast of veal and wine, cousins and class-
mates arriving with gifts of food and clothing as if to amend for all they had consumed
while Angelo did penance for their sins in
enemy clutches. The reckoning could wait.
Meantime, the delight at his return was so
spontaneous, the speeches so effusive, the
kisses so sweet, that he wept frequently during the celebrations, which continued for a
week, and stumbled from one welcoming
pair of arms to the next in a cavalcade of
consolations until he was ready to attempt a
resumption of normality.

His father took him to be fitted for new
clothes and he joined his uncle at his fruit
and vegetable stall, retuning his greyed-

down senses to the riot of colours and smells. The tasks were untaxing, the banter trivial. He wanted more. A cousin with political friends got him a job at the printing press of the town newspaper, a bit of fetching and carrying that would keep him in pocket money. School pals took him to see the new movies, an opera at the May festival, a garden in early flower, every day another joy, every gift a private guilt offering, every word a confirmation that he had nothing left in common with these light-headed people.

"And Renata?" prompted Paul, remembering his girlfriend's exuberant appetite for love.

"Renata was abundantly pleased to see me." Angelo grinned through gapped teeth. "She never left my side those first weeks. I was her Angel, descended from heaven, restored to her for ever more. She had worn black while I was away and never looked at another man, she swore, even though she had no idea if I was alive or dead.

"To be honest, Leonardo, her fidelity was not high in my catalogue of concerns. It would not have bothered me greatly or diminished me as a man if she had confessed that she made love with a lonely *partisano,* or even with many members of our group,

243

gripped as they were by constant fear of capture and death. Men and women cannot be judged by what they do in war. I would have forgiven her, desiring her as before, respecting whatever sacrifice she made to stay alive and sane. I found myself wishing that she had some transgression to confess. It would have put us on an equal footing of pain and regret, of compromise and shame, for I, too, did bad things to survive."

"You stole?" said Paul.

"Worse." Angelo shrugged.

"Don't tell me."

"Renata, my lovely Renata, had put on extra weight about the hips. She talked only of her love for me, her longing for my return, her constancy, as if nothing had befallen me in the meantime and I remained unchanged. She did not ask about the camp, changing the subject if I uttered so much as a hint of what she called 'the horrible history.' She kept saying that it was not her fault that I had been sent away, that it was all over and she wanted to hear nothing more about it.

"She repeated this so often that I became suspicious that maybe she did have something to do with it, for somebody in the group had certainly betrayed me, or failed to warn me of the trap that I walked into.

Renata insisted she knew nothing. Her two elder brothers, who were members of a certain society, said they had investigated the matter and identified a culprit, who was dealt with in the traditional way. Renata was innocent, full stop, yet her refusal to hear my story troubled me greatly and created a silence between us, as well as a mistrust on my part."

Paul nodded encouragement.

"It should not have disturbed me so much," Angelo continued, "but everybody else was acting the same way, putting their hands over their eyes to cover what they had not seen, like priests in a house of sin. They told me about their families, their businesses, their ailments, but no-one said a word about the wounds on my back that screamed in plain daylight when I went swimming. I had no-one to talk to in my town, in my dialect, no-one who saw that, though I wore the skin of Angelo, the inside had changed. I went to work each morning and, hearing about nothing but last night's football and fucking, I turned solitary and sullen. Lunchtimes, I went for walks down back alleys, watching women through open windows serve sweaty men in undershirts with steaming pasta and bowls of soup. I was not hungry for such things, for such a life. I had been spared, surely, for a better purpose.

"My evenings belonged to Renata, who was planning our wedding in exorbitant detail, attending fittings, examining household linens, viewing rooms for us to rent. She hardly noticed when I missed one appointment, then another, accepting my excuse that I had stayed on for a drink with the printers after work.

"In a bar at the Piazza Stazione, I got talking to a skinny waitress who came from a farm outside Trieste. When I asked how she came to our town, Jovanka gave a dismissive shrug. Everyone has a story, I said. Nobody wants to hear, she replied. I have nothing better to do, I told her.

"So she pulled up a chair — the bar was never busy — and let me have it, the whole story of how she was taken to serve on some Party chief's estate. I saw she had three black hairs sprouting from a mole on her chin, and shoulders that cringed so badly that her breasts drooped inwards into what had once been a cleavage. In dim light she could have been any age, from eighteen to eighty. She had suffered beatings every day — from the master, his wife, even from their little brute of a son, seven years old. We mocked our former hosts. I told her how they had kicked me along the ground; she told me how the boss and his friends had raped the household maids, shooting any who got pregnant. One girl aborted her foetus with a kitchen knife and died in agony. When Jovanka missed two periods, she arranged to escape in an empty milk churn. She walked a hundred miles back home, where her father took a look at her belly and slammed the door in her face. She carried on walking around the peninsula and far into our country, dragging herself from one drudgery to the next until a widow here, originally from her home country, gave her a job at the bar.

" 'And you?' she said to me — the first person who had wanted to know. I told her that I, too, had come a long way, and she listened to every word of my tale. A great relief descended on me, almost a religious absolution.

"To compress a long story, Jovanka's bar became my refuge. On her night off, I took her around the mediaeval quarter, showing her the church with the celebrated frescoes. She asked if I believed in an afterlife. I took her icy hand in the twilit chapel and said the only paradise I knew was the one we made for ourselves. We wound up in her airless room above a tannery. She was not attractive, not even pretty. Her face, sunken by hunger, tapered down to a V point at the mole on her chin. Her skin felt thin as parchment to my touch, and was much the same colour. I stared so long that she accused me of pitying her and pulled the sheet over her head. I said, 'Come out, Jovanka, come out. You are so beautiful. I am so fortunate to have found you.'

"I neglected my duties. I arrived late to work, was argumentative at home, abrupt with Renata. My father was upset, my friends concerned, my cousin angry. One night, leaving the café, I found my path blocked by two slaughterhouse workers with blood on their aprons — Renata's brothers. They demanded to know if I intended to marry their sister. For sure, I said, but I needed more time to settle some affairs. A week, they said, and no more visits to the station bar. I knew then what I had to do."

Angelo plunged his hand into an inner pocket and brought out a triple-folded leaflet advertising a new coffee machine that promised to sweep the world like the legions of Julius Caesar. A salesman had given it to Jovanka at the bar. The machine, he swore, magnified the coffee sensation tenfold and made it irresistible to men and women. One cup could turn night into day, gloom into joy. It was good for the complexion, and, by inference, for sexual performance. Angelo read the leaflet and was richly amused. The copywriter was a man after his own heart. He decided to find Signor Gaggia at his café address at the foot of the flyer. He went to a jeweller and bought a gold necklace from the window display, wrapped it in a multi-coloured silk square, and left it, noteless, at Jovanka's room above the tannery. The last to leave work that night, he rifled the printer's desk for cash and ran to the station to catch the night train to Milano.

Next morning, in his best suit, he walked into the Café Gaggia and asked to see the boss. The inventor, impressed by his interest, acknowledged that he was facing obstacles in his plan of world conquest. He could not get an export license because he had not found the right man to bribe and he could not see how humble café owners in other countries could afford the machine once all taxes, duties, and bribes were added on. "That's where I come in," said Angelo.

"You can get me a license?"

"I can get your machine into a big city where the authorities are too busy with war crimes and restoring order to bother their heads with import-export papers."

"You have somewhere in mind?"

"Occupied zone."

"You speak the language?"

"All of them."

Angelo returned that night to the land of oppression. To slip in unnoticed, he dressed in printers' overalls and hid in a coal wagon that clattered slowly north. The moment it screeched into the giant terminus, he leapt off and went scouting for a chancer who, in exchange for a jar of olives, would give him the lay of the land. Soon he was bartering in a shady corner with a Dachau man in the cigarette trade, who advised him that the man to meet was a gum-chewing corporal with a taste for gourmet delicacies; Bignotti, his name was. Angelo located the man and saw his surly look dissolve at the gift of olives and red Barolo wine. Bignotti asked what he wanted and, with a tick on his clipboard, allocated Angelo a hole-in-the-wall kiosk beside the station entrance.

Two days later, he opened at seven for breakfast coffee. By lunchtime, the queue stretched halfway round the forecourt. Bignotti, after one exquisite sip, demanded to buy Angelo's machine when he was demobbed. It would do well, he reckoned, in his brother's trattoria in downtown Milwaukee. How soon? asked Angelo. Six, seven weeks, said the corporal. Perfect, thought Angelo.

Selling the machine to Bignotti for a suitcase stuffed with dollar bills, he put a BACK SOON sign up on the kiosk and rode an empty coal wagon back south, all his dreams beneath his sleeping head. Next morning, he walked into Jovanka's bar as she was taking chairs off the tables and arranging them for business. She was wearing his necklace. "We leave tonight," he announced.

With a bundle of her meagre belongings and a potato sack with his cash, they caught the Milan train and, on arrival the next morning, showered in the lavish public lavatories of the monumental station.

"What now?" asked Jovanka.

"We go shopping."

In a glass-roofed passageway of fashion shops opposite the famous opera house, Jovanka stopped to admire a creation in light green and lilac with a huge cotton rose above the plaster-cast breast. Angelo whisked her indoors, a proprietary arm around her stooped shoulders.

"Try it on."

"I can't."

"Please, for me. . . ."

She emerged from behind the dressing-room curtain transformed, no longer cringed but haughty with erotic charge. "We'll take it," said Angelo, not bothering to check the price. "Lilac shoes to match?"

"But . . ."

"Please, for me. . . ."

"How can you afford it?" she whispered.

"Honest work." He winked. "And you're going to be my partner."

Stopping to buy himself a broad-brimmed dark hat, he led Jovanka to a beauty parlour for a full facial that would conceal the disfiguring mole. At dinnertime, they took a table in Café Gaggia. The owner, bowing deeply, complimented Jovanka on her classical beauty and impeccable complexion. He bowed double when Angelo handed over, in bundles, half the dollars he had earned from the sale of one machine. "Enough," exclaimed Gaggia, "to buy a family restaurant in Rimini."

"There's more where that came from," said Angelo.

With three machines and a sack of coffee, they took a first-class sleeper back to the occupied metropolis. "Here's the plan," said Angelo, holding Jovanka in his arms above the rattling rails. "Whenever we need machines or coffee beans, you will travel first-class to Milano in all your finery. Looking as you do, no-one can possibly take you for a smuggler."

"But . . ."

"And every time you visit, you will buy another outfit."

"But . . ."

"No buts, my love. You have earned the privileges of beauty."

They were installed in the kiosk and hard at work before Jovanka managed to alert Angelo to the flaw in his plan, and when she did, he struck his head in horror and dejection. "You're right," he said. "What was I thinking? How could I let a beautiful woman travel alone in these times? And it's impossible for me to come with you — we cannot afford to close the kiosk."

"Leave it to me," said Jovanka, "I think I have found a solution."

She sent him to meet a pair of Serb dollar rustlers on platform thirteen. "Wear your new black hat and some padding beneath the left shoulder," she instructed.

"What for?"

"I've told them you are Cosa Nostra — Sicilian Mafia. These boys are villains but not stupid. One look at your Borsalino and your bulge and they will be very docile."

She had an eye for male vulnerability, did Jovanka, allied to a cheerful disposition and restless ingenuity. She hung kilim rugs on the walls of the cellar they rented and served their evening meal on decorated plates. On Sundays, she baked bread. She was, by Angelo's account, a paragon of virtue, and he would have been happy to spend the rest of the waning afternoon expatiating on her innumerable qualities, exulting in his own virility at having conquered such a goddess in human form.

"You see, Leonardo" — he beamed — "your friend is a fortunate man, blessed with the love of a fine woman, successful at his business, selling cups of coffee from a window and coffee machines to the world. Already we have Gaggias in eighteen of the forty-eight states of America, where Marcello Bignotti is my agent. Soon the Yanks will go home and we will sell to the Swiss and the Swedes and the Saudi Arabians, anyone who has a taste for fine coffee and cash in hand. Next year, we will open a sit-down café on Prince Regent Street. In three years, we will buy a hotel in a town by the sea, Jovanka and me, and we will breed beautiful babies who will become tenors in the opera and models in the fashion houses, or just ordinary people without great ambition who will never need to know what their mamma and papa endured."

Paul gave a glance at his wrist, prompting Angelo to smite his forehead. "But you, *mio caro,* you must be exhausted from the train journey, and I don't let you say a word. So rude of me, but I am so excited. I stand here day after day at the edge of the station, watching all who come by, looking for old friends, old enemies. No-one escapes my eye."

"Who have you seen?"

"You remember Vremi with the bad foot? He came through on his way to France. Dragan the Serb, two or three others. But they are not my Leonardo, my master, my teacher, my friend. Tell me, *caro* Leonardo, tell me all that has happened to you since we were last together. Where do you live? You look well. Have you found work?"

Paul gave a curt, colourless account of his doings, pre-rehearsed for any encounter with those he had left behind. He spoke of collapsing after he had left the camp, being rescued and cared for, but he did not say where. He did not know how Angelo would respond to his staying on in the village, beside the camp. He confessed as he would to a customs inspector, confining himself to essentials, giving nothing away: married, with a child, working in his profession. Angelo, rinsing cups, did not interrupt. Paul knew he was being judged. He had never been able to read Angelo's expression or temperament, was not as close to him as he had been to the Professor and poor Janko, and was not interested in being his friend. He remembered Angelo as effusive and elusive by turn, never transparent in his motives. He had to be careful of where this might lead. Paul, as a public official, could not afford an entrepreneurial entanglement with past acquaintances; and as a survivor, the last thing he wanted was to recapitulate old scores.

Angelo was the first camp mate he had met in three years, and he had no urge to see him again. They shared nothing except an ordeal. Paul knew he ought to get up, shake hands, and walk away. That would be the sensible thing to do, he told himself, but desire detained him. His eye was transfixed by a gleam of steel and his nostrils trembled with coffee thrills. Paul had fallen in love with Angelo's coffee machine and wanted one for himself. He would set it up in the Laughing Hind and lure visitors from miles around. It was just what the inn needed to advertise its modern comforts. Paul shifted on his chair, wondering how best to make an offer. Angelo was talking again about his beloved, insisting that Paul come to meet the incomparable Jovanka — come for dinner and taste her unsurpassable veal cutlets and meringue desserts. Paul, ambivalent, professed himself a vegetarian. "No problem," declared Angelo. "She makes magnificent pasta pomodoro." They agreed on Saturday night and were on the point of locking up when Paul imposed a condition.

"No reminiscences at dinner, okay?" he stipulated.

"Just what Jovanka says," cried Angelo. "What is past is past and we who survive have no right to self-pity. The pity, and the stories, belong to those who died."

The café owner insisted on accompanying him to the address that Alice had given for the Hofmann cousin, near enough to the station to be reached on foot and perilous enough with robbers and potholes not to be walked alone. Angelo pranced on rubble with the adroitness of an alpine mule. Shattered houses on either side of the road were crawling with chains of aproned women and knee-bare boys who passed bricks and water wordlessly one to another. The centre of the city was rising, floor by floor, from the ruins of war.

Angelo deposited him with a hug at the gate of a two-storey house, its upper floor roofless but the frontage intact. A one-legged man came to the door, mumbling that he had been unable to meet the train on account of his invalidity. He showed Paul where to put his baggage and, at night, his head. A flourish of sausages and cheese from the country suitcase softened his welcome into a protracted moan about the worthlessness of his pension and the absence of his wife, who worked among the rubble women to keep them in food and fuel. Paul offered to pay rent for his stay, brightening the mood to near cordiality. A pair of beer bottles materialised from beneath the marital bed. Paul searched the cousin for a likeness to Alice and, finding none, dismissed the man from consideration and turned his mind to the torrent of work ahead.

Reimmersing himself in technical research marked a reversion to a student life that belonged to a different Paul. Finding the right books in a university library, sitting at a long table, and taking notes in a wire-hinged pad was a bifurcating experience, one half of Paul sweating under the pressure of exams, the other half in command of a town. Reconciling the two was impossible, but the experience was not uncomfortable. It felt, he decided, like an old married couple returning to stay at the hotel where they had spent their honeymoon and finding it substantially unchanged.

He met a ready ally in a monocled university librarian of the kind he had known back home, a man appreciative of solid scholarship, who directed him to the relevant planning literature and, appreciating his seriousness, made suggestions for peripheral reading that Paul would not otherwise have considered but which, the librarian felt, might broaden his perspective. Armed with a terrifying reading list, Paul was reluctant to waste time on a drink after work, but the librarian was insistent and, ensconced in his favourite *Stube,* introduced his country guest to a clerk at the housing ministry, half Polish on his mother's side, who promised to provide a tome of municipal regulations, past and present, underlining any that were germane to Paul's purpose. This was a welcome shortcut. Between them over several days, the two officials guided Paul through a thicket of constraints and enabled him to complete his research quicker than expected. A round of coffees at Angelo's and the gift of his last pork sausages elicited further benefits. The clerk promised to put his applications at the top of the pile. The librarian went one better. Before starting work the next morning, he walked Paul down a narrow side street to what appeared to be a mediaeval monastery, then down its cell-lined corridor to meet three men of no notable physical feature who, the librarian murmured, were the chief signalmen of good governance, able to flash a green light of approval at worthwhile schemes, eliminating months of committee hearings. These three grey mice had clung to their posts from one regime to the next, refusing all offers of personal advancement and enrichment. From within a monastic cell, they surveyed the shattered land from a pinnacle of principle. Paul asked, over a glass of weak tea, if the gentlemen were familiar with the works of Alvar Aalto. Two nodded assent and the third glinted encouragement. Paul related that he had written his doctorate on the Finn and was designing an Aalto estate for his new town, a development rippling with natural light and organic dimensions. A burr of approbation fluttered around the mouse hole and Paul sensed he was home and dry.

Success was accompanied by a sledload of stress. His head throbbed with an excess of information and traffic noise, and his back ached from being hunched over a library bench. He longed to be back in a country lane where he could order his thoughts to the chirping of chaffinches. The pressure was unremitting, the days too short. His hands shook with tremors of intensity. He had no place to unwind.

Every day, he would rush to the general post office, where a letter awaited him from Alice, full of Johann's doings; some days, there was also a report from Lisl on a book she had just read and others she would like him to buy. He replied on a postcard, one eye on the clock to catch the next collection. Hustling past the crowded counters, he made his way out into drizzling rain, watching where he put his feet while his mind whirred through layer upon layer of regulations, logical and petty, every one of which would have to be met before the first brick could be laid.

Paul liked rules. He enjoyed the collision between unruly vision and legal standards, for it was in the fulfilment of fixed laws that inspiration was tested and an idea could be proven as a project of general benefit. Every hurdle he overcame, each condition met, brought him one step closer to a goal that glowed like the Taj Mahal at dawn, the acme of architecture. He had once described the point where vision was endorsed by regulation as his "Leonardo da Vinci moment," the ultimate proof; and when his uncle had told him bluntly that architects were ten a penny and he was no blinding genius, Paul replied that any man who took a building from sketch to habitation had in him a gene of great invention, of *creatio ex nihilo,* making something out of nothing. No savagery or setback could depress Paul's pride in his vocation.

Sunk in thought, he walked each night to the hovel of Alice's kinsman, where a cold collation awaited him on a bare table. Knowing the food was unappetising and conversation with the crippled cousin pointless, he took ever-wider detours when walking home. Despite warnings from the librarian and the housing clerk, he had no fear of the lawless streets and little regard for personal safety. He had not survived a concentration camp to fall victim to urban crime. He walked with rising confidence in the rubble and did not look round at sudden noises, of which there were many. When a crackling of wheels brought a vehicle screeching to a stop beside him, he walked on, unheeding. A door gaped open and he was ordered to get in.

"I prefer to walk," said Paul, assuming this to be a prank of Angelo's.

"Your preferences are immaterial,"

drawled the voice. "Kindly get in."

"And if I refuse?"

Dashboard lights speckled off a polished gun barrel that barred his path. "I don't think you have that luxury," said the voice in an accent that sounded as if it belonged to someone of minor nobility, or the deputy manager of a grand hotel.

"My mother told me never to take lifts from strangers," said Paul. "Either shoot that silly thing at me or pull it out of my way."

The light was dim, the road deserted. He could be shot and bundled into the Buick or left unattended until morning. Whistling the opening phrase of a Chopin mazurka, he stepped around the weapon and strode straight ahead.

"Look here, my dear fellow," said the voice, wavering. "I was told you might be a bit obstreperous, but this is ridiculous. Be a sensible chap, climb aboard, and all will be explained. My apologies for the intrusion; formal introductions will follow. I have been sent to collect you by a friend of yours, a man of many names, one of which you will recognise. He is eager to renew your acquaintance, and I assure you that you will find him congenial. He is a man of taste and wealth, a patron of art. He will make your evening most enjoyable and ensure that you get home safer than you might have done had you continued walking this road into a veritable den of bandits — did no-one warn you?"

"I shall walk a little farther," said Paul. "You may collect me in five minutes at the bottom of the avenue, on the right-hand corner."

"I will take the liberty of driving right behind you with the barrel sticking out."

"As you please," said Paul.

Three men in double-breasted suits occupied the vehicle, each uttering "Good evening." They drove for a while in circles to confuse Paul with regard to his bearings. Arrival was announced by a screaming left turn and slammed brakes. "Allow me, sir," said the uniformed chauffeur, holding the Buick door open and shining a path with a handheld torch down a flight of steps to an unpropitious basement door. A series of knocks, seven and five, then three and four. The iron door chinked open and a pair of wary eyes surveyed Paul from head to foot. Inside, the decor was orange and mauve, the decadent hues of a sex club. There was a stage at the far end and a bar to his right, its high stools draped with girls in relative stages of undress. Framed movie posters crowded the walls and the floor space was dotted with tables for two, the chairs arranged with a view to the stage, where two women were locking tongues to the strains of a muted saxophone. The place was empty of customers, the night still young. "This way, please," drawled Paul's guide, leading him down the left-hand side of the bunker to a shellproof steel door at the end.

"Enter!" cried a voice. He was ushered into a neon-lit strong room, a cloud of cigar smoke obscuring its inhabitant.

"Ambassador," boomed the voice, "you have kept the cannibals waiting."

"Professor!" choked Paul, bear-hugged by a man in a three-piece suit, bespectacled and rotund. He might have guessed his old bunk mate would track him down, and he was not in the least surprised to find the former lab technician peddling stale metaphors and sexual favours in a seedy nightclub. Unlocking himself from the clinch, he sat down on an upholstered chair that could have been a Louis XIV but was surely a reproduction.

"Mind the legs," said his host, rubbing an imagined spot on the velvet livery.

"Court of the Sun King?" guessed Paul.

"A close cousin." The Rumanian grinned.

"Are you with the cannibals, Professor?"

"As you see, I trade in living flesh — more profitable than killing and eating it."

"That's unpleasant," said Paul. "Can we drop the joke? It's gone rancid."

"Like our former friendship," said the Professor, and Paul realised that he would be made to confront the bare truth, and whatever consequences it brought.

The pair glared at each other through a blue haze. A tall blonde entered with a bottle of sparkling wine and two fluted glasses on a silver tray. She wore, Paul could not help but notice, absolutely nothing beneath a short kimono of black-and-yellow design. "Want her?" said the Professor, oblivious of the girl's presence. "Ursula, her name is. Sixteen when she started. Her father, Count Waldstein, was the escort who brought you here. Blood as blue as ink, but a bit too keen on the ancien regime, if you catch my drift. Needs to keep his head down till the arrest warrant fades and he can show his face again at the casinos in Monte Carlo."

"You're sheltering a war criminal and pimping his daughter?"

"I give with one hand, take with the other."

"Whatever happened to 'Vengeance is mine, saith the Lord,' your war cry?"

"I did not bring you here to criticise me, dear Pavlov," said the Professor.

"So why did you go to the trouble of snatching me off the streets?"

"I wanted to see what had became of you."

"Well, now you know."

"I am told that you live at the inn in the village of death."

"Who told you that?"

The tubby man ignored him. "Why did you stay there?" he demanded.

"Because they took me in when I was dying."

"The same people who sat in the beer garden and watched us die every day?"

"The very same."

Paul blew his nose, relieved, as he returned the handkerchief to his trouser pocket, that his betrayal was out in the open. He had nothing left to hide, and the Professor was in no position to pass moral judgement. He figured he might as well go on the offensive.

"I guess it was worth surviving," he sneered, "to peddle flesh and protect murderers."

"It's a living." The Professor smiled.

"How did you know I was here?" asked Paul.

"Angelo told me. He works for me. Most people in this wicked city work for me. Or else they pay me for the right to work for someone else."

"What kind of work?"

"Currency markets, building materials, fuel. I keep the black economy ticking over and the prices reasonable. Thanks to me, things get built and people have somewhere to live. They no longer have to sell their furniture, their daughters, and their wives."

"Except to you."

"Soldiers need to fuck. Civilians need to eat. A transaction is effected and I take a cut. A working girl needs a doctor, I find one. The doctor needs penicillin, I get it. The hospital needs coal, I deliver. I am the central distribution point for basic needs."

"You're a pimp," said Paul.

"An impresario," said the Professor. "I organise entertainments of every kind, from classical concerts to live sex. I provide outlets for relief, without which the fabric of society would unravel and each would take as he pleased at the point of a gun."

"As you did with me this evening. . . ."

"Indeed."

"But you claim a dubious moral justification."

Paul remembered how much he had disliked the other man's penchant for airy and cumbersome locutions, a cover for an inadequate education. There was a lot about the Professor that he had never liked. They once kept each other alive. That did not make them friends. Suspicions that he had always tamped down now stormed to the fore. He should have been less amused by the other man's satisfaction at being called Professor when he was never more than a bottle washer in a path lab. He should have been more circumspect about the baby the Professor had fathered, when his description of the fumble in the Academy of Sciences broom closet sounded more like rape. He had trusted the Professor only so long as he had required his complementary qualities. Now the more he looked at the man, the less he wanted to be breathing the same stale air. He decided to terminate the encounter as quickly as possible, for his own good feeling and self-esteem.

"The world," drawled the Professor grandly, rolling ash from his cigar into a square glass dish on the desk, "is on the cusp of inexorable transition. We are gravitating from military rule to civil administration. A fresh start. Business must move with the times, so I am transmuting my operations into legal entities with limited liability, shareholders, and all accoutrements of respectability. I am going legit, as our Ami friends say."

"You'll be a pillar of the new society."

"If you like. Do I detect a subtext of condemnation?"

"Who am I to condemn?" said Paul.

"Who indeed?" said the Professor, and a silence fell between them, thick as fog.

"How —" began Paul, breaking the impasse.

"How did I become a gunrunner, a drug dealer, a corrupter of innocence?"

"I didn't mean that. I have no right —"

"I will tell you, anyway." The Professor smiled, as if he had been waiting a long time for the opportunity. "I will tell you from the time you so selfishly abandoned us."

Barely alive when the liberators arrived, "drained by dysentery and disillusion," as he put it, the Professor was rushed to the convalescent home, where he lay half-conscious for days. As soon as he could sit up and take nourishment from something other than a tube, he asked for his bed to be moved for privacy to the far end of the ward, against the wall of the nurses' room. There he lay and listened like a fox at a rabbit warren, alert to every sound. Something was not quite right about one of the male nurses, who kept dropping bedpans and lunch trays. Listening through the wall, he heard a doctor address the nurse by a famous name, one that belonged to a former political leader, notorious for his inflammatory speeches. The demagogue had got out in the nick of time and needed one last ally to get him across the southern border, where friends awaited. He had a heavy trunk and was looking for a truck to steal. An ambulance would be ideal. He offered the doctor two gold bars in exchange for a tranquilliser-loaded syringe that he could pop into the driver before making off with his truck. The doctor wanted five bars. They shook hands on four. The demagogue had no time to lose. His name was near the top of the occupiers' wanted list and his head carried a million-dollar reward.

The Professor knew that he had to move twice as fast. In the middle of the night, he bleated to be taken to the lavatory. The fallen minister was alone on duty at the nurses' station. Screwing up his face in disgust, he held the patient by the elbow and led him step by slow step to the cubicle at the end of the corridor. Once inside, the Professor grabbed the politician by the Adam's apple. "I am your hope, your salvation," he crooned.

"Wha-at?" croaked his prisoner.

"Half your gold, or I turn you in."

The ex-minister, five lines etched on his brow like a musical stave, pleaded for time. "An hour," said the Professor. "The commander comes on duty at seven. I have left a note on his desk, apprising him of your identity. Have the gold in an ambulance for me in an hour, and I'll exchange it for the note. I expect two hundred bars." Before first light, the Professor was being driven by an accomplice out of the forest at breakneck speed. "My first successful heist." He smiled.

"You had no right!" Paul spluttered.

"No right to what? To compensation? To take back what had been stolen from us? To take it before someone else used it against us?"

"You had no right to let the murderer off the hook."

"Save me the moral relativity, my friend; it cuts no carrots. Before the war, I heard a wonderfully inspiring lecture from the great Professor Einstein, and what did that giant give us? The mushroom cloud. So drink up and spare me the homily, because you have no monopoly on right and wrong, and any values we once shared went into a lime pit or were nailed to a church door somewhere in the sub-Carpathians."

"How dare you . . ." thundered Paul, leaping to his feet with outrage.

"Dare what?" retorted the Professor. "Dare to mention it, to remember, to get up in the morning, living and breathing and pretending to look forward to a new day? You may be right, Pavlov. I have no right to be alive, nor do you. What we have seen and done disqualifies us from inhaling O-two. But until we reach that conclusion, we may as well take what we can and live out our time, trying not to transmit the things we saw to another generation, limiting its expectations of life."

"Now you're being ridiculous," snapped Paul. "Of course we have a right to live and a duty to inform the next generation. I have a son. . . ."

"Congratulations. And what will you tell him?"

Paul dropped his eyes.

"Exactly," said the Professor. "You will tell him nothing, not him, not your wife, and not, on your deathbed, your confessor. You will take these things with you into the void because they cannot be shared with anyone who has not endured them at your side, as I did, and Angelo. We, the chosen few, are the only ones who may speak of it, and we do not speak even amongst ourselves, for fear of polluting the future."

"And you?" challenged Paul. "You also have a child."

The small man behind the desk took a watch from his waistcoat pocket. The rear flipped open to reveal a pretty gap-toothed smile.

"I am bringing her out," he grunted. "She is six years old; I have never seen her."

"How will you get her out?"

"The usual way."

"And the mother?"

"She has accepted a sum of money."

"You will separate her from the child?"

"She has agreed to the deal."

"Will she see the child again?"

"I doubt it, less distressing that way."

"First rape, then child robbery. Have you no feelings?" cried Paul.

"Only the ones I need to get me through each night, from dusk to dawn."

"You don't sleep well, then."

"Do you?"

Another silence fell, this time in solidarity. When the Professor spoke again, it was in the tone that company chairmen use when delivering an annual report to institutional investors, highlighting profit margins and glossing over misjudgements. Success, he related, had been hard-won. The post-war market was organised on strict demarcation lines. Former camp prisoners controlled girls and tobacco; army deserters from both sides dealt in building materials, motors, and visas; disgraced officials of the last regime held the liquor franchise and the foreign-currency racket. There were fortunes to be made. The *Stars and Stripes* newspaper reported that in six months American soldiers had sent home eleven million dollars in excess of their army pay — and that did not include the scientific equipment, precious antiques, and works of art they had looted. "Possession was eleven-tenths of the law," said the club owner.

Men killed at will, and for nothing. A gun was easier to get hold of than a good wine and just as easy to pump down a throat. At dawn, a dust cart collected bodies from the gutter. "I had some close shaves," confessed the Professor. "Friends of the demagogue-in-disguise were out to get me. They sprayed my vehicle with bullets, put a bomb by my club door, made things awkward. One of my barmen had his carotid artery severed as he stood in line for stamps at the general post office. He bled to death in silence on the marble floor as the queue parted left and right like the Red Sea for the Israelites. I was a marked man, in urgent need of protection. That's where Janko came in."

"Janko!" exclaimed Paul, "I thought he was dead."

"Not so far as I know. He's the one who drove me out of the forest."

"I heard he'd been killed by a farm woman screaming rape."

"No, that was Tibor, one of the Hungarian boys. And he wasn't killed, just peppered with birdshot. Too friendly, those Hungarian boys. Not like our pal Janko."

"Where is he? Can I see him?" demanded Paul, remembering the boy's avowal of love.

"He's around. In construction. Where was I?" said the Professor, irritated by the interruption.

"You were on the blood-soaked floor at the post office."

"Not me. That was my barman. Anyway, that's when Janko launched his defence campaign."

The young Czech, simmering with conflicting urges, formed a praetorian guard for the Professor. He recruited without prejudice — camp survivors, common criminals, and army-trained killers — and paid for their loyalty with ingots of gold. He formed two units of six men each and drilled them to operational precision. The first strike, made before the week was out, occasioned widespread comment for its barbarity. The

www.facebook.com/SnyderCountyLibraries
Like Snyder County Libraries on Facebook!

Total Items: 5

Due: 1/24/2012
Title: The dawn of probosties (LP)
Item: 31410548

Due: 1/24/2012
Title: The last gunfighter : Hell town (LP)
Item: 31882522

Due: 1/24/2012
Title: The scroll : a novel
Item: 31882522

Due: 1/24/2012
Title: The misfortune (LP)
Item: 31411520

Due: 1/24/2012

Check Out Receipt

Selinsgrove Community Library (SEL)
570-374

Item: 31449209
Title: Belle Ruin (LP)
Due: 7/24/2012

Item: 31477260
Title: The magicians (LP)
Due: 7/24/2012

Item: 31485259
Title: The scroll a novel
Due: 7/24/2012

Item: 31465255
Title: The last gunfighter. Hell town (LP)
Due: 7/24/2012

Item: 31476248
Title: The game of opposites (LP)
Due: 7/24/2012

Total Items: 5

Like Snyder County Libraries on Facebook!
www.facebook.com/SnyderCountyLibraries

recipe was duly repeated. Over the next six weeks, seventeen friends of the demagogue-in-disguise were found in various gutters with their throats cut, their tongues and genitals excised. A neat pack of gonads was delivered within hours by bicycle to the homes of wives, parents, and next of kin. "It had the intended effect," rasped the Professor. "Six former ministers gave themselves up to the occupation army rather than get winkled out of hiding by Janko's enthusiastic emasculators. Count Waldstein, emissary of a fugitive justice minister, came to my den with a peace offer, immediate and unconditional. I have the piece of paper in my drawer and I have cooperated with the bastards ever since without further trouble."

Paul spluttered an angry expostulation. "How can I let them live?" retorted the Professor. "Simple: I got tired of revenge. One killing is much the same as another, and organising them is a logistical headache. Although we had only two episodes of mistaken identity along with fifteen successful eliminations, the risk of error increased as it would in any game of Russian roulette. Anyway, the war was won. I had got all I wanted, which was to be left alone. So I called it quits and settled for coexistence."

"No more 'Vengeance is mine'?" said Paul.

"Enough," said the Professor. "It reached a point where I felt numb when a strike was concluded. That's not right. You ought to feel something when a man is killed, don't you think?"

"It was they who taught us to feel nothing," Paul objected.

"Not me," said the Professor. "I took it personally. That's how I am. When I felt nothing, I knew it had to stop. From that day, if anyone bothered me, I gave orders to have him hurt, but left alive. I couldn't face the numbness, you see."

"You wouldn't kill again?"

"No."

"Under any circumstances?"

"Never."

"What if you saw one of our guards, the baldie who set the dogs on Varady, or the fat one who shot Berkovich?"

"I'd ask if he was looking for a job. I can always use extra security. Listen, friend, the past is past. The century is halfway gone and the world is in recovery. Soon, everyone will be building and selling, buying and inventing. I want to be in on the boom, an investor, a facilitator, a responsible citizen who sends his child to a convent school and attends her Nativity play with a smile on his face as broad as the Bosphorus. I'm almost out of smuggling, the protection racket is over, and prostitution is just one headache after another, if you see what I mean. The girl who filled your glass, Ursula? She's a virgin, for all I know. I employ her in a decorative capacity. It impresses the nobodies who are going to be running the country by the end of the year to have their drinks poured by a naked young countess whom they can tip but may not touch."

"But you offered her to me," Paul protested.

"For friends, I make exceptions."

Paul could not decide what was believeable and what was a tease. A floor show was being staged for his benefit. The ringmaster was a man he had once known. Who was he, and what his game? He called Paul "friend," which was a lie and always had been.

"So what do you want of me, dear friend?" Paul asked.

"Why did I abduct you?"

"Correct."

"To verify that you are alive and well, dear Pavlov. To see if we had a dialogue worth continuing. To commend you on your construction project. To ask if you need my assistance in any way."

"As you can see," said Paul, folding his

hands tight to stop them from shaking with fury at the other man's presumptions, "I am alive. I have a family. I work in my profession. I don't look back. I have no desire for old-boy reunions and singsongs around the campfire. When the past is vile, erase it. Like you, I look ahead. As for my construction project, I would prefer if, with all due respect, you took no further interest."

"As you wish." The Professor grinned, stubbing out his cigar. "I am glad that you have found your feet and I shall not be dropping by your home to visit. I am sure you will understand the reason for my reticence."

"I collapsed there," protested Paul, "I was taken in and saved from certain death. That's why I stayed — no other reason — for the one person who was good to me."

"No need to justify yourself," said the Professor loftily. "A man does what he must."

"You don't understand," insisted Paul, impelled by a need to convince the shadow he had left behind. "I have an obligation to the person who saved me. I owe her. Why else would I linger in that place? And who knows how long I will stay?"

"No, you listen to me, Pavlov," said the

Professor, flushed and combative. "Don't explain, because we don't speak the same language, you and I. You were raised in comfort and had a career — two careers — laid out for you on a bed of lettuce. I grew up in a tin hut and had to fight for everything — work, women, money. We were tossed together by chance and torn apart by an act of egotism, your cruelty. Don't expect me to understand your fancy rationalisations for turning your back on friends to go and live in a charnel house. You tell it your way; I see it mine. Leave it at that."

They rose in unison, stretching out straw-dry hands. "Can I entertain you while you're in town?" said the club owner. "A floor show? A good meal? A girl? A better class of accommodation."

Paul shook his head.

"You don't fool me," said the Professor.

"I never did."

"If you want anything, let me know."

"Just one thing . . ." said Paul, clinging to the Professor's hand. It was not one thing at all but a thousand shards of memory that broke before his eyes, the mirror of their past compact shattered in an irreversible parting of ways.

"What is it?" said the Professor.

"What would you do if he turned up?"

"Who?"

"Hans."

The Professor scowled over half-moon spectacles as if Paul were a dim doorman who was refusing him entry to his own premises.

"What would you do if Hans came here?" Paul persisted.

"Why should I treat him differently from any other customer?"

"Because he is Hans, the maker of hell, our hell, yours and mine."

The Professor withdrew his hand from Paul's and reached into his waistcoat pocket for the chained watch, massaging the winding wheel with thumb and forefinger. He seemed disinclined to say another word, his ear to the timepiece to make sure it was ticking. Paul held his ground, forcing the proprietor to look up.

"What was the question again?" he said.

"What you would do if Hans were to walk in here, into your club?"

The watch was replaced in its pocket. A fresh cigar was lit. A puff of smoke burned the stagnant air.

"Ask me again," said the Professor.

"Hans walks in. What do you do — call Janko?"

"No, not Janko."

"What, then?"

"I'd kill him myself," muttered the Professor, oblivious to all that he had sworn before.

CHAPTER NINE

As the taxi entered the valley and began its ascent, Paul was overcome by a profound calm, a serenity so soporific that it took an effort of will for him to ask the driver to roll up his side window as the breeze turned mountainous and made him shiver in his short-sleeved shirt. Home was close, his tasks fulfilled, and he knew to the last statutory instrument and underground pipe thickness what was required to achieve his new town. The brushes with his past had been instructive and unthreatening. Dinner at Angelo's had been delightful, Jovanka proving to be an inventive chef and a good raconteuse with a throaty laugh and a healthy line in self-mockery. Angelo had basked in Paul's appreciation of his effervescent wife and promised to sell him the next coffee machine that came free, once he had got through a long list of overseas orders.

On his last day in the city, Paul had loaded up with gifts: a clockwork train set for Johann, silver earrings for Alice, a striped tie for Franz-Josef, a literary biography for Lisl, a monogrammed brass tankard for Papa Hofmann, and, overlooking no-one, a stainproof nylon-coated apron with a black horse on its front for Mathilde Zumsteig, whom Alice could not abide but who was worth keeping sweet through the months ahead.

All of his presents, without exception, would prove inappropriate or inconsiderate. Johann was a year too young to work the clockwork train and broke the handle before he had much joy from the toy. Alice, he should have noticed before, did not have pierced ears. Franz-Josef, with his one hand, was unable to knot a tie, and Lisl only ever read fiction. Papa Hofmann had more tankards on his bar than a smithy has horseshoes, and his partner turned out to be allergic to synthetic materials, sprouting pink rashes at the sight of a plastic wrapper. Despite these miscalculations, Paul's offerings were welcomed by one and all with squeals and rumbles of innocent pleasure and Paul was praised to the peaks for his loving kindness towards every member of the family, including Lisl's little twins, for whom he had bought transparently cheap (he had left the price stickers on) though timely woollen socks in, by chance, the right colour and size. The wholehearted reception of his presents was, for Paul, confirmation of his own acceptance by the family and the village. And when Alice on that homecoming night received him with renewed desire, he experienced a glow of well-being that, for one unbroken night's sleep, allayed his torments and allowed him the illusion of having found a perfect peace.

He had hoped to spend a leisurely day or two with his wife and child before getting back to work, but human need pressed at his door. There were children living in tents without adequate sanitation. Their parents, workless, were turning to crime. Barely stopping to ingest breakfast, Paul rushed to his desk and put together a project team from his displaced masses — a former building contractor as site manager, two trained draughtsmen, a pair of horn-rimmed bookkeepers, three typists, a courier-driver, a security officer — a list he modelled on his uncle's nefarious office. A float of state funding from the three grey mice paid ten salaries. Summoning the team, he told them to have all paperwork ready for submission and the ground cleared by New Year's Day.

or there would be no homes and future for anyone.

That night in bed, he promised to take Alice on his next official trip to the capital, where she had never been. Alice sharply refused, reminding him that everything they did, singly or together, had to be above suspicion if his plans were to succeed and their happiness endure. "We must never lose a wink of sleep," she warned, nestling a contented rump against his thigh, "worrying that we might be giving satisfaction to some bitter soul who is watching our movements, waiting to accuse us of nest-feathering." Paul kissed the top of her sleepy head, relishing his good fortune in finding a wife so prudent and clear-sighted.

Christmas was upon them before he noticed, preoccupied as he was by red-and-blue construction plans and the routine problems of running a busy office. His foreman fell sick; a draughtsman disappeared; one of the secretaries had twins and another could not spell to save her life. He shuttled twice more to the city, briskly in and out, like a squirrel carrying acorns to its lair. He stopped at Angelo's for coffee but had no further dealings with the Professor, walling off his past and failing to contact Janko, fond as he was of the young Czech. The

Christmas presents he bought on his second trip were conspicuously well chosen: a sterling silver necklace for Alice, wooden building bricks for the boy, a silver-tipped walking cane for his brother-in-law, and a Hemingway, the very latest, for Lisl — all received with cries of joy on the festive eve before the family set out together up the hill for midnight Mass. For the former Mathilde Zumsteig — lately married to his father-in-law in a purse-lipped ceremony with Alice and Franz-Josef in muttering attendance — he chose an elegant woollen head scarf, and for Papa he bought an English briar pipe until, remembering that the new Mrs. Hofmann had stopped his smoking and restricted him to one thin beer a night, he switched it for a smart felt hat in exactly the right shade and size.

As tallow candles sputtered on the outstretched arms of the living room tree, Paul was reminded of that boyhood glow when, treeless in regard for his mother's faith, he sat between his parents on a sagging sofa, unwrapping surprises that were no surprise at all but the affordable objects he most desired — things that hardly differed from the parental gifts that Johann would rip open with high-pitched excitement come the white morning. He ascended the stairs to bed, thigh by loving thigh with Alice, their knees and elbows finding harmony in motion. And when, bolt upright in the hour of blackness, he rose to relieve his bladder of the eve's excesses, he went stumbling down the bedroom corridor not in the usual vortex of self-torment but with a yawn of content and a pleasurable anticipation of holiday conjugality.

Shuffling back from the closet in his dressing gown, he heard sobbing in the corridor. "Lisl?" he whispered. "What's the matter?"

The girl was huddled at the foot of an armoured knight, snuffling into her sleeve. Paul sat down beside her, an arm around her shaking shoulders. The girl, in a transparent nightdress, trembled at his touch. "I should never have married him," she wept.

"You mustn't say that. . . ."

"Why not? He's not even half a man. He never talks to me. He drinks, like his father, and has no interest in anything. What kind of life is that for me and my children?"

"You must remember, Lisl, that Franz suffers constant pain. . . ."

"I know, and I make allowances. But he is getting more miserable each day, not less. I'm not doing him any good. Look at me," she cried, "I'm white as a turnip, thin as celery, sacrificing my vitality for no return."

She huddled closer to Paul, whispering into his compromised ear. "It's you I want," said Lisl with sudden urgency, her fingers scrabbling at the opening of his nightshirt. "I have always known that. I worshipped you from the moment we met."

"Don't be silly, Lisl," chided Paul, teetering between marital virtue and masculine vanity. "That's not going to solve anyone's problems. We are relatives, living in the same house. You are the daughter of my friend, my wife's best friend. We are forbidden to each other. We cannot be together, never in this world. That's a wild fantasy, too much sparkling wine at dinner."

"I didn't touch a drop," the girl protested. "I was too depressed to drink."

"Lisl, put these thoughts out of your head. It cannot be."

"But it can," she hissed, grabbing his hand and placing it beneath her nightdress, on her breast, its nipple pert. "Paul, my Paul, we are fish out of water in this place, you and I, dolphins in a pool of village dolts. When I talk to you, I see your mind flashing through choices, your eyes flickering with ideas. You are trapped here, a racehorse in a donkey harness. You should not be wasting your life on peasants. You have a brilliant mind. Use it where it can do the greatest good."

"I can do good here," said Paul, hunching forward to conceal his involuntary arousal.

"You can do so much more elsewhere," Lisl insisted. "We can run away and start again, you and I, in a big city. Together, tomorrow night. They'll never find us."

"But it would be wrong. . . ." said Paul, his hand cupped around her breast.

"Wrong? By what measure? What can ever be wrong in a country that wiped out whole races to prove its superiority? What are the morals by which the village can judge us, the village that watched as they hounded you poor prisoners like rats into a sack for drowning? Oh yes, they watched every day, they watched and they knew, and now they say nothing. Has Alice mentioned it? Ever?"

"I don't want to talk about that," snapped Paul, aware that by breaking the silence, Lisl had named the lie that kept him there, weakening the ground beneath his feet. He was being dragged, unresisting, to her view of the world, a seductive proposition in which the victim could do no wrong. He had to find a counter-argument, and find it fast, because the girl was smart and her case formidable.

"One w-wrong does not vindicate an-other," he stuttered.

"Unless it is an appropriate revenge," she replied. "An eye for an eye. You have a right to retribution."

"This family never harmed me. . . ."

"Hofmann offered free drinks to your guards. Alice served them."

"And your own father?" Paul retorted.

"Was forced to treat their colds and bruises," she retorted, but her face had reddened, and he exploited her hesitation to reclaim his hand, clamping it between his own jittery knees.

"This is not the time and place to discuss right and wrong," he began.

"What do *you* mean by 'wrong'?" she demanded.

"It is wrong to harm the innocent, wrong to abandon children, to afflict the ones who love us." He could feel the plates settling once more; he was on firmer ground. "You and I, Lisl, we know what is wrong. Adultery is wrong. Taking a best friend's husband is wrong."

"Wrong?" she retorted. "Night and day, there is wrong going on all over the valley. Ask my father; he deals with the consequences. Little boys get buggered on the open hills, men shove it up their sheep because they are incapable of human relations, and women ride horses to exhaustion. There are bad people in this village, sick people. You and I, Paul, are aliens from another planet. We belong in a greater constellation, out there in a world where people sit in cafés and discuss right and wrong in the abstract, untainted by personal experience. We belong amongst readers and thinkers, in the literary pages of great newspapers. I love you, Paul. You are my soulmate, my hope, my salvation. Take me away and I will make for us a life that is worthy of you. In ten years, you will be a world-famous architect and I will publish my first novel."

The ground was slipping again. She reached for his hand.

"What about your twins, your mother, your father?" he protested.

"The little ones will be looked after; my father will understand. He has other children. I have only this chance. I want to make you happy, Paul, to make you great. Happy — is that something you can understand? Is it not what you deserve?"

"But I *am* happy, with Alice."

"Really? I have seen you bite your lip when she opens her mouth to speak. Your condescension is obvious to me. She notices nothing. You like her, as I do, but that's not love — that's tolerance, affection, gratitude, coexistence. Alice is not the one for you, the one who will satisfy you, in work and in love. I can be the making of you, Paul. I will make you happy every minute of your life. I will devote my whole being to cultivating your fulfilment. Let me show you, Paul. Let me show you how. . . ."

She reached above his knees, stroking his renewed arousal. He could not deny the attractions of body and mind. Lisl was the physical type he liked — small-boned, dark-eyed, and swift, like his one and only true love, seething with boundless energies. She was intellectually ravenous, interested in every realm of ideas. She would challenge him, refine his plans, and push him to ever-greater heights. Naïve as she was, Lisl knew her strengths: She could be the making of him. He was filled with a desire to crush her in his arms, beneath his body, her submission a sign of his greatness, rampant and unleashed. They would have children of genius, a place in the sun, the world laying laurels at their feet.

Unthinkable, he knew. Beyond rational contemplation. He was married to Alice and could not leave her — not without losing whatever fig leaves of self-respect he had stitched together since his last great sin of abandonment and betrayal. He was Alice's for as long as she wanted him; he would not repay her charity with cruelty. He did not have it in him to do such a thing, and the thought of losing Johann brought tears trickling down his cheeks, even as he held the eager Lisl at half arm's length from his physical excitation.

Calmly and with the care of a surgeon preparing for amputation, he selected a low tone from his tray of measured expressions and applied it with emollient words to allay the girl's fevered delusion. He reiterated his love for Alice and his debt to her. He praised Franz-Josef's staunch and uncomplaining stoicism, his evident depths of character. He might yet overcome his hurt to become the man of her dreams.

"Don't patronise me," snorted Lisl. "You know he's a spoiled younger son, a weakling."

Paul tried again, telling her that every marriage had its troughs when the partners drifted apart and its summits when they joyfully reconnected. She should give it more time.

"Spare me the priestly sermon," snapped Lisl, "or is it psychotherapy? Of course, Father said you had studied Freud. Forget what you read — here's what I see. Franz is taciturn half the time, truculent when drunk. He cannot see if I am glad or sad. He has eyes for no-one but himself. He is melancholic, introspective, avaricious, egotistical."

"Don't you use those Sunday words on me, young lady!" exclaimed Paul, pulling away from her and seizing the chink of a pretension to assert seniority and authority, covering up his manifold confusions.

"Listen to me, Lisl," said Paul, "listen, for once, without interruption. You and I have no right to look down on anyone. Just because we read books, that does not make us better people than Franz and Alice, who have good instincts and kind hearts, and are brave, besides. We gave them our loyalty at the altar, and that's all there is to say. I love Alice with all my heart, and Franz is capable of proving that he truly deserves your love."

"No," cried Lisl, a cry of loss that rose from deep in her sparrow neck and threatened to wake the whole house. He put a hand over her mouth. She bit it below the thumb and, when he retracted, stretched up to press her lips to Paul's mouth, hauling him to his feet and pinning him to the cold wall for a sinfully long time before he contrived to break free. They faced each other, panting, partners in unfinished business.

"Here's where we stand," said Lisl, fixing him with glistening eyes. "We can return to our marriage beds right now and neither of us will ever mention this again. I am prepared to draw a line. But I want something in return."

"What's that?"

"Promise me something. Promise me on your son's life, your mother's grave, whatever you hold holy, that you will never leave Alice, that you'll stay here. Swear to me that you don't contemplate escape. Tell me that, hand on heart, and I will accept your rejection."

Paul said nothing.

"I'm going to count to ten." She smiled, taking his left hand and kissing each finger in turn, clockwise and in reverse. "Nothing to say?" she taunted.

Paul's legs trembled. His lips searched for the power of speech. On Johann's head, she had said, on Johanna's grave. He could not tell a lie, take a false oath on the two people he held most dear. The girl knew his weakness. She could do with him as she wished.

"Go back to bed," he said feebly, "please, Lisl. The children will be up soon."

"I am here when you want me," said the girl, touching his thigh. "But don't keep me waiting, Paul. We have a right to a better life than this."

Rattled to the roots of his ruined teeth, Paul dragged himself back to the four-poster bed where Alice slept, unheeding of his absence. He lay at the far edge, wondering what to do next. He might have an elliptical word with Lisl's father, alerting the old physician to her distress and reducing his own involvement by encouraging outside interference. The doctor had remarked on Lisl's negative attitude to Franz-Josef and his haggard despondency. Franzi had taken to banging his prosthetic arm around the bar, doubling the breakage costs.

Paul wondered if Alice was prey to the same genetic disposition. Would her face cave in if her husband were to leave her as he had left all the others in his life? Would she collapse and pine? Unlikely, Paul thought. Alice was a formidable person. She had nursed her dying mother and handled her difficult father with an inner strength and unblinking application. There was so much to cherish in his wife that Paul upbraided himself for letting Lisl distract him with fantasies of flight and fame. He cursed himself for letting the girl read doubt in his eyes. Lisl was Alice writ small, diminutive in name, shape, and nature. Two whole Lisls would not one Alice make, nor would Lisl bring him that blessed grace of conjugal bliss, that sighing catch of satisfaction, which was a mercy bestowed by Alice alone, she and no other.

That Christmas morning, Paul clung to his wife as to a life raft in raging seas, burying his head in her unknowing flesh, clasping her to his gaunt frame until their son came into the room dragging his teddy bear and they saw his oval eyes widen at the abundance of gifts. That shared spectacle was so intense that Paul had to pull on a dressing gown and step outside, unable to bear the possibility of happiness revealed.

After church and lunch, while Johann napped and Papa snored, Paul took a bracing, silent walk with Alice through light flakes of snow, two figures in a glacial landscape. As they turned back into the driveway of the Laughing Hind, they ran into Dr. Walters, who was bringing the twins home and asked if he could borrow Paul for "a few minutes — just a few minutes, I promise — of man-to-man conversation." Alice assured them of a hot punch on their return and they set out down the hill, united in festive well-being, each with an ulterior purpose in mind.

"I look at you, my dear friend," said the

doctor, "and I am reminded of Joseph in Mann's great trilogy."

"You said so once before."

"I know, I keep repeating myself these days, my wife says. But the story has acquired another dimension in my mind and I wanted to share it with you. Like Joseph, you came here a slave. You interpreted a dream, created a plan, saved the state. And then you let it be known that you would not be buried in this land, that you do not belong here. You have one foot in the saddle, poised for departure."

"What makes you say that?" said Paul, stunned by the perception.

"Lisl mentioned it. She's very astute, my little girl."

"I need to talk to you about Lisl."

"Not now," said the doctor. "I have a request, a favour to ask."

"And you are worried I might not be here long enough to grant it?"

"I don't know. Will you?"

"I expect so," said Paul. "I have commitments."

"I am glad to hear that."

"What is the favour?" The breaths expelled from his mouth glistened with suspicion.

"You remember how honoured I was to serve as best man at your wedding?"

"You did me the honour, Doctor."

"I need to request a reciprocal favour."

Paul said nothing. Surely the doctor was not planning to divorce his wife and re-marry? They climbed a stile and crossed a meadow. "I am dying, my friend," he told Paul. "A cancer, a fox in the chicken coop, has broken through the trusty bowel and at-tacked the liver. Look at my face. It's as jaundiced as Johannes Brahms's in that portrait that sits on my piano. The same disease, the same age, sixty-three. No point in treatment, nothing to be done. Morphine controls the pain. When it fails, my wife will administer a lethal dose I have prepared in the icebox. It's a matter of weeks, three months at most."

"I'm so sorry," murmured Paul. Walters was a fixture in his firmament, a moral compass. He would not know which way to turn without him.

"Spare me your pity, my friend," said the doctor. "I have led a rich life, full of foibles, blessed with children and other pleasures. In these last weeks of realisation, my wife and I are as close as two people can be, no regrets or recriminations, grateful for all we have shared. We are keeping the disease a secret, as if we are having an illicit affair. May I rely on your discretion?"

"Of course."

"Good. Then this is my request to you. The end will come soon, quite suddenly, and when it does, my wife may be unable to withstand social pressures for an appropriate disposal. I need you to execute my wishes in this regard."

"The funeral?"

"Very short. No eulogies. Not one word after the ashes-to-ashes babble from that decrepit bigot of a priest — I can't imagine why the diocese never replied to my letters — and nothing from the village elders, either. They are my patients, not my friends. I do not belong to them. Like you, Paul, I am a sojourner in this land, a city dweller exiled to Goshen. Remember Joseph on his deathbed? 'Do not bury me in Egypt,' he said; two centuries later, Moses brought out his bones. I want you to do the same for me, but don't wait that long. Take my bones that same day to the city that booted me out. Bury me near a café, with a good bookshop close at hand. That's all I ask, dear Paul."

The doctor stumbled on a snow-covered boulder. Paul caught him by the upper arm and clung to it as they walked on. He understood now why the older man had been so keen to accompany him to the city.

He must have wanted a friend at his side when he went to confirm his self-diagnosis at the university hospital, someone to hold his trembling hand as he received the verdict and prepared to face his end. Paul had failed this decent man on that request; he would not let him down again. "Tell me all the duties," he said humbly. "I will carry them out to the best of my ability."

The doctor produced a sealed envelope from the inner pocket of his overcoat. "Here is what I want you to do," he said in the tone he used to administer a cough tincture. "After the service in St. Ignatius, take the coffin to the capital and inter me in the central cemetery, in the Walters plot, among my ancestors, beside the main road. The only ones who may accompany the coffin, besides you, are my wife, my children, and their spouses — Alice as well, if you like. I don't like eulogies, but if something has to be said at the graveside, you are the one person I want to speak. You will give dignity to the occasion and comfort to my family."

"Why me?"

"I think you know why."

"I need to hear it from you."

"Like me, Paul, you have been familiar with death as a daily occurrence. You will not get flustered."

"Why not ask a medical colleague?"

"At the moment we speak of," replied Walters, smiling, "I shall be past needing a doctor."

"Thank you," said Paul forty paces later.

"For what?"

"For the privilege. I was unable to pay my parents that last respect."

"I thought as much," said the doctor softly.

At the next bend, before Paul could turn the conversation to Lisl's unsettled state, the doctor changed the subject to literary reputations, their everyday currency. Would any of the present crop be worthy to inherit the mantle of Mann, Zweig, and Hauptmann? They were still debating the merits when their feet mounted the inn's doorstep and the doctor laid a detaining hand on Paul's arm.

"There is a little game I play sometimes with the family," he related. "I invented it in the dark times, when we could not speak openly at table for fear of denunciation, and taught it to the little ones to keep their faculties alert and protect them from the platitudes of propaganda. It's called "the game of opposites."

"How does it go?"

"It's very easy — may I teach you? I say

Up, you say *Down.* That's easy: *Long* and *short. Acid* and *alkaline, poison* and *antidote,* those are simple antonyms. Got it?"

"I think so."

"I say Sons, you say Daughters. Though you could argue that they are complementary rather than polar opposites, huh? A bit like cats and dogs. Get the idea?"

Paul nodded, stamping his feet on the icy ground.

"Right, up to the next level. I say *Art,* you say *Entertainment* — ah, that's more interesting. Not art and ignorance, nor art and science. The opposite of art is the unserious, the trivial. Art is the difference between the essence and the inessential. Therefore, the opposite of art is ephemeral diversion. The object of the game is to challenge and explain these relations. Got the idea?"

"Getting there," said Paul.

"You try one."

"Black and grey," said Paul.

"Oh, that's good, that's very good." The doctor beamed. "White can't be the opposite of black because they both represent absence of colour. Both are nothingness. Black and grey, however, is the choice between an extreme and a compromise. Excellent, for a novice. Have another go."

"Tall and stooped."

"Nice. Why did you choose *stooped?* Let me work it out. Being short is not the opposite of being tall. They are unconnected states of being, one unimaginable to the other. A tall person cannot think what it is like to be short. But being stooped — that's tall brought low and therefore its opposite. I see you've got it. Let's go up another level."

Pulling up his overcoat collar, Paul fished for a philosophical polarity.

"Relative good and absolute evil."

"Oh, I knew you'd be good at this!" exclaimed the doctor, dancing a little jig of delight. "I see how your mind works. There is no such thing as perfect goodness — that's a tautology. Something is either good or it is not, full stop. Equally, there is no relative evil, only total and irredeemable evil, right? So relative good becomes the opposite of absolute evil. Splendid. Have you read Spinoza, my friend? I saw them burn his books in the city, outside the Café Imperial."

Paul pushed open the door to the inn and was thrust back by the heat and noise.

"Play this game on the last journey with my coffin," said the doctor, gripping him by the arm. "It will remind them of me, bring a fond smile to their lips, or maybe just a sigh of tolerance."

"Any particular riddle you'd like me to ask?" said Paul.

"What's the opposite of love?" said the doctor.

"Do you want me to try and answer that, here and now?"

"Have a go."

"Hate, most people would say."

"They would be wrong. Hate is a particle of love, bred of the same impulse."

"What, then? Lust? Indifference? Disloyalty?"

"All good suggestions," said the doctor, "but not the right one."

"What, then?"

"Keep trying. . . ."

"Abandonment."

The doctor gave Paul a searching look, causing sweat to sprout inside his collar. This man saw right through him, and so did his clever daughter. They knew that Paul was neither as resolute nor as capable as he pretended. In their eyes, he was maimed by guilt, easily manipulated by those with a stronger will. What was he going to do?

"Have another go," insisted the doctor. "What's the opposite of love?"

"I give up." Paul shrugged, shoulder to the door.

"The opposite of love," said the doctor, "is death."

CHAPTER TEN

He was taking Johann to his first riding lesson on the cart horse in the paddock when the mail van drove up with the documents he had been waiting for. Paul ripped open a square brown envelope smeared with official stamps and scanned the opening words of each paragraph like a child who scrapes chocolate topping off a fresh-baked cake. The pleasure was intense. Everything had been approved; every single design had met official specifications and earned a go-ahead from the three grey mice. Funding would be finalised following the imminent elections. The decision had all-party approval. Whatever the outcome of the voting, whoever formed the next government, and whoever became village mayor, Paul had permission to build a new town, a commission most architects would kill for.

The ramifications were so huge that he was left breathless and had to call out to the boy to stop running ahead while he assembled pieces of the vision in his throbbing head. Schmidt's field would be requisitioned and paved over as a central bus station, operating a local service every ten minutes and a twice-daily shuttle to the railway. The town hall would be repainted, an extension built to the police station to accommodate extra officers and a pair of lockup cells. There would be waste collection twice weekly, street lighting every thirty paces. A proper town.

Those were preliminaries. The second phase involved a cottage hospital behind Dr. Walters's clinic, a retirement home where the disused tannery now stood, but these could wait until he had finished the one project that validated all others — a brand-new school, staffed by hand-picked teachers who would introduce Johann to the plain truth about the world he would inherit, free of political modification and parental interference, scientifically proven and historically attested to the highest standard.

This, heedless of need, was Paul's driving mission. Two of the three grey mice had argued that both villages had adequate schools for eight classes of farm children, most of whom left to work at fourteen. A purpose-built school could follow as and when state finances permitted. Paul responded with a piece of high oratory, arguing that nowhere was it more vital to fight myths with modernity than in the heart of the rock-hard mountains, the source of the nation's darkest superstitions. His new school would be a beacon of enlightenment. The old fairy tales would have to go. The curriculum would be rewritten top to bottom. The buildings, rotted with pernicious lies, could be utilised as welfare centres until he was free to attend to their demolition. His new academy, free of tendentious associations, would be filled with natural light and intellectual freedom, a centre of inspiration, whose impact would flow far beyond the secluded region, into the national bloodstream.

One of the mice broke into involuntary applause and the other two covered their contentment with a shuffling of papers. Back home, Paul told Alice that the school was, for him, a sine qua non. He would not contemplate exposing Johann to the malign influence of unregenerate nostalgists. And perverts, she added. Quite right, said Paul, writing out an advertisement seeking teaching graduates with two foreign languages and a good knowledge of art.

Privately, in the black window, he admitted a second sine qua non. Unless he could be sure that his son was taught well, he could not stay. The school would be his purifying force, his cleansing of the past, his riposte to Lisl, demonstrating the benefits that he could bring to dark corners. Its success would allow him to stare into the black window one last time and attest that his work was good, and done.

Paul knew where he would build the school before he was aware of making a decision. Several scrubby fields had been proposed, but his mind was on two locations. Ruling out the camp site at the top of the hill because it was in the thick of a forest and kids could get lost or attacked by wolves, he settled on the land around the quarry for its proximity to water from the river and slate from the rock. It was just the right size for a school of six to eight hundred students. The half-finished storage depot would convert into an indoor sports centre and swimming pool; and the square into which slaves had dived headlong out of the sky would make a well-buffered infants' playground, buzzing with little fireflies at their games of hopscotch and catch, a protectorate of innocence.

On the school's foundation stone, at a corner where dogs would stop to piss and adolescents to tryst, Paul would hand-carve the names of all the men who died here, chisel on stone, before Johann's eyes, every name echoing with the pitter-patter of future generations. He told nobody of this memorial scheme, but, sitting late at his desk as the owls hooted and his eyes drooped, it gave him the last surge of strength to finish the paperwork and deliver the project in time to the three mice.

And now, with their authorisation in hand, he hopped with glee from one foot to the other until Johann, making him laugh, asked if he needed "to go somewhere." Paul heaved his squealing son off the horse and returned him, all jibbery-jabbery, to his open-armed mother in her kitchen. Sitting Johann at the table for a snack, Paul took Alice aside to share his good news and there, in a storage larder beside the canteen, made love to her upright against a bare brick wall, a reminiscence of their connective passion, a renewal of vows.

Flush-cheeked, he strode down to the village hall to congratulate his overworked team and out again onto the front steps to deliver an election address, drawing a substantial crowd to hear him promise an improved range of public services — kindergartens, care for the elderly, transport, and sanitation — to natives and newcomers alike. The applause was enthusiastic and, as he walked up and down the main street spouting pleasantries and pumping hands, it occurred to Paul that he no longer needed the kitchen knife up his sleeve: The fear had abated.

Election day came and went. As the votes were counted in the council chamber, one pile overtowered all others, and candidates from the national parties, bowing to the inevitable, slunk off before the result was announced. A roar went up as Paul was declared mayor, and Alice kissed him emphatically on the lips. As he wound up his victory speech, the first telegram was delivered: "MACHINA FIT FOR DEUS. STOP. COLLECT SOONEST BEFORE I SELL TO SWISS OR SWEDES." The mayor asked the postal messenger to wait for his reply: "DEUS DESCENDING TOWN THURSDAY. STOP. PREPARE SPEND WEEKEND WITH GODS IN EARTHLY HEAVEN."

Overcoming Alice's demurrals, he bundled her into a taxi and headed off to the capital to sign letters of agreement and create funding phases with the financial authority. While Alice went window-shopping, too shy to enter a grand city emporium without prior invitation, he laid gift-wrapped bottles of schnapps and mounds of cheese before the three mice, hoping they would not be offended (they weren't), and gave a thick roll of sausages to the university librarian, who was interviewing young schoolteachers on his behalf. He spent half an hour at the central cemetery, inspecting the Walters family tomb and rehearsing his sepulchral duties, as befitted the son of a former town registrar.

At the thick of the evening rush hour, he met up outside the railway station with Alice, who had conquered her shyness and was bent double under heavy shopping bags. Giggling, they walked over to the corner kiosk, where Paul presented his wife to Angelo and Jovanka, their guests for the weekend. Jovanka and Alice needed no introduction. Two country girls, flat heels to the ground, they eyed up each other's qualities and liked what they saw. Angelo loaded the coffee machine into a jeep he had "borrowed" from a two-pip major in exchange for a week's free coffee. "Let's go!" cried Angelo, hitting the road without a map. That night, in a country lay-by, the two couples lulled themselves to sleep in the jeep with long swigs of red wine and inconsequential conversation. In the morning,

Angelo sang operatic arias at the wheel as he overtook carts and horses on dwindling upland lanes.

The Laughing Hind was packed when they arrived. Alice had warned Lisl to expect an exceptional event, and the word had gone round the village like influenza. Paul and Alice lifted the coffee machine from the back of the jeep and bore it processionally into the inn. It took Jovanka no more than twenty minutes to set up the machine on the bar top, connect power and water, and set out the tiny cups for the premier libations. A throng of black bonnets surrounded the machine, tutting disapproval. Paul poured each of the ladies a tasting and was so preoccupied with holding their attention that an hour must have passed before he spotted that Angelo was missing.

"Where's the coffee king?" he demanded.

"Outside, I guess," said Jovanka over her shoulder, interrupting a ribald story she was telling Alice and Lisl. "Went for a gulp of fresh air."

"I'll go and find him," shouted Paul.

He did not have far to go. The Italian was standing in the forecourt, his back to the inn, staring up at the sign of the Laughing Hind.

"I can't go through that door," said Angelo.

"It's all right now," said Paul. "It's ours."

"I can't go in," repeated Angelo in a leaden, unarguable tone.

"I see. . . ."

"I can't stay here, either."

"It's all right now," Paul repeated.

"What's all right? The camp on the peak, the quarry down below? What can ever be all right in this charnel house? Why didn't you tell me where you lived?"

"I'm sorry."

"What are you doing here, Leonardo?"

"I told you: Alice took me when I collapsed. I was dying."

"Do you remember the ones who died," said Angelo, pointing at the ground, "who died here, and there, and just over there? What are you doing here?" There were tears in his eyes and a trembling in his voice.

Paul opened his arms, but the Italian stepped back, his palms in front of his chest, refusing to be touched.

"I won't go in there," he repeated, indicating the inn.

"I understand," said Paul.

"Tell my wife I am waiting in the jeep. We will leave right away."

CHAPTER ELEVEN

Obtaining coffee from an alternative source was no easy matter in those disconnected times, and Paul had to take the machine out of service once he had no more beans to grind. His shame and distress at Angelo's reaction had to be kept on ice while he wrote a flurry of letters and booked long-distance telephone calls to listed suppliers. He told Alice, not altogether untruthfully, that their guests had left because Angelo suffered respiratory difficulties at high altitudes. He told Angelo, on parting, that not every choice a man made could be justified to others. "Some are in-ex-cusable," came the emphatic reply as his recalcitrant visitor screamed on two wheels out of the forecourt and down the winding road, never, he swore, to be seen here again.

Before the month was out, Paul found a middleman with a line of Brazilian beans at an acceptable price and the machine went into business with a roar. The bar was full from breakfast to lights-out and Alice's kitchen staff worked double shifts, cooking three-course meals as a prelude to the celebrated coffee, the most talked-about beverage in living memory. Even morose Franz-Josef was stirred enough to mutter that they should serve fine mints with the coffee, just as he had seen done in an officer's mess somewhere in his army days. Paul welcomed the suggestion and was pleased to see that Lisl was looking a mite less drawn. She was going to need her husband's loving support on the day, quite soon, when her father died.

With the inn set to rights, Paul dealt with delayed guilt by telling himself he had been right all along about Angelo. The fellow was pompous, irrational, self-righteous, and inconsistent. He had insulted Paul's hospitality, while behaving no better than Paul himself — staying in the land of oppression and leeching off its people. Paul would have liked to tell Angelo he was a miserable hypocrite, but he owed the fellow a debt of gratitude for his wonderful coffee machine and quite a large sum in foreign currency. He would try to hand it over the next time he passed through the capital.

The coffee crisis resolved, there remained

one last obstacle. Papa Hofmann stormed into the inn one morning, thundering, "Litzi!" Alice was out, taking Johann to the clinic for a check-up, and Franz-Josef was dealing with a beer delivery at the back, which left Lisl to take the brunt of Papa's rage and blunt it by measure of her physical slightness and the social virtue of being the doctor's daughter. "Tell those racketeers," roared Papa, "that their foul coffee is taking away my best customers at the Horse. If this continues, we will cut beer prices by thirty percent."

"That would be war!" exclaimed Alice when Lisl passed on the ultimatum.

"Civil war," confirmed Paul. "It will set the two villages against each other, just before the minister arrives to perform the act of unification. The timing could not be worse. Have these people no sense of proportion? I'd better go over and pacify them."

He cycled across that evening, carrying in his handle basket a dish of pig's trotters, which Alice assured him would melt Papa's heart, and a kaleidoscopic silk scarf that he had been saving up for Lisl's birthday but which might put the former Zumsteig in a negotiable frame of mind. Paul had no gripe with this capable widow who had lost both husband and son on the Eastern Front and was applying herself with commendable diligence to rescuing Papa Hofmann from alcoholic suicide. Alice refused to acknowledge the woman as a family member. She would not let Johann call her "Grandma," and she resisted any cooperation between the two inns that did not bring superior advantage to the Laughing Hind. It was her resentful hostility that had fanned the flames of this unnecessary dispute.

Paul enjoyed his trips to Pringsheim, a place of no bad memories. Prisoners never set foot on that side of the valley, and its residents were excluded from their vengeance fantasies. He had an idea for developing on its slope one of those elite spas that attracted rich hypochondriacs in towelling gowns who were more concerned with being seen amongst their own class than with the efficacy of any proffered remedy — the kind of clientele who believed in magic mountains so long as they provided central heating. Pringsheim had the air quality for a health resort and its waters were not too brackish. Those plans, though, were far into the future. In the short term, he would promote it in the press as a stopover for summer ramblers, a spot for eagle watchers to rest their binoculars and for mycologists to find many varieties of Pilz mushrooms, including the Autumn Trumpet, the Parasol, and the splendidly named Flockenstiegler Hexenröhrling.

Intent on his plans, Paul skirted a construction barrier at the Black Horse's perimeter and, wobbling across a temporary bridge over a drainage duct in the yard, parked his bicycle outside the very room where Wierzbicki had given him the name to live a second life and the will to live it well. Greeted with chill formality by the landlord pair, he took less than ten minutes to end the coffee war, ten minutes and a large glass of red wine that he persuaded the former Zumsteig to let Hofmann quaff with his pig trotters and potatoes. To the echo of satisfied exhalations, Paul pledged that he would never permit unfair competition between the inns. He was scouring the world for an even better coffee machine for the Black Horse and, until he found one, was going to offer free coffees at the Laughing Hind to Black Horse patrons who produced recent meal receipts. Was that fair?

"Very fair indeed," spluttered Papa. "Splendid idea."

"What's it going to cost?" asked his wife.

"Nothing. We'll make money on it," said Paul. "The offer will not include dessert mints, which they will find painfully irresistible."

"Wonderful," murmured Papa. "My Alice makes such wonderful trotters."

"And what am I, an English fishwife?" cried the former Zumsteig.

"You, my Tilde, braise the tenderest venison. In our two houses, we have cooks fit for a king. Superb food, good drink, and strong coffee — what more could a man want?"

"We'll take on extra kitchen hands," enthused Paul. "There are young mothers and war widows who are looking for work. I might put in a government grant to start a catering school here, in your kitchen — it is certainly big enough."

"My Mathilde, a professor!" exclaimed Hofmann, exultant with the first alcohol to course through his veins in months. "She's bossy enough, that's for sure." He rose and excused himself for what Paul guessed was a raid on the schnapps shelf. When he was out of the room, Mathilde whispered something about a recurrence of bladder troubles.

It seemed a good moment to get close to the cuckoo, as Alice called her. Paul asked where she was born. Mathilde, charmed by his interest, told of growing up on the northern seaboard, dreaming of joining the ballet corps in *Swan Lake.*

"Have you seen the famous state ballet?" asked Paul.

"Never," said Mathilde, shaking a tight bun of grey-streaked hair.

"I will get tickets for your birthday," promised Paul. A grateful mist veiled her eyes and she pressed his hand with a gesture that signified alliance, one cuckoo to another. Paul was glad to have won her over so cheaply. Everything was going his way.

Beyond the peninsular lobe of Mathilde's left ear, his eye was drawn to an early diner, the first of the evening rush, his close-cropped steel grey head bobbing up and down over his soup until the bowl, tipped towards him, was slurped of its last spoonful and he was ready for meat. So close was the man's head to the bowl that Paul could not make out his features, but something in the way he ate struck him as odd or familiar, as if he had seen the same gestures acted out in another context, maybe on a cinema screen. He tried to avoid staring, but his eye kept straying back. As the main course arrived, the man raised his water glass and removed it to the far side of the table to make room for unhindered demolition. Forking a slab of flesh to the bottom of the plate, he sliced and severed, lengthways and across with his knife, covering the entire surface of the steak before the fork raised a morsel to bared brown teeth, then another, and another. His hands and mouth were a factory line, delivering materials to the assembly point and despatching them in an unstoppable mechanism. Paul wondered what would happen if a waiter removed the plate before the process was completed: would the hand continue to dip and rise, the mouth to open and chomp? Paul, hypnotised by inexorable motion, heard Mathilde reminiscing across the table, but his eyes could not budge from man and deed, their familiarity deepening and darkening.

The beard, that was it. The customer was, even by country norms, unkempt. He had not bothered to change clothes or wash up before sitting down to eat. His jacket was torn at the shoulder, his boots, beneath the table, were cracked, and his shirt was an indeterminate shade of dirty. This was a man who had let himself go. The way he held his upper body was a deterrent to human interaction. Back off, it said; I fend for myself. The one concession he made to politeness was his beard, which, a whole shade darker than the stubble on his head,

was trimmed around his mouth and jaw-
bone, neither straggled nor patchy but
covering every scrap of face below the
cheekbones. To look like that, a beard had
to be groomed in a mirror. This was the one
part of the man that was cared for, and it
stood out so incongruously from the rest
that it had to be a mask of sorts, a camouflage.

A reel of film clicked in Paul's head. He
saw on a parallel screen a man in a tin cabin
dissect his noon meal before the eyes of a
starving slave, consuming every last scrap,
smiling as he mopped up traces of gravy to
leave the dish shining white, like a desert
carcass after the vultures had been. The image was indelible, the parallel ineluctable.

This does not have to be what I think it
is, thought Paul, his heart pounding as Stub
Head swept his plate with bread and burped
on completion. It could be someone else altogether: another gustatory obsessive, a
brother, a cousin, a casual bastard. The
man's behaviour pattern indicated, according to a Freudian paper he had once read,
the after-effects of force-feeding in infancy.
A mother stood at this man-child's high
chair in the film, cajoling, enjoining, and
finally ramming food into its mouth until
every last speck disappeared; and there, on

an adjacent screen, appeared Paul's own sweet mother, spooning an egg mixture past the iron grille of his milk teeth, gulling him to open wide by ruses as old as motherhood itself — "One for Mama, one for Papa." Horrified, he tore his gaze away from Stub Head, fearing to put a name to enraged suspicion.

"Do you know that fellow back there?" he asked Mathilde Zumsteig, tamping down bile and panic at the base of his gullet.

"Him?" said Mathilde with a till keeper's derision for lone diners. "Comes in twice a week. Can't put a name to him. My husband might know. He's from your side of the gorge, they say. Never a word of thanks, and smells to high heaven. Come to mention it, where has he got to, that husband of mine?"

They found Hofmann in the kitchen, more flushed than before, pouring brandy over a fruit trifle. "We must celebrate our joint plan," he explained.

"Not you," scolded his wife, "you know what Dr. Walters said."

"Ya-ya," said Hofmann meekly. "I will nibble a biscuit while you enjoy my special trifle with our partner in crime." He never referred to Paul by name, or in any tone other than sardonic. Paul, by the same measure, had no mode of address for his wife's father, except "Opa" in the third person when Johann was present. The two men tiptoed around each other like rival thieves in a bank, avoiding recognition and complicity. Both had wartime cause for reticence. "How's your bladder?" queried Mathilde.

"Fine, fine," grunted Hofmann.

"Stick to your diet and it might stay that way."

Back in the dining room, the lone diner was gone. Pleading a late meeting, Paul left his dessert half-eaten and cycled home through low clouds, letting himself in through the back door and going straight up to bed without a good night to Alice, passing out as if slugged by a metal bar. The next time he crossed the valley, the kitchen knife was back up his sleeve. He was dressed in his wedding suit to welcome the minister of the interior to the unification ceremony. As the minister spoke, he scanned the crowd for a bearded face and saw nothing but a blur. He was not quite sure. He needed to be sure.

Confirmation came, as it so often does, when least expected. He was fetching Johann from a Sunday with the grandparents when, pulling out of the Black Horse yard in streaking rain, Paul clipped his bicycle basket against a short man in a greatcoat, arriving head bowed for his evening meal.

"Oops," bleeped Paul, preparing to apologise.

"Oops," mimicked Johann from his pillion seat.

"Watch where you're going, you bloody nuisance," snarled two wide lips from within the hedge of a beard, and Paul knew beyond doubt that his nemesis had returned. Head down over the handlebars, he swivelled round the man and wobbled down the slope as Johann giggled, thinking his father was playing a prank. Stability returned at the foot of the gorge and he began the slow pedal rhythm of the ascent home to the drumbeat of a leaden noise in his head. Hans, it went. Hans, hans, hans, hans, hans.

There was no more sleep to be had, that night or after. The skin on his face in the window drew tight and the flesh fell away from his ribcage. Alice asked if he was all right, and the doctor, passing by to see his grandchildren, ordered him in a tone that brooked no contradiction to drop by in the morning for a check-up.

"I'm fine," said Paul irritably.

"I shall be the judge of that," said Dr. Walters. "Nine o'clock tomorrow."

Stripped to the waist and tapped with a stethoscope, reduced to infantile responses by the physician's questions about coughs, pains, and bowel movements, he prepared to refuse further inspection if the doctor demanded that he drop his pants, having been well trained by a prudent Johanna to conceal his circumcised penis from prying eyes.

"You can get dressed now," said Walters, turning to the sink to wash his hands. Paul asked him what he had found.

"You are run-down," said the doctor, scribbling in his file. "I shall mix you a tonic, but I can't do much for the underlying condition unless you tell me what it's about."

Paul shrugged.

"I insist that you let me help you," said the doctor with some vehemence. "I have no wish to intrude on private matters, but I need to know that you will be fit and well on that day, not far off, when you will be called upon to perform a final act of kindness on my behalf. I am a member of the Hippocratic brotherhood, Paul. Nothing you say will shock or surprise me and no word will go beyond this room. You must give me symptoms so I can make a diagnosis. Is it an internal pain? Is it a crisis of self-esteem? A problem in your marriage, your, ahem, connubial relations?"

"None of those," said Paul firmly.

"What, then?"

"Unfinished business," mumbled Paul.

"The recent past?"

Paul nodded.

"An apparition? A nagging guilt?"

Paul gave two more nods.

"This is not a game, you know," said the doctor. "I am not going to run out of twenty questions and award you the prize for obtuseness. Come along, now. Be a man and out with it. What is troubling you?"

Paul mumbled alliterative words: *camp . . . commandant . . . come back.*

"Someone you've seen?"

Paul nodded.

"Hmm," said the doctor, tapping a pencil. "Sooner or later, it was bound to happen. It might as well be now, while you still have me around to help. Tell me: is it one man, or more?"

Paul nodded, just the once.

"Do I know him?"

Paul shrugged.

"If it's one man, you have nothing to fear. The whole village loves you and will look out for your safety. Only a lunatic would attempt an assault on you in daylight, and I am guessing that the man is not deranged? Good."

Paul swept a handkerchief across his brow.

"In that case, what we need to attend to is a phobia. I am going to send you to a colleague of mine, a consultant in the capital, a man of remarkable human insight and healing powers, not to mention good humour and extensive experience."

"A psychoanalyst?" said Paul.

"A genius, in his way."

"I can't see how talking about my infantile sexual development will help me deal with a war criminal on my doorstep."

Walters gave a sly, subversive smile. "You will find that Dr. Kovacs is not one of those doctrinaire therapists who do everything by the book. He does not believe, for instance, that every temperamental malfunction arises from frustrated genital urges. He broke away over that principle from his teacher, Sándor Ferenczi, and attached himself in Zurich to Professor Jung, who, as you know, argued that it is the inferiority complex which drives us to seize power and abuse it. Afterwards, he broke with Jung as well, accusing him of ignoring environmental causes in mental illness, the extent to which physical surroundings can provoke depression — the absence of light, greenery, beauty, and so on. He was attacked for that by Freudians and Jungians alike. When colleagues stopped sending him patients and he had nothing to eat, he went to work as a nurse in a mental asylum on the outskirts of Vienna, a place at the end of the longest bus line, where they kept cases who were likely to cause embarrassment. He found himself among survivors of the Turkish massacre in Smyrna, which officially never took place. The people under his care had been violated in body, stripped of their patrimony, and deprived of the right to memory. . . ."

"He sounds interesting," said Paul after a lengthy pause.

"The work he did with those patients and the study he wrote about their rehabilitation is world-famous. He's an old man now, semi-retired, but I'll see if I can get him, as a personal favour, to give you an appointment."

"What if I cannot talk to him?"

"Dr. Kovacs is a patient man."

"But what if I can't?"

"Then Dr. Kovacs will analyse your silences."

Kovacs, a quizzical gnome in pince-nez that he polished on a polka-dot silk handkerchief, said nothing for ten ticking minutes on the mantel clock. It was Paul, sunk in a high-backed armchair, who broke the impasse, remarking on the ugliness of the consultant's apartment, a corridor of matchbox rooms in a pre-fabricated block on the edge of the city centre.

"Ironic, isn't it?" chuckled Kovacs. "Once upon a time, I had the white coat ripped off my back by jealous colleagues for daring to suggest that bad buildings make people sick, and here I am practising medicine in an asbestos-walled excrescence that contravenes every principle of healthy habitation. Clever of you to spot that."

"I am, among other things, an architect," said Paul.

"How interesting. Is that the condition you came to talk to me about?"

Paul gave an involuntary laugh, his first since the rainy collision had plunged him into hell. He surveyed the room's furnishings with a lip curled in scorn: a bulky table from the late Biedermeier period surrounded by modern Bauhaus chairs on a rug of Balkan provenance that looked in need of a good beating. "The table belonged to my parents," said Kovacs, following his eyes around.

"Mine had a similar monster in the living room," said Paul.

"Antique or reproduction?"

"Who could afford antiques?" snorted Paul, drawn into describing the thick-legged table, the overstuffed sofa, the stifling warmth. "How many rooms in your parents' apartment?" queried Kovacs, and the floodgates of memory burst open.

It took three sessions on consecutive days — the doctor cancelling other patients and Paul cabling Alice that he was detained on official business — for a full account to come tumbling forth, from the morning he was knocked off his bike in the week before war to the collision with Hans in the courtyard of the Black Horse. Kovacs stopped him now and then for a tangential detail — the colour of Ewa's eyebrows (forest black), the exact distance in metres from camp to quarry (864), the payroll for his proposed school ($250,000 in the first year, $300,000 in the second) — beaming like a teacher when his star pupil gives a correct answer to the visiting inspectors. He seemed less concerned with emotion than with fact, taxing his patient with supplementary questions to establish consistency. "Just tell me how it was," he enjoined. "I can work out for myself how it felt."

"How can you know?" said Paul, enraged at the presumption.

"I am," murmured Kovacs, "no stranger to inhumanity. Apart from my asylum experience, they treated me to a full week of hospitality in Dachau, before my Hungarian passport came through."

"I see," said Paul.

"No more than I do." The therapist smiled.

Midway through the third session, he pronounced a significant improvement and told Paul that he was over the immediate crisis. He should go home and arrange to return in a fortnight. The brass plate at the entrance announced that patients were seen twice weekly, Tuesdays and Wednesdays, between one-thirty and five in the afternoon.

"But the problem hasn't gone away," Paul protested.

"What problem is that?"

"The devil on my doorstep."

"If that's a physical problem, it's nothing to do with me."

"It's the fear of him."

"The fellow you call Hans?"

"That's right."

"Well, what do you think *you* should do?" asked the Hungarian, his pungent accent curving upwards in an interrogative inflexion.

"I don't know," said Paul. "I must do something."

"Must you?"

"I can't carry on like this. Knowing he is nearby, breathing the same air, lurking around a corner, is like having a growth in the skull, pressing on the brain. It paralyses the functions, one by one, until you become a helpless object."

"That's very good," said the therapist. "With metaphors like that you could have joined my profession — which, I forgot, you almost did."

"To no useful purpose."

"On the contrary: All learning is useful. Your readings in psychology will lead you to an objective understanding of your situation. Unlike many survivors, you are not frozen like a rabbit in searchlights. So long as you have this awareness, you will not feel powerless."

"So what do you expect me to do, Doctor?"

"That's for you to decide."

"As I see it, there are three possibilities."

"Namely?"

"One, I kill Hans. Two, I run away. Or three, I do nothing and end up killing myself."

"There may be other ways," said Kovacs

softly, "but let's regard yours as the organic remedies, for you might say they are drawn from nature."

"What do you mean by that?"

"What choices does an animal have when it faces a predator?"

"I don't know. Never thought about it."

"Well, living in the country as you do, you should take a walk with my friend Walters and observe the cycle of life. A rabbit, for instance, seeing a fox, has three choices: fight, flight, or hide. Agree?"

"I guess."

The therapist creaked up from his armchair to pour himself a glass of water that he did not really need, savouring the woodland metaphor. As a third-year medical student, smitten by a charismatic professor who was later exposed as a fraud, he had switched his registration to the faculty of zoology until his father, a socially ambitious tailor, threatened to cut off his allowance unless he finished medicine. Later, hounded from his practice, he found solace in the Vienna Woods between one victim's rape and the next man's unspeakable torture, each stroll a refuge and a reference point for healing. Now nearing the end of his therapeutic practice, Kovacs amused himself with analogies drawn from birdsong and the mating rituals of small mammals.

"We," he surmised with an inclusive wave at Paul, "ignore nature at our peril. For the animal under threat, there are three choices: fight, flight, or hide. The first two give the embattled creature some say in the outcome. The third is inertia, all motion suspended until hunger drives the animal into the open, to eat or be eaten.

"The human choices are not dissimilar; you have just described them. One, fight — we risk all in attack. Two, flight — we retreat, yielding ground, plotting a comeback. Three, hide — we enter a state of suspended animation, hoping the danger will pass. The first two are positive actions. The third is called depression. I do not recommend it. If those are your options, let me suggest that you choose a or b. Come back in a fortnight and let me know what you have decided."

Paul burrowed into his chair. There was thunder in the air, and his skin crawled as if with vermin. He had a train to catch. He tried to rise, but his legs were floppy. "I don't understand," he bleated, playing for time.

"Are you unclear about the choice between a and b?"

"I understand the choice. It's you I can't

figure out."

"How so?"

"You're a shrink. You're meant to listen, not tell me what to do. That's unprofessional."

"For Freud, perhaps. For Jung, anathema. For Kovacs, quite normal."

"I'm not sure I'm comfortable with your method."

"Surely," said the old therapist, "you have worked out by now that Imre Kovacs doesn't follow anybody's method, even, at times, his own. Wolfgang Walters knew that when he sent you to me. Life is too short to let patients waste my time and their money finding a cure by talking without direction, which was Freud's device. I am a doctor; I prescribe. You decide whether to take the medicine, or to go out and get a second, more orthodox opinion. You have identified remedies; now, you have a decision to make."

Paul shook his head, ridding it of cobwebs. He was not sure if Kovacs was charlatan or wizard, but his apathy had lifted and he was prepared to give him a try. There was just one residual doubt.

"Dr. Kovacs?"

"That's the name on the door."

"Are you telling me, Doctor, that if I

decide to kill this man, you will give me therapeutic permission to go ahead?"

"Let's not hypothesise, Paul, or you will miss your train. I want you to choose between fight and flight, that's all. We'll take it from there next time."

"But if I killed him, you'd be an accessory to murder?"

Kovacs, with the patience of an old eagle on a mile-high crag, walked him through an empty vestibule to the apartment door. "You, Paul, are my patient," he explained. "My concern is your recovery. We have reached a point in the treatment where you will bring me a decision and we will discuss it. Whatever you decide, you can be sure that I am on your side, and will be for as long as you need me."

"But . . ."

"Hypothesis is the brother of hypocrisy. Neither takes responsibility for an idea. Kovacs, you will learn, does. Now mind how you go on those broken pavements."

Recharged, Paul raced to the station and arrived in the nick of time for his train, only to find that the timetable had changed and he had an hour to kill. Buoyed with confidence, he marched over to the coffee kiosk and shouted, "Angelo!"

The Italian appeared at his window.

"Come out here," called Paul. "We need to talk."

"I have nothing to say," said Angelo, wiping wet hands on the front of his coat, then shuffling hastily out of customer earshot.

"I have cash for you."

"I don't want it."

"And I have something to tell you."

"Make it quick. I have customers waiting."

"He's back!"

"Who's back?"

"Hans, who else?"

"My God . . ." A train whistled hoarsely in departure.

"So that's . . . why you stayed," said Angelo. "You waited for him all this time, waiting until he came back like a dog to its vomit, waiting to deliver justice."

Paul said nothing, allowing his friend to spin a vengeance fantasy, elaborating all the vile and excruciating things that he would like to see done to the monster before he was allowed to die. "Patience," said Paul, "patience, my friend," and Angelo began to weep, large storm-cloud tears that plopped to the ground without touching his cheeks.

"I am so sorry," he sobbed. "I cursed your name, Leonardo, and told Jovanka you are a despicable traitor for staying there, that we must never see you again. I should have known that you are a deep one, Leonardo. You do not show your hand. You wait like a bandit, and when the moment is right, you strike. How could I have doubted you? Can you ever forgive me, Leonardo? Jovanka, she wanted many times to write to your dear wife . . . but I forbade her. Please, tell me what I can do to earn your pardon. . . ."

"Two things," said Paul equably.

"Anything you ask, *mio caro*."

"I want you to promise that you will come straightaway if I call. To help me deal with Hans."

"Day or night, I drop everything and come."

"And I need another coffee machine. It's for my second hotel."

On the train home, Paul drew a line down the back of a used brown envelope. In the left-hand column he listed seven ways of carrying out a silent killing on a dark country night. Easily done. The snag was getting rid of the body. Burial was insecure; foxes would dig up fresh corpses. Dismemberment was untenable. A fire would attract attention. Frustrated, he turned to the right — the escape option.

Having killed Hans, or perhaps without

killing him at all, he would flee somewhere beyond trace, somewhere on the right of the envelope. He could slip across two borders to the town of his birth, where they might welcome him as a former resistance icon. He could seek out that distant cousin on the far Canadian coast, or join Captain Wierzbicki in the wide-open American flatlands. He could sail to the survivor state at the edge of the Mediterranean, where, on a Sabbath promenade, he might see a man or woman who bore a heart-stopping resemblance to Ewa or Johanna and turned out to be a relative, a brand plucked from the burning. He, like them, could be — what was the pulpit phrase? — gathered unto his forefathers in an eternity of rest.

In short, there were any number of places he could go and enough money in his safe to pay for his passage and a new identity. The trouble was, none of the destinations was inviting. His mother country was yoked to an oppressive ideology; life in North America was, from what he had read of it, too frank and confrontational for his retiring nature; and as for the sunny survivor state, it seemed to be perpetually at war with its neighbours. Paul could not face another war on his doorstep.

Anyway, if he did not commit murder,

there was more to keep him here than to make him flee. There was Johann. What would become of him without Paul to guide him to manhood? Alice was a magnificent mother, intuitive and loving, yet alert to the boy's shortcomings, but she might make an unsuitable remarriage after Paul was gone. Johann could be corrupted, brutalised, made into another Hans. Paul had to stay on, come what may. He could not abandon his child.

Striking a line through the right-hand column, he turned back to the left. There was no fail-safe way of killing Hans and getting away with it; therefore, why bother? He had survived the camp by refusing to kill; must he now forsake his principle just to have the comfort of knowing that Hans no longer existed? He could ask Angelo to do the job, of course, but that would be evasive. Hans was his to kill, or not to kill, and in the cold light of reason, the killing of Hans seemed less and less necessary.

That left him one last option: lying low, doing nothing, waiting for Hans to wilt or die. Hiding, Kovacs had said, was a passive act, courting depression. *Deep-pression,* the therapist had pronounced it, a sinking into the void. Paul could not face more darkness than he already saw. What, then? Nothing he had discussed with Kovacs seemed to work. Everything was hopeless, pointless, insoluble — or was it? Something had shifted. The act of acknowledging that he could do nothing about Hans left Paul feeling neither impotent nor defeated but liberated, relieved of the responsibility to act. Freedom shuddered through his frame. He crumpled the envelope into his pocket and turned with relish to the pack of novels that he had bought at a station stall as a gift for Wolfgang Walters, by way of thanks.

He reached home late, long after the inn was locked up. Tiptoeing into the kitchen, he munched an apple from the larder and mounted the stairs, tapping his spare hand blindly up the banister, his eyes half-shut in anticipation of a good night's sleep. Two rungs from the top, he touched a shock of human hair and the back of a cold hand. Startled, he peered into the night-light and saw Lisl's spare frame in a dressing gown two sizes too large, hunched over a newish book by Hermann Hesse.

"What are you reading?" he said automatically.

"*The Glass Bead Game.*"

"Any good?"

"Haven't decided yet."

He had avoided the girl since Christmas,

fearful of destabilising the household. When their hands touched along the bar or, as they did now on the banister, an electric charge ran up his fingers and his heart heaved with excitement. He could not deny his desire for this girl with the dancing eyes, but he was doing his best to subdue it, in the hope that it would die of inattention. He had taken the third option. He was hiding from Lisl, and it seemed to be working.

"Is Alice asleep?" he enquired before Lisl could initiate anything.

"She asked me to wait up for you."

"That was kind of her."

"Have you eaten? Alice said I should make sure you'd had something to eat."

"Thank you, yes."

She was not making it easy for him, the girl. Heavy as he was with travel fatigue, he was susceptible to her touch, afire with the smell of her skin. If she kissed him now, he might not have the strength to resist.

"Alice is not why I waited up," said Lisl softly, looking him square in the eye.

"I was wondering . . ."

"It's my father," she said. "He said to make sure I caught you. He needs you to go and see him tonight. No matter how late, he said."

"I see," said Paul, concerned for the doctor, who must have taken a turn for the worse.

"Shall I come along?" asked Lisl, slipping her small hand into his.

"Better not," said Paul. "It will be a confidential matter, between him and me."

"I see," she said, echoing his phrase.

"I will ask him to tell you himself, if he wants to."

"Good, so will I."

And with that, without so much as a good-night peck, Lisl climbed the stairs, leaving Paul to stumble back down, put on his shoes, and drag himself up the wet slope to the doctor's house, fearing the worst as he went. The door was flung open before he could knock and Walters greeted him, a flute of pale champagne in his hand. "Why didn't you tell me?" he demanded as soon as they were shut behind his soundproofed surgery door.

"Tell you what?"

"That Hannes Kerner is back."

"I assumed people knew."

"How would they? He cannot set foot this side of the valley. Not after the scandal with the two scouts he is supposed to have buggered and the way he lorded it over the village when his pals were in power. He was a menace, a misanthrope, despised by one and all. People would cross the road at the sight of him and cross themselves when he was out of sight. Everyone was happy when he went to work in that camp and had no more time for pestering us in the village with his political conformities."

"Your loss, our gain," said Paul sourly.

"You could say that."

"How well did you know him?"

"Enough to be arrested on his orders. My wife, too."

"On what grounds?"

"Sedition. Promoting defeatism. Refusing to sing the blood-spurt song. Who cares?"

"I'm sorry," said Paul in his softest voice. "I wasn't aware."

"Nothing to be aware of. We got off lightly. A patient of mine with gout, a police commander, let us out before the secret police arrived to start the beatings. Said the paperwork was faulty, so he let us off with a warning."

"How did you know Hans was back?"

"I had a call a few hours ago from Kovacs. He wants me to keep an eye on you, to make sure you do nothing rash until you have seen him again. Paul, are you sure this is Kerner?"

"How could I be wrong?" cried Paul. "With my own eyes I saw him kill men, standing no farther away from me than you are now."

"In that case," said Walters, "we had better deal with him."

"What do you mean?"

The doctor raised the lid of a large icebox where he kept perishable medicines and a permanent bottle of champagne. He extracted a long glass syringe, loaded to the brim.

"This is the one I've been keeping for myself," he said, waving the instrument in the air. "Take it. I can mix another solution for myself."

"What am I supposed to do with it?" asked Paul.

"Find Kerner, take him somewhere quiet, and stab this into his arm, leg, anywhere. Put a hand over his mouth. He will croak within a minute."

"What then?"

"You walk away. When the gendarmes find the body, they will bring it to me and I will certify cause of death as a coronary attack. Quick burial, no family, end of story."

Paul could not assimilate the things he was hearing. For the second time in a day, a medical man, sworn to do no harm, was inciting him to kill. First Kovacs, now Walters — only Walters had gone further by providing the means and offering to organise the cover-up. Paul could assassinate Hans and get away with it. No-one need ever know.

Fearing that he had misheard, he asked Walters to repeat himself. "Get rid of him," said the doctor. "Kill him."

"How can you, of all people, tell me to do that?"

"Sometimes a doctor has to eliminate a life when it endangers another's. I abort a foetus that puts the mother at risk. I help the mortally ill to die when all that remains is agony for them and those round them. We are called upon from time to time to make judgements, for the good of the individual and the community. It is our job."

"Hans is not a dying man," Paul objected.

"He is a pestilence, a plague carrier, a danger to society. He has forfeited the right to live by the murders he committed. The Bible says that he who kills shall surely be put to death. Kerner killed many times. We have the right to kill him before he strikes again. I would do it myself, given the strength and the opportunity."

"That's outrageous," said Paul. "You have a grievance against Kerner for arresting you and terrifying your wife. You might like to see him dead, but you cannot act at once as

351

prosecutor, judge, and executioner. You must be drunk to suggest such a thing."

"Look at me," said Walters, stretching out a tremor-free hand. "Is this the hand of a drunk? I have hardly the liver function left to sniff a bottle of champagne without passing out. I like to watch the bubbles in the glass, a souvenir of better days. Shall I tell you why I am convinced that this man must die?"

"I think you had better."

"In a short time, Paul, I shall account to my Maker for my earthly deeds, the lives I saved and the ones I failed to. Many a time, an extra effort on my part, a quicker tumble out of a warm bed on a snowy night, might have made a difference. I have things on my conscience and I shall confess them when asked, the ones I can remember without my wife at my side as a prompt. Am I rambling, Paul? Indulge me, please.

"Where was I? Ah, yes, the recording angel. My guess is that the scales will be fairly evenly balanced for me, as they are for most people. I've done some good, some bad. I tried to be a good doctor, a good husband, a good father. There were times I failed. You don't need to know more.

"So when I come up for judgement before the seat of glory, it could go one way or the other, if you believe in the whole metaphorical courtroom setup, which I am not sure I do, at least not in the literal sense the church teaches. In any event, if in such a Dante scenario the difference for me between an eternity in hell or a seat in heaven hangs upon this one act of helping you to kill Hannes Kerner, I would go to hell with a song on my lips, knowing that it was the right thing to do. Heaven can wait for me. This man took lives, tortured innocent people, brutalised children. He does not deserve to outlive me, and he will continue to haunt you, my friend, so long as he survives. Get rid of him, Paul, for your sake and mine, for the sake of our families, for God's sake. Do it without delay, and we will both feel better for it."

Somewhere in the woods, a wolf let out its lonely cry. Light blazed over the doctor's desk, sparkling off the syringe in his hand.

"Put it away," said Paul, neutralising his voice.

"Take it," the doctor insisted.

"I'm not going to kill Kerner."

"But you must."

"No, I must not," said Paul. "When I told Dr. Kovacs I must do something, he replied, 'Must you?' He was right. I don't have to. This man cannot hurt me anymore. His power is gone, his friends dispersed. So long as he poses no threat, I shall let your friend the recording angel handle his personnel file in due course."

"And if —"

"If he gives me trouble? I shall get the police sergeant to pull him in for drunken conduct, trespass, theft, any number of overnight charges, until he learns to make himself scarce. I am not afraid of him, not anymore. He is a broken reed. So put away that syringe, dear doctor, and pour me another glass of Krug. I came here to ask what you thought of that fashionable Hesse book that I caught in Lisl's hand."

The friends clinked glasses, surveying each other with wary respect. A line had been crossed, and they had ended up on the same side of it. Both had contemplated killing; both had conscientiously abstained. They had joined the same club, were drinking at the same table in an existential boulevard café, a Paris of the mind.

"You saw Lisl tonight?" said the doctor.

Paul nodded.

"She is a good girl, my Lisl, impetuous and strong-headed but fundamentally *good*. Look after her, Paul. Protect her, when I am gone."

"I'll do my best."

"Do you understand what I am saying?"

Paul avoided the doctor's eye, fearing what he might find there.

"Be her friend is what I ask. Nothing more."

"I understand," said Paul, shifting in his seat. "Tell me about Hermann Hesse."

"*Glass Beads*? Too austere, for my taste. Give me a good story, any day. I am reading Hermann Broch's *The Death of Virgil.* Much more cheerful."

CHAPTER TWELVE

The doctor's death was announced by a howling in the hallway. Paul, sipping his breakfast coffee, stepped out to find Lisl huddled in the crook of the bottom step, the telephone receiver swinging pendulum-like from the table. "I'll come right away," he said into the receiver, and, calling for Alice to attend Lisl, who was tearing her cheeks with red fingernails, he grabbed a coat and ran. He raced up the hill, then checked himself to a walk, remembering his panic on the morning of Alice's miscarriage and his solemn role in the coming ceremonies. He had been charged with carrying out the doctor's last wishes and he knew he must do so with decorum.

The door was opened by the widow, who led him to the bedroom, where Walters lay in striped pyjamas, eyes shut, face ashen, the sheet pulled up to his chin and tucked in at the sides, his cultivated moustache arrayed, lifeless, on the coverlet.

"He did not want to be seen in disarray," said the widow.

"You got rid of the syringe?" asked Paul.

"Pounded with a mallet, the fragments buried in a flowerpot, as instructed."

"I'm so sorry. . . ."

"He was ready," said the widow.

Paul planted dry lips on his friend's brow and pulled the sheet over his head. "Leave everything to me."

"I know," said the widow. "He told me you would take care of the . . . arrangements. I have telephoned Lisl; I must tell the others."

"Leave the rest to me," said Paul.

Downstairs, he used the surgery phone to summon the on-call locum. Tobias Strauss, stiff, in rimless spectacles, came up, inspected the body, took its temperature, calculated time of death, and signed the certificate that Walters had thoughtfully prepared in advance. The young physician was new enough to consider each death a personal defeat; Paul remembered the coal miner whom Ewa had failed to save on the operating table. The thought crossed his mind that his affection for Walters might have been conditioned by his love for the doctor he had lost; he dismissed the thought.

The funeral, held early one morning to allow time for the long drive to the city, was brief to the point of perfunctory. "He never liked my preaching, did he?" cackled Father Hitzinger when Paul asked him to desist from obsequies. At the service, the old man took clerical revenge by gabbling the rites and whisking off in his egg-stained cassock before the last amen faded. Everyone in the whole village, old and young, walked in step with the cortège from the church of St. Ignatius down into the bottom of the ravine, where Paul told the driver to pick up speed.

Paul sat in front of the hearse with Alice and the driver. At the back was Lisl, crushed between her black-veiled mother and Franz-Josef's lone protective arm. Paul, his eyes paper-dry, was hearing the priest jabber: *Our beloved brother Hans Wolfgang Walters, who has returned his soul . . .*

Another Hans, then, if the old cassock had got the name right. A good Hans, if there was such a thing. Hans, his friend. What's a name, after all? he thought. No more than a parental whim, a registrar's scrawl. A name is neutral; it does not define character. Hans means nothing. Maybe he was getting over his Hans fixation.

As the car sped down wintry lanes and

onto broad highways, he regretted the things they had left undone, the doctor and he. They had never collected herbs and fungi in the woods, though they talked of it many times; they had never argued about God; never, not once, had they discussed his friend's understanding of the recent horrors. Walters, in their final conversation, had acknowledged Paul as one of the damned who had marched past his door. But he had judiciously avoided direct recognition, whether in protection of Paul's dignity or of his own embarrassment at not having done more — anything at all — to help the oppressed. How could Walters have called himself a friend of a man whose life he had refrained from saving?

Paul put himself in the doctor's place. What would he have done, faced with a victim of his own inaction, his instinct for self-preservation? Would he have confessed his cowardice and sought forgiveness, or pretended at a lack of recognition? What, he asked himself, playing the doctor's mind game, is the opposite of recognition? Amnesia, abstraction, unawareness, misperception, disavowal — no, none of those. The opposite of recognition must be discretion — a trait he first admired in Alice, and one so innate to the poor soul in the coffin behind them that Paul plunged into his pocket for a handkerchief to staunch his sudden gush of loss.

They pulled up, wordless, at the cemetery gates, where a knot of city folk were gathered in dark finery. Medical acquaintances, Paul assumed, erstwhile colleagues who had forsaken Walters in life and were here to see him buried. He spotted a brown hat bobbing at the fringe, unmistakably belonging to Imre Kovacs. An oration might be required.

Outside the family catafalque, Paul addressed the assembly without recourse to the notes in his wallet. "Our dear friend asked that nothing should be said here," he began, "unless the mourners felt it was essential. He hated pleasantries and platitudes, as you know, and was impatient with songs of praise. But what he hated above all else was being bored, and he would not want us to leave him at this place without food for thought on his journey into the everlasting."

The widow gave a little smile. Alice pressed Paul's gloved hand to urge him to get on with it. It was lip-freezing cold and the light was fading.

"On his bedside table," Paul continued, "I found a book, *The Death of Virgil,* by Hermann Broch. It is quite a recent publication and I have not yet read it myself, but it appears to be a novelised account of the philosopher's final hours, which Dr. Walters chose as his last reading. I skimmed through five hundred and fifty pages, looking for any corners he had thumbed down, any passages of significance. On page sixty, he had underlined one phrase in pencil: 'Not quite here, and yet here already.'

"Those words are Wolfgang Walters to the life — slightly abstracted yet totally engaged, whether in a medical emergency or just as good company."

Paul looked around to see if his voice carried to the rim, where Kovacs stood. He particularly wanted the old shrink to hear this. "The other phrase he marked was the last line in the book: . . . 'it was the word beyond speech.' That was his lifelong quest, the idea that lay just beyond human grasp, the decisive last word."

Except for Lisl and her mother, he had lost his audience, its frozen faces buried in coat muffs. He would have to be quick about it, he realised. "He asked me to play a game with you," Paul cried. "He said most of you would know the rules. It's a game of opposites that he played at the dinner table, to sharpen people's minds."

"Boring," groaned a mechanic son-in-law.

"Shut up," hissed Lisl, kicking the nearest ankle.

"What," Paul said, "is the opposite of love?"

"Hate," piped Lisl.

"Absence," grumbled one of the sons.

"Indifference," said the sterile Tobias Strauss, who had driven up in a white coat in case any of the mourners collapsed and required his attention.

"None of those," said Paul. "The opposite of love is . . ."

"Marriage," suggested the widow, chuckling behind her veil.

"War," muttered Franz-Josef.

"The opposite of love," announced Paul, "is death. That was Walters's solution, or so he told me at Christmas."

The cemetery janitor approached, jangling keys.

"But he left a doubt in my mind when he said that," said Paul. "I knew that by naming death as the antipode to love, Walters had left the game unfinished. There has to be another antonym. If the opposite of love is death, what, dear friends, might be the opposite of death?"

"Life?" asked a married daughter.

"Too obvious."

"Birth?" said one of her sisters.

"Not bad . . ."

"The Resurrection," spouted a pious voice.

"The morning after . . ." said Lisl, her brow furrowed tight.

"That's good, that's very good," said Paul in a passable Walters imitation. "Your father would have liked that, Lisl, but he would have said you're not quite there yet. If death is unfathomable, if death is 'the word beyond speech,' as he indicates in the clue — then the opposite of death, the defeat of death, must be —"

"Knowledge?" said Alice.

"Science," pronounced Strauss.

"Understanding," declared Lisl.

"That's it!" cried Paul. "It's accepting that we cannot understand."

A light buffet had been laid on in the dining room of the small hotel where Paul had booked rooms for the night, and three sons-in-law were getting merry on wine before the last of the mourners had shed their coats. "Come join us, Paul," called Franz-Josef. "A toast to the departed."

Paul hung back. Emptiness gaped within him and he was grateful when Alice said they should go up to rest. No sooner had he shut the bedroom door than she pulled him onto the counterpane and into an act of love, her affirmation of life, a carnal opposite to the idea of death. Alice was wise in so many unexpressed ways that Paul wondered how he could ever have allowed Lisl to challenge the aptness of their marriage. Alice responded to emotion with healthy action, not measly equivocation. She had no need to verbalise, internalise, or rationalise — unlike Paul, who addressed life on the one hand, then the other, and could not let vital moments pass without context and comparison. "Was it," he asked as they lay there, limbs entwined, "anything like your mother's funeral?"

Alice rolled away from him with a sigh. "You spoke beautifully" was all she managed to say before her breathing relaxed into a soporific rhythm.

They overslept in the morning and dressed in a rush. Alice was meeting Jovanka for shopping and Paul was due at Dr. Kovacs's, although he told Alice he was seeing a surveyor of buildings.

"So what have you decided?" asked the psychiatrist with more anticipation than seemed appropriate in a professional relationship.

"None of the options." Paul smiled. "Not

fight, not flight, not hide."

"What, then?"

"Nothing. I don't have to do anything."

"At all?"

"Only if he confronts me."

"Which, given your relative circumstances, seems unlikely?"

"Correct."

Sunlight streamed into the room like an impartial adjudicator. "What led you to this tranquil resolution?" asked Dr. Kovacs, breaking the silence.

"Something you said."

"What was that?"

" 'Must you?' you said."

"Ah, the eternal interrogative."

They chuckled together, more colleagues now than therapist and patient.

"So where do we go from here?" said Paul.

"We can explore, deeper and wider, the roots of your neurosis."

"Is that all it is, a neurosis?"

"When we take into account the traumas of recent years, that's all it is."

"That's rather disappointing. It sounds as if I am making a fuss about nothing."

"On the contrary, there is nothing more interesting than neurosis."

"Have you reached a diagnosis?"

Kovacs took out his polka-dot handkerchief and wound it round a nicotine-stained index finger. "I see a man who longs to be liked. I ask myself why a person of such talent and attraction should suffer such a need. I suspect that he has been conditioned to dislike himself, to castigate himself for faults, real or imagined. The insomnia that he inflicts on himself is as great as any objective suffering he has been made to endure. That makes him, in his own eyes, worse than his tormentors. This is remarkably interesting. He does not like himself; *therefore,* he must prove that he is a very bad man. The only way he can disprove this is for someone to love him. Hence his desperate need to be loved. Might that be a basis for discussion?"

Paul glared at the therapist, outraged at the clarity of his perception.

"What's to discuss?" he sulked. "You've told me what I already know."

"Sometimes it helps to say it aloud."

"Why do you think I am unlikeable?"

"I didn't say that — you did."

"But I don't think so."

"Good, then we can discuss it objectively."

"Does that mean more animal tales?"

"If you like," said Kovacs. "There is much to be learned from an outcast, thrown out

366

of the wolf pack because of genetic difference or disruptive potential."

"A misfit? A mongrel?"

"Exactly, just like you and me. We hover at the margins of society, observing from without what cannot be seen within, improving our survival chances at the expense of permanent exclusion, a price we willingly pay. Shunned, we flaunt our difference as a special mark of superiority and we are then surprised that no-one loves us — so we hate the pack but cannot tear ourselves away from its habitat."

"What's the cure?"

"Adjustment. Getting to know, and like, ourselves a little bit."

Paul had no response to that. He shifted from buttock to buttock, staring at his fingernails as if they were to blame for his exclusion, scratching the cuticle on his thumb until it bled. "Adjustment won't be easy," he said.

"Or quick." Kovacs smiled.

"But worth trying?"

"Did Freud cure the Wolf Man?" chuckled Kovacs. "Of course not. But in the course of their transaction, they both learned an awful lot about themselves, even if Freud could not admit that to the Wolf Man as freely as I do to you."

"What have you learned from me, Dr. Kovacs?"

"That suppression need not be harmful."

"Am I allowed to keep buried memories?"

"As many as you like."

"Shall we give it six months?" said Paul, trying to take control.

"Fortnightly," said the therapist, unmoved, "every other Wednesday at three."

Paul made a note in his diary. "Before you go," said Kovacs, "there are a couple of things I'd like you to think about for our next session."

"Go ahead."

"Consider this, please. Wherever you live, whether in the village or on the other side of the world, you will always live near the camp and the quarry. The trauma can be held in check, but it cannot be erased altogether."

"I understand. That is why I seek your help."

"Second, I need you to ask yourself if, in your nights at the window, you ever think of hurting anyone else in the village — apart from Hans, that is."

"No," said Paul, responding a little too quickly.

"Really?"

"Who would I hurt? The storekeeper, the

washerwoman, my father-in-law? My rage is general, not particular; it is a collective anger."

"What about Alice?"

"What do you mean?"

"Do you ever think of harming Alice?"

"Alice? Harm Alice? She loves me. How could I hurt her?"

Kovacs creaked out of his chair and limped to the window. Arthritis had made it impossible for him to sit through a whole hour, and retirement could not be deferred much longer but, so long as he continued to practise, he tried to work the leg-flexing interval to the patient's benefit, allowing a difficult insight to settle in.

"Sometimes," Kovacs muttered, his back to Paul, his words barely audible, "sometimes the ones we want to hurt are precisely the ones we love."

"Wanting is not the same as hurting."

"So you do want to hurt her?" asked Kovacs, swivelling round on screaming knees.

"I didn't say that. . . ."

Kovacs hobbled over to the bookshelf and extracted a slim volume. "Yet each man kills the thing he loves/By each let this be heard . . ." he recited.

"Who wrote that?"

"Oscar Wilde, the Irish outcast, in *The Bal-*

lad of Reading Gaol. It's about a man who is waiting to be hanged for the murder of his wife."

"What are you getting at?" demanded Paul.

"Think about it."

"I have."

"Do you ever, in the act of love, think of killing your wife?"

"How can you ask such a thing?"

"Because people do. It is not just for the moment of oblivion that making love is known as 'the little death.' In congress, we dominate and submit, as beasts do in combat. Some creatures kill their lovers after sex. You've heard of the praying mantis? It bites off the partner's head. We humans mostly sublimate — we have a fleeting urge, and draw back. We put hands to throat, press head to pillow, and then let go. Have you felt that, Paul? Do you want to punish your wife during love?"

"I don't think so. Not consciously. Not that I can honestly recollect."

"Think carefully."

"Are you suggesting I am a danger to Alice?" His voice had risen to a squeak.

"Not necessarily." Kovacs sighed, exhaling tired air. "Or even knowingly. Everyone gets angry at times with a loved one. If we cannot find a way to let it out, the emotion turns inwards and reinforces feelings of inadequacy and self-hatred, yes?"

Paul grudged assent.

"You never show anger towards Alice, no matter how much she provokes you. You walk out of the room rather than shout back. You will not express what you feel. When she calls your little boy Hans, what do you feel, Paul? Don't you want to throttle her, to choke that sound before it leaves her throat?"

Paul said nothing, fingertips to his lips.

The shrink quoted:

Yet each man kills the thing he loves,
    By each let this be heard,
Some do it with a bitter look,
    Some with a flattering word,
The coward does it with a kiss,
    The brave man with a sword!

Paul shot to his feet. "I don't get it," he cried. "Last time you encouraged me to kill Hans. Now you want me to kill Alice? Are you mad, Kovacs? What kind of therapy is this? Let me out of here." He moved to the door, but the doctor barred his way.

"When I told you it was all right to kill Hans, did you proceed to kill him?" said

Kovacs. Paul, an inch from the old man's watery eyes, shook his head.

"If I tell you to kill anyone else, will you do what I say? I doubt it. You have a will of your own and a cautious mind. You will act according to character and do what the situation demands. What I am asking you to consider is your feelings towards and against your wife, your child, your therapist, yourself. That's what I can do for you, Paul. I can release your safety catch and allow you to play with a loaded metaphorical gun without anyone getting hurt. Your time is up. I will see you in a fortnight."

Trembling with confusion, Paul ran to the railway station, where, finding Alice with Jovanka at the coffee kiosk, he flung his arms around his tranquil, unknowing wife and smothered her in boyish kisses.

"One for me, too?" cajoled Jovanka.

Paul raised her chapped hand to his lips, conscious of Angelo's eyes on the back of his neck. "Angelo," he told her gallantly, "is a very lucky man."

In an otherwise empty carriage on the long train journey home, Paul held Alice's hand and talked about Johann. Such a clever child, he chortled, such curiosity. He could grow up to be a scientist, a great artist, a statesman. "He could even be an elder brother," hinted Alice.

"Are you sure?" Paul cried.

"Quite sure."

"How far gone?"

"Nearly four months."

He drew his wife to his ribs in a crushing embrace.

"Does anyone know?"

"Only Dr. Walters," panted Alice. "He examined me two days before he died. He said, if he didn't see you first, I should congratulate you on his behalf."

CHAPTER THIRTEEN

Three weeks before the summer solstice, a postcard arrived from Angelo saying that he had a second coffee machine ready for delivery. Mathilde Zumsteig, ecstatic, asked Paul to delay its arrival so that she could get the Black Horse painted, pasting over the last cracks of military damage, incorporating the antiquated bridal chamber into the main dining area, and presenting a brighter face to new customers.

"Good thinking," said Paul.

"I am just copying what you did," said his mother-in-law.

"You are a quick learner."

She blushed a deep red, confirming Paul's conquest. Another pawn on his chessboard.

Notices went up announcing that, on production of a recent receipt, Black Horse patrons could eat at reduced prices in the Laughing Hind during the week of closure.

Mathilde volunteered to come over and run the kitchens, coping with the overflow and relieving Alice to devote attention to Johann, who had turned petulant as her pregnancy progressed. Alice, exhausted, raised no objection. Mathilde, exuding goodwill, promised to bring over traditional Pringsheim recipes that had never crossed the gorge before.

On the fourth night of the week the Black Horse was shut, a Thursday, Paul returned home late from a fractious council meeting about footpath maintenance and entered the bar of the Laughing Hind a few moments before closing time. He was milking a pair of mild coffees from the Gaggia to share with Alice in their sitting room upstairs when a crawling sensation at the left-hand side of his neck made him turn around, knocking over the jug and swilling milk along the counter. Even as he registered the thing that had made him turn around, he knew that he should have been expecting it.

In the alcove that usually accommodated carrot seller Schreier's old man and his best pal, the blacksmith, the hulk that Paul knew as Hans was mopping up the gravy of Mathilde's pigeon roast with a gob of white bread, his head so close to the plate that the fork moved no more than ten centimetres, up or down. Paul squeezed his eyes shut, opening them as he mopped the last of the milk to confirm that he was not hallucinating with fatigue, that the squat creature in the filthy torn shirt sitting in the snug of his own bar was none other than his nemesis, the commandant of life and death. As the man leaned back with a satiated sigh, Paul knew that this was no mistake. He should never have allowed this to happen. It had to be stopped.

He reproached himself for not having prepared a contingency plan. He should have known the creature would come salivating across the gorge in pursuit of a cut-price offer of the widow Zumsteig's grub. He should have been ready for him. As he threw the milk-sodden rag into a laundry basket beneath the bar, his stomach heaved and he barely reached the hallway washroom in time to retch its contents over an enamelled hand basin that he had been meaning to replace with modern steel. A glass of wilting violets on the shelf above winked at him in the vanity mirror.

Paul washed his face and, drying it on a towel, emptied his mind of other thoughts. Hans was in his house, under the roof where Johann slept and Alice awaited his baby.

Hans had invaded his home, destroyed the calm that every man has the right to expect on crossing his threshold. He would have to be removed: first excised, then exorcised. His presence contaminated all it touched. His plate and glass would have to be smashed, the cutlery thrown away, the bench and tabletops stripped and revarnished, the floor scrubbed. That would come later. First he had to evict the intruder. Grey-faced, Paul went to the kitchen in search of Mathilde. "That tramp of yours is in there," he told her. "Could you get him to finish up and tell him we're shut? Be as rude as you like. I don't want to see him in here again."

"Easily done," said his latest admirer. "Are you all right, Paul?"

"I'll be fine. Just a little tired."

He sat down and laid his head on a pine table in the kitchen until the pounding stopped and Mathilde returned to say she had got rid of the nuisance. "I told him he was too shabby for a nice place like this, and that he smelled besides." She smiled.

"Has he ever given you trouble at the Black Horse?" asked Paul.

"He's always on his own," said Mathilde. "Never says a word. Hides a multitude of secrets behind that beard, if you ask me.

Useless fellow."

"Has he gone?"

"He is using the lavatory. Give him a couple of minutes. Then we can lock up."

"Had a good evening, Mathilde?"

"Outstanding. Not a spare table, rushed off our feet. Only really slowed down in the last half-hour. Have you eaten?"

She ladled a bowl of dumpling soup and placed it, unasked, in front of him. Paul sipped motorically, calming himself down with broth, whispering a mantra: Hans is going; he won't be back. But even as he said the words, he knew that they were false. Hans was back in his life. There was only one thing he could do about it.

"Why don't you go home," he told Mathilde. "I can finish up on my own."

"You sure?"

"I could do with some physical activity, actually, to take my mind off the highways and byways debate that has been running all evening."

"You work too hard," said Mathilde.

Paul shrugged.

"You will overheat that brain of yours one day," she warned, kissing him on both cheeks before pulling on her coat and darting out to her reconditioned Volkswagen, an early reward of the prosperity to come.

Paul double-locked the front door behind his mother-in-law, stacked the dirty glasses in the sink, threw the implements that Hans had used into a bin outside the kitchen door, and drew the heavy bolt. He wiped the bar top until it shone, shut down the coffee machine, stacked the day's newspapers beside the coal grate, and flicked up several sets of switches in the fuse box, all but the one in the hallway that would light him up the stairs and home to the safety of Alice. As he passed the washroom on his way to the staircase, he stuck his head inside to make sure no-one had fallen asleep there, as sometimes happened with elderly men who had drunk too much. The four lavatory doors yawned open, but a tap had been left drip-dripping. As Paul reached an arm inside to turn it off, he saw that someone had left an object on the rim of the washbasin, removed while a customer was washing his hands and forgotten on departure. Holding it to the hall light, he recognised a crisscrossed strap and a heavy, scratched glass face.

He knew without knowing whose watch it was, knew also that it had been left there with intent, as a message to Paul that Hans would return, to haunt him, taunt him, provoke him into acknowledging that Hans was there, that he was not going away. Paul did not understand why Hans needed to manifest his presence here, but need it he must if he had left that accursed watch behind. The Tissot was the same one that had lain across the commandant's file on the day Paul uncovered his name. It gave off the same whiff of unwashed intimacy, of unsought proximity, an aura he could neither resist nor ignore. He was going to have to do something about Hans.

He sniffed the glass of violets to mask the smell of Hans, then flushed them down the toilet pan, as if the flowers were to blame. He returned to the bar, extracted two brown paper bags from beneath the counter and, grasping the watch in one piece of paper as he dropped it into the other, took care not to let it touch any part of his clothing or his skin. Behind the bar, at floor level, stood a safe, which Franz-Josef, despite repeated exhortations, refused to use for its designated purpose of keeping the night's takings. The safe served as an occasional lost-property store. It opened to Paul's touch. He flung the bag deep within, shut the door, twirled the dial on the front panel, tested the door to make sure it was locked, switched off the light, and went upstairs with a leaden tread. He thought he could hear the watch tick-tocking, mocking his every step, and he knew that he would know no peace so long as it lay there, unredeemed.

An image of his cherished Tissot slipped into mind. For an instant he wondered if the two watches might be one and the same, if the object ripped off his wrist on arrival in camp had not been retrieved by Hans off a pile of looted property, furnished with a runic strap, and worn day and night to tick the toll of deaths. He was half-tempted to go back downstairs and examine the back for Johanna's loving inscription — *To my darling Paul, on the day he becomes a man* — but decided it did not matter. The watch could not be his. It was Hans incarnate. It would have to disappear, along with its owner.

Removing his outer clothes, Paul lay beside the sleeping Alice in sweaty underwear, stiff as a plank, blanking his mind. Less than three hours later, long before first light, he faced the black window on fidgety feet. There was no-one in the world to share his pain. Walters was dead, Kovacs saw patients only on Tuesdays and Wednesdays, the Professor was a pimp, and all Angelo would tell him was: kill, kill, kill. Tiptoeing into the bathroom, Paul showered, dressed, and went downstairs in stocking feet. He drew three short coffees in quick succession, stroking the machine as it sputtered and squirted, encouraging it with soft murmurs. Lisl, a light sleeper, came into the room, disturbed by the hissing, she said. She was wearing a floor-length flannel nightgown and a look of friendly concern. She offered to cook him breakfast.

"Not hungry," said Paul, "but nice of you to think of me."

"I do" — Lisl smiled — "often."

He could confide in Lisl, so long as they did not touch. She was smart, loyal, discreet as her father. But even as he entertained the comfort of a burden shared, he knew that a secret would complicate their precarious connection. He had promised the dying doctor to protect her from impulsiveness, hers or his.

"Did you see that tramp on Schreier's table last night?" he asked, testing, testing.

"The one who limped? Yes, he ponged."

"Ever seen him before?"

"No. Refugee, is he?"

"Not sure. He left a watch in the washroom. If he comes back, it's in a brown bag at the back of the safe. Just give it to him and throw him out."

"Anything else?"

"I don't think so."

"Paul?" she said, her tone softening.

"No, Lisl."

"There's something the matter with you. I can tell. Come here. Sit down a minute. . . ."

"No, I must go. I'm running late."

He raced out of the door in shirtsleeves and uphill to the town hall, banging on the drawn shutters to hasten the caretaker. He demolished his in-tray in a fury, jotted notes in the margins of a pathways manual, barked at a secretary who arrived at three minutes past nine, and, when she burst into tears, picked up the telephone receiver and ordered the long-distance operator to connect him to the number he had for Imre Kovacs. It rang eighteen times before he agreed with the operator that there seemed to be no answer.

His head splitting, he went home and put himself to bed with what he said was influenza. Alice plied him with soup and brandy and he slept. In the evening, feeling calmer, he read *Pinocchio* aloud to Johann, and *The Death of Virgil* to himself until he dozed off without extinguishing the bedside lamp.

He was first down on Saturday, checking the safe, finding the watch still there. After breakfast, he took Johann riding, then to his flute lesson, his grandparents. Mathilde asked if he was feeling better. Paul growled, the watch tick-tocking in his brain even though he knew it must have stopped by now for want of rewinding. He rang Angelo from the hallway of the Black Horse, decorators clattering around him.

"Is the machine ready?"

"Anytime you like. Monday soon enough?"

"Fine. I might need a Hans with installing it."

He had meant to say "hand." Angelo understood the slip.

"Anytime," said Angelo. "Day or night, just call. I can be there in six hours."

Saturday evening he spent with Alice, putting crinkle-edged photographs into paper corners and sticking them, page by page, into the family album they had been filling up before the baby was born. Paul, said Alice, was hardly to be seen in any of the pictures. Only at a distance, a pinprick against a mountain slope, half a head in the rear row of a Christmas grouping. He was either behind the camera, arranging others, or so far off, he might have been a member of a different party. Alice went through the album from start to finish, counting. Paul was in twenty-six photographs, but in none of them was he distinct and recognisable.

"We must do something about that," she said.

Sunday he went with Alice and Johann to church as usual, then joined the extended family at lunch, where he seemed so much his usual controlled self that Lisl was the only one who noticed him leaving the room three times during the meal, unable to sit still. After Alice went up for a nap and the grandparents took Johann for the afternoon, he walked downhill in grey drizzle, following the path he had taken with Walters towards the quarry. He stood beside the stream, soaked in penitential misery. The inn lights went on at five-thirty, amid grumbles from Mathilde that business would be slow in such weather. At six, Paul retrieved the brown paper bag from the safe and sat himself in Schreier's alcove, watching all who came and went from behind a cardboard file of planning applications. Hans entered the room at seven thirty-four on the plastic wall clock between the two stags' heads above the bar. Paul sprang up and stopped him at the door. "You've come for the watch? Come with me."

He walked out into the forecourt and, as the man drew beside him, took the knife from his sleeve and, ten paces from the front door, jabbed it below his ribs. "Straight ahead. Do not look back. Turn right at the road," said Paul through clenched teeth.

"Where are we going?" asked his victim, unshaken by the assault, which pierced neither garment nor flesh. His tone of voice, had Paul bothered to analyse it, was on the verge of jocular. There was no fear to be heard.

"We're going down," said Paul.

"Do I know you?"

"Don't play games."

"Why would I do that?"

"You know damn well who I am."

"I don't recognise the name. Paul Miller," said Stub Head with a sly elision in his pronunciation. "I can't call to mind any Miller."

"You gave me a number: ten, sixty-six, five three seven, forty-four."

"Ah, so it *is* you," cried the prisoner, stumbling on a pothole but keeping his feet. "I thought it must be you, but you can never know these days, with people changing their names and faces to suit the new conditions. Your name is not what it was — something -owski, wasn't it? — and your face has fattened out. I was fairly sure it was you when you nearly knocked me over with your bicycle outside the Black Horse. But since you showed no sign of recognising me

386

behind my hairy hedge, I thought I'd do nothing about it until you did."

"I would know you anywhere, Commandant, beard or no beard."

"Then you have a good eye. I've been back for months, on my farm, in the shops, and nobody has said a word. Neither enemy nor friend — not that I ever had friends here. These people are passive as sheep at pasture, unmoved by great events. They are not men of destiny like you and me, architect. They see no evil, hear no evil, and do no bloody good at all, and that's a fact."

"Shut up, Kerner, and keep walking."

"No need for the knife, architect. I cannot fight a big strong fellow like you. And you know damn well, I cannot run, with my bad leg."

"Just walk."

The rain had penetrated one of Paul's boots, and his head, heavy with residual flu, was hearing every word blurred. His control was tenuous and his reflexes blunt. The man at the end of his knife was chatting away, as if he had been waiting for ages for such congenial company.

"I decided to make myself known to you, architect," said Hans, "because the disguise was unnecessary. I had not expected to find camp survivors in the vicinity when I came home and was greatly surprised that you, of all people, were still here. A pleasant surprise, if I may say so. Even more agreeable to discover that you are now mayor. I thought I had better make sure you knew me, before I approached you in your official capacity. But we can do that another day. I need better housing. I have neither electricity nor gas in my miserable stone cottage, you know. It's not right."

"Walk, don't talk," barked Paul in a voice that was not his own.

"It puzzled me at first," said Hans, unmoved, "that you stayed put. I had trouble understanding your motives. But then I reckoned you had nothing to go back to after the great destruction, and it can't be too bad living above a pub, eh? I guess you got used to us, attached even. Certainly, I tried to treat you well, at least in comparison to some of the others. One way or another, I saved your life."

"What are you saying? You nearly killed me."

"Don't be so naïve. Who was it, do you think, who kept you off the rock face? There was not enough work for you in the cabin, so I had to come up with constant amendments to the plans for you to draw. It wasn't easy, I can tell you. But I was determined that you should survive."

"Shut up," said Paul, jabbing the knife into wet serge.

Both Mathilde and Lisl had remarked on the man's unwashed smell, but Paul, sniff as he might, caught no odour beyond soaked wool and muddy boots. He had the beast at his mercy. It was a moonless night, ideal conditions. In a few moments, it could all be over. But he needed a sensory stimulus, some reminiscent smell, sound, or sight before he could strike. Nothing in this garrulous, bedraggled bundle aroused any feeling in him. Those twisted features were buried beneath the beard, the voice had modulated from bark to whine, and there was no detectable stench to him in the relentless rain. Like a devil or angel, Hans lacked earthly attributes. Were it not for his odious table manners, he might never have caught Paul's eye in the first place.

The road ahead glistened, dirty and deserted. The only sound was the slap of their soles on the tarred surface and the rain splattering on corrugated fencing at either side of the tarmac strip where construction was taking place. "I can't go fast," said Hans, slowing down. "You remember, I have a short leg, from polio. A bad hip. Soft bones. Not easy to run a military installation when you are in pain, but I did my duty, my best."

"You're wasting your time looking for sympathy," snapped Paul.

"A little understanding, perhaps . . ."

" 'Understanding'?" exploded Paul. "Understand what — murder? starvation? Forced jumps over a sheer cliff?"

"I have to stop," said Hans. "I need a piss."

The prisoner fumbled at his buttons and micturated carelessly at the side of the road, forcing Paul to retreat, for fear of being splashed. "That's better. Now where are we heading?"

"Take a left at the next path," said Paul.

"A walk down memory lane, eh?"

"Shut up!" cried Paul, punching the man on the side of the neck and again in the kidneys, the best he could manage from behind. Hans tripped, caught himself, and straightened up as far as his stoop would permit. "Good to see you learned something from us," he muttered. "You didn't waste your time in camp."

"Will you shut up!" growled Paul.

"Or what?" mocked the prisoner. "You'll kill me? Go ahead. See if I care. Alive, I'm a burden to myself. Dead, I become your responsibility, Mr. Mayor. Do you think I have anything left to live for? I am a useless relic of a failed experiment, glorious but flawed. A crippled leftover, that's what I am. Go ahead, Mr. Mayor. Relieve my pain. Get rid of the nuisance. What's stopping you?"

"Stop right here," said Paul, reaching the end of the world.

They were at the top of the cliff, above the quarry. Paul quaked at the knees, remembering the men who had flown off the precipice. Hans limped on, two paces farther, placing one heavy foot teasingly at the jutting edge. He turned to face Paul, mocking him through a bead curtain of rain.

"What now, little architect? What do you want from me: a confession? An apology? That I should go on bended knee and beg for my life? Lick your boots? You know I'll never do that. Times have changed, but not you and me, draughtsman."

"Just be quiet," said Paul, his authority draining away.

"Why should I? Give me one reason to be quiet. This is the first good chat I have had in years. I'm enjoying myself. I have no-one else in the world to talk to. You must know that from the file I left you to read. I had a wife once; the slut ran off. I had a son; they put him in a home. Then they drove up a gas truck and suffocated him — was that in the file? Euthanasia, they called it. Part of our leader's vision of purity, perfecting the species. No-one asked my boy if he wanted to die; no-one asked me, either. Fate took charge in those days. We were chaff in the wind of fate, me and my boy. You, too. The wind blew. For a while, I was up and you were down. Then it stopped and we're the other way round. Such is fate. So what am I supposed to regret? Staying alive? Keeping you alive?"

Paul reached into his jacket for a handkerchief to wipe his sopping face. Though he gripped a weapon, he was powerless. Hans ruled, just as he had done in the camp, stripping Paul of dignity, manliness, and the right to make a decision. He had taken away everything, even the superiority of suffering, by making a preposterous claim to equal persecution, a commonality in misery. Paul was losing every round in this grotesque dialogue. He could not let it continue and yet he had no way of making it stop.

Hoping Hans would wear himself out, he let him embark on an odyssey of self-pity that began with his flight from the camp and wriggled along under various disguises, fixed up with menial jobs by former Party brothers in different countries, themselves out of hiding and living off war spoils. Year after year, he kept his head down and obeyed orders, until something snapped in his skull and he decided to take his chances back in the village where he had been born, on his own farm, behind a full-bearded facial mask that would protect him from casual recognition.

His anecdotes were random, without chronology or a connecting thread, leaping from a market tiff two days before to the night the leader called out his name at the Party rally and decorated him, to the roar of millions. That moment, as the gold badge was pinned to his lapel and the great man's hand was in his grasp, his pretty wife was riding through a mountain pass with a subversive writer of the forbidden race, leaving their boy alone and helpless in the cottage and Hans a public cuckold. None of this was Hans's fault; fate was working against him. "I tried to see the leader when my problems became intolerable, but he was fenced off from true believers like me by opportunists, arse lickers, paper pushers. I waited four days in the anteroom and had to leave when I rebuked a typist girl who was mocking me. Back in the village, people were against me. When I annexed a patch of adjacent land — the owner died in prison — I had the taxmen on my back before I could put up new fencing. When I reported unpatriotic talk to the police, the market women stopped buying my produce. When I set up a scouts group for farm boys on Sundays, the priest accused me of filthy things. It was him, not me: I never touched them. But who is going to believe a poor cripple's word against a man of God's? The church closed ranks, the police were hand in surplice with the priest, and as for the examining doctor, that Walters —"

"Shut up," said Paul, roused by his friend's name, "shut up before —"

"Before what?"

"Before I smash your teeth."

"Something else you must have learned from us."

"Listen, Kerner," said Paul, a surge of current reconnecting him to the power grid. "I don't want to hear any more. I don't need excuses. I am not interested in your story. I don't want to know why you're here. I am a practical man. My aim is to rebuild this community. I care less about you than I do about the row of thatched cottages I demolished the other week to make space for an apartment block. You want new housing? Be my guest. Two-bed, top floor, brand-new. Just to show I hold nothing against you. There is nothing between us, you and me. You belong to the past, and the past is past.

You are right. Once you were on top; now you're down — you lost; I won. Satisfied? You can go now."

A crease flickered at the edge of the bushy beard, a curl of triumph, victory for the little man over the mayor: The canny peasant outsmarts the city professor. Paul willed himself to turn and walk away, but something held him back, a glimmer in the other fellow's eye. He could not let it shine.

"I have one last question," said Paul.

"Ask," laughed Hans, "I'm in no hurry."

"I need to know why?"

"Why what?"

"Why did you kill men for no reason?"

"It was not without reason. I had orders. Population control. Keep them working; get rid of the unproductive ones. There's plenty more where they came from. That's what the minister in charge of munitions told me — nothing in writing, you understand, just an intimation between comrades, a nod and a pat on the shoulder. The job was my second lease on life, a gift from the leader himself after he asked about me one night at dinner. Finally, after years of loyalty, I was rewarded with an important mission. My orders were to rule by terror. That way, we got by with a lower ratio of guards to prisoners. Had I shown pity, my officers would have reported to the army high command and I could have been removed from my position. They were out to undermine me, those shirkers and malingerers on my staff. I had to show toughness, demonstrate that I was a man without weakness or sentiment. When I had you flogged, little architect, it was to save my skin as much as yours."

"You were protecting me by beating me almost to death?"

"I could not be seen to have favourites. If the guards had thought you were my pet, they would have set the dogs on you the moment I was out of sight."

"And the skydiving?"

"My deputy's idea. Very wasteful. I had it stopped."

"Only towards the end. Before that, you seemed to enjoy it."

"I put on a show of enthusiasm — I was being watched. You read my file."

"When you shot men, they were never killed outright. You winged them in the leg or thigh and called the dogs to tear them apart."

"I was a poor shot," said Hans. "Bad squint. Had it since I was a boy."

"Why did you keep me alive?" said Paul after a long pause.

"Those were my orders. You were category B, punishment, not category A, disposal. An influential relative, I was told, was paying to have you disciplined but not killed."

"That was it, you were obeying orders?"

"There were other reasons, as well."

"Such as?"

"I am glad to see the past still interests you, little architect. You were useful to me in the office. You were intelligent and you had a nice presence, even in prisoner stripes. I thought that maybe, someday, you might understand what I was trying to achieve and, if called upon, would testify on my behalf. I was a diligent and effective commanding officer. Just imagine: If I had received the wonder weapon in time and stored it properly, we could have changed the course of history without a rocket being fired. The weapon was a deterrent, a bargaining chip, a chance for an honourable peace instead of chaotic, abject surrender. I was a patriot, I did not want my country to be crushed. I wanted us both to walk away from that place on the day of peace, heads held high. That's why I left the file for you to read. So that one man would know who I was and that I had done my best for peace."

"That's all you wanted?" asked Paul.

"Those were my goals," said Hans.

"You want sympathy for your bid to escape the consequences of defeat?" gasped Paul, disarmed by the insanity of the man's reasoning. "You want me to *understand?*"

For the first time, the hunched figure at the cliff edge hesitated in his reply. "Nobody," he finally mumbled, "is beyond understanding."

"God's understanding," said Paul, "not man's. Certainly not mine."

"Where was God when they gassed my boy?" the man cried.

"Where was God when you made men jump from the cliff?"

"Exactly," cried Hans. "Just as I said. Those were extraordinary times. God had removed himself from the world. It was up to each of us to do as he saw fit. We survived, you and I, because we knew how to adapt, to manipulate a situation to our advantage."

"I do not accept any comparison between you and me," said Paul icily.

"As you wish, architect. That's how I saw it."

The rain had eased and in the pale evening light he saw his enemy's face, not contorted and terrifying as he knew it from the cabin and the parade ground, but sunken and sorrowed, emptied of solid purpose. He felt a wrench of something like pity for this son of Cain, condemned to drag his twisted body across the earth until the day he died because God's laws were back in force and men could no longer kill a stranger without a second thought. It felt almost like justice, a harmonic resolution.

"I want you to walk away from here now," said Paul with quiet certainty.

"Right now?" asked Hans.

"This very minute."

"I'm not begging," said Hans.

"I'm not bothered. All I demand is that you stay out of my sight. Understood?"

"If you like. From tomorrow, I'll go back to eat at the Black Horse."

"You do that," said Paul, turning to leave.

"Just a minute," the commandant called after him.

"What is it?"

"You've forgotten something."

"What's that?"

"My watch. I want it back."

"How do I know it's yours?"

"You saw me wear it, day after day in the cabin. I wore it right through the war, the occupation, the years of hiding. Its ticking is all I have to keep me company."

"Why did you leave it behind, in my wash-room?"

"To make sure you knew who I was, who I am."

"Where did you get the watch?" asked Paul. "In the first place, I mean."

"Originally? Off a mound of prisoner's possessions — we used to take our pick when a new transport arrived. My old watch never kept time. This one was sleek and stylish. I had a thick strap put on to offset its feminine look. The glass face got scratched by a rockfall at the quarry. But it still works very well. Why do you ask?"

Paul fished into his jacket and extracted the Tissot. "Is this it?" he demanded.

"You know damned well it is."

"And you want it back?"

"It's mine," said Hans.

Paul held the carved leather strap between contemptuous fingers, turned it over, and spat twice on the despoiled face. "Here," he called out, "catch!"

The man lurched forward, then swayed back. The soaking ground gave way beneath his maimed feet. There was a pause, longer than a jackal's howl. Then a thump at the foot of the quarry and an echo that thudded around the hills. Paul took himself to the lip of the cliff and looked straight down. The body lay below, its limbs splayed out in a crazy parody of the crooked Party emblem. "Shit," he swore, "the bastard was right." Hans alive was no-one's problem. Dead, he became Paul's immediate responsibility.

Clambering down the winding path beside the rock face, he lost his foothold twice and had to clutch at an outcrop of shrubs to stop himself from falling. Looking down, he felt no fear. He was in a different place now, a world without Hans. His reactions were being retuned. Nothing would feel the same again. He was living minute by minute, step by precarious step.

At the bottom of the rock, he went over to the corpse and touched the artery at its broken neck. Confirming that there was no pulse, he fumbled in the man's jacket pocket, taking out a wallet, an identity card, and a wrinkled square photograph of a fat-cheeked boy. Paul tore up the papers and threw the scraps into the stream. Six paces to the left, he found the fallen watch in a patch of heather, miraculously unbroken. Without forethought, he buckled it onto the dead man's left wrist, where it belonged.

The rain had brought down birch and pine branches in abundance. Paul, panting, dragged one branch after another towards the body, covering it perfunctorily, so that it could not be seen from a distance. He thought of setting light to the pyre with a box of matches that he found on the corpse, but the foliage was too wet to burn. He had done all he could for the day and it looked like the rain clouds were regathering.

Dusting bracken off his jacket, he took the riverside path up to the main road and walked vacantly back home, entering unseen by the side door and slipping upstairs to shower and change clothes. Bundling his soaked garments into the hotel sack for the laundryman to collect in the morning, he descended the staircase to the hallway and, checking that he was unobserved, lifted the telephone receiver and asked the operator to put him through to the Grey Cat club in the big city.

"I should like to speak to the proprietor," he began, forgetting which name the Professor was using these days.

"Can you tell me who's calling?" said the receptionist, sceptical and sour.

"Tell him it's . . . Pavlov."

He heard a hand placed over the receiver and a hundred other calls crackle on the line.

"He's in a meeting," came the reply.

"When will he be free?"

"I can't be sure."

"Can you tell him it's urgent, a matter of life and death?"

"I wasn't expecting to hear from you," said the Professor after a while.

"You said to call if I was in trouble."

"What can a humble impresario do for a grand developer like you?"

"I have a disposal problem."

"I'm sorry, we don't do disposals anymore. Not part of our business."

"It's to do with the person we discussed."

"I understand."

"And?"

"The answer is still no."

"I see."

"No, you don't, Pavlov, never did, never will. I could help if I wanted, but I won't."

"And why is that?"

"Because I want you to know what it's like to be let down the way you left us that day, totally dependent on a man we thought we could trust."

"It was not like that; you know it wasn't."

"Have it your way, Pavlov, you always do."

"So this is revenge at last, Professor. 'Vengeance is mine,' and all that?"

"How little you know, Dr. Pavlov, with all your hoity-toity degrees. If I wanted to teach you a lesson, I could do it with a snap of the fingers — but, no, I don't do that sort of thing anymore. I am standing for election to the state legislature. Did you hear about that? I can't be bothered with kicking over traces of the past, mine or yours. Stand on your own two feet, dear Pavlov, and good luck with the job."

"Are you still speaking?" said the village operator after half a minute's empty crackling.

"I don't think so," said Paul in a gravelled monotone. "I'm not sure we ever did."

Replacing the receiver, he stepped outside through the kitchen door that he had first entered, upheld on that occasion by Alice's strong arms. The circle was closing and he did not want to get trapped. It was raining again, a thin drizzle like the mewling of a baby that is wet but not hungry. Not a good night for running away. Turning abruptly, he walked back inside and played his last card on the phone.

"Can you get me a cement mixer?" he asked.

"When do you need it?" said Angelo.

"Immediately, by daybreak."

"Where?"

"The quarry. There has been a spot of skydiving."

"I can deliver the coffee machine at the same time," said Angelo.

"But not Jovanka this time."

"Just me and a friend," said Angelo. "We'll drive all night. It will take six hours. We'll be there by five in the morning. Trust me."

Lisl entered the hall as he finished the call. Turning on his winning political smile, Paul bid her good night and went up to join Alice on the sitting room sofa for the end of the radio news. Pleading influenza, he apologised for his daylong distraction and urged her to turn in with him for an early night. Alice levered herself up, smiling and satisfied, from the sofa. Paul put his arm in hers and led her to their suite with a show of solicitous affection. She said she would only be a minute, but he was fast asleep before she had finished in the bathroom.

CHAPTER FOURTEEN

At four in the morning, an hour before the cement mixer was due, Paul crept downstairs in woollen socks and pulled on his trousers in the wood-panelled tavern bar, the air heavy with the past night's conviviality. Fumbling past the silent coffee machine, a stair light winking off its steel wall, he brewed himself a small black pot on the old crusted hob and sipped the scalding bitterness through a rock-hard almond biscuit, the last of the batch that Alice had baked for Easter.

Upending his cup on the drain board, Paul shrugged on his dried-out outdoor jacket and tiptoed to the front door, shoes in hand, raising the latch without a creak and shutting the door with a muted finality. "Time to go," he murmured, planting thick rubber soles on a road that his feet knew by rote and following the steps that memory dictated. He reached the quarry at four twenty-eight by the luminous watch that Alice had given him on their first Christmas together. It was the hour he knew best, the hour before daybreak. Pulling out a pocket torch, he checked that everything was as he had left it the night before. No wolves had come scavenging from the woods. The body lay beneath its canopy of fallen branches and the ground around it was drying out in a light breeze.

A crew of eighty builders was due at six. If Angelo arrived on time, they would have an hour to run the mixer, throw Hans into the school's foundation, and cover him with fast-setting cement before the first helmeted labourer set foot on the site. Paul would tell the foreman that he had ordered the mixer as a surprise, to eliminate the arduous business of mixing cement by hand. The growling mixer would have novelty value. A crowd would gather to watch it turn and spout. It would be the talk of the village, another welcome mayoral innovation.

An owl hooted. Paul looked at his watch. Ten minutes to five. Getting close.

A murmur came to his ear, a purr that turned to thunder. "They're here!" exclaimed Paul, swinging open the heavy site gates to salvation. Two trucks pulled into the yard, a trim van with CAFÉ ANGELO on its sides and a potbellied monster caked in grit. Beauty and the Beast, thought Paul as Angelo sprang from the van and folded him in an embrace, kissing his cheeks with abrasive stubble.

"Who's the guy in the cement truck?" Paul murmured, breaking free.

"You don't recognise him?"

"Pavel!" came a flat voice from a common grave.

"Janko!" choked Paul as the screen split before his eyes.

To the left, in grainy silent monochrome, was an emaciated Czech boy on the bunk below, prudent and solitary, tortured by his secret love for the man above. To the right stood a construction boss, thick of waist and coarse of face, Janko, the liquidator, who cut off men's gonads on the Professor's behalf and delivered them to wives and loved ones. The two Jankos, tender and brutal, were not easily conjoined into one, but Paul knew which of them he most needed at this moment and he was grateful for the man's gruff taciturnity. The former bunk-house mates shook hands with grave formality, as if concluding a contract.

Angelo had begun unloading. "Best cement mix," declared Janko, rolling himself a cigarette as the café owner dumped two white sandbags onto the muddy ground. "Two sacks of sand," he said, counting. "Gravel and water, you have here." Paul, torn between fear and relief, was grateful for Janko's practicality. Janko was one of those Paul had left behind in the camp. He had no idea how far he could trust him and was grateful that Janko fixed his eyes on the cigarette, oblivious to Paul's guilty glances.

"So where is he?" demanded Angelo. Paul pointed his torch at the mound. Angelo flicked open a cigarette lighter and cupped it for Janko. By the flare of a small flame, Paul and Janko tugged off two branches and turned the crunched face upwards for close inspection. Janko stared down, then kicked the body without much vehemence.

"Did he jump?" he asked Paul in a clinical manner, "or did you push him?"

"What does it matter?" insisted Angelo. "He's gone. It's over. We got him."

"I'd like to know," said Janko in a flat, emotionless tone.

"He fell," said Paul.

"What does it matter?" insisted Angelo, "It's getting late."

"The workforce arrives in an hour," added Paul.

"Plenty of time," drawled Janko, taking an

extended drag on his cigarette. "It takes five minutes for my machine to warm up, ten for us to load it, five more for the mixing. Your foundations will be half a metre thick before any of your crew pulls on a hard hat. But first I need to know if you had the guts to do the right thing."

"I brought him here," said Paul, refusing to lie.

"And then?"

"He fell."

Janko raised his eyes and held Paul's in a vise. "Let's get cracking," he said.

He mounted the truck and switched on the ignition. The engine chortled into life and the barrel on the back slowly turned. "See those?" Janko called out, indicating four sacks of sand. "Tip them in separate piles and scrape together some gravel. Angelo, get that bucket and fill it from the stream.

"My new shoes," wailed the café owner.

"Italian?" yelled Janko above the machine's roar.

"What else?" Angelo sighed, polishing a ruined toecap on the opposite trouser leg.

Jumping down from the cabin, Janko strode over to the corpse, lifted it as if it were another sack of sand, and carried it to the edge of the foundation pit of the school that Paul was building for the enlightenment of future generations. "On a count of three," said Janko, beckoning Paul to help him with the last rites. "One, two, three . . ." and the body of Hans flew and then fell ten feet below to its final resting place.

The mixer growled in contentment on its diet of sand, water, and cement. "I am going to drive the truck to the side of the trench so we can pour the stuff directly where we want it," Janko announced. Paul and Angelo skipped aside as he steered the ugly behemoth around them.

"All we need to do now," said Janko, "is pull this lever, and the cement will drop in great dollops into the pit."

The three conspirators surveyed one another in the truck lights, requiring a ceremony of some kind. "Shall I pour?" Angelo giggled, as if he were the hostess at an English tea party.

"No," said Janko. "Paul did the job. Let him finish it."

"What do I do?" asked Paul.

"Throw this switch on the dashboard and the mixer will tip over," said Janko, taking his hand and placing it on a lever. Paul's knuckles whitened, locked with Janko's in the act.

"Up or down?" asked Paul.

"Up," said Janko, pushing firmly upwards.

The mixer stopped in mid-turn. "Shit," said Janko.

"What's the matter?" Paul asked in a quavering voice.

"Probably nothing. It seizes up sometimes. Par for the course with army-surplus machinery."

"Was it something I just did?"

"Nah, just happens."

"What do we do now?"

"We wait ten minutes, then start again."

It was five twenty-two, time in hand. While Janko and Angelo shared another cigarette at the front of the vehicle, Paul walked around in circles, a knot forming at the base of his stomach.

At five thirty-two, he said, "Time's up. Let's try again."

"Give it another minute," said Janko, climbing into the driver's cabin.

"Let me throw the lever this time," said Angelo. "We Italians are the best drivers."

Janko turned on the ignition and the mixer whirred. Paul, his nerves fraying, stood at the brink of the foundation pit, clenching fingernails into his palms.

"Ready?" asked Angelo.

"Ready," said Janko.

"Andiam!"

The barrel stirred from its base like a bear disturbed in hibernation. With a rising roar, it lifted itself ten, twenty, thirty degrees above the horizontal, ready to pour. Then, in midair, it stopped.

"Fuck," said Janko.

"What is it?"

"Dunno. I'll switch off for ten minutes and try again."

"We haven't got time," said Paul, ashenfaced. "My crew will be here in a quarter of an hour. They will see — that — and then we're all done for."

"Can't you stand at the gate and hold them off for a bit?" asked Janko, wrenching a jammed lever at the flank of his machine.

"It won't work," said Paul, taking charge. "I want you to leave right away. Drive out and go home. I will not put your lives at risk. I'm the one responsible for this mess. I'll handle it in my way."

"Are you sure?" said Janko, his voice soft with admiration.

"He's sure," said Angelo, shifting from shoe to sodden shoe.

"Leave now," said Paul. "Just go."

"Come with us," said Janko. "I can get you a new identity, fly you to Canada, America, somewhere safe."

"Thanks," said Paul. "But no. Go now,

my friends, go in peace. I know what I have to do."

It was five fifty-two on Alice's watch as they pulled out of the gate. Paul locked it behind them without regret. He must have been mad to involve others. This was his job, as Janko had said. He would have to see it through to the grim conclusion.

A sparrow chirped. Paul was alone in the quarry, alone with Hans on the patch of ground where they had once shared a stuffy cabin. He sat on a pile of bricks and waited for events to run their course. In eight minutes' time, the foreman, unerringly punctual, would let himself in, throw both gates wide open, and enter the site. He would greet the mayor with a surprised "Good morning," look around to see what he was doing there, and cast his eyes down into the pit below. Then he would march over to his site office and telephone the police. That was how Paul's story would end. Arrest, questioning, relocation to a city jail, trial, sentence, appeal, verdict, justice, the end. He looked at the watch Alice had given him for Christmas, full of love. His life was measured in two watches. He had four minutes to go, from now. He started to count the seconds backwards: 240, 239, 238.

An arresting hand descended on his shoulder. It's too early, thought Paul. Three and a half minutes too early. The foreman was always on the dot. The hand squeezed hard, hauling him to his feet. "What's going on?" said a heavy voice.

A dawn chorus of larks and cockerels speckled the damp air. Clouds swirled; there was more rain ahead. Papa Hofmann clutched Paul's shoulder, as if to prevent escape.

"What are you doing here?" Paul demanded.

"Lisl called me. She saw you sneak out of the inn and got suspicious."

"Nosy girl."

"You should be grateful."

"How did you know I'd be here?"

"There are no secrets in a village."

"You mean everyone knows?"

"About him?" said Papa, pointing downwards. "Pretty much."

"And about me?"

"Those who don't know, guess. We're not as dumb as we look."

"I'm sorry," said Paul.

"No time for that," said his father-in-law. "We'd better get our sleeves rolled up."

"Doing what?"

"Getting a cement mixture going by hand. Ever done it before? Watch me. It won't take long. I've brought a pair of shovels."

"But the crew will be here in a couple of minutes."

"I put Franz-Josef at the gate to head them off. Feed them some bullshit about bad smells, health inspection. Work cancelled today. Come back tomorrow. Free breakfast at the Laughing Hind."

"The foreman won't believe him; he'll want to see for himself."

"Franzi's got a sheet of paper with your signature. The foreman's a foreigner, don't read too good. Now stop your worrying and start shovelling."

Sweat had soaked Paul's shirt. He tore it off and, bare-chested, churned a conical pile of grit with his shovel, digging and mixing, churning and overturning, twice refreshing the mixture with water that he fetched in a bucket from the stream. His father-in-law hummed as he worked, a tuneless, rhythmic burr. Paul could not grasp how a man so rough could produce a daughter as delicate as Alice. Hofmann smiled with approval at Paul's naked efforts.

When the two piles reached a finger-tested consistency, the two men began shovelling the cement dollop by dollop, side by side, onto the corpse at the bottom of the pit. The dollops were haphazard, more falling around the head than at the feet.

"Climb down the ladder and rake it over with your shovel," directed Hofmann. "When no part of the remains is uncovered, I'll drop another few shovelfuls of cement and you can spread it evenly across a wide area to make it look like drainage treatment."

"Like this?" Paul called from below.

"Perfect," said Hofmann. "A professional job, I'd say."

"Any more?"

"That'll do."

"Help me out."

The older man hauled him up by the hand at the top of the ladder, holding on to him again by the shoulder to steady him on safe ground. They had never touched flesh to flesh, so far as he could remember. Feeling suddenly frail, Paul lurched down for his shirt and pulled it across his bare shoulders.

"Better?" said Papa.

"You've done this before," said Paul accusingly, a statement, not a question.

"Cementing?"

"Getting rid of bodies," said Paul.

"Sometimes things need to get looked after without fuss," said the older man, rinsing his hands and face in the stream. The clouds had passed and sunlight streaked the gorge.

"And this fellow?"

"Someone would have got rid of him, sooner or later."

"Natural justice?"

"He had it coming."

"But why help me?" Paul persisted.

"What do you mean?"

"You could have let me take the rap for his death, killed two birds with one stone. Why come down here to get me out? You don't like me, don't approve of me and Alice. You've never looked me in the eye or called me by my name."

"What's that got to do with anything?" said Hofmann. "You're family."

"And what does that mean?"

"It means you're not alone."

"Thank you," said Paul.

"Forget it, Mr. Mayor."

"My name is Paul."

"Whatever," grunted his father-in-law.

The faint chatter of disputation could be heard at the gates, fading away in a patter of departing feet. Franz-Josef must have held off the workforce with a flurry of false documents and an offer of free grub. The day stretched ahead, mute and golden, there to make of it what Paul pleased. Life, too, seemed open-ended.

"What about the fellow we've buried?" Paul asked by way of valediction.

"Scum," said Hofmann. "That's what my wife called him — *'Scum'* — when he marched past our windows, whipping you poor fellows up and down the track."

"So you knew?"

"Like I said: In a village, everyone knows. Now dry yourself on this towel and we'll go home for breakfast."

"How can you think of breakfast in a place like this?" exclaimed Paul.

"Damson-jam pancakes, Lisl promised. My favourites." His father-in-law gave a broad grin, before plodding his heavy way uphill.

■ ■ ■ ■

PART THREE:
HIDE

■ ■ ■ ■

CHAPTER FIFTEEN

One crisp noon, forty-two years after the events related, an air-conditioned coach pulled up in front of the Laughing Hind and disgorged a late-spring dribble of elderly tourists. Off-peak, the hotel accommodated discount visitors who were past their prime — blue rinse and blazer groups on a lakes and mountains fortnight that they had booked out of loneliness, boredom, a quest for lost times, or the urge to take leave of earthly splendours before the last, grim confinement. In the hilly chill, a busload of seniors formed two gender lines for the ground-floor washrooms before moving on without curiosity or real hunger to a pre-ordered three-course lunch served with a minimum of fuss, the dishes designed for the geriatric international palate, being free of salt, sugar, cholesterol, and any discernible taste.

One tourist detached himself from the

straggled line and stepped outside to gulp thin air, telling the others that he needed to encourage an appetite. A sturdy man of medium height and weather-beaten skin, he wore his age with soldierly erectness and paced the tarmac with the air of one who knew his way around the world and was not inclined to follow the herd. Stopping at the centre of the forecourt, he turned in three directions, raising his eyes to admire the mountain peaks. At the fourth compass point, his eyes rested on the eight-storey concrete building where he was booked to eat two standard meals and sleep the night. A grimace creased his craggy features. The hotel had been erected round and above what must once have been a mediaeval inn, its gabled wall incorporated into the right-hand corner of the façade. This was the sort of thing that infuriated him, the reduction of organic heritage to tourist kitsch, and he railed about it every night of this dehuman-ised Calvary when the more alert members of the party repaired to a bar where lads in leather pants leapt and slapped one anoth-er's butts and girls in dirndls poured litres of a putatively local beer that had been brewed two thousand miles away. The disgruntled traveller did most of the railing to himself, since half of his companions fell asleep on the second litre, and because, a nurturer by nature, he did not like to appear unappreciative of the athletic efforts of young people, doubtless underpaid. He was not, he muttered, a crusty old curmudgeon. Not quite yet.

Shaking his cropped grey head, the stray passenger marched back indoors and wound up at a reception desk that was identical in height, colour, and texture to every other front counter he had confronted on a tour that he'd regretted purchasing the moment a Rockefeller Center travel agent swiped his American Express gold card and wished him a pleasant trip. What the hell was he doing here?

"The group lunch is in the dining room over there," said a voice behind the reception desk, a paper shuffler to all appearances, fortyish, corpulent, and officious.

"May I ask you a question?" said the awkward visitor.

"No problem, sir."

"Can you tell me: Is there a Paul Miller here?"

"A guest in the hotel?"

"No, he used to live here."

The fat deskman shook his head without raising his eyes. "It's a common name, Miller," he muttered. "We must get twenty,

425

thirty such guests a year by that name. I'm sorry, I can't help you."

"Not a guest, I said. He was once the landlord of this place."

The hotelier's eyes rose to counter level, truculent and heavy-lidded. "This house has been owned by my family for three hundred years, sir. Our name is not Miller. Sir."

"May I ask what it is?"

The hotelier jerked his thumb over his left shoulder at a hand-painted wooden sign above his head. KARLHEINRICH HOFMANN, PROPRIETOR it said on a neat bed of poppies, lilacs, and gentians.

"Nice to meet you, Mr. Hofmann," said the visitor.

"Are you here on official business?" asked the hotelier, alert to the authority in his voice and suspecting the presence of one of those inspectors who could reduce your place from four stars to three.

"Not exactly."

"May I ask the reason for your question?"

"It's private. I passed through here a long while ago. Before your time. Thought I might tie up some loose ends."

"With a man called Miller?"

The visitor nodded.

"Nothing to do with me," said the proprietor. "Shall I make enquiries?"

"That won't be necessary. Probably best left forgotten."

"I can ask," the man offered, twitching with anxiety.

"Don't bother. It won't make a jot of difference to your life. Thank you for your help. I think I'll skip lunch and take a walk."

Bypassing battered chicken and insipid apple strudel retrieved from the deep freeze, the visitor stepped back outside and cast a professional eye over a town that covered two convergent slopes with identical twin-storey cottages, speared at indecent intervals by medium-rise hotels of the kind he had once been asked to build in Milwaukee and had honourably declined. A steeple caught his eye and he wrestled with recalcitrant memory to retrieve the church's name — St. Ignatius, that was it.

He decided he could do with a drink. There was a bar at the far end of the building, a stainless-surface utility for local idlers. He ordered a beer for himself and whatever anyone else was having. "Schnapps" — four sets of false teeth grinned — "and beer to wash it down." He asked, after the schnapps was downed and replenished, if they remembered the landlord, the one who had run the Laughing Hind after the war. "Coffee machine," they cried in jocular chorus.

"Popular, he was."

"What happened to him?" the visitor asked. Change of dialect. Slurp of beer. The locals were giving nothing away.

He wiped his mouth and was about to leave, when a low voice at his elbow said, "I hear you have been asking about Paul Miller."

The woman was short, slight, and snow white above the hairline.

"That's right," he said.

"It's a common name, insignificant you might say."

"The man I knew was not insignificant."

"We don't talk about him anymore."

"I see."

"Some people forget; others would rather not remember. Can I get you a coffee?"

She walked him out into the courtyard, round the perimeter of the hotel, and into a side entrance that revealed the old saloon bar. "It's the only part of the building I kept unchanged." His hostess smiled. "Did you say you were here before?"

An espresso machine hissed at the touch of her fingers, beneath the dead eye of a decrepit stag. "It's an antique," said the woman, "one of the oldest still in public use. Experts have come twice from Milan to inspect the mechanism. They want to buy it for a design museum."

"These things used to be on every street corner in Chicago when I was in college."

"They had their day," said the woman.

"Like us, you mean?" The visitor laughed, enticing her into reminiscence.

"Speak for yourself," she flashed back. "I still make myself useful."

"I'm sorry, I didn't mean you were decrepit."

"No offence." She smiled. "I'm Elisabeth Hofmann, by the way."

"Ed Weaver."

"Nice to meet you, Mr. Weaver. Where are you from?"

"Iowa, Illinois, Milwaukee, California, New York, all over. And you?"

"I've lived here all my life."

"You wouldn't be Lisl, would you?" guessed Weaver, not knowing where that inspiration had come from.

"Have we met before?" she retorted, intrigued by his presumption.

"We danced together once. At a wedding."

"We have five bookings here every weekend. Whose wedding was it?"

"A flash of fantasy and romance into this overcast day. . . ."

He was playing all or nothing on the recognition card. If she blanked him, he was out of the game.

"You're Captain Wierzbicki," said Lisl.

"I wore a longer name in those days."

"And a well-pressed uniform. Captain Wierzbicki, the district commander . . ."

"I had to change the name when I got home," explained Weaver. "Wierzbicki was fine for a gas station in Iowa, but when I went into practice and tendered for multimillion-dollar commissions, it was easier to give New York and D.C. a name they could spell. I was the man who got Paul Miller to change his name, start over. So I did the same for myself. Took a pin to the telephone directory —"

"And chose Weaver, a defunct country craft."

"Pretty much like Miller, Mrs. Hofmann."

"You may call me Lisl. Not many people do anymore."

Her eyes were unclouded, her movements uncluttered, her English textbook-correct. She was alert and intelligent, exceptionally so for a tourist-trek hotel owner in a folksy flounced skirt with matching short jacket — an outfit on sale at her own gift store for a price beyond rational consideration.

"You must wonder what I'm doing here," said Weaver, inviting the question. Lisl laid coffee and cakes on an alcove table and motioned him to sit on the opposite bench.

"I retired last year," he explained, unasked. "Sort of retired, semi. Had some health setbacks and thought I'd retrace a few steps, tie up loose ends. You never know what lies ahead. Touch wood."

"Cancer?" said Lisl clinically.

"Triple bypass. A major artery furred up and was ready to blow."

Lisl gave the wooden table a superstitious tap.

"I've had a good life," resumed Weaver. "Got my name on a few buildings, saw the world for what it's worth, spent a night at the White House. But once you've had the exhilaration of high achievement and recognition, you know it'll never be that good again. And then you look back and ask, What was all that about? Did I make much of a difference to anyone, anyone at all? Right now, I can't get much of an answer."

"No family to share the success?" asked Lisl.

"Two ex-wives. A daughter, somewhere. A Christmas card from her, if I'm lucky."

"I'm sorry."

"Don't be. That's life."

"The buildings?"

"Someone else could have built them. It didn't have to be me. I'm not an original. I did what I was paid for. I kept the clients happy and the income coming in. The fame? Ephemeral. Looking back, I've gone through life without touching the sides."

He took a nip at the coffee, scalded his tongue, and asked for a glass of water. As Lisl went to fetch it, he found it easier to talk without her staring him in the eye across the table. By some unexpected empathy, she appeared to feel the same, taking up a protective position behind the bevelled bar.

"I came out of the hospital with a transistor ticking inside of me and no-one waiting at home," said Weaver. "I ran through a lot of conversations in my head, the ones that had been left unfinished. Paul Miller most of all. We exchanged cards for a while, then lost touch. I wrote here a couple of years back, inviting him to an awards ceremony. I was being honoured for a building in Miami that I thought he might appreciate — all white and glass, just like he used to dream of. First-class flight, expenses paid. Got no reply. Wrote again. Still no answer. Then I thought, Hell, I'll go and see for myself what this here place looks like after all these years."

"As you can see . . ." said Lisl.

"It's like everywhere else." Weaver

432

grinned. "The tourist gets fleeced and every mouse hole with running water is designated 'deluxe accommodation.' "

"That's the name of our business."

"No place for a midnight dreamer, then, like Paul."

"Only for a nightmare manufacturer."

"What do you mean by that?"

"Never mind."

Weaver was good at extracting information. He knew when to press for details and when to change tack. He was a good listener, attending less to what a client was saying than to the gaps and hesitations in the speech pattern, the chinks through which he might penetrate. Patience, he reckoned, was his greatest talent.

"Paul was responsible for modernising the place, wasn't he?"

"I just told you," said Lisl, her voice a shaft of steel, "I'd rather not talk about that."

"I guess he moved on, then?"

"People do," said Lisl.

"I'd better go," said Weaver.

"So soon?"

"I don't want to press on painful memories."

"Why do you assume they are all painful?"

"Can you tell me about the non-painful ones? In general terms, without causing distress or breaching any confidences. Just so I know if he's alive or dead."

"It's all a long time ago," said Lisl. "A long, long story."

"I've got all day and all night," said Weaver, "before I get moved on to another beauty spot that's been blighted beyond redemption by concrete hotels."

Lisl laughed, a guilty giggle that called to mind a skittish girl with dancing eyes who used to flutter, book in hand, around copper-bottomed Alice. Weaver tried to remember what Paul had told him about Lisl, some double-edged compliment, but he failed to connect two memory cells and gave up.

"I won't discuss Paul," she stipulated from the safety of the bar.

"Tell me about yourself, then." Lisl shrugged.

"Look, why don't I go first?" proposed Weaver. "I was a hick kid with officer's pips and two hundred men at my command. Paul Miller looked at me from where you're standing now, thin as a centipede, stared at me with moonscape eyes and made me feel like an ant that shat in the Sistine Chapel. He had this air of experience and moral rectitude that I could never match if I lived for a millennium. The best I could do was look, listen, and try to be like him.

"When I came to say goodbye, he told me to get an education. He told me I had a gift for leadership, that I could leave a mark on the world. Anything was possible, he said. A man could shed his past and start over. I was young, gullible, malleable. I cast off my roots, quit the gas pump. It killed my poor old pa inside a year, but by then I was up and away. Chicago was brain heaven, a gathering of the elemental and the ethereal. I hung out with philosophers and appropriated their ideas. I became a pioneer of ethical architecture, championing beauty and energy efficiency in a wilderness of builders' greed. I shamed billionaires into building for posterity. I thought Paul might approve."

"And you achieved great success," Lisl confirmed.

"I was famously quixotic and furiously fashionable, with enough commissions to fill three lifetimes. Four of my buildings will stand the test of time. One is a landmark, protected under international law."

"Congratulations."

"Thank you. Every single one of them is fatally compromised."

435

"By failing to meet your ideals?"

"By failing to meet the ideals that Paul Miller imprinted on me. I added nothing of my own. Can you imagine how it feels to be showered with awards when you're forever looking over your shoulder, wondering what the true originator would make of it? That's why I wanted to bring Paul to Miami, to confront myself with my compromise — which was indirectly his."

Lisl smiled. It had been a while since she had shafted a man with a well-aimed barb and drawn a red flood of emotion. She was enjoying herself. When Weaver paused, she pressed for more.

"But you are famous for your work?"

"Moderately."

"Money, property, presidential medals, television . . ."

"Yes, all of that. When the transistor they planted in my chest packs it in, I won't have to be flung into a pauper's grave like Mozart. The French government have offered me a plot in Père Lachaise, across the aisle from Oscar Wilde."

"*'For each man kills the thing he loves . . .'*"

"I turned them down."

"The French Republic must have been devastated."

Weaver remembered now what Paul had

436

said about her. Lisl was acerbic in tongue and mind, a stickler for literal meaning, a ferret who never let go until she had nailed truth to the wall. She was a misplaced peg, a jagged rectangle in this round hole of a hotel. Jammed here for life, it seemed, stuck in the spot where he had twirled her around at Paul's wedding, brighter than any girl in miles, yet unwilling or unable to tear up her roots as he had done.

Whereas Weaver had filial cause to regret his uprooting, Lisl did not seem to mind the opportunities she might have missed. Her manner was calm, her eyes vivacious, her tongue rapier-sharp, her face crinkled with mirth. She was nothing like the women he dated back home, puffed with platitudes and smoothed out by surgeons. She liked getting a rise out of a man, not just a buck or a bang. He had already told her more about his aches and aims than he had to any other woman in years. And she was testing him, teasing him, demanding more. He needed to keep her interested in him if he was going to get anywhere near the information he had come to find.

"Who is to blame for your angst?" she enquired.

"Myself," said Weaver, "and Paul. I told you: I am what he made me. Before I met him, I was a blank sheet. If he were to walk in here right now, he could claim credit for everything I did. He was not shy in taking possession of other people."

"You can say that again," said Lisl, an unforced admission.

"And I owe him a lot. If I had never met him, I'd have gone back to the gas station, married the girl next door, and lived drearily ever after. Paul got me to make choices. He rewrote my script. To some extent, I'm still speaking his lines."

"Sounds familiar," said Lisl.

"What do you mean?"

"Nothing."

"Come on, you must mean something."

"A cadence, a turn of phrase . . ."

"Can you be specific?" he asked, pressing her.

"I told you: I am not going to talk about Paul Miller. It's off-limits. We don't talk about him. Is that understood?"

"Understood," said Weaver. "Then tell me about you. You agreed to tell me."

"It's a long story." She smiled, coming out from behind the bar. "I don't know where to begin."

"Begin," said Weaver, "at the beginning."

"*Alice in Wonderland,*" said Lisl.

" 'Begin at the beginning,' " quoted

438

Weaver, " 'and go on till you come to the end: then stop.' "

"I wish I could," said Lisl with a look he could not interpret.

She was a natural storyteller, structuring events to raise and lower narrative tension and minimise the risk of inattention. She had a velvety voice and a precise turn of phrase, depicting Alice as "the heart in our family" — *in,* Weaver noted, not *of* — and Franz-Josef as "half a man, before he ever lost his arm."

"Pardon me if I'm mistaken, but didn't you marry him?"

"My mistake, not yours." She grinned, the skin around her eyes wrinkling. "It lasted five years, gave us three children — including the fat, surly one you met out front. But it was not made in heaven. Franzi drank a lot and stayed out nights. I heard he had a woman across the valley. There was no shortage of lone women in those days. I told him to move in with her, said he could keep his job here — I was running the business by then — but he would be happier away from me. After that, we were friends until he died."

"Did you remarry?"

"I had offers," said Lisl coquettishly, "and

involvements, but there were only two real men in my life."

"Your father, I remember, was an impressive man. . . ."

"A good man, and wise."

"And the other fellow?"

She rose from the table, stretched her arms above her head, and said nothing for such a long time that Weaver wondered if she was about to throw him out.

"Not here," she announced.

"Where, then?"

"I take a daily walk, on doctor's orders, for the blood pressure. You can walk me to the top of the hill, if you're quick enough on your feet."

"I work out twice weekly," said Weaver, stung into defensiveness. There was a calf muscle that had been twingeing on the long bus journey. He hoped he could make it up the hill.

"Then let's go, before the place gets overrun by tourists — begging your pardon, sir."

"No offence, Mrs. Hofmann. And, please, call me Ed."

"Ed it is."

They marched to the crest of the hill, past a white-walled hospital and the old church, up to where the road had once vanished into woods and was now a four-lane highway adorned with four-colour advertisement hoardings for a health spa, "Recommended by physicians in 26 countries — Neustadt for the best of health."

"Pampering the rich, it's our second-biggest industry," explained Lisl.

"You bring them here, to the concentration camp site?"

"Every triple-cursed centimetre of it. A healthy restorative."

"Not a very sensitive use, if I may say so."

"Why not? They taught us at school that people got sent here for the health of the nation. Life is full of ironies. Anyway, don't be too shocked by this. Wait till you see our number-one service industry."

"What's that?"

"All in good time . . ."

"You mentioned the other man in your life," said Weaver, tantalised beyond endurance.

They sat down on an olive green bench, overlooking a stretch of sun-blessed valley that had been turned into a fenced-in wild park, "safe for families with small children." Sipping a glass of outrageously priced tap water that Weaver had fetched from the spa hotel, Lisl fast-forwarded without prelude to her father's funeral, speaking in a tone of reverie, oblivious to her companion. "That's where my love for the other one died," she began.

She had planned to say a few words about her father at the family tomb, to say them aloud among his loved ones, but before she could step forward, this outsider usurped her right to speak, perverting the occasion into a set of party games. "I was furious," said Lisl. "Furious at my father for arranging this charade — he had a warped sense of humour — and furious at this other one who had taken over Papi's funeral just as he had taken over Alice, the inn, the village, and me. My feelings for Paul ended there and then. I saw him with unerring lucidity as a predator, a mortal threat to us all. It made me grip my mother's thin arm so hard, she let out a little cry, poor thing. But I had received a premonition and I needed somehow to share it. I was stricken by a different sense of loss — no longer for my father, but for the tragedy that was about to befall us all."

Lisl clamped her lips to the rim of the glass and drank, eyeing Weaver without focus as she might look upon a bird pecking at a worm. Ed hunched forward on the bench, rubbing the back of one big mitt against the other in a vague consoling motion. He wondered if he ought to take her hand — she seemed so upset — but he decided against it, not that he ever got these things right with women. He guessed she was talking about Paul. She had been in love with him, that was for sure. And now she had shut up. He had to keep Lisl talking.

"You speak pretty good English," he said with a B-Western accent. "*Predator, premonition, lucidity,* them's fancy words for a country lass. Cain't remember ever having had cause to use such fine words myself."

"I beg your pardon?" He'd got it wrong again. This was no time for jokes.

"Sorry, that was inappropriate. When I am taken aback by something and need to dissimulate, Mrs. Hofmann, I slip into a hick accent. I guess you do the same, only you use long words to hide behind."

"You're quite a sharpshooter, Mr. Weaver."

"Takes one to know one, Mrs. H."

"Touché."

"Lisl," he said, trying once more, his hands wrapped around each other, all fingers and thumbs, "have you talked about this to anyone before?"

Lisl shook a head of spray-set, fine-spun white hair.

"Given the opportunity," said Weaver, "what would you have said at your father's sepulchre?" He cunningly insinuated the classical noun to suggest a literary affinity. It seemed to work, lulling Lisl into a zone of trust. She stared ahead into the picture-postcard view. "I was going to tell them a story that no-one knew but me," she whispered, "about the day Papi told me he was going to kill himself."

She was back in childhood now, on her last day in the fourth grade. Ten years old, she had come top in literature and won a life-size head-and-shoulders photograph of the leader as a prize for her essay on flower metaphors in a poem by Goethe. Bursting with pride, trophy in hand, she dashed home and, knowing that surgery hours were over, ran into the doctor's room with the merest gloss of a knock at the door. Her father was slumped across his desk, head down on the writing mat, his bald crown exposed. Seeing Lisl, he motioned her to come in and shut the door.

"We have to be careful," he said.

"What's the matter, Papi?"

"I have received a warning from the future."

His last patient that morning had been a boy one class above hers. He presented with a monorchic irregularity. "That's when one testicle is missing, or has not descended," explained the doctor pedantically. He had taught all of his children the proper names for body parts, nothing to be ashamed of. The boy patient, dressed in a brown youth-movement shirt, his mother in worried attendance, dropped his pants for the doctor. His foreskin was mildly inflamed, perhaps from excessive masturbation, but before he could climb onto the couch for a full examination, the lad pointed at an object on the sideboard.

"What's that?" he demanded to know.

"A book," said the doctor.

"Whassit called?"

"*The Interpretation of Dreams.*"

"We burned one of them. It's banned, y'know. You don't wanna have one a them in the house, Doctor. Not good for you. Give it to me, before you get in trouble."

"Erwin, that is no way to speak to the doctor," whispered his mother.

"People gotta learn," the boy continued. "Things are different now. It's the leader what makes the rules, not doctor this and doctor that — begging your pardon, Doctor. You know what I mean. Lawyers, doctors, priests, clever clogs, they don't count no more. It's the people what decide."

"At that illiterate moment," said the doctor to his daughter, "I decided I must die. If I'd had a gun in my desk, I would have shot the boy and his laundry sack of a mother, then myself. If I'd had morphine in the icebox, I would have loaded a syringe as soon as they were gone, and plunged it in a vein. I cannot bear to live in such a world, a world that teaches children to read just enough so that they can know which books to burn. For the first time, I could not bear to touch a patient. I thanked Erwin for his kind advice and, after a perfunctory glance at his weenie, told him to get dressed and go to the surgeon with a letter I would provide, shamefully gratified that he turned pale at the cutting noun *surgeon* and forgot to take the Freud with him when he left. I scrubbed my hands red at the sink and sat here, as you find me, waiting to die."

"You mustn't," lisped Lisl, but the doctor hardly seemed to hear.

"This lout befouled my sanitary space and made me break the sacred oath of care. I failed myself and failed him. I wanted to die, wanting it with the greed of a man who grabs the last slice of cake on the breakfast table."

"You can't die, Papi. . . ."

"Yes, you're right, little one. Of course I cannot die, because that would mean leaving my family undefended and my world of ideas in ruins, abandoning my loved ones,

446

not sticking around to see the return of reason. So I have no choice. I must live. But how? How can I get through each day? How can I preserve a store of knowledge for the day of eventual reenlightenment? How am I to save our precious books?"

"That's easy, Papi," said Lisl, flourishing her autographed potrait of the leader. "We hang this on the door to the attic and behind it we hide the forbidden books. If Erwin and his gang come to search the house, they will see the photo, salute it, and forget why they came in the first place."

"You think it will be that simple?" said her father.

"If those boys were bright, they wouldn't be looking for books to burn."

The doctor burst into full-throated laughter, hugging his daughter to his scratchy whiskers and promising to double her pocket money if she swore not to tell anyone about their conversation. "Let's do it," said pigtailed Lisl, solemn in her precocity. "Let's do it now, while everyone is out. It'll be our secret. Not a word to Mother — she worries too much."

"Like squirrels," said her father, "we hide things until the weather changes."

"Like bunny rabbits," giggled Lisl, "and lazy old badgers."

447

"One day," pledged her father from beneath an armful of books, "we will free these works from captivity and release them into the wild." He carried up Sigmund Freud in marbled frontispieces, followed by a set of Heinrich Heine and some sheet music by Mendelssohn, finishing with a mingling of the brothers Mann (who loathed each other, he told her), a play by Bertolt Brecht, well-thumbed paperbacks of Kafka, Lessing, and Wolfskehl, an uncut book by Walter Benjamin, a pouch of poems by Else Lasker-Schüler, and the dour-looking works of a man called Magnus Hirschfeld — "not to be read until you are twenty-one, Lisl," said her father as they sat in the kitchen afterwards over hot chocolate and a glass of wine respectively, with her prize certificate on the table to show what had passed that day between them, the act they had sealed.

"That's what I should have said at the funeral," declared Lisl, staring Weaver in the eye for the first time. "Books were life and death to my father. They were not a source of silly riddles, as they were to Paul. They were the breath in his lungs, the bread on his plate, the jam on his bread, the brimming of ideas that gave him impetus to face each day, no matter how vile the world beyond. Books were the sum of him, the stuff he carried from childbirth to deathbed on his daily rounds, the source from which he dispensed comfort and relief. Paul never understood the essence of the man who was my father. He spoke at the grave like a stranger, and for that I could not forgive him. From the minute we left the cemetery, I felt nothing towards him. Neither love nor lust, hate or revulsion. I was as neutral as a Swiss."

"Did you say anything to Paul?" prompted Weaver. "Did you protest his intrusion?"

"I was going to, but Franzi took me away after the funeral and cared for me as a husband should. Next morning, at breakfast, I caught sight of Paul hurrying away from the hotel, his scarf flapping in a strong wind. As he ran, I felt a wrenching fear for Alice, who had given him her life. He could have been an axe murderer, for all she knew. I used to laugh when she told me that they never discussed anything that happened before the day they met. Now I wanted to raise the alarm, to warn her that he was a destroyer. But I couldn't. Anything I said would have been construed as emotional, a jealous reaction to my father's misplaced trust in this man. I had to bide my time. Had I known that Paul was rushing off at that very moment to see a psychotherapist who treated only what my father called 'the most interesting cases,' I would have thrown a fit. But I didn't find out until much later."

"Hang on," interrupted Weaver. "How did you know he was seeing a shrink? Isn't that supposed to be confidential?"

Lisl laughed, that fetching, self-mocking chuckle he remembered from their long-ago dance, an embarrassment at her own cleverness. "Of course it is supposed to be privileged information, but I am a doctor's daughter. I get to know things."

"How did you find out?"

"Some months after my father died, a letter arrived from a Dr. Kovacs, informing honoured colleagues of his immediate retirement and asking if they wanted him to return patient files. The letter should have gone to the clinic, but the postman dropped it by mistake in my mother's letter box, and I, wanting to protect her from unpleasant surprises — you never know what men have been up to — opened all official-looking mail. I saw Paul's name in the Kovacs letter. I wrote back, using my father's rubber-stamped signature, asking for the file to be sent to my address."

"That's illegal," protested Weaver.

"It was a family emergency," said Lisl.

"It's unethical."

"Questionable, I agree. But I was frantic with grief and fear. Can you grasp that? And I thought — who knew? — that a peek into Paul's head might explain the hold he had over my father and give me some idea how to protect Alice. I knew she was at risk. That was my concern, making sure no harm came to poor Alice."

"And did it?"

"I kept the file under my bed and sneaked out to read it on the landing, beneath the stair light. By the end, the words were so familiar, I could have set them to music."

"What did you discover?" probed Weaver.

A chaffinch gave a lyrical trill, letting the other birds know that it was around and ready to defend its territory. "Enough, enough, enough!" cried Lisl in response, her voice rising to a shriek, her compact body recoiling from Weaver's adjacent presence on the bench. "Didn't I tell you I don't want to talk about him? Do you think I can't see through your tricks, your techniques for teasing things out? Enough! I have met men like you before, Mr. Weaver, seedy little gropers, always wanting more. Well, that's it. Not another word. It's been nice meeting you again. Good of you to drop by. Have a lovely vacation in our hotel. If you want more information, I suggest you consult the public archives in the town hall."

Her anger was high and real, two crimson points on her cheekbones and a pair of eyes dancing with agitation. This was no longer playful Lisl, cocky in her cleverness and self-control, but a woman hurt and resilient, an opponent capable of self-defence and counter-attack. Weaver risked turning her into an enemy if he was not careful. That would leave his trip a write-off and himself more of a mess than before.

He had to win Lisl back, and he thought he knew how to do it. Three decades of running a practice, maintaining a team of highly strung professionals, and beating off tough competition had left Weaver in command of as neat a set of operating tools as any brain surgeon in mid-section. He was no longer the shallow uniform that had danced with Lisl. Life and Paul had taught him a few lessons. He had learned from Paul to search people for entry points that would respond to his suasion. He had learned from life never to give up, to decide at each setback when to be forthright and when to simulate contrition. This, he reckoned, was a moment for strategic humility.

"Hey, Lisl," said Weaver, retracting his arm from the back of the bench and rising to his feet in front of her in an attitude of sincere abjection. "That was unforgivable. I got carried away by natural curiosity and pried into your affairs. I should never have done that. I am truly sorry and I promise it won't happen again. I'm not a man who takes advantage of women. You must believe that."

Lisl appraised him with steady, sensible eyes. "I do," she said. After a pause, she added, "I went too far, as well. You're not an exploiter."

"No," said Weaver, "I'm the one that went too far, and I'd like to make amends."

"What do you have in mind?"

"Dinner for two tonight in the best restaurant in the valley. A good meal, fine wines, light chit-chat, nothing painful or inquisitive, just two old acquaintances having a night out in candlelight."

"Not so much of the old."

"Delete the old."

"You make it sound moderately appealing. I'll think about it." The edge had gone from her voice, replaced by a hint of flirtation. His shrewd apology had worked.

"How will I know your decision?" asked Weaver.

"I'll leave a message at the front desk."

"Did you say seven o'clock?" He smiled, pressing home the advantage.

"Seven-thirty's better."

"I kiss your hand, ma'am — as folks say around these parts."

"Kiss my ass, Ed." Lisl grinned in prompt imitation. "I'm not that easy a pushover."

The town hall, she had said. Why hadn't he thought of that first? The town hall would have all the answers about Paul, the first mayor of Neustadt. As soon as Lisl left, Ed half walked, half ran down the hill towards the pillared building in the reliquary square of the overbuilt village. He had enough words in the native tongue to ask the reception clerk to direct him to the archives. "Closed," sniffed the clerk. "Budget cuts. Open only on Mondays."

Weaver was not much of a liar, but he was in no mood to be deterred. "I have a letter from the director. We made an appointment for today. I'm sure it was today."

"When did you write?"

"Six months ago."

"That would be before the cuts?"

"I see. I'm only here for twenty-four hours. Is there anything you can do to help me?"

"Which university did you say you were from?" asked the clerk, a battered-looking man of pensionable age.

"Princeton," said Weaver, thinking the fellow must have heard of Albert Einstein.

"Let me try calling His Honour, the mayor."

"Tell him I'm researching the post-liberation era, nothing controversial."

Minutes later, Weaver was sitting in a basement amidst stacks of the local newspaper, which had ceased publication twenty years before, and the unlocked cabinets of the village photographer, likewise defunct. Resisting the lure of documents that bore his own young stamp of authority, he quickly found Paul's election result: 2,847 votes, against 316 for the Christian Democrat and a derisory 85 for the Socialist. Procedural reforms followed thick and fast. Council meetings became quarterly instead of monthly and a two-thirds majority was required to overturn a mayoral decision. This mayor was ruling practically by decree.

Weaver skimmed a year, two years. Suddenly a gap. He rang the clerk.

"There are five years missing."

"Conservation," came the reply.

"I beg your pardon?"

"They are being microfiched in the state library."

"Sh—" said Weaver, suppressing the expletive.

Beyond the gap, Paul was gone, never mentioned again. His erasure was so thorough that his name was not to be found even in a half-page obituary of the former landlord of the Laughing Hind, the genial Ludwig Hofmann. The omission reminded Weaver of a certain asphyxiating atmosphere.

"Where are you from?" a newcomer would be asked in those dark times.

"Over there" was the ultimate conversation stopper.

"Over there" could mean a time or a place — the time before the present, or a place beyond the rye field not far to the east, where the fertile soil was furrowed with barbed wire and machinegun nests. The border was over there. The past was over there, a place apart, a no-go zone. This country had an infinite capacity for suppressing past and place. Or so Weaver seemed to remember.

He called the clerk and asked if there was a photographic archive. "You're in luck," said the man. "We ran out of funds before we could put them on fiche." A cellar wall was lined with metal cabinets, each of them stuffed with mud-coloured envelopes bursting with prints, undusted in decades. Weaver pulled out the year in question and was

456

flung back four decades. In the photos, Paul is out on the streets, canvassing votes. People are pleased to see him. His hand is pumped by a man in a striped apron, a butcher proud and astonished that a man so able should come within his grasp. Paul is retracting his hand, his eyes searching for escape.

Photographs proliferated. In them, Paul is talking to tradesmen and labourers on victory night. A farmer bestows on him a home-cured ham. Someone from a women's deputation spoons him a dab of home-made jam. A priest invokes a blessing. Paul addresses the camera. The reel of handshakes runs on. Paul is relaxed, basking in approval. The old men in the bar were right: Popularity became the man, defined him.

And there was more. Glass negatives from the village photographer reveal the mayor as wedding host at the Laughing Hind. Paul is behind the bar, never among the dancers. A bride tumbles to the floor in mid-waltz, her plump haunches comically flared. Two youths haul her up by either arm, mimicking a tug-of-war for the reward of a pouting kiss. Paul's expression conveys a fastidious distaste.

Weaver, struck by a familiar face in the background, extracted a magnifying glass from the drawer and held the shot beneath the desk lamp. There was no mistake. There he stood, unformed and in uniform, with a look so naïve, he might have been a newborn babe. What did he, this pre-Weaver, know of life? He had fought and killed and governed, but he remained, at twenty-four, though no-one knew it, a virgin. He had never stopped long enough in one spot for romance, and when sex was available, it was of the sluttish or mercenary kind. He did not get around to consummation until an infirmary nurse, bored and overweight on the homebound troopship, put him out of his misery with swift despatch in an upper bunk, allowing him to return home a man and not, as he appeared in these photographs, an acolyte — always looking to Paul for guidance in the higher realms of human experience.

"What am I doing here?" he hears Paul saying as the last drunken farmer bangs the door on his way out. *"Why is a man with two doctorates plying drink to the peasantry?"*

"There are worse fates in life," says the young officer.

"How's that?"

"Think of your fellow professors, starving under communism, and ask yourself what they would give right now to be living above a

fat country pub."

"You're right," says Paul. "I should enjoy myself more."

"I didn't mean that," says Ed.

"Neither did I."

"What, then?"

"Nothing."

Ed does not know what Paul means by "nothing." "Nothing" is like "over there," an insurmountable barrier to conversation. Paul is the cleverest man Ed has ever met. He has been to hell and back. Ed observes his every word and move. He is the light that shines, but how? In his eyes? To deceive?

Half a lifetime later, Weaver had come back to find out. If he could crack the enigma of Paul, he might begin to understand why his own life had turned out the unsatisfactory way it did, why he had made such a hash of his ideals, never finding a loving partner, never achieving the perfection that glinted in his mind's eye. Was the fault innate to Ed, or did it stem from the inequality of his transaction with Paul? Had he been dazzled out of his own identity by his friend's irresistible personality? These were not questions of little consequence. They governed his life and work. They made it impossible for him to offer guidance to interns, fearing to bear responsibility for their possible dependency. They ruled out trust in love. One girlfriend had called him a hit-and-run lover; that hurt, but she was right. He had only to feel strong need for another person and he was on the run again. He was nearing the end of his useful life, with a beeping pacemaker in his chest and a vacant space in his bed, and still he had no idea who he really was or which part of himself he preferred, the Ed part or the Paul. And which was which.

The more he struggled to separate the parts, the more they fell into direct opposites. What had he derived from Paul — was it the will to do good, or the fear that nothing could ever be good enough? Was Paul a good influence or a malign shadow at his shoulder, willing him to fail? Was he a nagging conscience or the very opposite — a nudge to opportunism and amorality? It was to clarify these dichotomies that Ed had signed up for this caricature of a coach tour, where half the party talked only of their ailments and the other half were too far gone to remember what was wrong with them. He had considered bailing out at the next city they passed through, booking a business-class seat back to Kennedy, and impressing the air crew with his business-like manner, a man at the peak of his powers. The only thing that kept him on the bus was the chance, faint as it was, that he might find out what had happened to Paul and, from that result, separate his wreckage from the other man's sufficiently to allow himself a fair crack at an independent life. There was a woman he wanted to see again back home — two or three, actually — to see if he could find a soulmate for his remaining years. But to form a loving relationship, he needed first to exorcise himself of the other. That was what he was doing here. He needed to break free of Paul's shadow, to be Ed.

And to be free, he required the full story. The archive had given him a useful memory jerk, but Lisl held the real key. He had to make her loosen up, to yield the truths she had teased him with. He had gained one evening to work his charms on her — no second chance. He had to get it right first time, this time.

Returning the archive keys to the reception clerk, he strode down the hill in sunshine and was sweating heavily as he entered the air-conditioned lobby of the Laughing Hind hotel.

"Weaver, room three four two. Any messages?" he asked the paunchy desk clerk.

"Your afternoon excursion was delayed,"

said Karlheinrich Hofmann, "by your forgetting to tell the tour leader you wanted to miss it."

"Does that mean I get sent to bed without supper?" Weaver laughed.

"There is a message for you from my mother," said the manager. "She will meet you down here at seven-thirty."

Weaver beamed his biggest smile and patted the sullen fellow on his pudgy hand.

"Thank you, pal." He winked. "Tell her I won't let her down."

CHAPTER SIXTEEN

Ed dressed for dinner in a white button-down shirt, a mauve silk tie, a dark blue blazer, and grey slacks, the best he had packed. Lisl met him in a flowery dress that showed off her trim form and clear brown eyes. He bowed low and kissed her hand, whisking from behind his back an outsize bunch of pink roses. "They are lovely," squeaked Lisl in surprise. "I'll have them put in water right away in my living room."

"I booked a table at the Italian restaurant in Pringsheim," said Weaver. "It's the only one in the area that's listed in my guide-book."

"Then let me get the desk to cancel it," said Lisl. "It's pasta, pizza, tourist junk. I've arranged for us to dine in my apartment. My treat. I owe you an apology."

"Whatever for?"

"I shouldn't have bit your head off when you said something I didn't want to hear."

"We all have things we never want to hear about again."

"I was too sharp with you. It's a problem of mine. So allow me to make it up to you with the best cuisine in the region. I have asked our chef to prepare something special. He came within sniffing distance of a Michelin star last year. He's also the only one I trust with my diet — low salt, low everything."

"Sounds good to me," boomed Weaver, holding the elevator door open.

The apartment was on the tenth and top floor, furnished in international showroom style with reproduction chairs and tables and cream flounced couches, a determined absence of character. "I kept up appearances for major customers while I was running the business," said Lisl, "and now I'm retired, I can't be bothered to change it."

"Are you looking for a redesign?" suggested Weaver.

"What would you do with this?"

"Me? I'm hopeless with interiors. Every few years, I move into the Plaza for a month and let the boys loose on my place; the only room they can't touch is my study. When I move back in, I hardly notice the difference. Still, you gotta keep it looking good, for self-respect. Here, you've got this fabulous penthouse with a mountain view. You could make more of it. Open out the brickwork here, picture window here. Let in more light."

"Goethe's last words," said Lisl.

"What were?"

"More light."

"He'd have done well in my profession, that Goethe." She was still a big reader, he noticed, taking in the crowded shelves that lined three walls of the living room.

A table had been laid for two with shining silverware and a candelabra. Lisl struck a match. Flames danced on the cut-glass outline of an antique water jug. Ed held out a chair and she spread her skirts fetchingly as she sat down. A teenaged waitress in black and white shimmied in from the kitchen with chilled wine in a napkin-clad bottle.

"Your good health," toasted Lisl, raising a glass of tart Gewürztraminer.

"What's left of it." Weaver grimaced.

"Do you want to live forever?"

"Just long enough to sort out a few things."

Over a stew of fresh field mushrooms in the lightest choux pastry, Weaver emitted appreciative grunts, encouraging Lisl to make small talk.

"My granddaughter, Maria-Alice," she announced when the waitress returned to clear plates. Weaver rose, kissed a hand. He remembered how things were done here.

"Every bit as beautiful as you," he said, just stopping himself from adding "were."

"Thank you," said Lisl, with the faintest of blushes. "Not bright, though," she added when the girl was out of earshot. "Boys are all she has got on her mind."

The soup was a pellucid vegetable broth, the main dish a pink roast of lamb, served with root vegetables and a severe though complex Alpine red, whose name Weaver jotted down from the label. "Magnificent," he said, imbibing with restraint.

"Drink up," said Lisl. "The bottle has to be finished. I'm going away tomorrow for the rest of the week. You were lucky to catch me at home."

"I was," said Weaver.

"You are," corrected Lisl with a pedantic frown.

"Tell me about the business," said Weaver, a diversionary tactic.

"What's to tell?"

"Whatever you're comfortable telling me."

Lisl took a slow sip of red, wiping her lips on the crisp napkin. "It began a few months after the disasters," she began, "when everything was shit and Papa Hofmann was in hospital with a bladder cancer that they had not yet found. One afternoon, Mathilde came over and plonked herself down at a table. 'It's down to you and me, Lisl,' she said. 'Papa is sick, Franzi is weak, and we have children to feed. You and I must take charge. We have a business strategy and we must make it work. Read it tonight,' she said, slapping the document on the table, 'and I will come by in the morning.'

"What she had found in Papa's desk was Paul's master plan. It was a good plan, a challenge, a chance to take my mind off the futility of everything else. I thought, I can do this. Next morning, we agreed, Mathilde and I, that she would look after the inns on a day-to-day basis while I put my mind to growing the business.

"I caught a train to town, kitted myself out in a two-piece suit and nylon stockings. Then I went round all the real-estate offices and put a bid on every inn that was for sale within a hundred-kilometre radius. No-one else could see the potential, and I was able to make the deals without competing bids. Each inn I bought, I mortgaged at a different bank, raising funds for the next. Within two years, we had twelve properties."

"Impressive." Weaver whistled.

"Nerve-racking," said Lisl. "It was a pack of cards that would have come down with the first economic sneeze, but I was so ignorant, I never thought about a downturn, and the men at the banks mistook my confidence for acumen and my legs for a promise of something else. I was nominated businesswoman of the year by a newspaper and money flooded in. I invested it in customising the hotels, making each look exactly like the next, the same room sizes, cotton-mix sheets, breakfast menus, shoeshine machines, and lobby design. I was banking on the resumption of business travel and the return of foreign tourism, and sure enough, just as Paul predicted, both clicked in within a year or two and we were booking heavily. I flew to travel conventions, selling neutered rooms from glamorised photographs. One by one, the hotels filled up. With the profits, I bought more inns.

"I left the Hind to last, until after Papa was gone. When the wreckers moved in, I found myself yelling with joy as the staircase came down and the vast kitchen was stripped bare, expurgating the building, expunging its curse on us. I went, I think, a bit mad. At the last minute I saved the mediaeval entrance as a photo opportunity for tourist cameras, and the old bar with the coffee machine as a piece of personal sentiment.

"That's all there is to tell. Three years ago, when I merged the business with a Swiss chain, we were the fifth-largest hotel group in the country. Now, we are the second. Mathilde, I have to say, was magnificent. Apart from running the Black Horse and the Laughing Hind, she brought up my children while I was away. She was more of a mother than I was to poor Karli, downstairs."

"I like the brand name on my booking form," said Weaver. "Sleep-Easy."

Lisl roared, much as she must have done when the staircase came down. "I needed a name that said we were Anglo-friendly and conscience-clear. It fitted the bill. Nobody from abroad has ever asked me or my senior staff what we did in the war. Not that it's any of their business."

"So I can expect an undisturbed night's rest?"

"Not if you're me." Lisl chortled. "I get four hours a night if I'm lucky. Too much on my mind. Still, they say you need less sleep as you grow older."

"Among other things," replied Weaver, wondering if he was softening her up.

He veered off into a story about a palace

he had built for an Arab sheikh and his harem on the ruins of an old convent on the Corsaire in Cannes. It never failed to get a laugh at architectural conventions, but Lisl gave no more than a smile, and Weaver feared he was losing her. It was now or never.

"Don't answer if you don't want to," he murmured, walking round the table to refill her glass. "But, leaving Paul aside, do you think you could tell me what became of Alice? She was such a warm presence in this house. A good person."

"She was" — Lisl sighed — "the sweetest soul I have ever known."

The silence that descended with her verdict was unoppressive, neither resentful nor reflective, but the kind of lull that falls between old friends who have no high expectation of each other.

"After," said Lisl. A tense silence followed.

"After what happened." Another long hiatus.

"After . . . that," she finally began, "Alice fell into a deep melancholy, a place I could not reach her. She wore black and spoke to no-one except Johann, whom she called Hans, always in a low singsong voice like the Norns in Valhalla — you know, in Wagner's operas. I took her to the doctor, hoping he would give her what my father used to dispense to women after childbirth who suffered from their nerves — a listening ear and a nettle potion that did no harm except for making them pee a lot. Tobias Strauss, though, was a believer in Science. He declared that she was severely depressed and drove her himself to the university hospital, where three psychiatrists in white coats bullied her into submitting to mind-altering drugs and electroconvulsive therapy. She came home after a month or so wearing a fixed smile, unrecognisable.

"Life went on. One year, another. When the cancer took hold — Johann was nine — Alice kept it inside, telling no-one until it was too late for treatment and all Dr. Strauss could do was palliate her pain. She asked me in her final weeks to bring up Hans — Johann, that is — for her. I said: Is there anything you want me to tell him when he asks about his parents? She said: He must not idealise us. He should think of us as good people who did their best in circumstances beyond their comprehension. Those were her words. I remember them because it was so unlike Alice to use an alliterated polysyllabic construct. She must have heard it from Paul and held it to her breast as the cancer crunched away, dragging her to the earth before she reached thirty."

"I'm so sorry," murmured Weaver.

"Of all the people I knew," said Lisl, dry-eyed, "she was the acme of goodness. I knew it from the day she took my hand at kinder-garten and declared herself my friend."

"And Johann?"

"Why do you need to know?"

"No need, don't bother."

"I may as well tell you," said Lisl. "Johann was a quiet, considerate boy, a pleasure to bring up, never a brat. He was bright. At fourteen, he was ready to matriculate in mathematics. I did not know what to do with him. A professor in the city, a friend of my father's, took him under his wing, put him through an elite academy and into the university, where he acquired a passion for archaeology of the Palaeolithic period. He talked to me about it for hours when he came home, how the ancients in northern Africa made tools and weapons out of stone. He could light up a room with his enthusi-asm. Johann did not like to be touched, but when he left on the last trip to northern Kenya, he said, 'Thank you, Auntie,' and stroked my hair as I kissed him goodbye. That I will not forget.

"One day, the state police rang from the

capital, asking for me by name. I drove to the city like a robot and identified the remains in a morgue — scraps of white bone and scattered fabric."

"What happened?"

"We shall never know. He had stayed on, late, alone, one evening at a remote dig. They found his remains the next day in a lay-by on the eastern coastal highway. Road-kill, the police said. Hit by a truck in the dark. The driver probably never noticed, and the vultures had stripped him clean by daybreak. I went out there to see for myself.

"An English lawyer told me there is no such thing in Africa as an accidental death. Johann must have been murdered, because his knapsack was never recovered. I offered to pay for a private investigation, but the lawyer said it would be expensive and futile. The pursuit of justice is a European indulgence. Africans are much less bothered. He did make the point, though, that if Johann was murdered for his possessions, why did they leave this behind?"

She held out her right hand with a ring on the fourth finger. Weaver ambled round the table to examine it, holding it close to his face before asking — certain of her answer — if it was not the same gold band that Paul had given to Alice on their wedding day. Lisl left her hand inert in his, pleased at his recognition.

"I can understand now," rumbled Weaver in a low, confidential tone, "why you're so reluctant to revisit those events. I won't press you for more, and I apologise again if any of my questions has caused you distress. I am grateful for your forbearance, Lisl, truly grateful. It sets a few things in my mind to rest."

"I'm glad."

"Just one thing . . ."

"Enough," she said, withdrawing her hand. "Not. Another. Word. Understood?"

"I understand," said Weaver, desperate for her to continue.

"You don't," she said. "Understand. You think it's painful for me. Not so. It's point-less. So many lives cut short. So much goodness reduced to dust. So many funerals to arrange. It makes me feel ashamed sometimes that I am still alive."

"And secretly pleased that you have sur-vived?"

"Exactly. That's where the shame comes in. Why me? Why you, for that matter? What's the point of it all? Let's change the subject."

"Of course," said Weaver.

"I wonder what has become of our desserts?" said Lisl.

She tinkled a silver bell on the table and, when no waitress appeared, strode out of the room. "Just as I thought!" She chuckled, returning with a slip of paper in her fingers. " 'Sorry, Oma — I've got a date. Desserts downstairs. Lots of love, Maria-Alice.' "

"That's kids for you these days," said Weaver.

"Were we any better?" Lisl smiled.

"I guess we didn't involve the rest of the family in our love lives."

"I'll go downstairs to get the desserts," said Lisl. "It may take a few minutes. Make yourself comfortable on the sofa. We'll eat at the coffee table and the house staff can clear up in the morning. If you want to freshen up, by the way, it's at the end of the corridor."

Weaver needed no second invitation. The moment the door clicked behind Lisl, he leapt into search mode. It was not going to be on the living room bookshelves, the thing he sought. There were two bedrooms and a study. The desk in the study was locked. Damn, damn, damn. Where else might she have put it? Where does a woman hide something that she doesn't want anyone to see? Caroline, the one he should have married, Caroline with more skeletons in her curriculum vitae than the anatomy room at Mount Sinai, used to cram secret papers in her underwear drawer. He had no time to strip Lisl's penthouse. Make a guess, he told himself. She'd be back any minute. Where would someone like Lisl keep her smalls?

The bedroom had a queen-size orthopaedic mattress which looked like it was not used for much other than sleep. Beneath it, four capacious drawers. The first shoes, the second sweaters, the third underwear, mature and sensible. A fastidious thief, Weaver averted his eyes as his hand rummaged through intimacies of silk and cotton.

Nothing, nothing, nothing. He went back to the desk and sat there drumming his fingers on its leather top. There were two document piles on either side, right and left, incoming mail and out. The file on the top of the left-hand pile was thick and forbidding, legal deeds, he assumed, until he looked at the top right-hand corner and read a familiar name in cursive script. Eureka, he whispered, Eu-bloody-reka.

He could not take it outright. Lisl would be sure to notice its absence. But if he removed its contents and replaced them with papers from the other pile, she might not find anything amiss until morning, by

476

which time he would know what he needed and be ready to leave. It took him less than a minute to empty the folder and stuff it with household bills. He slipped off his blazer, opened his shirt, and rammed the sheaf of papers into the top of his pants, beneath the belt, buttoning up with trembling fingers and seizing his jacket by the collar just as the front door clicked open. "Berries from our Hansel and Gretel woods," announced Lisl, "with home-made vanilla ice."

"Would it be terrible if I skipped dessert?" said Weaver, bulging at the waist. "It's been a lovely evening, but I'm suddenly totally bushed."

"Of course," said Lisl. "Are you unwell?"

"No, but the energy levels are not what they used to be."

"Don't let me detain you," said Lisl.

"I'm really sorry."

"Don't be. I enjoyed myself. Let's have coffee in the morning, before you go."

She held a hand out at the door, only for Weaver to reach across and kiss her on the cheek. She smiled. Weaver let her lips gloss his close-shaven skin but pulled back from a risk of embrace, fearing she might discover the theft on his guilty body. The elevator whisked him four floors down to his room, with the truth at his fingertips.

Paul's psychiatric dossier lay on the table, thick and forbidding. Weaver hung his jacket over the chair, switched on the desk lamp, and checked the door again to make sure it was double-locked and chained. Sitting in the circle of light, he untied a brown cloth ribbon and raised the front sheet, rocking back at a billow of dust, as if horses had thundered through the room. When his coughing abated, Ed walked away from the file, fearful that he had disturbed dead spirits. Ridiculous, he muttered, there's no such thing as ghosts. Pull yourself together, man.

Forensically, like the first detective at a crime scene, he noted the physical disposition of objects. The pile of papers was five inches thick and contained 318 pages, about half in typescript, the rest in an antiquated hand, nearly unintelligible. The paper was poverty-era issue, crumbling at the edges. It appeared to consist of notes relating to a man's psychoanalysis with a therapist, Professor Imre Kovacs, whose methods appeared to be far from orthodox. His reports, alternately terse and discursive, were speckled with abbreviations, Latinisms, and hyper-accented words that might, conceivably, be Hungarian and were sometimes transcribed and translated in a neater hand. "Complains of nightly awakening, one hour before dawn; neaurasth.? dysautonomia?; fantasies of *keresztre feszités.*" A second hand noted: "self-crucifixion," followed by an exclamation mark in parentheses. There was no structure to the reports, and most were undated.

A reader unfamiliar with the sluggish rhythms of the talking cure would have given up after a dozen pages of discursive thoughts, tumbling like torn-off tree branches over a waterfall. There was neither rhythm nor tune to the flow of unreason, forcing the reader to concentrate twice as hard as he would have done with a novel or a newspaper. Weaver, however, had been sensitised to the literature of psychiatry by an Upper East Side Jungian who cured him of post–second divorce blues by getting him to read case histories that were invariably more tortured and exotic than his own. He took an indecent pleasure in peeking into other persons' psyches. A tremor of wicked curiosity shook him as he began to read the dossier. He consumed it fast and with intense fascination, admiring the sabre play between two masked experts, thrust and parry, occasional stab. One passage, sixty pages in, made him pull up and reread. Patient and therapist were discussing popularity, a quality both of them considered distortive and overrated.

PATIENT: It doesn't come naturally to me.

KOVACS: How do you know that?

PATIENT: Being popular is not how I recognise myself — not how I was, when I was growing up, or as a young adult.

KOVACS: Could it have been latent, then, developing in a different place and time?

PATIENT: No. Categorically not. I was a confirmed loner, and not by choice.

KOVACS: You tried to be liked, and were rebuffed.

PATIENT: Correct.

KOVACS: So if you become popular, you would not be yourself?

PATIENT: Correct.

KOVACS: What is wrong with being liked?

PATIENT: It is obviously not me that people like, not the real me.

KOVACS: Who is the real me?

PATIENT: I wish I knew — that's why I am here.

KOVACS: Tell me, Paul: Which is worse for you, being liked by men, or by women?

After a page and a half of equivocation, the patient responded.

PATIENT: Women.
KOVACS: You're sure?
PATIENT: Positive, but I take no advantage from being liked by them.
KOVACS: Really? That's unusual.
PATIENT: How so?
KOVACS: Most men feel good to be desired by women.
PATIENT: Not me.
KOVACS: Not at all?
PATIENT: By my wife, yes. Before, by my fiancée.
KOVACS: And by others, here and now?
PATIENT: No.
KOVACS: Never?
PATIENT: On one occasion.
KOVACS: Would you like to tell me about it?

A stark confession followed — how, on Christmas night in a dark corridor, his kittenish sister-in-law had pressed herself against him, her lips to his, tongue protruding. She'd worn a flimsy nightgown, nothing beneath. Paul had uncoiled himself from her clutch. "We mustn't," he'd told her. "Think of the scandal, of our children. Let's pretend it never happened, a Christmas-night kiss, nothing more."

KOVACS: And was it?
PATIENT: No. I let the kiss linger. It felt good. I was aroused, both physically and in the proud knowledge that I could have this girl, any woman I wanted in the village. Lisl, sensing advantage, put my hand beneath her nightie and said she loved me, that we must elope. We kissed once more; I touched her bare flesh, caressed her. And all the while, another me was looking in at us from the outside, the real me, the unpopular one, the unde-sired, jealous of my conquest, eager for involvement. So which am I, Doctor? The watcher or the watched, outcast or participant?
KOVACS: Which would you rather be, Paul?
PATIENT: You tell me; that's what I am here for.

Weaver pulled up once more, hearing his own voice in parallel situations, observing himself in the tumult of sexual congress as if through secondary glazing, unable to engage wholly, recklessly, in the act of love.

KOVACS: Surely it is better to be loved than unloved.
PATIENT: Not at all. I know who I am when I am unloved.
KOVACS: The real you.
PATIENT: Correct.
KOVACS: Unloved by whom?
PATIENT: Just unloved.
KOVACS: By whom?
PATIENT: You know what I mean.
KOVACS: I'd like to hear it from you.
PATIENT: Is that necessary?
KOVACS: I think so.
PATIENT: I can't. . . .
KOVACS: Fine, then let me summarise. You are not yourself when loved; you are when you feel unloved. Is that right?
PATIENT: Correct.
KOVACS: Unloved by whom, Paul?

The typescript stopped, pencilling off into twenty lines of crabbed scrawl, too spidery for decipherment. At the foot of the page, the therapist reiterated his question, with a coda: "Unloved by whom, Paul? Who dislikes you most?" Finally, ten, fifteen, twenty pages later, into another session, came a whispered answer, so hesitant that Paul has to be made to repeat it.

KOVACS: By whom, Paul?
PATIENT: By me.
KOVACS: Again?
PATIENT: By myself.

Kovacs's notes followed in an italic type-script.

To describe Paul as a man consumed by self-hatred understates the complexity of his condition. He is quite the most challenging case I have seen: intellectually and emotionally articulate, anticipating my questions and forever trying to manipulate my responses. After sessions, I am in low spirits, fearing that he has transferred onto me something of his disabling sense of inadequacy. His will can be stronger than mine. He makes me feel that I am not fit to be his doctor. Even if I heal his soul, I will emerge hurt and full of doubt. Why, Saint Sigmund and Saint Sándor, did you train poor Kovacs in this unprotected cure? I could have been a happy cardiologist or a wealthy dermatologist. Instead, I am sicker at heart than my patients, and thinner of skin. Often I wish I had never met this man, much as I like and admire him.

My problem precisely! exclaimed Weaver to the empty room. He stood up to reread the last sentence, stumbling, as he walked around the room, towards an aperture of self-knowledge. This was Paul exactly as he remembered him, charismatic and aloof, irresistibly imposing, a smiling sphinx who could not receive love. When he was loved, he turned it back against the giver. " 'Yet each man kills the thing he loves,' " quoted Kovacs. So true, thought Weaver. True of Paul, true of himself, true perhaps of Lisl, living out her days in lofty disenchantment.

Worn-out as he was, Weaver forced himself to read on, intrigued by a dialogue that the therapist headed "Good Paul, Bad Paul." The patient is concerned about his moral balance. The therapist nudges him away from self-castigation. "We are all made of good and bad in unequal measure," he advises. "You, Paul, are no different from anyone else." But when the patient is gone, the old man torments himself.

Which Paul did I see today, Good Paul, or

bad? Is there a Jekyll and Hyde aspect to him? Is he a danger to himself, to others? Somehow, I don't think so. What I see is a man who blames himself unreasonably and fears that he is cursed to harm all whom he loves. That fear, paradoxically, renders him harmless — except to himself. What was the famous phrase about Lord Byron: "Mad, bad and dangerous to know"? Paul is not mad, nor bad. The only danger in knowing him is the way he zones in on vulnerability in others. He leaves me with an exaggerated sense of my inadequacy and yet a great warmth towards him. Is that his fault, or is it mine? I think we know, dear Sándor, I think we know.

What's this guy going on about? snapped Weaver silently, reordering the pile and slipping it into the bottom of his suitcase. Is he saying Paul was some kind of plague carrier, a Typhoid Mary who meant no harm but who infected half of New York in the summer of 1907? Good Paul, or bad? Who cares? thought Weaver, brushing his teeth with an electric rotator head. There was one last thing he needed to know, and he had just enough time to track it down.

CHAPTER SEVENTEEN

At five in the morning, Weaver's feet hit the carpet before he knew he was awake. Checking the digital bedside clock, he stumbled to the bathroom, emptied a hesitant bladder, washed, shaved, took his blood-pressure pills, and dressed in checked shirt, jeans, and rainproof jacket. Clicking the door shut, he tiptoed down the fire stairs and past a sleeping African clerk at the reception desk, through automatic glass doors and out into a starry night.

He reached the church gates with the first streak of light and, finding them locked, vaulted over with forgotten agility and headed left, to that part of the churchyard where he had met Paul on his wedding day and where he hoped to settle the last doubts about his fate by reading the inscriptions on the family tombstone. This was the place of truth, the unalterable text. The slab of marble would surely reveal all.

But instead of hearing the crunch of gravel beneath his soles as he walked towards the grave, he found himself on tarmac. Shining the pocket torch that he carried on site visits, he found this part of the cemetery paved over as a car park, no doubt for tourist coaches. He remembered that graves in this region were assigned on short leases. Unless the family paid for renewal every ten years, the bones were removed and the tombstone uprooted, left to fade against the cemetery wall, or used as paving underfoot. Something of the sort had been done to a man as important as Mozart. No pay, no rest in peace — that was the rule.

Rigid with frustration, Weaver swore with sudden vehemence. "-uck, -uck, -uck," came the echo from the brightening slopes. He swore again. "-it, -it, -it." How the hell was he ever going to find out what had happened to Paul if there was no grave and Lisl clammed up like a virgin oyster every time he broached the name? "Not. Another. Word. Understood?" That's what she'd said. In six hours from now, he'd be waving from a coach window and his last chance to know would be gone.

"-Uck, -uck, -uck," said the mountains again, and the unaccustomed profanity flicked a file of memory, calling to mind something a woman had once said to him, not one of his wives but a fellow architect in a foreign hotel, a woman whose name momentarily escaped him. "Ed," she'd said in bed, her bare breasts reproaching him with raspberry eyes, "you're a great guy, but you're not your own man. You're always looking some place else for approval. It's a disabling feature. You need to put your hand up, Ed, take credit for success and owner-ship of failure. Accept that it's you who did it, whatever it was: you who fucked up, you who fucked me, no-one but you, Ed Weaver. You see what I'm getting at? You're never there, not at work and not in bed. Not for me. So get out of my life, Ed Weaver. Get out before you wreck it."

It had started to rain, as it does in the mountains without warning, and the squelch of dismissal — Caroline, was it? Penelope? no, Ingrid — caused a shiver of misery to run down his spine. Ed was good at getting dumped. He attracted women easily, but the ones he wanted to get close to dropped him like soiled laundry after a short acquaintance. His Jungian therapist had asked him to think about Ingrid's ac-cusation and he had, for a bit; but there was Penelope soon afterwards, and Caroline, and he'd never got quite to the bottom of it. Not until he read Kovacs's file did he realise that he shared with Paul the same disabling hole in the heart, the inability to receive, to let himself be loved. That, he understood, was the real reason he had come here — to trace the fatal flaw in Paul before it was too late to save some life for Ed. His job was almost done.

Lisl was at reception when he returned, replacing the somnolent African. "I thought you were meant to be retired!" Ed exclaimed.

"Someone has to keep a check on the staff," she muttered. "Look at you — you're half-soaked. Get your coat off and I'll make us a coffee."

She walked him round to the museum bar, where the machine was spluttering its first of the morning and nothing had changed since the day they first met. "Before you ask," she said, sitting him in the widow alcove and barely changing her tone, "I've got security searching your room for the object you took from me last night, and I am considering calling the police."

"I see," said Weaver, a muscle trembling at the wall of his heart.

"What did you think you were doing, going through my desk?"

"I had to know," he said, "and you weren't telling."

"You have no right to know!" she exploded. "This is our story, not yours, and if we choose to keep it quiet, that's our prerogative. Who do you think you are? You came, you saw, you conquered, you left forty years ago. What claim have you got to know?"

"What claim?" thundered Weaver, unleashing the righteous rage that had terrorised billionaires into endorsing his boldest visions. "What right? I'll tell you what fucking right — excuse my French. . . . If it hadn't been for me, none of this would ever have come to pass. If I'd obeyed my orders, I would have hauled Paul right out from behind that bar the first time I clapped eyes on him and shut this place down for the duration. He'd have been trucked to a DP camp and you would never have seen him again. There would have been no big town here, no health resort, no hotel chain, no multinational Lisl chain, nothing but a sleepy hole in the hills with more darkness to it than Goethe's fucking light.

"I broke the rules at that time and — yes — I walked away from the consequences. But I'm back now, ready to take responsibility for the decision I made, right or wrong,

491

a decision based on personal sentiment, which changed the course of your life, Lisl, and mine, and Alice's and everyone else's. That's why I'm here, and that's my god-damned right. Will you grant me that small human decency, Mrs. Superior Hofmann?"

"I will," she said, not in the least bit cowed. "Have a biscuit."

"A glass of water," he requested. His chest was pounding and he needed to pop a pill.

"I didn't mean it about the police," said Lisl in a conciliatory tone.

"It's your call. Do what you like."

"I was not surprised, or upset, that you took the file last night. I knew the moment I disclosed its existence that it was no longer a secret. A man of your experience and ingenuity would find a way to read it, if you were determined enough. That's why I left it on the desk. I needed to test the strength of your determination."

"You left it there for me to find?"

"If you like. . . ."

"Where have I heard that story before?"

He gulped the pill down with water, sipped the coffee, and bit gratefully into Lisl's rock-hard biscuits.

"I guess I passed the test?"

"With that blaze of passion, yes. I needed to know that what happened here, to us, means something to you."

"It's my story, too."

"I know."

"So what happens now?"

"I'll show you what you came to see."

They were plodding down the hill in thick traffic, the streets on either side lined with identical trees and houses. "Acacia avenues, we'd call them," Weaver said with a smirk. Lisl took his arm and made no attempt to speak above the noise until they reached a children's park on the right, just as the road began snake-winding down to the river. She unlatched the low gate and headed past an enclosure of swings and roundabouts to a stone bench at the far end of the civic amenity.

"Isn't this the path that led to the quarry head?" he queried.

"You've got a good sense of direction, Mr. Weaver."

"I used to lead an army of invasion, remember?"

A tall metal fence, the spikes placed too close together for a child to insert a hand, walled off the park from the sheer drop into the gorge without obliterating the breath-catching view of the river below. It was a bad place made safe, a suitable disposition.

The bench had an inscription carved into its white stone headrest in small square letters: *Requiem aeternam dona eis, Domine, et lux perpetua luceat eis.*

" 'Give them eternal rest, Lord, and let perpetual light shine upon them,' " Weaver translated in a schoolboy recitation.

"Not bad," said Lisl, squeezing his arm. "The Pope won't let us pray the good old words any more and the town council wouldn't let me add another line, not one mention of the cruelties that took place here. It might give offence, they said — meaning to the rich who come to gasp our air and swill our water. Don't cause trouble, said the council. Let the past be past. That's our motto: Let the Past Be Past."

"But you remember, don't you, Lisl?" said Weaver.

"Less each day, Ed. You know how it is."

"The important things?"

"As if they were yesterday."

"Tell me."

"Not yet. First you must witness our shame."

She led him to the fence and pointed down. The base of the quarry was occupied by a circular building as garish as any he had seen on the Jersey seafront or the Vegas Strip, three bars of neon running around its brow and a crown of flashing gold as cara-pace.

"W-what?" he stuttered.

"Our premier industry," specified Lisl, "our disgrace."

"A casino?"

"Twenty-four hours, three hundred and sixty-four days a year. Credit card only. No cash on the premises. Even the prostitutes take plastic."

"Wasn't this meant to be a school?"

"And before that, it was a killing ground, but who cares? Now it's apple and cherry machines, rooms by the half-hour, duty-free beer, a palace of empty promises."

"No different," murmured Weaver, "from joints I know back home, including some I built, places where guys go to forget their pain. No harm in that."

" 'I do declare,' " sang Lisl, wallpaper lyr-ics from the middle of their different lives, " 'there were times when I was so lonesome I took some comfort there.' "

"Not me, personally," said Weaver. "But lotsa guys with no-one else in their lives. Nothing wrong with it, as such. . . ."

"Men died here," said Lisl.

"A long time ago, during the war . . ."

"And after."

"What do you mean, 'after'?"

495

"Hans," she said.

"He came back?"

"And Paul. That's what you wanted to find out, isn't it?"

The sun was high and she had brought a bottle of water for them to sip, two people at the cusp of their leisure years, sharing a quiet reminiscence. The time was past for hesitation, denial, and prevarication. Lisl was ready to start, had been waiting for years in some corner of her soul to present her evidence, the only eyewitness at the close.

The three men, she reported, returned that morning from burying Hans with grit on their boots. It took some minutes to kick it off. They had been mixing cement, said Papa Hofmann. Lisl served pancakes and coffee. Papa tucked in. Mathilde had driven over to lend a hand, and her cheerfulness in the kitchen counterpointed the cataleptic stillness that arose from the table where the three conspirators sat, father, son, and son-in-law. They chomped, slurped, burped, and looked straight ahead — anywhere but into the women's eyes.

It was Johann who cracked the tension, coming down at seven-thirty and wolfing Paul's untouched pancake, chirping about his day ahead. Papa clasped a mighty arm around Franz-Josef and gave Lisl a nod of thanks. Franzi went out back to check an incoming delivery. Paul sat on, staring through the window, ignoring Lisl's exhortations to go to work so that she could set up the room for the lunchtime rush. He sat there for an age, until she kicked him out. He left with a dragging foot, an empathetic limp.

His lethargy refused to lift in the following weeks. Gloom shrouded the inn, causing the lights to dim above the smirking Hind. Lisl did her best to whip up a happy whirr of activity, but every foot tread, each rat-a-tat at the front door filled her with a nameless dread. She lost her appetite and slept in fits and starts.

One night, huge hailstones fell from the sky, and Franz-Josef, clinging to his wife in bed, confessed what they had done that morning and shared his anxiety that the cement under which they had buried a man might break open in the storm. Hearing what the three men had done settled Lisl's nerves. Don't worry, she told Franzi, the dead man won't come back to haunt you. Still, she made sure of being first to the door when the postman knocked, the first to receive any conceivable threat. Hans would not be missed in the locality, but there might be others beyond who were looking for him — a cousin, a war comrade, a tradesman, the tax collector. Their first move, if they planned a visit, would be to book a room at the village inn. Lisl examined every reservation as if it were a ticking bomb.

Four weeks passed, then five and six. Mathilde, emptying vases of dead flowers, asked if Lisl knew what had become of that smelly tramp, not that anyone in her place missed him. Papa had driven up to the fellow's farm and found no livestock in the cowshed, the house dilapidated. He set the thatch on fire to discourage squatters. A missing man was no big deal, Papa assured Franzi, not even a statistic. Soon, when prosperity returned, individuality would regain its value, but not yet. Soon, said Papa, things will pick up. There were three private cars parked in the forecourt. The carrot seller was replacing her straw roof with Italian tile. The inn was getting bookings for birthday parties. The good times were coming back. Papa gave Lisl a brooch for her birthday and Franzi talked of having another baby. Alice, impervious to most events around her, stopped work in the seventh month of pregnancy to give her unborn child the best chance and Johann his last kingdom as a beloved only son.

Alice spent long hours watching the boy as he rode nags around the pasture and did his homework on beer-garden tables. Paul worked at the town hall each morning and spent afternoons at the building site, where work was halted by a run of misfortunes. Strange smells were sniffed by workmen and had to be officially investigated — a rotted tree stump, an animal corpse. The join between two walls needed adjusting to allow for a steeper incline than Paul had envisaged. The soil was too soft on one part of the site. And when the two walls were realigned, the foundations reinforced, and the sanitation inspector satisfied, half the hard hats walked out over a foreman's slur on a bricklayer's war record — a flash strike at first, but one that escalated into a full-scale wage dispute, with huge cost implications and an indefinite postponement of the school's opening. The foreman blamed the disruption on Communists. Paul took every setback as a personal failing. He looked haggard and he spent little time with Johann and Alice. His breath took on a sour tang. A kitten that nuzzled his leg as he came into the kitchen for a bowl of soup was savagely kicked away. Alice said nothing; Lisl frowned.

A month before her due date, Alice went into labour. "Everything's fine," said Tobias Strauss, in a spotted bow tie, joining the family downstairs for supper. "The midwife will call down when mother is ready to deliver," he assured them. "I will leave the door open so we can hear everything." The baby, a girl, was born with the umbilical cord wound around its neck. The doctor got upstairs too late to get a living breath out of the child.

There was no funeral, no opportunity for consolation. After three weeks, Alice returned to work. When Franz-Josef offered a hug, she went stiff as a corpse. Lisl, she barely noticed. Johann frisked round her, not knowing what he had done wrong. Paul was out and about, seldom to be seen.

One night, as Lisl sat on the stairs reading a John Steinbeck novel, she saw him creeping out of his bedroom in underpants, his shoes and trousers in hand, his spindly legs rattling like birches in a blizzard.

"Where are you going at this hour?" she whispered.

"Lots to do," he mumbled.

"It's four in the morning."

"I know."

"Sit down a minute," she said, patting the

step. "We haven't talked for ages. . . ."

Paul pulled on his trousers, put a finger to his lips, and motioned downwards. They tiptoed to the tavern room and nestled into a corner table.

"What are you reading?" he said, half-interested.

"Steinbeck, Hemingway, Chandler, the literature of the victors."

"It will come in useful when the tourism resumes," said Paul.

"I know," said Lisl. "It *is* going to be all right, you know. Alice will get over the loss. There will be another baby. The school will get built. There will be much to celebrate." She took his hand in hers, a sisterly gesture.

Paul twisted her fingers around his, this way and that. He could not agree. Nothing was getting better. It had all gone wrong since her father's death. The good doctor would not have guzzled supper while their baby died, would he? He would have been there for the birth and, if anything went wrong, he would have made Alice smile again, given her hope for the future. He would have known what to do when bad things happened, and now no-one knew, no-one at all.

"You do, Paul," said Lisl, but he ignored her, rumbling on about a fellow called

Hans. Who's Hans? asked Lisl. Kerner, he grunted, Hannes Kerner.

She knew the name: a childhood ogre. Hans had returned, said Paul. They had got rid of him. With help from Papa and Franzi. "I know." Lisl smiled. Paul glared at her, resenting interruption. "What do you know?" he demanded. "What can you know about any of this?" Lisl squeezed his hand, encouraging him to say more. When he stayed silent, she kissed him, a peck on the cheek, a token of support and solidarity.

"It will get better," she said, repeating Papa's mantra.

Paul twisted his neck towards her and planted a kiss on her lips. No harm, thought Lisl, letting the poor sap have some feminine affection. His tongue came stabbing at her teeth and she decided to ignore it. He was upset, disoriented, in no state to cope with an unpleasant confrontation. She caressed his protruding cheekbones, hoping to infuse him with positive feelings. Only when his hands grabbed at her breasts did she say "Stop," confident that he would respect her wishes.

Paul stared back with uncomprehending eyes, looking not at but through her. He lurched once more at her breasts. "That's enough," said Lisl, pulling away and out of the alcove. Paul came after her across the room, pressing her against the wall and tearing at her nightclothes, forcing his hand inside her gown, between her legs.

"What was he thinking?" cried Lisl, turning to Weaver for male interpretation. "That I was chattel, his to use as and when he pleased? That he had a right to hurt me? That my feelings for him remained unchanged after the funeral fiasco? We had not exchanged a friendly word in months, and here he was expecting instant love, a love he himself had declared forbidden. What was I meant to make of this?"

"What did you do?" asked Weaver.

"My best in the circumstances. I held him off until he went too far. Then I reached back with *The Grapes of Wrath,* the hardback in my hand, and cracked it against his skull. He glared at me for a minute, eyes wide open like a fox in headlights. Then he heaved on his jacket and walked right out of the door. That's the last I saw of Paul Miller, alive."

Voices floated up from the bottom of the quarry. A flock of tourists was being ushered into the casino.

"They're taking my herd in for milking," said Weaver.

"You have a caustic tongue," said Lisl.

"Two-edged. Cost me a couple of mar-riages."

"But you always had the last word."

"As you're doing now."

"Do you want me to continue, or not?"

Lisl straightened her back against the bench, took a sip of water, and picked up from the scene she had left. "I went into the kitchen and prepared a pancake mixture, my stress therapy. Then I sat down with Steinbeck, waiting for the children to stir. I must have sat for twenty minutes before the alarm went off in my head, just as it did on the night that Paul crept out to bury Hans beneath a cement carpet.

"There was no time to call Papa Hof-mann. Yanking a greatcoat over my night-gown, I raced down on my bicycle to the top of the cliff. It was getting light and I knew by instinct where to look. Down there, right where the woman in the brown cardi-gan is standing now, is where I found Paul. He was crumpled on the ground, face up. I scrambled down the side path and ran towards him. The back of his head was smashed like a breakfast egg."

"But he was still alive?" prompted Weaver.

"A few halting breaths. I took his hand, pressed it to my cheek. It was cold, white, unmoving. I held it there while he died, telling him he was loved, and forgiven."

"Did he say anything?"

"One word. He shaped a word with his lips and I could not decipher it. It wasn't Alice, I know that. It wasn't *sorry,* or any message. It wasn't anything I recognised. Maybe it was a word from his other life, the one we knew nothing about. Even when he was gone, it stayed shaped on his lips."

"What did you do?"

"What had to be done. Got on my bike, went home, phoned Mathilde, went to the police station, came back, told Franzi. Together, we went to the kitchen to find Alice, knowing she would never forgive me so long as I lived, the bringer of evil tidings. I had tried so hard to protect her, and all I could do was give her disasters."

"How'd she take it?" asked Weaver.

"With a look of complete and utter emptiness. No tears, not a single tear. All she said was, 'I'd better fetch Johann,' and off she went to the kindergarten to collect the boy before he heard anything in the playground. I ran after her, but she waved me back. She wanted to be with the boy. The police came by, asking questions. There was a postmortem and a hearing, before a district judge; an open verdict. 'While the balance of his mind was disturbed,' said the judge.

505

The pathologists butchered the body, so we had it cremated. I have no idea what Alice did with the urn."

"You must be cold," said Weaver as Lisl blew her nose. The sun had gone behind a cloud and the birds had stopped their singing. "Here, take my jacket."

"It's time we were getting back," she said.

On the walk uphill, she described Paul's funeral. "The new pastor spoke, fresh out of a seminary. He chose a verse in Deuteronomy about the body that is found outside the city walls and the elders declare, 'Our hands did not shed this blood.' It felt like an epitaph, not just for Paul but for the times we had lived through — before, during, and after the war."

"A collective pardon for the community's sins."

"If you like."

"And did you feel absolved?"

"I tried. One part of me tried. The other cannot forget. I lie awake some nights asking myself where I failed them — Alice, Johann, and Paul. Am I in any way to blame? Was there anything I could have done to prevent this?"

Weaver was about to put another question, when she demanded, "Is that it? Is that what you wanted to know?"

"It is."

"Does it make any difference?"

"It already has. I know where I came in, where my responsibility lies. And you?"

"Me? I tried for years to wipe Paul from my memory, as he erased our village. I yelled for joy when the old staircase crashed down, because I thought it would take away the stigma of our . . . embraces, and bring me some peace in amnesia. It didn't. I know now that peace lies in truth, and I am grateful to you, Ed, for reinforcing that belief by the persistence of your interrogation. That's it. I need never speak of it again."

They were back at the hotel, their lives forking apart. "I'll fetch the dossier," said Weaver.

"Keep it, if you like," said Lisl. "I won't need it anymore. One last coffee for the road?" They reentered the mediaeval barroom, its suspended stag heads threatening, as ever, to fall off the wall and inflict injury. "This room is the one area for which I can't get third-party insurance," said Lisl in her business voice. "So I keep it for special guests. Ones I think I can trust. Can I trust you?"

"I guess so," said Weaver.

"It's too late now to take it back." She shrugged.

He had already decided that the television documentary the British company wanted to make about his life would not contain reference to any of this, and that his soldierly past would be sanitised of any reference to Paul. This could be his last gift to Paul, a blessed oblivion. Their friendship would have made a good story for the fifth channel, or whatever the intrusive thing that wanted to show his life was called, but the more he thought about it, the less inclined he was to let himself be numbered in a series of *Ten Men Who Changed Our Skylines*. If there was one discovery he had made here, it was the confirmation of his insignificance in the events of his own life.

"Do you think," he tested Lisl, "that he slipped at the edge?"

"The ground was dry, Sahara-dry."

"Then he jumped?"

"Unlikely. Paul was not the kind to do away with himself. But what do I know? What can anyone know of another? With Paul, truth slips through the fingers like water. My father liked to say that every human quality can be quantified, and each has its moral opposite. He was wrong. There are shades of meaning, hairline cracks, invisible gestures, unheard words, through which we grasp, or fail to grasp, the essence of another person's life. There is no opposite to the immaterial."

"That's pretty deep, Lisl," said Weaver. "Do you still think in opposites?"

"Let me tell you about a dream I had," she said. "One hot Sunday that awful summer, the new priest tried to impress us with a sermon about goats, something he expected a rural congregation to appreciate. He was wet behind the ears and full of enthusiasm. He had a live goat led in to the altar and talked about the Day of Atonement ritual in Leviticus, where a goat was taken from the Temple with a scarlet thread around its neck and led into the desert to be hurled from a cliff, its death relieving the whole community of its sins. The goat of Azazel, it is called."

"I remember it from Sunday school," said Ed.

"The priest tied a thread around it and had the farmer lead it outside. Nobody saw what he was getting at. People stood around afterwards asking what was he doing, in God's name, bringing a goat into God's house?

"That night in bed, I had an Azazel dream, in which Paul stood before me, stark naked, with a red strand around his —"

"His neck?"

"No, his —"

"Oh, that."

"Yes."

"And?"

"That was it. He just stood there, upright, and as my eyes opened as wide as they could go, he turned away from me, until all I saw were his haunches, tensed on the point of flight. And I prayed, Dear God, please save him. He means us no harm."

The hissing of the machine and the trembling of cup on saucer in Weaver's hand were the only sounds to be heard. Lisl sat against the alcove wall, patting her cheeks, which had reddened with faint embarrassment.

"You had a vision of him, as a saint and martyr?" asked Weaver.

"Not a saint. I told you: He was sexually aroused."

"What, then? As Christ, who died for our sins?"

"Don't be ridiculous. That would be blasphemous."

"How, then?"

"As an emissary, an epitome of the human condition. The good and the bad in us, the holy and the hellish, all in one. Here was a man who was trying to be good and, like all mortals, failed at the end. Failed nobly, I think. I hope. I believe. I cannot know."

Ten minutes, announced the public address speaker. *All members of the Academy of Third Age kindly have your bags in the lobby in ten minutes, ready for departure. The coach is leaving in ten minutes. Ten. Minutes.*

"That means you," said Lisl.

"I guess."

They stood in the centre of the room, uncertain how to part. Weaver stuck out a hand. Lisl took a step forward. They fell into a hug, like people crawling out of a collapsed building, two blinking souls who had been given back their lives by chance or destiny and did not quite know what to do with them. They clung to each other in relief, and bewilderment, and, inevitably, a stirring of desire. It was Weaver who broke the clinch.

"I'd better go," he said, kissing the crown of Lisl's head, her widow's peak.

"Go." She smiled, patting her hair.

"I'll write."

"No need," she said.

"I can see some daylight," he said.

"It could be a false dawn." Lisl laughed.

Taking her hand, he kissed the Alice ring. Lisl ran her fingers with a flicker of fondness over his tight, iron-gray hair. They might never meet again, or perhaps they might. Too soon to determine, too much to absorb and reconfigure. Weaver had a Caroline and a Penelope and an Ingrid on whom to work the benefits of his newfound self-knowledge. Lisl owned this place, and the past, and probably a greater share of the peace they had earned from the telling of her story. It seemed a fair trade.

She walked him out to the coach park, where the luxury bus was purring and the Laughing Hind shield moaned in a low-cloud easterly breeze with a hint of rain, insistently, as it had done from the day Weaver first heard it. "All it needs," he declared wistfully, "is for some bright fellow to shimmy up a ladder and drip oil on the squeaking hinge."

Lisl flung him a quizzical look, frozen by the image, staring beyond the moment into another frame of time. Weaver gazed back at her from the top step of his bus, waiting for a reply. He required, she realised, a meaningful valediction. He was looking to her for some phrase, a blessing that would allow him to leave with a sense of mission accomplished. As a leader in the hospitality industry, she knew how such things were professionally done, with tart clichés and gift-wrapped souvenirs and a smile of impermeable superficiality. As Lisl, she knew that nothing ever ended neatly, and she was damned if she'd give some crock of a man the unearned satisfaction of a job well done. Rival impulses warred in her mind and a sharp word flickered at the edge of her tongue. Then, thinking better of it, she turned on her heel and, waving at Weaver with the back of her Alice-ring hand, she vanished into the hotel by the side entrance, where the kitchen used to be.

ACKNOWLEDGEMENTS

The author wishes to thank his close and immediate family for unfailing support, and the following for practical advice and moral encouragement: Shirley Apthorp, Nicole Bachmann, Lin Bender, Catherine Best, Lexy Bloom, the late Jonathan Carr, Tony Cheevers, Aviva Cohen, Attila Csampai, the late Anneke Daalder, Eythan Elkindi, Victor Eskenasi, Brigitte Fassbender, Ines Feuerstein, Stephen Games, Medi Gasteiner-Girth, Jane Gelfman, Jonny Geller, Jeffrey M. Graham, Michael Haas, Nick Hirschkorn, Tatiana Hofmann, Fiona Hughes, Ernest Keeling, Douglas Kennedy, Esther Klag, Sylvia Laqueur, Walter Laqueur, Richard Mabey, Fiona Maddocks, Claire Meljac, Nicola Milsom, Rowan Moore, Christopher Nupen, Berenika Osvacova, the late Andrzej Panufnik, Zdena Posvicova, Thomas Robosz, Fiammetta Rocco, Michael Schachter, David Sexton,

Sonia Simmenauer, Ivana Stehlikova, Alice van Straalen, Mihaly Szilagyi, Veronica Wadley, Lisa Weinert, Arnold Wesker, Yun Sheng.

ABOUT THE AUTHOR

Norman Lebrecht is the author of eleven books about music, including the international best sellers *The Maestro Myth* and *Who Killed Classical Music?* He is a music columnist for the London *Evening Standard,* a cultural commentator on Bloomberg.com, and presenter of *The Lebrecht Interview* series on BBC Radio 3 in Great Britain. He lives in London.

www.normanlebrecht.com

SNYDER COUNTY LIBRARIES, INC.
ONE NORTH HIGH STREET
SELINSGROVE, PA 17870

The employees of Thorndike Press hope you have enjoyed this Large Print book. All our Thorndike, Wheeler, and Kennebec Large Print titles are designed for easy reading, and all our books are made to last. Other Thorndike Press Large Print books are available at your library, through selected bookstores, or directly from us.

For information about titles, please call:
(800) 223-1244

or visit our Web site at:
http://gale.cengage.com/thorndike

To share your comments, please write:
Publisher
Thorndike Press
295 Kennedy Memorial Drive
Waterville, ME 04901